More Praise fo
Ten Girls to Wat

"Lively, smart, and funny . . . What I loved about this coming-of-age story was its realistic and confirming celebration of female resilience, brilliance, and generosity. Not your stereotypical single gal novel, Shumway's book is a passion-stirring breath of fresh air."

–Helen Schulman,
bestselling author of
This Beautiful Life

This novel captures that time ght after college, when we all feel verwhelmed and adrift. Shumway xpertly guides us through a young woman's love life, her family, friends, and career as she proves that perfect endings aren't the only happy ones."

–Lauren Weisberger,
bestselling author of
The Devil Wears Prada

"A thoroughly charming, sassy, highly satisfying debut from a writer with a rare gift: She sounds like your best friend, telling a story you don't ever want to end. I adored this book."

–Sarah Pekkanen,
author of *These Girls*

"A heartwarming story about a gathering of extraordinary women who offer wisdom, warmth, and humanity. I can't wait to give this book to my sisters and best girl-friends."

–Nicolle Wallace, bestselling
author of *Eighteen Acres*

CHARM · 15

TEN
GIRLS
to
WATCH

TEN
GIRLS
to
WATCH

— a novel —

Charity Shumway

WASHINGTON SQUARE PRESS

New York ▪ *London* ▪ *Toronto* ▪ *Sydney* ▪ *New Delhi*

WASHINGTON SQUARE PRESS
A Division of Simon & Schuster, Inc.
1230 Avenue of the Americas
New York, NY 10020

First Washington Square Press trade paperback edition July 2012

WASHINGTON SQUARE PRESS and colophon are registered trademarks of Simon & Schuster, Inc.

For information about special discounts for bulk purchases, please contact Simon & Schuster Special Sales at 1-866-506-1949 or business@simonandschuster.com.

The Simon & Schuster Speakers Bureau can bring authors to your live event. For more information or to book an event contact the Simon & Schuster Speakers Bureau at 1-866-248-3049 or visit our website at www.simonspeakers.com.

Designed by Jaime Putorti

Manufactured in the United States of America

10 9 8 7 6 5 4 3 2 1

Library of Congress Cataloging-in-Publication Data

Shumway, Charity.
   Ten girls to watch : a novel / Charity Shumway.—1st ed.
      p.   cm.
   1. Single women—Fiction.   2. Women authors—Fiction.   3. Women college graduates—Fiction.   4. Self-acceptance—Fiction.   5. Self-actualization (Psychology)—Fiction.   6. New York—Fiction. I. Title.
   PS3619.H866T46 2012
   813'.6—dc23
                                                              2011048888

ISBN 978-1-4516-7341-8
ISBN 978-1-4516-7342-5 (ebook)

For Donna and Loa Jean

Chapter One

*T*he Internet told me the temperature in Brooklyn was ninety-three degrees, but my fourth-floor apartment wrapped those ninety-three degrees in ancient plaster, a sweaty hug that pushed things that much closer to triple digits. The large windows could have helped, but this was a day when flags hung limp on their poles. Instead of offering a breeze, all the windows did was lap up sticky sunshine. Even standing motionless in front of my blaring fan, perspiration trickled down my temples and pooled around my waistband. Still, before I dialed, I flicked off the fan. I didn't want to risk missing a word, and the beauty of phone calls is that the other person can't see how damp you are.

I rehearsed what I'd say to whomever answered the phone. *Hi, this is Dawn West. Regina should be expecting my call.* Too formal. *Hi, Regina asked me to give her a call this morning. My name is Dawn West.* I said that one over and over a few times. If I got the words out fast, it sounded okay. And what to say to Regina? *Hi, we met this weekend? You said to phone your office Monday?* Why was I making everything sound like a question? And surely she'd remember me. It'd only been a day. Cross-legged in the corner that got the very best cell reception, I punched the numbers slowly, my mouth moving as I checked each digit against the ones on the card I held between my fingers: Regina Greene, Editor in Chief, *Charm*.

Her assistant answered on the first ring.

A whole new line of sweat bloomed on my upper lip. The words blurred together. "Hi Regina asked me to give her a call this morning my name is Dawn West."

"What was your name again?" the assistant asked. I wiped my lip and enunciated a bit more clearly.

Moments later, Regina was on the line. "Dawn!" She answered like we were old friends. "So glad you called!"

Since college graduation more than a year earlier, I'd applied for 116 jobs. (I knew the exact number because I'd kept scrupulous track of every application in Excel.) I might as well have been paper-airplaning my many résumés into the Grand Canyon for all the good my rigorous applying had done me. But now, I was on the phone with Regina Greene, and surely she hadn't asked me to call just to say hello. I could feel disappointment poised and ready to fire—after all those months of trying and trying and failing, I was riddled with bullet holes—but right there beside the potential dashed hopes was so much pulsing want and need that even if it had been fifty degrees, I would have been sweating.

We exchanged a pleasantry or two, and then she got right to it.

"Have you seen our Ten Girls to Watch issue, Dawn?"

Regina explained that every year *Charm* picked ten remarkable college women—violin prodigies who also discovered vaccines, Olympic archers who also ran orphanages, things like that—and this year marked the contest's fiftieth anniversary.

"We're looking to do some special coverage for the magazine," she said. "Plus something for the web, and then an event. A fun gala or luncheon or something for all the past winners. The only trick is that we don't know where the winners are. I mean, we know where a few of them are. For instance, Gerri Vans was a winner in the eighties."

Gerri Vans, the talk show star turned media empress. I glanced over at my coffee table—a generous description of the cardboard box over which I'd thrown a folded sheet. There, like millions of other American women, I had multiple copies of both *Gerri,* Gerri's original magazine, and *G-Talk,* her interview spin-off. Each issue featured Gerri's beaming face on the cover, angled just so to show off her trademark dimples. On the cover of the *G-Talk* topping my pile, Gerri leaned her less dimply cheek on Bill Murray's shoulder.

"Gerri Vans," I said reverentially. "Wow."

"I know. She's great," Regina said, pronouncing the word "great" as if she were Tony the Tiger: "Grrrreat!" The way you would say it if you were talking about an old pal you hadn't seen in awhile but were dying to catch up with. From which I inferred this was exactly the case.

I drew the perfect picture of Gerri and Regina, giggling in a discreet corner of some swank, downtown restaurant. Then for good measure I made the table four-top, added some candles, and popped me and Bill Murray into the picture. I told a joke. They all laughed and laughed.

Regina went on. "So we know where the winners like Gerri are, but most of them are a mystery to us—1957 was a long time ago. And that's where you'd start. Tracking down all five hundred of them, or as many as possible, interviewing them, and figuring out who's worth featuring. And then figuring out what sort of celebration makes sense."

That's where I would start? Had she really just said that?

It was like a cold hand had grabbed my heart, like icy air had just poured through the windows. I felt like I might cry. I didn't breathe for a few seconds. I closed my eyes.

Yes, she'd really just said it.

She didn't get around to telling me when I would start. Or

whether I'd work from home or get a desk at the office. Or how much *Charm* was planning to pay me. And it was pretty clear that whatever this was, it was temporary. But I said yes as fast as I could.

During the one year, two months, and fourteen days since college graduation, the closest I'd gotten to anything other than office-drone temping was a web marketing company I'd found on Craigslist that hired me as a "lawn care writer." They paid me eleven cents a word to write columns and answer questions on their lawn care website, with the understanding that I would use the search engine keyword phrase "lawn fertilizer" as frequently as possible. I'd baked a cake the day I'd gotten that gig. This, though, *this* was worth a real celebration.

After I hung up, I leapt to my feet and hopped across the room, flinging droplets of sweat as I danced. I turned on the fan and said *"I have a job"* into the blades, the words echoing with grand Darth Vader distortion. I was tempted to shout it out the window, but I'm not really a shouter. Instead, I paced my apartment in giddy shock, hands held over my mouth like a girl who has just been given an engagement ring.

What I felt was something close to pure delight. Close to, but not quite pure delight, because there was a slight complication, above and beyond the fact that this job wasn't a long-term proposition and might pay close to zero dollars. For this job, I had two people to thank: my ex-boyfriend Robert and *Robert's new girlfriend,* Lily.

––––––––

Robert Rolland and I met second semester freshman year on a shared overnight shift at the student-run homeless shelter. We'd walked back to the dining hall together, shared waffles (I doctored mine with sloppy syrup, he carefully and lightly applied powdered sugar to his), and gone hardly a day without seeing each other for the rest of college.

It had taken him six months to admit to me that he was a pret-zel baron. Pretzel baron, pretzel mogul, pretzel heir, however you said it, Robert was in line to inherit the Rolland Pretzel empire. His great-grandfather, the one who got the family into the pretzel business in the first place, owned just a single pretzel shop. But after World War II, his son, Grandpa Rolland, came back from France determined to do something big. He turned out to be a uniquely gifted pretzel entrepreneur, and anyone who's ever been to New York and had a soft pretzel from any street cart has contrib-uted to the Rolland family fortune. They expanded the empire to hard pretzels in the sixties, but only folks in the big beer-drinking states (the Rollands have beer-consumption coded maps up on the walls at HQ and also in their billiard room at home) get to see the full range of their products, readily available at grocery and liquor stores.

Over the four years of college, Robert and I broke up two or three times a year, then got back together, more or less instanta-neously. We always broke up because of small things that really stood for big things. For example, Robert approached the world in a smooth-sailing, moneyed way. Whenever he needed help, be it movers, caterers, delivery services, he could buy it. I, on the other hand, could not. Once, we broke up because I walked home from a party at two in the morning and he thought this demonstrated incredible irresponsibility. What if we had kids? Would I traipse all over the city at night then too? I said wasting twenty dollars on a taxi was what was really irresponsible. We'd sharpened the tone of our voices and assessed our utter incompatibility as life part-ners from there, and though we'd gotten back together in less than seventy-two hours, it wasn't like the argument went away.

But he was funny and handsome and almost painfully smart, and I'd never thought anybody smelled as good as he did. Undoubt-edly it was something to do with his soap and deodorant and fabric softener, but it was more than that. I wanted to nuzzle my face between his neck and collarbone and breathe in that exact smell forever. That seemed important, not trivial, like the deep animal part of my brain had zeroed in on him and millions of years of evolution dictated that we belonged together.

He felt the same way about me, or so he said. "There's no one for me but you," he'd written, just a one-line e-mail, after a breakup junior year when he'd said my parents' divorce made me skeptical and mistrusting. And since then, every so often, he'd say those words to me, never in a whisper, but always in a low voice that caught just the edge of his vocal cords, like sawteeth catching in wood. "There's no one for me but you."

And so, despite the fact that after graduation Robert's parents had sent him on a six-week trip to Asia, then set him up in a nice apartment on the Upper West Side so he could take his place in the family pretzel empire—the exact opposite of my postcollegiate setup (which was limited to the twenty-five-dollar Red Lobster gift certificate my mother had sent along with her "Congrats, Grad!" card; nothing from my dad)—we persisted in our back-and-forth.

Until Lily.

During one of our postgraduation breaks, Robert started dating some nineteen-year-old NYU freshman, which made steam shoot from my ears and hot fountains pour from my eyes. I particularly hated that she was nineteen. Four years past being a college freshman, I would never date one. What would we talk about? Homesickness and final-exam jitters? But apparently that didn't matter to Robert. I felt like a jilted middle-aged wife whose husband has taken up with some young trollop. I was only twenty-three, and already I was being cast in that part? A few friends tried to set me up. I went on a date or two, and even though I didn't like the guys, I turned into a puppet, tap-dancing my way through the part of a girl pretending to have a good time on a date. When they phoned later, I dodged their calls. How was Robert so easily finding other people he wanted to date? Fortunately, the freshman didn't last long, and, perhaps unfortunately, Robert and I continued "hanging out" until we lapsed into dating again.

Which had lasted a few months. Until nine weeks ago, to be precise. And yes, I was keeping track. Inside my head there was a mechanism like one of those elaborate clocks in the town squares of German villages. Each week, it was like a bunch of birds and a little wooden girl dressed in a dirndl whirled out of the clock and yodeled a bit, then announced how long it had been. One week, two weeks! With each calendar marker, I was supposed to feel better. And I kind of was feeling better, until week three, that is, when Robert started dating Lily Harris. Week three! The dirndl girl's weekly cuckoo had not prepared me for that. At least Lily was our age, even if she was a University of Texas debutante sorority girl. Not that I'd Internet-stalked her and seen any stupid blowing-kisses-at-the-camera sorority-girl photos . . .

As always, Robert and I kept having dinner or going to the movies. Now, as "just friends," though of course "just friends" had devolved back into more than just friends a dozen times before. I kept waiting for it to happen. At the movies, my arm next to his, tingling with anticipation. At dinner, waiting for the invitation to go on a walk after dessert or to go for another drink or to "watch a movie" back at his place. But he hadn't leaned into me, and the invitation back to his place hadn't come either, and even though my brain knew we were broken up and knew, furthermore, that he was seeing someone else, the loud glockenspiel of reason didn't keep me from feeling rejected anew, every time.

Then, two weeks ago, Robert had phoned. "I hope it's not weird," he said. "I invited Lily to the Pretzel Party. I mean, I hope you don't think it's weird that I invited *you* too. I want you to come. I want you to meet her."

Every summer Robert's parents threw a party at their house in the Hamptons, which they called the Summer Party, but which everyone else referred to as the Pretzel Party. Robert had called to tell me I'd be getting an invitation in the mail. I'd never gotten a formal invitation before. I'd just gone as Robert's girlfriend.

Trying to pretend, to myself most of all, that I was cool and totally over it, I said sure, of course, I'd love to meet Lily. And then I put on my sneakers and ran four miles to try to shake off the awful feeling. It didn't work. Robert was really, truly dating someone, who was not me. And I wasn't dating anyone. Not that I would be guaranteed to feel better if I were, but that was the thought that reverberated in my head, like some big flashing scoreboard. Robert, 1; Dawn, 0. Or more accurately, Robert, infinity; Dawn, negative infinity.

The fact that Lily was going to be at the Pretzel Party meant I definitely shouldn't go. Yet there I'd been, the morning of the party, getting ready in the so-hot-you-might-pass-out heat of my banged-up old Brooklyn apartment with my fan blowing straight into my face in order to avoid sweating off my eyeliner before it even dried. Anyone sane in New York has an air conditioner. I was sane—it was just that expenditures of more than, say, nine dollars weren't in my temp-and-lawn-care-writer budget. My dress, a blue polyester number pretending to be silk, had, in fact, rung up for precisely nine dollars at H&M. With a vintage gold pin my grandmother had given me and a yellow belt I'd had since high school, I liked to imagine it could pass for Anthropologie, but that might have been wishful thinking.

"You look nice," my roommate, Sylvia, said, standing at my door with a bowl of Cap'n Crunch in her hand. She took a slurpy bite, a Crunch Berry falling to the floor and rolling toward the center of the living room.

Turns out a lot of people will say no to an apartment with a twenty-degree slope to its floor. Not me, and not Sylvia, another Craigslist find. I'd rummaged her up with a posting that did its best to match honesty ("near the Brooklyn-Queens Expressway, so a little noisy") with salesmanship ("vintage details"). Other than the fact that Sylvia never, ever wore a bra (despite her rather voluptuous form) and sometimes went a day or two past the point where hair washing was truly necessary (even for a girl whose curly brown mop masked a lot of grease), she was all right.

That said, certain things about her frightened me. For instance, she was twenty-eight, and although she'd been working at a marketing firm in Soho for a few years now, she didn't seem to have any more cash than I did. That seemed a worrisome indicator of what I could expect in New York in years to come. And then there was her boyfriend, Rodney, a linebacker-looking fellow she met back home over Christmas and who now flew in from Ohio every month or so. He responded to all my attempts at cordial conversation with one-word answers and a blank face, his eyes flashing to wherever Sylvia happened to be, whether she was grabbing her coat or behind the bathroom door. I'd never seen a single slitty-eyed look silently yell "hurry up" in another person's direction quite so loudly.

"Where you going?" Sylvia said now, but since she had cereal in her mouth, it was more like "Wuh yu gwon?"

"A friend is having a party out on Long Island," I heard myself say.

Ugh. "A friend." And, ugh, "Long Island." My first Pretzel Party, the one right after our freshman year, Robert told me his parents were having a get-together in the backyard of their house on Long Island. I'd never been to the Hamptons, but I'd watched a VH1 celebrity special or two, so a more specific geographic reference might have given me some hint as to the true nature of this party. But Robert wasn't up for saying the H-word, which meant I got ready for this party like I would have any backyard barbecue back in Milldale, Oregon—just a T-shirt and jeans. When Robert picked me up for the drive from our summer dorms in Boston down to New York, the fact that he was outfitted in a sharp white linen concoction should have tipped me off. I did feel instantly nervous that perhaps the party was going to be a little fancier than I had guessed, but still, I didn't quite get it.

When did I actually get it? Was it when we pulled up to the house, or should I say, estate? Not fully. Was it when we walked into the little backyard party, or should I say, extravaganza on the grounds? Nope. Was it when the first person at the party I made eye contact with was Alec Baldwin? Yes, I'd say that was the moment.

"Is that Alec Baldwin?" I whispered to Robert.

He nodded, and then a second later as a waiter passed by with little spoonfuls of caviar on a silver tray, he whispered ferociously, "This is all tax deductible." And I suppose he was trying to say that otherwise it'd be Ma and Pa Rolland flipping burgers themselves, which I almost believed until I met Ma and Pa Rolland.

But apparently, now I said "Long Island" too.

The fan blowing in my face didn't do much good. Sweat ran from my upper lip into my lipstick, and the whole thing smeared when I attempted to wipe away the moisture. Thankfully, it was a mercifully short walk from my building to the subway and from the subway to the Long Island Rail Road. I cheered for every bit of air-conditioning along the way. Yay for air-conditioned train cars. Yay for the air-conditioned cab from the train, and yay for the waves of icy air I could practically see pouring from the Rollands' house as we pulled up. I would have cheered more had I been arriving in Robert's nicely air-conditioned BMW two-seater, which he undoubtedly drove in from the city that morning, but alas, my seat was taken.

Mr. and Mrs. Rolland hovered near what looked like wicker thrones on top of a fancy Oriental rug near their koi pond, greeting throngs of guests with cheek kisses for one and all. I joined the queue, ready for the somewhat strained familiarity that had marked our interactions since they'd first become aware of the turbulence of Robert's relationship with me sometime during sophomore year. Before I got my chance to say hello, Robert and a woman who could only be Lily swooped in.

All lean angles as usual, Robert looked appropriately like a pretzel heir in his trim tan suit. His dark brown hair had a few lighter brown streaks, and his skin had a slightly golden, baked quality to it. He and Lily must have been picnicking or hiking or doing other summery, coupley activities for the last several weeks while I'd been inside doing single-person things like cleaning the hair out of my brushes.

"Dawn, darling, how lovely to see you," Robert crooned.

Lily elbowed him. "He thinks it's funny to imitate his parents. He's been doing it all day to see who calls him on it and who takes him seriously." She said it with such jocular ease, like the most popular girl at summer camp.

I looked her up and down. I should have been discreet, but I don't think I was. I'd imagined being calm and cool, so cool and lovely that the Texas tart would walk away feeling wholly inadequate, trembling at the thought of trying to measure up to me. But I didn't feel calm and cool. The sight of Lily in real life standing next to Robert tripped my adrenal glands. I felt shaky with nerves, like I was barely holding the reins of rearing horses. She was petite, or normal, but compared to my gangly five-nine she was a diminutive little darling. And while my wavy red hair was piled on top of my head in a way that seemed to advertise what a sweaty morning I'd had as well as what cheap spangly earrings I was wearing, her sleek brown bob announced an invincibility to summer humidity, showed off what I couldn't imagine were anything other than real pearl earrings, and led your eye straight to her dainty freckled nose. (Of course her nose was that cute. What else could it be since my slightly crooked nose was one of my prime insecurities?) Decked out in a flip-collared seersucker jacket over a white cotton dress and a Tiffany charm bracelet, I thought she looked like polo-pony puke. I was glad to note she wasn't skinnier than I was. Then I felt bad for noting this, like I was so brainwashed I thought that mattered. Though even after I felt bad, I noted it again from another angle.

"Lily," I said, doing my best to impersonate a gracious person. "So nice to meet you."

"So Robert tells me you're a writer," she said, leaning in like we were actually friends, not just people badly faking the parts. Her voice was lower and more compelling than I would have thought, a little husky even, without a trace of Texas in it. She sounded like she should be reading the news on the radio.

"That's very generous of him," I said, my own voice all of a sudden sounding tinny and irksome to my ear, the way it does when you listen to recordings of yourself.

I might have been flattered by this line of conversation, or relieved, since it at least steered us somewhat delicately around the topic of my actual employment, but instead, I cringed because I knew exactly where it was headed.

"He says you write wonderful short stories," Lily said, carrying on politely.

"It's true, she does," Robert piped up, as if he were just getting his bearings. Usually, when Robert and I were together we generated a sort of undeniable heat, like the waves that radiate from the hood of an idling car. You could practically see it, and everything got hazy, and breathing in the haze was like breathing in a potion that magically pulled us together again. But with Lily here, the heat was diffuse, whatever waves were there refracted and sent bouncing in strange directions. At best, you could get a whiff of the magic. I detected a definite note of fluster in Robert's voice, and it was like he didn't know which one of us to look at when he talked, me or Lily. He kept shifting on his feet.

"So have you published any of your stories?" Lily asked, all innocent-like. And there it was, just as predicted: the dreaded moment. Almost as bad as "So what do you do?" Not having an answer you can be proud of for questions like that makes ordinary conversation agonizing, like having a blister on your heel and a shoe that cuts further into your skin with every should-be-painless step.

"Ah, well, I'm still working on the publishing part . . ." I said.
Robert fiddled with his drink.

"I'm sure it'll be any day now," Lily said, like she was some wise
old woman who knew the ways of the world and was patting naive
little me on the head.

I flashed a look of recrimination at Robert while Lily flagged
down a waiter with a tray of champagne. He wouldn't let me catch
his eye, and he had a single flushed spot on one cheek.

As we drank our champagne, I shifted the conversation to law
school. Lily had just finished her first year at Columbia. I would
have been starting law school in the fall, except that I'd decided I
just couldn't do it.

I'd been very close. As a teenager, I'd been hooked on shows
like *Ally McBeal* and *The Practice,* and maybe the more reasonable conclusion to draw from being attracted to TV programs
about lawyers is not that you want to be a lawyer, but rather that
you want to be an actor or a writer of shows about lawyers. Alas,
that hadn't occurred to me at the time. Peering into those big-city
lives through the television screen was like watching my teenage
dreams line up on a slot machine, each piece like a cherry inex-
tricably tied to the next. Ambition 1: Glamour. Ambition 2: Pres-
tige. Ambition 3: Lawyer? Bingo! There weren't a lot of competing
bingos presenting themselves to my imagination in small-town
Oregon, other than being a writer, which seemed about as unlikely
as being a movie star, and was therefore off the list. Being an attor-
ney seemed exciting *and* attainable, so the idea stuck.

My first two summers of college, I went home and worked at
a law firm in Eugene, drafting affidavits and motions for summary
judgment for workers' compensation cases. I liked it, or liked it
well enough. Figuring out the formal structure of each document I
had to write was like solving a puzzle, satisfying and vaguely enjoyable in a crosswordy sort of way, and I lapped up all the "Good
job, Dawn!" comments my work garnered. Plus, it was my first

experience with business attire—turned out pencil skirts and I got along quite nicely. Junior year, I stayed in Boston so I could be with Robert. He spent the summer interning for a business school professor, and I got a job as a camp counselor at a city camp for low-income kids, but I still spent my every free moment studying for the LSAT. And then I did the whole thing. I took the test, I applied, and I got in. I had options in D.C., Boston, and New York. But a strange thing happened. Spring of senior year, I stared at the "Yes, I will attend" box on each of the acceptance forms, and I couldn't bring myself to check a single one of them.

I'd always told myself writing was just a hobby, but it had started to feel like more than that. I'd been churning out stories during creative writing seminars all through college, and a few of my professors had made "I think you have talent" type remarks. They probably thought nothing of their words, but I couldn't let them go. It wasn't just their compliments; it was the way I felt when I was writing. When I put together a fifteen-page paper about imagery in Gerard Manley Hopkins's poetry, the whole point was breaking down and analyzing his ideas. When I wrote a short story, the whole point was breathing life into *my* ideas. It was like the difference between rummaging around in someone else's old house and designing and building a whole new house of my own. There is pleasure in rummaging, but nothing like the grand, expansive feeling of creating.

Bit by bit, writing dreams crept into my brain, and now, those dreams were like squatters yelling loudly for their rights. When I looked at law school acceptance forms, it was as if the "Yes" box did not say "Yes, I will attend," but instead boomed in a draconian voice, "Yes, I will crush all the creativity in my soul." I checked the "No" box. Robert had applauded my creative ambitions. My parents, on the other hand, fell into a category closer to worried-slash-perplexed. Maybe they were right, after all, since that pen mark had led me directly to the delightful world of unemployment and disappointment I was currently enjoying. My various collegiate activities were fine for grad school, but if you want a job, turns out some summer experience in fields other than playing at law or playing with kids can be helpful. Oops.

But Lily had checked the "Yes" box. Looking at her was like looking into some sort of fun-house mirror. If I'd gone to law school, would I be her right now?

At the very moment I was thinking this, Lily said, "I'm summering at Craven & Swinton, in their tax practice." She actually used the word "summering." From which I inferred—as if the seersucker and pearls weren't enough—that she belonged to the class of people for whom "summer" was regularly employed as a verb. So really, it would take a lot more than some fun-house glass to turn me into her.

My face was starting to hurt from smiling so pleasantly.

"Let's find some food," Robert said during a conversational lull. "There's this new mustard we're testing."

After every Thanksgiving, Robert had returned to school with a case of different mustard types to sample. We'd sat on his futon and carefully tried out various mustard and pretzel combinations—Bronson's honey mustard with the garlic pretzel. Heneman's dijon with the low-sodium pretzel twigs—Robert writing notes as if it were a wine tasting. When he said "mustard testing" he looked at me, and it felt like the first time he'd actually *looked* at me since I'd arrived. We exchanged knowing half smiles. How much mustard could he and Lily have shared? Certainly nothing to rival our mustard history.

I wanted to interpret the moment to mean he didn't love Lily, he still loved me. But after our glancing exchange, he took Lily's hand, which I knew, coming from Robert, was not uncalculated. He'd grant me our history, but he was with her. I wanted to walk away without saying a word, hail a cab, and disappear. But that would have been so dramatic, so over the top, so final. Instead, I followed along as if I hadn't noticed the gesture.

We'd just started across the lawn together, me a step behind, when Lily planted her feet and spun around dramatically. "Dawn, there's someone you have to meet!" she said.

I felt like all sensation had already left me, like I was an empty piñata. "Okay" was all I could muster. She looped her arm chummily through mine, and I let her lead me toward a small circle of partygoers a few yards away.

"Regina," she said, gently touching the arm of a lovely and somehow vaguely familiar petite, dark-haired woman in red silk. "I want you to meet Dawn. She's an old friend of Robert's and the most terrific writer." Then she turned to me. "Dawn, Regina just moved in down the street from the Rollands, and she definitely knows a thing or two about the magazine business." And then Lily winked and walked away.

Off-kilter and dazed, I stood there, trying to return to myself and marshal my forces to attempt a passable rendition of a charming person. I'd applied for dozens of magazine jobs, most of which asked for experience I didn't have. And then there were the internships. What a great idea, except most of them didn't pay, or required that you were a college student receiving credit for the work, which I wasn't anymore. While the engine of my brain tried to chug forward on these unhelpful fumes, Regina, who actually *was* a charming person, provided the conversational fuel to get us going.

"So what kind of writing do you do, Dawn?" she asked in the most warm, interested way, like she'd just made me tea and cookies and now we had an entire kettle's worth of chitchat to enjoy.

"Well, lots of things." I laughed a little. "Short stories, you know, for the money. Ha-ha. But mostly, well yes, mostly, I'm a lawn expert."

I'd expected questions along the employment line, and I'd prepared my "lawn expert" answer in advance. LawnTalk.com hadn't given me a title. It wasn't like I had business cards. I didn't even use my real name. And it certainly wasn't a full-time gig. But I couldn't stand saying "Well, actually, I graduated a year ago and I'm still looking for a real job." That either stopped conversation or unleashed a river of comforting, even wistful advice from older adults, intoned as if my problems were a quaint reminder of their younger years.

"A lawn expert?" Regina smiled and leaned in. "Do you take care of lawns? Do you have a lawn?"

This was a much better approach.

"Actually, don't ever tell anyone"—I leaned in conspiratorially—"but I've never had a lawn. I mean, my parents had a lawn for a while, though I never helped take care of it, but eventually my mom ripped it out and put in a rock garden. And now I guess I can *see* grass from my apartment window in Brooklyn . . ."

"So how did you become a lawn expert?" she asked, wide eyed.

I heard myself taking on a slightly swashbuckling tone. "Well, actually, Craigslist . . . This website was looking for a writer who could write about lawns, and I told them I'd seen neighbors mow their lawns, I'd run through sprinklers on lawns, I liked lawns, and somehow they were hard-up enough that they signed me. I have about half the Brooklyn Public Library system's lawn care books on my floor at home right now. But I've been doing it for a few months now. I write a little weekly column and then answer all the questions users post, and somehow, it's worked out."

I expected a "Gosh, that's kind of funny" reaction, but that's not what Regina was giving me. As I talked, she actually bent toward me like a tennis player, crouching and tensed, ready to spring at the ball the second it left my racket. It made me nervous, and I wondered where things had gone wrong.

"I'm sure the lawn care expert world must be pretty small," Regina rushed, "so I have to ask, do you know a writer named Kelly Burns?"

I felt a terrific zing all the way from my toes to my fingertips. "Kelly Burns?" I said. "I'm Kelly Burns! That's my online pen name."

She snatched my forearm. "No way. LawnTalk.com Kelly Burns? We just bought a house down the street, and my husband is obsessed with having the perfect lawn and has this total crazy need to do it himself. He seriously reads your site every night. He actually says 'Time for Kelly Burns' and cracks his knuckles as he sits down with his laptop. You're Kelly Burns?! Oh, he's going to love this."

A few users on the site had sent me nice thank-you messages after I helped them diagnose their mysterious lawn diseases or choose the best grass type for their yard, but a real-life, in-person fan? I felt a glow of pride, the first time I'd felt any such thing in a long, long while. Forget my air conditioner–free digs, forget that Robert seemed to have found his dream sorority-girl counterpart, forget that I still wasn't getting interviews and that the idea that I'd ever publish any fiction seemed totally laughable. Someone in this world cracked his knuckles every night, logged on to LawnTalk.com, and said "Time for Kelly Burns."

Regina released her grip on my forearm, only to grab my bicep, mafia-escort style. "I think he's out back. Let's go find him," she said, and just like that we were swerving through the crowd (I saw Alec Baldwin out of the corner of my eye), out onto the deck by the pool, and from there down to the west garden. We stopped at a table up near the band, where a group of handsome men, one of whom was apparently Regina's husband, were sitting around enjoying fancy foreign beers and a bowl of Rolland's Bavarians.

"Tony," she said, looking at the curly-haired one with super-thick-framed nerd-cool glasses, "I'd like to introduce you to Kelly Burns, the lawn expert." She waved her hand up and down over me, like a manic version of a model on *The Price Is Right*. The other men looked a little bewildered—who was this slightly sweaty, blushing lawn-expert person?—but Tony jumped up to shake my hand.

"Kelly Burns? Kelly Burns of Lawn Talk?" He beamed. "No way. I'm Buddy 7468."

"For real?" I answered giddily. "Have you treated the bindweed yet?"

"Oh yeah, did exactly what you said. Double treatment of dicamba, cut off their water supply. Worked like a charm." He turned to his wife. "How did . . . ?"

"Robert's girlfriend just introduced us," Regina said.

Robert's girlfriend. Robert's girlfriend. Robert's girlfriend. The words were a cartoon echo in my head.

"And actually," Regina continued, "it's not Kelly Burns, it's Dawn in real life, right?"

I nodded. "Kelly Burns is just a pen name."

"Crazy," Tony said. "I always figured Kelly Burns was a fifty-year-old dude living in Ohio."

"Don't tell anyone I'm not," I whispered.

Just then the band started playing "Blue Skies," and Lily swung by our table and touched my shoulder, a dainty interruption. "Dawn, I wondered if I could grab you for a minute."

I could have said no, but anything other than gracious acceptance would have sounded strident after Lily's dulcet request.

"So great meeting you, Regina, Tony, everyone." I put my hand up in a wave and turned toward Lily.

"I'm sure we'll talk again before the night is over." Regina smiled.

I nodded, smiles all around, and let Lily take my arm.

"I'm sorry to pull you away," she said in a low tone as we made our way across the lawn. "I got stuck talking to this horrible horse-radish distributor, and I needed an excuse to leave and I saw you across the way and told him I had to give you a message. I think the horseradish guy is still looking, so try to look superengrossed in conversation."

Confident presumption seemed to define Lily. She talked to me like she naturally deserved to be in charge. And I recognized it because it reminded me of Robert. Like the time Robert picked me up after my last final sophomore year and drove us straight to Portland, Maine, where he insisted on instructing me in perfect lobster-eating technique. He'd sat down beside me and practically moved my hands for me. I'd loved it. It had felt so caring and fun. On the way home, though, he'd told me I should stop holding my head at an angle when I talked, and I felt assaulted by such minute criticism, so there'd always been both sides. But there was a gleam to it, being singled out for attention by someone so obviously striding wherever he pleased. I didn't want to feel drawn in by Lily. I wanted to find her undynamic and dismissible. But she wasn't either of those things.

Lily led us to a place by the pool, where she sat on the edge, took off her shoes, and dangled her feet in the water. I joined her.

"Robert says that after you guys broke up, you didn't talk for a little while, but then it was pretty much normal and friendly." She kicked the water and little droplets splashed back onto our dresses.

So, she wanted to get right into it, did she? I was surprised Robert had told such a massive lie. I held my breath, waiting for whatever was coming next.

"I think that's awesome." She splashed the water with her feet again, this time a little harder. "The guy I broke up with before Robert and I started dating—or who broke up with me, actually—I sent him squirrel heads in the mail and programmed my e-mail to send him a message every single morning for a whole month that just said 'Fuck you,' nothing else. I'm sure he figured out how to block it, but it felt great sending it anyway."

None of this was what I expected from the rose of Texas.

"Rewind," I interrupted, "squirrel heads?"

"Oh, it's the best thing I ever discovered. Roguetaxidermy

.com. They've got amazing stuff. Bags of bird wings. Pickled sheep brains. You can do cleaned squirrel heads so it's just the bones, or mummified squirrel heads. Mummified is the way to go. Much freakier."

"Wow." I nodded with real admiration. "I mean, I guess the most I've ever really done is write mean e-mails, but then not send them."

"You're a killer, Dawn," she said, and then after a long and what seemed appraising pause, "I think we should be friends. That way you can give me the dirt on Robert."

I smiled without saying anything, then looked away, almost embarrassed. Announcing friendship felt like too much, not just for us but for anyone. What was I supposed to do if I didn't want to be friends? Say no? Then I'd seem confrontational when in fact she'd introduced the demands.

Robert arrived just then. "I wondered where you two disappeared to!" he said in his jocular host voice. I watched his eyes flick between us while his mouth held a steady smile.

He gave a flourishy little bow and offered his hand to Lily to pull her up. She took his hand and glided to his side. Before Robert could extend the same courtly hand to me, which would have been awkward, or leave me to get up from the pool deck by myself, which would have been even more awkward, Lily reached her own hand down to me. "Heave-ho, up we go!" she groaned as she pulled me up.

There was nothing dainty about her grip, and when I was finally standing beside her, she smiled and nodded, like we'd just sealed the deal on our agreement to be friends. I glanced at Robert. He looked away.

"Come on," he said, "let's get some dinner." And again, it was diffuse, an invitation to Lily, to me, to the air.

We got some of the chic pretzel pastrami sandwiches, put our feet in the pool again, and talked to Alec Baldwin. (In all my years at the party I'd never talked to him before. In real life he was nicer and had fatter fingers than expected.)

After sunset, crickets now chirping all around us, guests began to leave. Still in our awkward but seemingly inescapable trio, Robert, Lily, and I were sitting near the koi pond when Regina and Tony walked by. I popped up, and Regina saw me, waved, and quickly walked over. Gosh, she was stylish, her red dress swishing around her legs like she was some jazz-era singer as she moved across the lawn.

She gave me a quick air kiss on the cheek, then took a card from her purse and leaned in close. "Call me Monday, Kelly Burns."

She pulled away and walked off with Tony, turning back to wave over her shoulder. I looked at the card. In big pink letters it said: Regina Greene, Editor in Chief, *Charm*. For years, I'd been reading *Charm* magazine in doctors' offices and hair salons, and even, occasionally, off the periodicals shelf at the library when I just couldn't study for one more second. (I'd always hid in one of the carrels in the back when I executed that move, since reading about lip liner and layering when you were supposed to be reading critical interpretations of *King Lear* struck me as embarrassing.) Surely, I'd seen Regina's photo inset on the editor page any number of times. I felt dopey for not recognizing her.

"Looks like you sure *charmed* them, ha-ha, get it?" Lily said.

"Or was it *bedazzled* them?" Robert said.

"Wait, did Tony invent the bedazzler or something?" I asked, ready to be astounded if Tony or Regina were somehow affiliated with such a wardrobe revolutionizing tool.

"Uh, no," Robert said.

"Then I don't think I get your joke," I said.

"I guess there wasn't really one. Just that bedazzled is a funny word?" He shrugged and flashed a supplicating smile.

Lily splashed Robert with water from the pond, and I plopped back on the grass, turning my face away from them. The grass was soft and deep green—the loveliest fine fescue blend around. It hadn't been so long ago that I'd imagined Robert and me getting married and having kids and our kids running around on this lawn. In fact, I could still imagine it. But as Lily moved, her silver kitten heel sandals flashed into my periphery, and I suddenly had a crystalline vision of their wedding, right here, in this same yard. In the rest of my view, though, I saw fireflies, more and more of them every second, rising out of the grass with perfect blinking zips of gold.

Just a few minutes later, I said my good-byes. Robert offered to drive me to the train. I said no. He didn't insist. The walk to the train station was just under a mile, but with Regina's card tucked in my wallet, it felt like just a few blocks.

When I called her office Monday morning, she offered me Ten Girls to Watch.

And like I said, I danced and power-pumped my fists the second I hung up. I wanted to sing. I did sing! But after the initial bright white surge of delight dimmed slightly, I saw a few other colors.

A job you find online and apply for and get through your own shining résumé—no one can say anything about that except congratulations, you deserve it. A job you get because you met someone at a party in the Hamptons—it has the taint of privilege, as if Regina hadn't chosen me because I'd wowed her but because I'd been vouched for by the *right* people. I knew "that was how the world worked," and after a year of searching, it wasn't like I was going to turn down the job. It was just that this was the sort of thing I'd resented most about Robert. When he wanted a summer job on Capitol Hill, his dad called some friends. When I wanted a summer job anywhere other than Oregon, my dad said good luck. Meaning, I was usually the person who got screwed by "that's how the world works." Just shrugging and taking advantage of it now made me feel a little like I was pocketing an envelope full of dirty money. Pocketing gratefully, but still.

And then, of course, there was the fact that Lily had introduced me to Regina, which meant I now owed Lily. Lily, a woman I didn't exactly wish bodily harm, but whose sudden disappearance from the world I would not mourn. I'd have to thank *both* Robert and Lily. Should I send one e-mail or e-mail them separately? Together felt like it solidified their status as a couple. Separately felt like I was attempting to further forge some sort of independent relationship with Lily. Bah, I'd figure it out later.

I marched out of the house to buy an air conditioner on credit. A much sweeter celebration than any cake.

That night, I sat on a blanket directly in front of the newly installed window unit and lapped up the cool while earning my day's wages on LawnTalk.com. Even with the vague promise of a future *Charm* payday, I still desperately needed my eleven cents a word.

After a solid chunk answering questions about grubs and crabgrass, I gave myself a little e-mail break. I'd gotten this:

Dawn, Regina asked me to e-mail you
please come in tomorrow at 10am with the following
    1) your resume
    2) your passport
    3) a working knowledge of excel
    4) a can-do attitude
XADI Crockett
Senior Editor
Charm magazine

From this e-mail, I determined the following:

1) Regina worked fast.
2) Xadi was my new boss.

3) Xadi liked lists.

4) Xadi didn't like punctuation.

5) Xadi imagined that if I didn't know how to use Excel, I would learn overnight.

6) XADI expected others to capitalize her name too.

I felt weird about all-caps names, so that was going to be an adjustment, but I was just the can-do girl she was looking for, so all caps it was. But those were the subtleties. What beamed out from the screen was this: I hadn't made it up. The job was real.

Helen Thomas,

Harvard University, 1972

THE CAMPUS CRUSADER

This straight-A history major is one for the record books herself. As president of Harvard Earth Day, Helen led a march of more than three thousand students in support of the environment. Next up, she worked with a local union to organize university service workers in a successful campaign for higher wages and increased benefits. "When I see problems, I can't just sit around and do nothing," Helen says. We can't wait to see what she'll tackle next.

Chapter Two

*R*egina Greene's call wasn't the first time I'd heard of the Ten Girls to Watch Contest. The first time was a year earlier, in the home of Helen Hensley, my college thesis advisor. Helen Hensley, née Helen Thomas: 1972 Ten Girls to Watch awardee.

In a national poll from a few years back, 68 percent of US liberal arts colleges reported assigning their incoming freshmen to read one of two essays: "Self-Reliance" by Ralph Waldo Emerson or Helen Hensley's 1978 essay "Must We Find Meaning?" about the cultural and spiritual fallout of World War I. I was one of the college freshmen assigned to Helen's essay.

"Remembering the Great War," the essay opens, "requires modern man to face twin compulsions: the compulsion to find sense in tragedy and the compulsion to insist on its senselessness." Ordinary enough, but by the time she was describing the smell of old artillery rust in the soil, farmers turning up gas masks in their fields fifty years after the war, and the way she tried to cope with the death of half her family in a fire when she was a teenager, I could feel the tops of my ears tingling and my entire body humming along with the resonance of the unfolding sentences and paragraphs. I was so enthralled that I hated to finish it, and when I came to the end of the essay I turned right back to the beginning and read it all over again.

And then I read it about twenty more times over the next four years. It turned out Helen Hensley was a professor in the history department at my university, a discovery that led to my near hyperventilation in the library—certainly the last time the course catalog got me *that* excited. I took every class Professor Hensley offered for the next six semesters, and, after many nervous courting visits to her office hours, finally asked her to be my thesis advisor, which, despite the fact that I was a literature major, was possible if I wrote a "History and Literature" thesis. (Literature major didn't exactly spell postcollegiate big bucks, but history and literature? A combo that ensured I'd have to beat away employers.)

During our first official weekly thesis meeting my senior year, she told me to call her Helen. I was the equivalent of a screaming Beatles teenager. The second I left her office, I called Robert to tell him the news. "Call her Helen?!" I screeched. "Does it get any better than that?"

Helen won the Pulitzer for the book *Must We Find Meaning?* of which "Must We Find Meaning?" the essay, served as the introduction. In addition to being a public intellectual and the chair of our university's history department, she's also a master glassblower. Did I mention that she has long, flowing white hair and wears green eyeliner and Chanel No. 5 at all times? I believe my hyperventilation over the course catalog was well merited.

During the year, we grew closer, and I calmed down a little, though never enough that the thrill went away completely. Helen grew up in Oregon too, in a town only about an hour from mine. Like me, she'd grown up secretly wanting to be a writer, and again, like me, her hair had once been a firebolt of red (hers had gone white; mine had lightened into a shade I called "strawberry blonde"). In addition to slogging through my thesis chapters on

"Regret versus Remorse in the Works of Thomas Hardy and Wilfred Owen" (a topic for the ages), she generously volunteered to read and comment on my fiction. "I can smell Oregon when I read this," she wrote in a note on a story about a girl who spends her summer working at a saltwater taffy shop on the waterfront in Yachats, only to find the shop burgled on her last day of work and then to discover months later that the burglar was her brother.

Midway through the year, Helen invited me to dinner at her home with her husband, Paul, and a few of her grad students. After a glass or two of wine, at the end of the night, standing next to her at the sink drying dishes, I goofily said, "You know you're my hero." She laughed, then turned serious. "That works very well, since I've started to think of you as my protégé." I felt pinpricks of delight.

The summer after graduation, when I'd turned down law school and gone from being her bright protégé to being her ailing graduate who couldn't get a job, she offered to let me stay with her and Paul, for free, in the glassblowing hut in their backyard.

I took them up on it for a few months. To be clear, "glassblowing hut" was a misnomer. Complete with two floors and indoor plumbing, the hut was a beautiful, scaled-down version of one of those ornate winter greenhouse palaces that make it possible for Icelandic princesses to eat oranges all year long. On afternoons when she came out to the glassblowing hut to work, she graciously listened to every sob story I had about jobs I wasn't getting and Robert-related melodrama. On the nights she and Paul would invite me over to "the big house" for dinner, they offered thoughts on careers and grad school and writing.

At one of our dinners, when I lamented for perhaps the millionth time that *maybe I should have gone to law school*, Helen had finally had enough. She was gentle, but I remember her exact words. "You'd make a great lawyer, Dawn," she said. "And you haven't closed the door on law school. Not by a long shot. But if you're going to try something else first, you need to stop second-guessing yourself. There's a time for reflection and course correction if necessary, but *you're not there yet.*"

When October arrived, I finally decided to move to New York, job or no job, and Helen left a note on my cot. (To be clear, "cot" was also a misnomer. It had feather padding and one-thousand-thread-count sheets.) On simple cream stationery in Helen's sloping script, the note was just one line: "D, I believe in you, and what makes me really happy is I think you're starting to believe in you too. Love, H." I folded it and tucked it into my copy of *Must We Find Meaning?* and I've kept that book by my bedside every night since then.

On my last day before decamping to New York, I was poking around in Helen's library (a favorite activity, made even more favorite by the fact that her library had one of those rolling ladders), when I found the framed Ten Girls to Watch award certificate on one of the upper shelves, *Charm* scripted out in vintage magenta font. She'd giggled and gushed through the details of the contest when I'd asked her about it the next day. She still remembered the platform boots they'd outfitted her in for her photos, seeing *Grease* on Broadway with the other winners, touring the UN, and lunching with Betty Friedan. When the magazine hit newsstands, she'd enjoyed the glow of minor celebrity. The suitcase full of beauty products she'd gone home with hadn't hurt either.

I knew Helen would be thrilled to hear about my new job. That night, just after I got the e-mail from XADI that assured me I hadn't been hallucinating, I zipped off an e-mail:

Helen, you won't believe it. I just got a job. An amazing job. A real job. I'm working at Charm Magazine, and my first assignment is to track down all the past Ten Girls to Watch winners for the contest's 50th anniversary this year. TGTW winners—that means you! Talk later this week? Love, Dawn

After that I called my older sister, Sarah.

There were a few reasons I was in New York. One was Robert. Another was the ostensible possibility of writing-related jobs. A third was Sarah. She'd never left Oregon. I mean, she'd left for vacation, but she'd never *left* left. It wasn't supposed to be that way. Her plan had been: New York City. She was five years older than me, and as a twelve-year-old listening to her talk about all the clubs she was going to sing in someday in Soho and the East Village, the place names had taken on the power of incantations. When she said "Manhattan," I conjured people with sleek black forms, like ghosts, gliding down streets that glittered in the dark. I pictured Sarah becoming one of them. I could feel all those ghosts in the room when she played her guitar, their misty hands clapping when she finished each song. But then she'd gone to U of O, and then she'd met Peter, and then they'd moved to Eugene and gotten married and had kids. Sometimes I felt I was living in New York for both of us. And sometimes I thought I was in New York out of some sort of perverse sibling rivalry.

"Hi, Dawn!" Sarah said in a staccato when she answered. "I've only got like five minutes. Dinnertime." I heard Peter murmur something in the background and one of their girls begin to howl. The twins, Holly and Hannah, had come a few months before I graduated from college.

"Takes less than five minutes to tell you I got a job!" I announced.

"Oh my gosh, I want to hear everything," she squealed with real delight, and then, away from the phone, "Baby, just put it in for a minute and then pull it out to see if it's hot. Yeah, just a minute, I promise."

"Well, it's at *Charm* magazine," I said in a ritzy voice.

"Really? An assistant job? An editor job?" She got dimmer as she spoke—the telltale sign of the receiver slipping away. She must have been holding the phone with her shoulder, probably a kid in each arm.

I talked fast. I considered leaving out the part about meeting Regina at Robert's Pretzel Party, but in the end I left it in, and she groaned at Robert's name, as expected.

"Have you told Mom or Dad yet?" she asked.

"Not yet," I said.

The phone clattered from her ear to the floor. I listened to the faraway sounds of the kitchen, scuffling of feet, beeping of microwave, Sarah and Peter sweet-talking the twins as they buckled them into their high chairs. Only then did Sarah pick up the phone again.

"Sorry, sweetie," she said.

I said it was okay and promised to tell her more after my first day of work.

"At least call Mom. She'll be upset if she finds out you didn't tell her right away."

"Of course," I said, though, in fact, if Sarah hadn't ordered me to do it, I might have waited a day or two before calling.

I read in some women's magazine (maybe it was *Charm*) that it takes fifteen years for a kid to get over a divorce. So maybe in seven years I'd dial my parents right away. For the time being I was grateful Sarah always answered, even if she dropped the phone on me a few minutes later.

My dad was a high school history teacher. He'd been at the same school, in the town over from ours, for twenty-nine years, since just before Sarah was born, and his job advice always had a local slant. He'd heard they needed a secretary at the Ford dealership down the road from his school, or, if I was ever interested in selling insurance, Sherry Fogel, from church, had a good business and she was looking to bring in some new blood . . .

My mom, on the other hand, hadn't worked until the divorce, when I was in high school, at which point she'd become a Mary Kay lady, and her advice had a manic salesy tinge to it. *You just have to march into the offices where you want to work with your résumé in hand, then wait till someone will see you!*

My dad and I only spoke sporadically. Every month or so I'd call to update him. He never called. My mom, on the other hand, called a few times a week to share the latest town gossip. You got a lot of it as a Mary Kay lady. Sherry Fogel's business must really have been doing okay, because rumor had it she'd gotten a face-lift, and if my mother's powers of detection were as sharp as ever, breast implants too.

A couple of days before the Pretzel Party, my mom had called to tell me she had a great idea for me: "Have you thought about creating flyers? Just dropping them off at every business you can think of. Flyers have really done so much for my business," she said.

I explained that résumés were sort of like flyers.

"Well, just think about it," she implored.

You'd think I'd be thrilled to share the job news with her. But landing a job at a party was way too Mary Kay. I could already hear her crowing voice. *"See! It's all about putting yourself out there!"* It sounded just like "I told you so," with that little barb wrapped up in a big hug. The big hug almost made it worse, since it's hard to stay irked at someone who's smooshing you so energetically into their arms, even if you're feeling the prick all the while.

But my big sister was right, you can't get a job and not call your mom.

I dialed, and the phone rang and rang. Leaving a message—the best of both worlds!

"Guess what? I've got some good news for you. A job! I got a job!" My voice went into a singsong, exactly like my mom's when she knocked on a door and said "Yoo-hoo! Mary Kay!" I couldn't help it.

It was late, and I turned my phone to vibrate for the night. I knew she'd call back but I'd listen to her message later. And I'd call my dad soon enough.

Then I sent one more e-mail, to Abigail Wei, my best friend and college roommate. She was marooned in the jungles of El Salvador working for the Peace Corps, and it might be a week, or maybe two, before she was able to take the seven-hour bus ride to town to check her e-mail. But I knew, when she finally did, that she'd sleep a little easier in her hammock knowing something had finally happened for me.

———

Charm magazine is a Mandalay Carson publication. I'd applied for at least ten jobs at the company (everything from assistant to the editor in chief of *Outdoor Living* to web marketing assistant at *Modern Mom*), and while I'd seen photos and walked by the Carson building and looked through the windows, I'd never been in. Apparently, they were interviewing recent grads who had previous experience doing something other than writing legal briefs. The outrage. At the center of the all-white five-story atrium lobby stands a sixty-foot silver tree sculpture by Guier Loudon, complete with thousands of delicately carved silver leaves individually attached with tiny hooks so that they shimmer and quake in the artificial breeze circulating through the atrium's upper levels.

The next morning as I walked through the doors, I avoided all staring and gasping so that anyone who happened to be looking would think I was an old pro rather than some neophyte. At the front desk I asked for XADI Crockett, and after flashing a photo ID I was directed up to eighteen.

Like the main lobby, *Charm*'s waiting area was bright white, and at the far end behind a shiny bright counter sat the receptionist and, behind her on the wall, a giant blowup of *Charm*'s most recent cover featuring Reese Witherspoon, hung in a way that gave the impression that Reese served as a coreceptionist, but one whose choice of workplace attire might be suspect, boobalicious purple satin dresses typically not on the list of office-approved apparel.

I asked for XADI and took a seat as the receptionist called back. Of course I'd googled XADI that morning. The Internet had very quickly verified that she was indeed an editor at *Charm,* but that was about it—my image search had been fruitless. I perched anxiously on the chair.

And then, there she was, holding open the glass door that led to the offices, the word CHARM in giant letters emblazoned on the wall behind her. XADI Crockett. The second I saw her, any remaining strains of resistance to capitalizing her name vanished. In her forties, with solid square shoulders, she looked like a masseuse at a Turkish bath, the kind whose massive hands could really work out all your kinks. Her hair was mousy brown and bluntly cut to her chin, with wiry strands of gray running through it. Her facial features were broad and unmitigated by makeup, save one savage dash of magenta lipstick. Her black shirt and slacks hung shapelessly on her broad frame. She had the sort of presence that could quiet a whole gym full of unruly seventh graders with one blow of a whistle. Not exactly the woman my teenage self had imagined on the other side of the *Charm* advice I memorized monthly, but clearly a force. She radiated competence. Meanwhile, the white pencil skirt, green tank, and yellow cardigan I'd come up with that morning, feeling like an ad for a bright young working professional who knew a thing or two about color blocking, suddenly seemed cartoonish.

XADI led me down a long hallway adorned with photo after photo of old *Charm* covers—Grace Kelly with red lipstick in 1960; Candice Bergen with a staggeringly tall updo in 1964.

"Amazing photos!" I said. Nothing like a little winning chitchat to break the ice.

"Aren't they?" XADI said, her tone clearly ending that line of conversation. Apparently she didn't hail from the chitchat school of get-to-know-you.

As we sped along I imagined that the hallway would soon open on a buzzing newsroom where, in my dream version of the day, I would first be shown into Regina's office for a friendly tête-à-tête, following which I would be presented with my shiny new desk. Alas, no such thing. XADI led us immediately to an internal office.

"You're just here today to fill out paperwork," she said. "You'll be starting tomorrow at the archives warehouse."

"Archives warehouse?" I said as cheerily as possible.

"It's on Fiftieth and Eleventh. The address is in your packet. They'll be expecting you in the morning. I thought it would be easier for you to work from there. They have all the back issues and the relevant Ten Girls to Watch materials."

I nodded as my dream of a shiny new desk shriveled up and disappeared, leaving me feeling embarrassed to have had the vision in the first place.

"Your first job is to get to know all of the Ten Girls to Watch back issues," XADI continued. "You'll start in the fifties and work forward." At this unnecessary chronological guidance, I felt a pang of worry—had I come across as incompetent? Already? I did my best to look alert and alive.

"The contest ran in the August issues until 1973," XADI continued in her stern voice. "Then it moved to September until 1981, and it's been in March ever since. Just to orient you."

I nodded vigorously and jotted notes. The note taking seemed to garner some approval.

"I'm not actually going through any of the paperwork with you," she said. "HR takes care of that. They're expecting you in a few minutes. I just wanted to meet in person since I'll be your editor for this project."

Ah, so here came the get-to-know-you. I cleared my throat and smiled eagerly in preparation. But no. With that, XADI stopped. When she said "meet in person," apparently that's all she meant. Just meeting.

"Well, it's great to meet you," I said, trying to build a bridge over the awkwardness.

"You too. This should be fun," she said, smiling without showing her teeth. And then she stood up and walked me back to the reception area. "They're expecting you on ten. Just tell the receptionist your name, and she'll know what to do. And they'll be expecting you at the archives tomorrow at nine a.m."

So that was *Charm* Day One. It could have gone better. It could have gone worse.

Day Two began with the long walk from the subway to the distant fringes of Hell's Kitchen. When you get that far west the city gets scrubby, the office towers giving way to barbed-wire-protected parking lots and hulking windowless warehouses. I double checked the address, then rang the buzzer at one such warehouse, though this one was on the diminutive side compared to some of its neighbors, more like a sliver of a warehouse, the width of a town house. Somebody somewhere in the building pressed a button that buzzed me in, and I walked into a small gray room, with stained industrial beige carpet and no receptionist in sight. It felt like the waiting area at a car mechanic's garage.

I looked around expectantly, not sure what to do next. After a minute I contemplated taking a seat in one of the chairs. Certainly I was on some sort of surveillance camera, and whoever had buzzed me into the building would send someone to the waiting room eventually? Mindful of the theoretical cameras, I avoided worrying my cuticles or looking for split ends or any of the other biding-time behaviors I typically engaged in when unsurveilled. I smoothed my skirt and adjusted my cardigan (today's outfit was a combo of red, pink, and tan, which was hard for a redhead to pull off and which may have made me look like a valentine, but which

I hoped nonetheless read as capable with a side of pizzazz), and then I waited with what I believed was a look of polite expectation on my face.

At last a door at the back of the room opened, and in walked a toweringly tall forty-something man who bore a notable resemblance to Eddie Munster in a tan cardigan, though a friendly-seeming Eddie Munster to be sure.

"Dawn?" he said.

I nodded, noting our matching cardigans, and we shook hands vigorously as he said, "I'm Ralph, the head librarian. Pleased to meet you. If you'll follow me back, I'll show you where we've got you set up."

He held the door for me, and I followed him into an expanse of neon lights, buzzing above steel cages that separated us from shelves and shelves of books and magazines. Our footsteps clicked and clacked on the cement floor. The smell was the exact slightly musty but glittering-with-possibility smell of the stacks in my college library.

"The archival materials for *Charm* are all on level two," Ralph said, passing me to take the lead. My, what a lot of neck hair he had.

When we entered the elevator, he pressed –2, which seemed to imply that level two was in the basement. Down we went. So far, Ralph and I appeared to be the only two people in the building, no other signs of life. I expected that maybe level –2 housed all the action, but when we arrived, the elevator opened on an identically barren-of-persons-but-full-of-books landscape. He unlocked one of the steel cages, and I followed him through sets of shelves. Upon closer inspection, I realized that all the books were bound volumes of magazines. First we passed the back issues of *Invest,* then came the back issues of *Couture.*

After these shelves, we reached an open area with a grouping of four desks, all equipped with computers and scanners. No sign or sound of people near the desks, however.

"We're working on digitizing everything," Ralph said. "In addition to overseeing the library, I also oversee the online archives project." And then perhaps sensing my confusion given the lack of bodies, he said, "Most of the scanning team works the night shift."

So maybe it really was just me and Ralph, and "head librarian" actually meant "only librarian." Finally, we reached the shelves where the back issues of *Charm* resided. The warehouse archives had up to this point proved far from the gleaming Mandalay Carson experience I'd fantasized about, but the bound volumes of *Charm* gleamed in their own way. White spined, with the capital letters C-H-A-R-M emblazoned in gold down each one, they looked like treasure.

"We've got ten copies of every issue. The loose volumes are on the shelves over there," Ralph said, gesturing to the row behind us. "And we've got photos and correspondence and all sorts of other materials there too. But the bound copies are here. And they're the easiest to work with. Every copy since 1946, with a book per year."

"Great!" I said, truly excited by the reams of materials, but in the quiet, it sounded louder than I'd intended, like a strange yelp.

"Let me show you where we've got your desk," Ralph said eagerly. I'd figured I'd be using one of the four desks back in the middle of the floor, but Ralph led me past the shelves and out of the cage and opened the door to what was clearly a storage room, half full of boxes. On one wall, amid the boxes, a computer and a phone were perched atop a small table.

"They set you up with a login and everything yesterday, right?" Ralph said.

I concurred.

"Good. I'll let you get started then. Oh, before I forget, you need your keys." He reached into his pocket. "This one is for your office." Generous use of that term, I thought, as he set the silver key on my desk. "And this one is for the security screen on this floor." By which I figured he meant the steel cage. Apparently my access was limited to this floor only. And with that, Ralph gave me a big pearly smile and said, "I'm upstairs if you need anything. You can also just call my extension. I'm extension 1. You're extension 2." Which sounded suspiciously like he might just be the only other extension in the building.

After Ralph's departure, I plunked down in my swivel chair and gave it a slow spin, taking in the 360 view. Yes, it was a closet, but it was *my* closet. I had *a job*. And yes, there were boxes, boxes, and more boxes, but I like the smell of cardboard boxes and have a long and loving history with cardboard in general. My current coffee table was just the start of it. My "nightstand" and all the "end tables" in my apartment were made of cardboard too. In college, I'd been even more of a cardboard connoisseur. As far as I was concerned, a sturdy box plus a folded sheet equaled completely passable furniture.

But perhaps most important, in my first glance at my new office space, I'd overlooked the bulletin board. I loved that scene in the *Sabrina* remake where Sabrina posts a photo of the man she's obsessed with on her bulletin board and then, in subsequent scenes, tacks other pictures up until he's completely covered, thus physically manifesting her psychological transformation. What other Staples product can do that for you? With visions of color copies and thumbtacks dancing in my head, I headed to the shelves and loaded myself up with the 1957, '58, and '72 volumes—1972 because, if I remembered correctly, that was Helen Hensley's year.

I hadn't heard back from her yet, which had me a touch worried. She usually wasn't the sort of person who didn't return e-mails.

When I returned with the '72 volume, I flipped pages until I landed on the TGTW coverage. Our gals were looking pretty groovy, long hair, a few showings of fringey vests . . . And then, as I'd known I would, I saw her face. She may have been wearing the Muppetiest brown and white pile coat ever, and her hair may have been topped in a knit cap, but there was no doubt about it. It was

Helen, who had apparently been Miss Social Action back in the day. Why had I never heard a single thing about her marching history? I didn't want to pester, but I imagined she'd get a kick out of my discovery, and somehow I suspected that whatever was going on with her, she might need to smile.

Helen, You won't believe what I'm looking at. You! "Helen Thomas: Campus Crusader." Yes, it's your Ten Girls to Watch contest photo! Nice coat.;) And I had no idea you were such an activist! I'm sure you're swamped, but just had to pop into your inbox again to share!

With that done, I began at the beginning, per XADI's explicit instructions. *Charm,* August 1957.

The very first spread of the inaugural Ten Girls to Watch featured a brunette girl in a red coat, cinched at the waist, walking down the stairs outside an ivy-covered building, amid a throng of smiling fellows, all with Ken-doll hair. Headline—"Let Her Inspire You."

A page over, another pretty girl, this one in a blue velvet tea-length dress with a huge diamond brooch, peeked out from under an umbrella held by a tuxedo-clad gent, her palm up, testing for rain. Beside her, a list of the official criteria by which *Charm's* Ten Girls to Watch had been selected:

1. *Her grooming is not just neat. It's a picture of perfection.*
2. *Her hair is glossy, gleaming, and well kept at all times.*
3. *Her figure is well proportioned and appealing.*
4. *Her posture and poise are impeccable.*
5. *Her use of makeup is deft, highlighting her best features. She never wears too much.*
6. *Her campus attire is in keeping with local customs but is never rah-rah.*

7. *Her weekend and party attire is stylish, flattering, and reflective of good taste.*
8. *Her clothing is not just attractive; it is in pristine condition at all times. Wrinkles and runs are unthinkable.*
9. *She is an individual dresser with a unique look and an awareness of her fashion type.*
10. *She represents the best in college girls today.*

It was hard to tell which rule pleased me most. Gleaming hair? Campus attire that was never rah-rah? The individual dresser who was nonetheless aware of her fashion type?

And then there were the descriptions of the winners that year. Charming young ladies, one and all. For instance, the dark-haired beauty from the red-coat-walking-down-the-stairs photo:

> *Janet Bell is as sweet as a spoonful of ice cream (not surprising given that her father owns Bell Creameries, one of the biggest dairies in the South). But when it comes to completing her degree in English before setting off to spend a year in Europe to study painting, Janet is a woman of unmelting determination.*

Why modern editors trimmed away such high-flying rhetorical flourishes I simply couldn't understand.

In 1958, the rules ran once again (as I soon discovered they would every year until the contest got all academic-merity in 1968) and the girls were photographed in locations around the United States. "She is you, from Sea to Shining Sea," read the headline above the spread of the winners in technicolor skirts and jackets, arm in arm along a rocky outcrop on the California coast. A page over, the caption beside two girls photographed on the steps of the Jefferson Memorial read, "She is monumental in spirit," following which the girls' coats, hats, gloves, shoes, and so on were described in detail. At the end of the color photos was a black-and-white page with detailed diagrams of curler patterns that readers could use to achieve the girls' hairstyles.

I wanted to cut out every page and frame it, and I also wanted to hunt down a number of the outfits. The bouffantish hairdos, well, I could pass on those, though I had to admit that upon close inspection the "Winged Peak" curler pattern used to create one of the girl's wavy little bobs was not without merit.

I swiveled my chair around, readying myself to retrieve more issues, but then, outside my door, in the stillness of the archives, I saw something move. I froze, startled. We'd had rats in my apartment, honest-to-goodness-much-bigger-than-mice rats, so I'd developed a keen eye for scuttling movements. But what caught my eye had been too big to be the darting of a rodent. I rolled my chair so I could see down the rows of shelves a little better. And just like that, it became official—I hadn't made it up. I was not alone. There, in the *Charm* aisle, was a man. Who was not Ralph.

He was tallish (taller than Robert), and nicely angular, in a button-up shirt and jeans. From his profile, he looked young, thirty maybe, with dark hair and preppy good looks that leaned away from frat boy and toward struggling poet. I made lots of noise, clearing my throat and stepping loudly out of my office, hoping not to startle him. I ran my hand through my hair to give it a quick fluff.

"Hi there," I said, cautiously stepping into the aisle as if I were Robinson Crusoe approaching some unknown intruder.

"Oh, hello!" He held one of the white *Charm* hardbound books open in his arms, and juggled it from right to left so he could shake my hand.

"I'm Elliot," he said, smiling.

"Dawn West." I smiled, suddenly feeling a little warm. "So what brings you to the forgotten land of the magazine archives?"

"Ah, well, do you read *Charm*?" he asked, then continued without waiting for me to answer. "I'm the dating columnist, Secret Agent Romance. Sometimes I come here to read the columns of the various Secret Agents Romance from eras past, so I can subtly steal their best ideas. That, and it's a quiet place to work."

"I see," I said.

"Though now that I've admitted my secret identity, I might have to lock you down here unless you swear never to tell. No one wants to know that the laudable male opinion is coming from Elliot Kaslowski. It's much more compelling coming from a mysterious everyman."

The sleeves of his blue Oxford shirt were rolled to just below his elbows. It may be based on some leftover *Dead Poets Society* crush, but I almost always think rolled-up sleeves are hot. Is it because I like wrists? Forearm hair? The teacher-really-getting-into-the-fray look? Robert always wore his sleeves this way. I loved Robert's wrists and hands. He had nice pronounced wrist bones and long fingers that would have made him a good pianist, with just enough hair to be manly but not enough to be hirsute. Elliot's wrists shouldn't have been making me think of Robert. Why was I still thinking of Robert?

"Your secret is safe, I swear it," I said to Elliot, closing out my internal melodrama.

"And what brings you to the *Charm* archives, Dawn?" he asked in a mock overdone tone, like he was asking me my sign.

"Well, turns out this is my new office. You know *Charm*'s Ten Girls to Watch contest? I'm working on the fiftieth anniversary of the contest, tracking down all the past winners. I'm set up right back there in the fancy storage closet."

"Ah, very nice," he said.

"Well, nice to meet you," I said, abruptly ending things.

I hadn't meant to do it! But it just slipped out thanks to a very bad habit I'd developed in elementary school, a surefire cover for all my embarrassing crushes called "being mean so they'll never sus-

pect you like them." Unfortunately, unlike most people who out-
grow this behavior after age eleven, I never got over it. Spending all
four years of college with one person had further stunted the growth
of my game. Clearly, I needed to work on my flirting abilities.

Elliot looked at me curiously as I awkwardly grabbed another
couple of volumes and headed back down the aisle to my office.
This was the exact sort of social faux paus Ms. Lily Harris would
never commit.

"Well, good luck," he called. "See you around."

Once back in my office, I intended to get right down to business, but alas, I didn't succeed. I felt edgy, wondering how long
Secret Agent Romance Elliot Kaslowski was going to be lingering on floor −2, and I turned myself into a little actress in a play
just for him. Just in case he should come around the corner and
peek in, I flipped pages with the most graceful wrist movements.
I thumbed through the volumes just so. I posed, looking at the
covers with an appreciative face. I typed with immaculate posture.
Because, of course, people fall in love with your posture.

After twenty minutes of such nonsense, I finally decided to
see whether Elliot was still around. This I did with a notebook in
hand, so it might appear as if I were on a journalistic foray. Shelf
after shelf, no Elliot. And no one else either. Passing the shelf with
the current year's issues, I noted that they were as of yet unbound,
and I grabbed June, July, and August. Just a little homework reading to find out the latest and greatest in Secret Agent Romance's
dating life.

Then back I went to the sixties. After the sixties, despite
XADI's instructions, I skipped to the eighties, then the nineties.
I'd brought a sandwich with me, so I didn't even leave for lunch—
just reading and note taking and typing names into a spreadsheet
for hours on end. At six, I turned off my lamp and didn't see a soul
on the way out of the building. When I emerged onto the street, I
squinted like a mole coming into the sunlight.

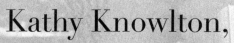

Kathy Knowlton,
Ohio State University, 1969

THE GLOBETROTTER

Brains or beauty? With her top-of-the-class grades and her sleek chestnut hair, Kathy is a clear case of the obvious answer: both! Future work: Kathy wants to be a teacher or a doctor. Epidemiology—the study of the spread of diseases—excites her the most. Future play: There's no place she doesn't want to travel.

Chapter Three

*I*n the end, I'd e-mailed Robert to tell him the news about my job and had asked him to forward along my profuse thanks to Lily. I'd said it just like that: "Please pass along my profuse thanks," which you could read with utter sincerity or with an edge, like lace so starched it scratched. I meant it more or less both ways, because even if I didn't want to be indebted to Lily, even if I wanted to dismiss and ignore her, she'd done something major for me, I had to begrudgingly acknowledge it. Though that didn't mean I had to correspond with her directly.

Lily, however, didn't seem to feel any such desire for distance. That night when I got home, she'd sent me a note from her fancy Craven & Swinton law firm e-mail:

Dawn, Robert told me the great news. I'm so excited for you! Also, another connection, turns out my sister's college roommate was a Ten Girl. You know TheOne.com? She founded it. She's in town from Dallas, and Robert and I are having her over for dinner tomorrow. I know this is absolutely last minute, but Robert and I are wondering if there's any chance you're free to join us?

Friendliness at the Pretzel Party was one thing. We all play parts at parties. But this? Was she really so secure that she didn't see me as any sort of threat? Or maybe she was masking over a sort of perverse curiosity, wanting to know exactly what Robert's old girlfriend was like, the way, in high school, I could never help looking at the disturbing pictures in my biology textbooks—burrowing parasitic worms, birth canals. I felt that way about Lily. Thoughts of her and Robert together were like a sore in my mouth I kept worrying, unable to keep myself from the precise and reliable pain they delivered.

Or maybe she was just generous. One of those famous connectors. Not that I read them, but I knew there were business books that categorized people like that. She was a maven or a hub or an axle, some moniker, the discussion of which was supposed to be worth the cover price. Maybe that was it.

But there was something else I didn't like: "Robert and I are wondering . . ." I could just hear the words in her husky, alluring voice, the ease with which joint invitations were already rolling off her tongue. *Robert and I would like to invite you to dinner. Robert and I would like to invite you to our wedding. Robert and I would like to console you on the lifetime of loneliness ahead of you.*

I thought about the time I had tried to host a party with Robert. A Christmas party, sophomore year of college, in his room. I'd used the dorm's kitchen to bake cookies and cakes and cream puffs and thought it was all just spectacular. The pièce de résistance, just before guests arrived: I whipped up the punch my mother had made for every special occasion at home: four liters of Sprite with a half gallon of rainbow sherbet scooped in. I loved this punch. I made it without thinking that it might not fit in my new world. When Robert came into the room, he looked at the punch, and an awful smirk took possession of his face. I felt like I would have at age fourteen had someone caught me stuffing my bra—embarrassed for the act itself, but even more deeply humiliated to have been exposed as a person who wants to be something she's not. I was a person who thought sherbet punch was elegant and festive, masquerading as someone who ordered cheese plates for dessert. The unmasking of my aspiration was horrifying. Lily, undoubtedly, bought cases of fine wine, and all their future parties would be smashing, catered affairs.

Enough reasons to decline the invitation right there. But the list went on. There was, of course, the other guest: the founder of TheOne.com. The company's ads, plastered all over the subway, traumatized me on a daily basis. Each one was a famous painting, like Seurat's *A Sunday Afternoon* or Hopper's *Nighthawks*, edited so that two individuals in each picture, inevitably individuals who weren't paying any attention to each other, were outlined in glowing white auras, with taglines like "Where's Your One?" "Help Her Find Her One," or, more ominous, "Don't Miss Your One." Mutated versions of the ads made their way into my dreams. I'd be glowing, a la TheOne's Ones, but it wasn't a good thing—I was always trying to escape from something and the giant aura made hiding impossible.

Self-preservation dictated that I should thank Lily but let her know I was busy tomorrow night and for the foreseeable future. But that's not what I did. No, instead I disregarded all those rational instincts and wrote back saying I'd love to come to dinner.

Being upset by my boyfriend's new girlfriend just felt so *typical*. I wanted to be the sort of self-possessed person who didn't have such feelings or, at the very least, kept such feelings folded up and tucked in a private closet. And finally, though undoubtedly there was an element of masochism in it, I wanted to see Robert. Or maybe more than to see him, to smell him. Why I thought *that* was a good idea was a real mystery.

E-mail answered, I microwaved a veggie pattie and continued my pretending by faking that I wasn't depressed by my dinner. Then I headed off to the coffee shop around the corner to dole

out lawn care advice. On one of the eight or so ratty couches at
Tea Lounge, I sipped a café au lait (a whole dollar cheaper than
a latte!) and took advantage of their generous seating policy (one
hot beverage bought you as many hours of free Internet and blaring Fugees music as you liked) to struggle through some brutal
weed identification questions. Next, I wrote a column on planting
a new lawn, complete with ample keyword usage. The sort of *lawn
fertilizer* typically sold for mature lawns won't give newly seeded
lawns the boost they need. Starter *lawn fertilizer,* which has more
potassium and phosphorus than the average *lawn fertilizer,* is key.
Starter *lawn fertilizer* should be applied at the same time you seed.
Somehow the soft, yellow lamplight and the company of strangers
and Lauryn Hill almost made me feel like I'd had a night out on
the town rather than a shift of work.

Once my search engine optimization efforts were over, I
headed home and climbed right into bed. Had I not snagged back
issues of *Charm,* I might have spent some time on sites that I'd
become quite familiar with in recent months, like adoptapet.com
or cashmerebathrobeemporium.com, researching the possibility
of cats and warm and fuzzy clothing as reasonable alternatives to
human companionship. Instead, I flipped pages till I found Elliot
Kaslowski's old columns.

August's column was cute, but ho-hum. Your basic, went on a
date, it was pretty bad, here's how, ha-ha. July was pretty similar.
But June, oh, June had meat. The column told the tale of a night
out with an old flame, code name "Boots."

> *Boots looks good in all lights, but in candlelight she's like
> a painting. When she looks at me across the table, her eyes
> brown and glowing, I don't know why we're not together.*

He rambled on for a bit about commitment and temperament,
standard stuff, then got back to Boots.

I kept wanting each part of the meal to last longer—no, don't bring the dessert yet. Yes, pour another cup of coffee. But finally the check arrived, that dread signal of the end. Boots reached for it. "No, let me," I said. And she shot me back a withering look. "I don't think so," she said, and put down her credit card.

Why are checks so fraught? I knew Boots thought that I thought that if I paid, I'd somehow taken her on a date and that I'd expect something, but if she paid, she was in control of the night. I've never been any match for her withering looks—I learned that long ago—so I sighed and said fine. She signaled the waiter right away.

I had fooled myself into thinking she was having the same kind of night I was—a night of longing and wondering—but the speed with which she disposed of the bill put an end to the illusion. She stood up and reached for her bag. "Nice seeing you," she said. And only a few seconds later she was walking down the sidewalk away from me.

Reading Secret Agent Romance's dispatch, I did a calculation. If the June issue went to press in May, that meant the night out was probably sometime in March or April. Which meant he was possibly over this woman by now . . . or possibly still deeply into her. I also calculated that this woman and I were likely about 180 degrees apart in personality. I wanted to give withering looks, I practiced giving withering looks in the mirror, but when faced with withering-look-inspiring situations in real life, my face always failed to fully cooperate. Or less my face, more my whole person.

After spending a few minutes trying on various expressions, I finally called my mom back and listened to her crow. In actuality, that part of the call only took a minute, though as predicted, she seemed to think I'd done some sort of soft shoe followed by a hard sell.

"Well, I don't know exactly how it happened," I said, "but I'm excited."

Then she sighed, her voice cracking a little, and said, "I've been so worried."

With his constant, lowing "come back home," I'd known my dad had been worried all along (though never quite worried enough to offer to help with rent), but my mom had always sounded like she thought I was some sort of plucky adventuress, even if her idea of what it meant to be a plucky adventuress was straight out of *Thoroughly Modern Millie.*

"Don't be worried, this is a great job," I told her. I left out the part about the job being temporary.

"And they're paying you good money?" she said.

"Enough," I said. Though, of course, I had yet to find out how much "enough" was going to be.

After we said our good-byes, I texted Sarah. "Did you tell Dad about my job yet?"

My phone buzzed hours later, in the middle of the night. "Yep. He's really excited!"

Maybe one of the reasons my parents hadn't been a good match was that my dad could be really excited but would probably still wait three weeks to call, whereas my mom had left three voice mail messages the night I phoned with the news.

The next morning I buzzed at the archives warehouse door, and the mysterious someone let me in again. No sign of Ralph or anyone else as I made my way back to my area and unlocked my door to find everything just where I'd left it. The trash had not even been emptied. Fortunately, that meant only that my empty sandwich bag and a few scraps of paper had spent the night, but I made a note to carry anything with rot potential to a more central trash in the future.

All this solitude might have made me lonely, but in fact, I liked it. Unlike all the offices I'd painfully temped in over the last year (the law office, the life insurance office, the accounting office) where I'd been a ghost, the girl no one really notices or acknowledges—you'll be there a day, maybe a week, who wants to exert effort for that?—here, I was official. I had keys. I belonged. And as the only person in this office, other than Ralph, I was the alpha ruler of my domain. No gingerly stepping, no polite, restrained smiling. In the quiet of my new office, I could roar. Not that I did, but I felt myself uncoiling.

All year, everyone had said "You'll see, it'll all work out in the end," and I'd wanted to throw things at them and remind them that was easy for them to say since they were in the enviable positions of having more than twenty-eight dollars in their bank accounts. All year, it felt like I was barely catching shallow, ragged breaths. But as a sense of command over floor −2 seeped into me, I could feel a physical change. I knew this job wasn't permanent—that after I found these five hundred women I was most likely going to find myself hurling résumés into the void again—but finally, at least for the moment, the buzz of anxiety lifted.

I needed to spend the day photocopying the collected TGTW coverage so I'd have handy access at my desk, but before I did anything so boring, I wanted to further put down roots and actually talk to one of these women. I went to the shelves, pulled a volume from the seventies, and picked a winner. Cicely Ross, '78. She'd do just fine. *Charm* had done her up in a long prairie dress, which drew my eye, but I also zoned in on Ms. Ross because she'd gone to my college, which meant that, unlike the other women I was going to have to aimlessly google, for Cicely Ross I could simply log in to the alumni directory, type her name, and voilà. Which is exactly what I did. And just like that, Dr. Cicely Ross Rumbachand appeared, complete with street address, e-mail, and phone number.

I dialed and a man's voice answered. When I asked if Cicely was available he said, "I'm sorry, she's not."

"It would be great if I could leave a message," I cheerily replied, just thrilled with myself for having so swiftly and successfully tracked her down.

"I'm sorry," the man said. "That won't be possible. Cicely passed away a few weeks ago."

I put my hand over my mouth. Then I apologized and got off the phone as quickly as possible, all the gusto drained right out of me. Maybe I was by myself in this basement, but XADI and Regina were out there, and at some point they were going to want to know how things were going. And suddenly, it seemed possible my reports might not be so great. Not that all the women were going to be dead, obviously, but there was a chance these conversations might be a little less smooth and sunny than I'd imagined.

I should have just moved right along and dialed another woman, but I felt suddenly phone shy. I tried to practice a theoretical call, rehearsing lines. "Hello, I'm calling from *Charm* magazine. Hello, I'm calling about *Charm* magazine's Ten Girls to Watch contest." I even mouthed the words. Nope, still not ready to dial again.

I needed something repetitive and calming to ease me back into it. I needed to make copies. I grabbed a couple of the bound volumes and walked quickly away from the phone.

One full track around the perimeter of floor −2 confirmed that there really was no one else down here, and I hadn't found any signs of copy machines either. I didn't feel an entirely rejuvenated sense of confidence yet, but I felt collected enough to at least reach for the phone. From his outpost somewhere in the building, Ralph answered . . . halfway through the first ring. Which made me wonder what Ralph did all day, other than wait for his phone to ring.

"Well hello there, Dawn," he said before I had a chance to say anything. The copy machine, he informed me, was on floor −1, on the east side, and it was unlocked. I thanked Ralph and made my way upstairs.

After graduation, Helen had encouraged me to send pitches to magazines. I'd whipped up dozens of story ideas. Not a single editor replied to a single one of them, but I still liked some of what I'd come up with. Like "Tone Your Calves While Copying," tip no. 6 in an article on office exercises I'd pitched to *Girl Talk*.

During one particularly bleak stretch of temping as a legal secretary at a law firm (a job made all the more depressing by my decision not to go to law school, as if the universe had fated me for legal work and all I got by attempting to escape was a kick down to the lowest paid rung on the ladder), a junior associate had finally talked to me in the hallway. I said I'd just graduated, or graduated eight months earlier and was temping while I looked for a job, and after I revealed where I'd gone to school, he'd incredulously said, "What are you doing here?" A mad streak of toe raises in the copy room that afternoon was the only thing that kept me from turning into a fountain of tears, or at least postponed the outburst till I was out of the office.

The toe raises I did in the archives copy room today were similarly soothing—three hours of copying later, I'd done about three hundred—but the pages of TGTW were the real boost. I made eleven trips up and down the stairs and copied about thirty years of TGTW coverage, lovingly lingering over the best years. Like 1986.

That year, *Charm*'s editors thought the college girls of America should be using their smarts to rake in some extra cash. Suggestions included tutoring (yawn), typing (yawn), and my two favorites (no more yawning): selling art class seconds and late-night snacks. That ceramic pot may not have made the grade for class, but it could fetch a pretty penny as a "dorm decorator's item," and grilled ham and cheese sandwiches, which *Charm* assured were a breeze to make with just a little tinfoil and a hot iron, were sure to be top sellers.

I took my own sandwich break around lunch (a grilled ham and cheese would have been a real upgrade from my pb&j), but by midafternoon even the fabulous oversize sweaters of the nineties weren't enough to keep me interested in more copying, so I decided to take a quick break and look at the coverage of the most recent TGTW winners in last March's issue. At least that's what I told myself, but it was a total lie. I'd been listening for Elliot's footfalls all day. A flicker of lights, the slightest hint of a sound, and I braced for him. But nothing. Now, I sat down at my desk with the issue and turned straight to Elliot's March article. Secret Agent Romance's dispatch title for that month: "I'm Finally Ready for a Real Relationship."

> I just turned 30. And somewhere between the cheesy party and inspecting my scalp for signs of thinning hair, I realized something: I'm finally ready for a real relationship. I'm not suddenly financially secure or mature or any of the other things that supposedly make guys get serious, and I'm not losing my hair either, thank you very much. I didn't wake up one day transformed. It was more like I woke up day after day and realized I wasn't quite as happy on my own as I thought. Turning 30 finally made me wake up and smell the stale coffee.

> "I'm not ready for a serious relationship." That's the number one excuse guys give for breaking up. But I'm here to tell you, it's not an excuse. It's the only real reason I've had for breaking up with anyone for the past ten years. The actual excuses are a lot more ridiculous. In the spirit of looking back and seeing how far I've come, here's a sampling of the totally bogus explanations I've had for breaking up with some pretty wonderful women when the real reason was my immaturity.

- *Willow—Started wearing cutesy aprons while cooking. Looked too much like my mom in them.*
- *Roller Girl—Beneath those roller blades her ankles were a touch thick.*
- *Banking Beauty—So driven and productive she was bound to have a breakdown sooner or later.*
- *Speed Racer—All that running, what was she really running from?*
- *Dandy Lion—Tone-deaf but loved to sing.*
- *Mandolin—So much crying. Why so much crying?*
- *Velvet Ropes—Knew way too much about celebrities.*

What an idiot I've been. I met someone new a few weeks ago. Let's call her Boots. She flips her hair. Her lips may be a little too glossy. I'm giving it a real go anyway. Mature of me, right?

Secret Agent Romance

First off, Elliot was thirty. Officially, too old for me. But much more than that, it was easy to imagine, after that column, why Elliot was lurking around at the archives rather than hanging out in the Mandalay Carson building. He had to be running scared. Half the women on the list were probably *Charm* staffers or friends thereof. Thick ankles? While Secret Agent Romance claimed that was the excuse, what woman hears a single thing after the sonic boom of thick ankles? I had no idea who Roller Girl was, other than that she certainly wasn't me. Nonetheless, I crossed my ankles as I read the words. How thick is thick? How much crying is too much crying? Was it bad that I knew Angelina Jolie, Brad Pitt, and their kids liked to picnic? The column was insidious.

I smacked the magazine closed as if it were the pages' fault and not Elliot's. I needed some positive, supportive womanly cheerleading immediately.

I picked another winner, Kathy Knowlton, '69. I'd waited long enough.

You can do this. I actually whispered the words, psyching myself up. I started with Google, hoping that if there were an obituary to be found, I'd find it before calling the grieving spouse. No obituary, but Kathy Knowlton's faculty profile at the University of Minnesota came right up. *You can do this,* I mouthed again. I dialed.

"Hello," a woman's voice answered.

"Hi, is this Kathy Knowlton?" I hated the timid sound of my voice.

"Yes."

I consciously spoke a touch louder, with a slight salesy lilt, what I thought of as the voice of enthusiasm. "Kathy, this is Dawn West, I'm calling from *Charm* magazine. I'm hoping I have the right Kathy Knowlton—were you one of *Charm*'s 1969 Ten Girls to Watch?"

"Well, I certainly was."

Success! I explained it was the fiftieth anniversary of the contest, that we were doing a retrospective and were starting by tracking down all the past winners, that we were trying to figure out where all those incredible young women had ended up.

I looked at her college photo as we spoke. She had long, dark hair, full, pretty lips, and was posed leaning against a tree. In the photo, she appeared to be wearing tweed bell bottoms.

"How wild," she said, clear delight in her voice. "It's such a funny coincidence, actually. My mother passed away recently and I was going through her attic with my sister just the other day, and we found a big stack of *Charm*s up there. Copy after copy of my Ten Girls to Watch issue. I hadn't thought about it in years, and I just laughed and laughed. My mother must have bought every issue in the county. And then there was that photo . . ."

"I'm looking at it right now. Groovy pants."

"Oh, they were awesome."

We both giggled, and then she went on, no prompting necessary. "The thing that was funniest, though, was looking back at
what I said I was going to do."

I glanced at the block of text alongside her photo: "Future
work: Kathy wants to be a teacher or a doctor. Epidemiology—the
study of the spread of diseases—excites her the most. Future play:
There's no place she doesn't want to travel."

"It was a little crazy how close I got to describing my life now,"
she said. "I didn't remember having said all that stuff. But here I
am now. I actually *am* an epidemiologist. What made me think
I wanted to be an epidemiologist back then, I can't tell you. But
somehow I said it. I teach and I travel too, and I've been incredibly
lucky—I don't think I said this in the article, but I always wanted
to have a family, and I've been lucky enough to have four wild and
crazy kids."

"You have four? That's wonderful! How do you—"

"I always say you have to pick them right, and I lucked out. My
husband's a peach. And then we were also lucky—my mom took
care of the kids for a lot of years."

We talked through the ages of all the kids (thirty, twenty-six,
twenty-four, and eighteen), how Kathy met her husband (grad student bowling league), how her mother died (a stroke), Kathy's best
family vacation (a safari in Kenya with her mother and kids in
tow), and her academic and practical focus, which had started out
as asthma and moved to AIDS.

We made our way to talking about her teaching; she was
restructuring her Principles of Epidemiology class for the fall.

"Here's an epidemiology metaphor I always found interesting,"
she said. "Back when cars first hit it big-time, there weren't traffic
lights. There weren't stop signs. When there were crashes, and
there were lots of them in those years, people always tried to frame
the crashes as a moral issue. They'd say, 'People just need to slow
down and stop being reckless. The value of courtesy and caution

has eroded. If only we could bring back those virtues we'd be just fine and these tragic automobile deaths would go away.' And those sorts of arguments went on for a while until we came up with stoplights and installed them all over the place, and then lo and behold, people stopped smashing into each other quite so often. I always remember that when I think about diseases today. We always want to blame people and their morals and say that we just need to be careful. But there's usually more to it, so when it comes to any disease-related issue I'm working on, I always like to ask myself, 'What are the stoplights in this situation?' and then once I start to figure those out, I have something to really talk about."

I came to the end of the page in my notebook and flipped it quickly so I could write down every last word she was saying. And then I made her promise to send me her syllabus.

She asked me whether I'd found anyone else from her year yet.

"Not yet," I said.

"I have always wanted to get back in touch with Susan Frock. When you find her, please give her my information. We roomed together during our week in New York and our trip to Europe, and she was just amazing."

"Wait, *Charm* sent you on a trip to Europe?"

"Oh, it was this grand tour. Paris, Rome, and then sort of weirdly backwater Ireland, which I think was just because one of our chaperones was from there. I distinctly remember our bus getting stuck in the mud and sheep swarming us. But I have to tell you my best Susan story. In New York, *Charm* sent us to all sorts of shows, and one night after a play we were at Sardi's, and across the room there was Paul Newman. We all started tittering and looking over, and Susan just got up, walked over, and said we were the *Charm* girls and would he come have a drink with us. Poised as can be, like she was asking a schoolboy to dance. And of course he said yes, and I will never forget the way he smelled. Like Old Spice and cigarettes. When that man went into food it was a terrible thing for me. I slather on his dressings. I pop all his popcorn. I just can't get enough of his face in my cupboard."

After joining her in another few moments of rhapsodizing about the particular pleasures of Newman's Caesar, I told her how glad I was I'd found the right Kathy Knowlton and that I'd be back in touch as our plans for the anniversary celebration shaped up. We were planning something big. We just weren't sure what yet.

She told me to come visit if I was ever in Minneapolis. It was the lovey-doveyest of good-byes. I hung up smiling. And I couldn't stop. It was just one call, but it had gone well. If I had to report to XADI or Regina now, I could say I'd "really been hitting it off" with the winners. It gave me hope for all the hundreds of calls to come. I didn't need to say much, just Ten Girls to Watch, and the floodgates opened. It was like being in *Ali Baba and the Forty Thieves,* except I would always remember the magic words that opened the treasure cave. Kathy had been so happy to reminisce. Listening to her filled me with energy. Instead of my earlier, tattered self, I felt buoyant, like a pumped-up tire, ready to ride smoothly over whatever rocky roads came my way.

Yes, I was also a tiny little bit worried that I might be doomed because unlike Kathy Knowlton as a young woman, I couldn't say exactly what I wanted to do with my whole life, other than something vague like "be a writer" or "give back somehow" or "make enough money so I don't have to move home." But that was niggling. After melting away that morning, my confidence wasn't quite firm yet, but it was re-forming, like Jell-O poured back into the mold and setting again quite nicely.

XADI hadn't given me any instructions for how to keep track of my interviews, but after Kathy I decided on an approach. I added a few short notes to my Excel spreadsheet, "Kathy Knowlton, Epidemiology Professor, University of Minnesota (married, four kids)," plus all the address, phone number, and e-mail information. Then I wrote up a profile. Nothing fancy, just a page, but I spent more than a few minutes on it, making sure I had Kathy's quotes right, coming up with the right words to describe her enthusiasm for her research and her family. Who knew what good these profiles would do—I suspected XADI only wanted the spreadsheet—but after everything Kathy had told me, taking a little time felt appropriate. Besides which, wasn't writing what I wanted to do with my life? Surely if Kathy Knowlton had wanted to be a writer, she wouldn't have waited for an assignment. She would have seized whatever material came her way. I imagined a tidy pile of profiles, growing taller and taller. For just a second I pictured handing them all over to Regina, who'd read them in awe and immediately offer me a staff job.

If I'd wanted someone to talk me further into fantasies like that one, I'd have called Helen. If I wanted someone to talk me back to reality, I'd call my dad. I decided a little reality was in order.

Walking to the subway that night, I weaved past the tourists slowing up midtown's pedestrian traffic, and then, hoping not to slow foot traffic myself, I stepped to the side of the sidewalk at a quiet spot between a Rolland's Pretzel cart and a fire hydrant and dialed my dad.

"Hello?" he said, as if he didn't have caller ID.

"Hi, Dad, it's Dawn."

"Oh! How nice to hear your voice."

He was only in his fifties, but he'd been playing the part of a sweet old man for years. He got away with a lot because of it. *"It was your birthday? Well, I plum forgot."*

"So I guess Sarah told you my news," I said.

"That's right! I was so pleased to hear it. So, tell me about the job."

When I talked to my mom, she always got a thrill out of the New York details—*"They have sushi in convenience stores? My gosh!"*—as if even the dingiest aspects of my life (like eating questionably fresh bodega sushi) were dusted with glamour. Not so with my dad. New York had no appeal for him. A fishing cabin on a lake in upstate New York, maybe. But the city? Nope. Add to that the fact that he just wasn't a phone talker and could handle maybe seven minutes of chitchat max, and you had conditions that led to the development of good summarizing skills on my part. I hit the high points: fiftieth anniversary of contest, calls to women, office in basement of warehouse archives.

"How nice that you have your own office," he said.

"I know," I said. I'd been pretty impressed by that too, even if it was in a basement. If I'd had to pick one detail out of everything I'd said, I probably would have picked that one too. Just another data point proving my dad and I shared more brain waves than I sometimes liked to admit.

"Are you walking home right now?" he asked. The city's geography wasn't his strong suit. For all he knew, midtown and Brooklyn were just a few blocks apart.

"Well, not quite walking home, but walking to the subway that will take me home."

"I better let you go so you can watch out for traffic then!" he said.

We'd reached seven minutes.

"All right, Dad. Glad to catch up a little."

"Dawn," he said, then paused, as if he were working himself up to say something big. "You know, I'm proud of you."

It was the first time he'd said that since I'd moved to New York.

That one sentence meant more to me than my whole gushing love fest with Kathy Knowlton.

"Thanks, Dad," I said.

"Love you, sweetie."

"Love you too."

Jean Danton,

Radcliffe College, 1960

THE ELEGANT ORIENTALIST

A true world traveler, Jean has visited more than 30 countries. Growing up in Hong Kong helped (her father is in international business). A political science major, she has a keen interest in international relations. This summer, she will study painting and language in France. Free-time pursuits: art, poetry, and sewing. "I was wholly unprepared for Massachusetts weather." She quickly adapted, sewing herself an enviable collection of conservative wool dresses and tweedy British jackets, spiced with Oriental silks and real jewelry. In sum, her style is both artistic and mature. Above all, Jean impresses with a real *womanliness*—at only 20, she seems truly wise beyond her years.

Chapter Four

*T*he next day, working away in the little circle of light from my desk lamp, I tracked down three winners, including Jean Danton from 1960. She'd grown up to be just about as worldly and sophisticated as *Charm* had expected.

I found her at home, in Washington, D.C. She and her husband had moved back in 1990 after spending twenty-plus years off and on stationed in Russia with the foreign service. At first she hated Russia, or the USSR, as it was back then. "All I wanted was to get back to East Asia," she said, laughing at the memory. "I actually fought learning the language and refused to remember even the simplest words. But bit by bit the country wore me down. And my children too, I suppose. They were all speaking Russian by then." She took her first baby steps by reading Russian poets in translation. "Anna Akhmatova, Sophia Parnok . . . they were wonderful," Jean reminisced. "As I became better with the language, I began to read their poems in the original Russian, and that's how I first began to translate—painstakingly poring through my dictionary." After their return to the States, Jean translated Anna Akhmatova's collected works, the publication released to great fanfare in the poetry community. She told me about her current project, collecting and translating works written under Stalin by female Russian poets.

I typed fast as she spoke, trying to capture every word for my profile and hoping I'd somehow be able to interpret the gibberish of typos later. "Three of my children now live in Russia, and the oldest is here in D.C. but works on Russia-related issues with the State Department. I would never have predicted it. In our early years in Russia I would have cried if you'd told me. Russia? What an insidious love! It took root against my will, and now its vines are in and around my heart and the hearts of my family. What you grow to love . . ." She drifted off, as if she were reflecting on this all for the very first time. "That might be one of life's biggest surprises."

That great, life-changing happiness could come from something you started out thinking was terrible was a pretty comforting idea. The words "you never know what you'll grow to love" echoed in my head as I walked uptown in the cloudy August heat that night for dinner with Robert, Lily, and Ms. Rachel Link, matchmaker to millions. Of course I'd looked up Rachel's Ten Girls to Watch profile in advance of this get-together: "Rachel Link, Rice University, 'The Computer Whiz.'" She'd been programming since age thirteen, and by the time she hit college in the mid-nineties, *Charm* reported that she'd won just about every computery competition you could think of and was also a softball star.

I'd also done a little extra research on TheOne.com in anticipation of meeting Rachel, and the articles I'd browsed made three things clear: (1) TheOne was far and away the web's most popular dating website, beating out Meet.com by more than a million users (largely, I wager, because of Meet's unfortunate homophone); (2) Rachel Link was rolling in dough as a result, evidenced not only by the feature I found in *Fine Living Decor* on her faux home-on-the-range manse in Dallas and her so-shiny-it-looked-slippery pied-à-terre in San Francisco but also by the no. 3 listing I found for her in *GRID*'s "Where the Money's at on the Web" rankings; and (3) as I had already been well aware, liberals of all stripes—in particular liberals who wrote for magazines, newspapers, blogs, television, or radio—loved to hate her because of TheOne's old-school matching style. Interracial dating? Interclass dating? Homosexuals? All rabble-rousing nonsense in the world of TheOne.

Dinner was at Robert's place, and Robert lived in a fancy building near Columbus Circle with not one but two, sometimes three, white-gloved doormen. I'd never once had to turn the revolving door that led to the oh-so-elegant lobby thanks to said doormen. I'm just lazy and germ-phobic enough that I'm often a revolving-door freeloader, letting the folks in front of and behind me do the real pushing, but having a formal pusher so I didn't have to go through the pretense of leaning into the push bar? Now that was something.

But there's also something weird about doormen, other than the weirdness of having people to wait on you—they remember you. And I knew that all three men on duty that day knew that not so many months ago, I'd been spending night after night in Robert's apartment. And that I had then stopped spending nights. And now Lily was spending nights. And now Lily and I were both arriving. Plus some other chick. I smiled somewhat grimly when they said hello and tried to pretend I wasn't pained. Undoubtedly they'd brand Robert a Lothario and give him high fives later. The female role in such dramas is much less flattering.

After one of the doormen called up and gave me the go-ahead, I took the elevator up to the seventh floor. When Robert's parents bought the apartment for him, he'd earnestly explained their bargain-hunting prowess: "I get the exact same service as the guy who lives in the twenty-million-dollar penthouse, but the price goes down a few million every floor. It's really an unbeatable deal." This was while I was staying with him and apartment hunting, with a negative budget. The bargains I was looking at were more like "Who needs a pesky window in their bedroom?" or "Not exactly a bedroom, but the ladder is sturdy, the crawl space fits a mattress, and you can almost sit up without hitting your head on the ceiling." The moderately wretched though to-my-standards livable apartment I finally found cost less than Robert's parking space.

Outside the door of 7C, I adjusted my dress, a simple black sheath that no one would think much of, except Robert had said I looked beautiful in it every time I'd ever worn it. Lily opened the door a mere second after I knocked. "Perfect timing!" she said, kissing me on both cheeks. She smelled like perfume. Not the sort of lightweight perfume I dared to wear. Something muskier, woodsier. It gave her a gravitas and sexiness I resented. "Robert is just finishing up in the kitchen, and Rachel already arrived. Don't worry, she just got here. She's freshening up." Her delivery was so breezy and comfortable, her lines delivered like we were best friends, and like a forensics team wouldn't turn up many more of my fingerprints in the apartment than hers.

Despite the fact that the knot in my stomach—which had been present since the day I first learned Lily existed but which had been growing increasingly tangled all the way up the elevator— was now tightening even further in the face of her ease, I managed to lob the polite, charming, so-cool-with-everything ball back at her. "Excellent," I said. "What's cooking? It smells great!"

"I'm not sure," Lily said. "Robert's in charge of dinner."

Robert? In charge of dinner? In all our time together, Robert's being "in charge of dinner" had involved, at most, choosing a restaurant. Though that wasn't quite fair. He'd extended himself to boiling pasta . . . once.

We walked by the kitchen and Robert, in an apron, with green beans in one hand and kitchen scissors in the other, semishouted hello.

"Need any help?" I said, slowing at the door.

Before he could answer, Lily looped her arm through mine. "He's fine. We worked it all out. He's on last-minute meal-prep duty, I'm on entertaining-our-guests duty."

"I have my orders!" Robert cheerily said.

I'd never given Robert orders. That just hadn't been how it worked. It had always felt like he would have bridled had I even thought to. Though he'd condescended and dominated me plenty. But with Lily, it was clear he liked it. Like he could trust her to captain. And in painful contrast, I thought, like he'd never trusted me. She'd probably grown up yachting or horse jumping or some other similarly chichi hobby that had instilled her with the power to jauntily shout commands.

The living room looked just like always, meaning complete with real rugs and furniture and artwork as opposed to my apartment and the secondhand Ikea furniture I'd prayed didn't have bedbugs before I bought it off Craigslist. It looked like always, that is, except one change I noticed immediately: on the wall by the bookshelves, the grouping of nicely framed photos of college friends—which had prominently featured me—was gone, replaced by a big art photo of a diner.

Lily walked straight to the sideboard and poured a couple of glasses of wine for us, again with complete ease, as if she had already moved in, as if it were her apartment as much as Robert's. I wondered whether she'd had anything to do with the changing of the photos or whether Robert had undertaken my removal all on his own.

Before Lily and I had to sit down and undertake our not-at-all-agonizingly friendly tête-à-tête, the bathroom door opened down the hall, and a moment later an extraordinarily tall woman—she must have been six-one—walked into the room. She hadn't seemed so tall in her old *Charm* photograph.

"Rachel," Lily said in a glittering tone, "I'm so excited for you to meet Dawn. Dawn, this is the amazing Rachel Link." She handed Rachel a glass and poured another one for herself.

Rachel's dark hair had grown more voluminous since her photo—she now gave it the sort of height typically reserved for the pageant circuit. She had one of those full, almost exaggerated faces—a little like Geena Davis. Just a lot of everything. Not in the old photo, but in person now, with all of it put together, she reminded me of my cousin Renee, who, while going to community college, had briefly lived in an extra room in our house (this just before my parents' divorce, when it was still *our* house, not my mom's house; the extra room was, in fact, my sister Sarah's room, only "extra" because she was already away at college). Renee had been queen of this, princess of that, and was in the running for Miss Oregon during her guest-room sojourn. In one of the most mortifying moments of my teen-age years, my father had one night during her stay suggested that "Maybe Renee could show you a trick or two. Do up your makeup and hair. Maybe set you up with a nice boy she knows." I did my chemistry homework with a special fervor that night.

"Rachel, it's so good to meet you," I said as we shook hands.

"I cracked up when Lily e-mailed me," Rachel said. "I can't believe Ten Girls to Watch is turning fifty."

"I just started working on the project this week, but I finished going through all the coverage today. It's such good stuff! You were a winner in 1996, right?"

She nodded.

"I believe that was the year of the mom jeans?"

She grinned without showing her teeth. Was that smile good or bad? Hard to tell, so undaunted, I forged ahead.

"I think the shapeless white sweaters were even better than the jeans. Cable knit is so underrated."

Lily laughed and Rachel half laughed, or more like quarter laughed. It could have been a hiccup.

Since my tepid attempts at humor weren't doing it for her, I took the more serious tack. "Have you kept track of anyone from your year?" Stories about other women from her year had been such a winning line of conversation with Kathy Knowlton, I figured it might get a little something from Rachel.

"I actually worked with Donetta Allen for a few years after college," she said, "but we haven't really kept in touch since then." Again, she seemed rather unenthused.

"Where were the two of you working?" I asked.

"Zing.com," she said, her smile spreading wide for the first time.

"No way," I chirped. "I loved you guys! I had my order down. Diet root beer, kettle corn, and a DVD. All at my door at ten thirty every Saturday night."

Robert came in from the kitchen, carrying a tray. "The rest of us were going out at ten thirty," he said. "Dawn, she was settling in with a nice cold diet root beer."

"Hm. I'm having this memory," I said. "Wait, wait, it's becoming clearer. Oh yeah, it's you, insisting that I rent *Big* like four different times and then—why am I becoming thirsty all of a sudden?—oh, probably because I'm remembering you drinking all my root beer."

Whoa—where had that come from? It was rare for me to have a sarcastic retort at the ready, and I immediately wondered whether I had gone a little too far, whether I was somehow rubbing Lily's face in our four-year romance. Then I suddenly had a profoundly disorienting thought. Maybe Lily was so cool with me because Robert had downplayed our whole relationship as much as he'd downplayed our breakup. This didn't sit well. Though I didn't exactly like the present, I could adjust, or at least pretend to adjust. But I couldn't adjust away the facts of the matter. We had a history. Robert wasn't allowed to simply erase it. I turned a scrutinizing eye on him.

"I have no idea what you're talking about," Robert jokingly said, not really clarifying anything. Last time he'd been in close quarters with me and Lily, he'd seemed flustered. This time, not at all. He set the tray he was holding down on the table and went to stand next to Lily. His lack of confusion felt like a betrayal.

"So Rachel, what did you do for Zing?" I asked, trying to plaster over the leaks in the dam of my heart with the quick cement of ordinary conversation.

Rachel took a sip of her wine and tipped her head coquettishly toward Robert, leaning languidly against the sideboard so that she was, for the moment, just a bit shorter than he was. And suddenly I saw it, like the clouds parted and a ray of sunlight flooded down, and there, illuminated for all to see: Rachel Link was one of those. A woman who only cared about men. The way she suddenly moved and glowed, it was like Robert had pulled the string and started the doll walking. I would have been more bothered by this had I not been distracted by Robert's hand. It dangled next to Lily's silk skirt, the backs of his fingers ever so slightly brushing up against the fabric and her thigh beneath it.

"I was a web engineer," she said, to Robert, not me, and she said it with a drawl that I swear came out of nowhere.

"And then after Zing you started TheOne?" Robert asked intently.

"Excuse me," Lily whispered, slipping away to the kitchen. Robert moved his hand to his pockets.

"That's right," Rachel continued, but she'd turned all Georgia peach again so it came out "rahyt." She giggled, and then, thankfully, Lily rescued us by returning with the rest of the food.

"It's filet, Dawn," Lily said, "but it's nice happy filet from a farm upstate." So Robert must have told her that, at least—I'd been a vegetarian for most of college, but I'd recently started eating meat again, if it met certain criteria. It was thoughtful of her to mention, the act of a gracious hostess, which should have engendered gratitude and graciousness in me, but which was instead like a match to the tinderbox of my feelings. Why was Robert flaunting all this in my face? Why was I letting him? I wanted to furiously storm out of the apartment, slamming the door behind me. Instead, I robotically and politely took a seat.

"I just love a good filet," Rachel crooned in Robert's direction.

I finished my glass of wine before the beans and the potatoes and the rest of the meal made its way around the table, and I felt the loosening in my joints and muscles.

For a few minutes no one said much, which helped as well. There was general mming and aahing about the meal, which was indeed delicious.

I applied myself assiduously to a second glass of wine.

Between bites, Robert, always one for delicately probing a subject, said, "So is TheOne really the evil social engineering scheme people make it out to be?"

I glanced at Lily, who took another sip of wine, seemingly unflustered by her beau's charming approach.

Rachel put down her silverware and sat up to her full height. "I've always been an engineer," she said, "and I built TheOne just the way I've tried to build everything else—so it would work. The fact that what works makes a few people uncomfortable? Don't shoot the messenger is all I can say."

I had the feeling she'd delivered those very lines innumerable times.

Lily jumped in. "So we have to back up. I actually don't know very much about TheOne."

Without a pause, Rachel launched into her full stump speech. "I'd say there are four secrets to TheOne's success. The first is that you can't sign yourself up for it, someone else has to sign you up, so it takes away all the stigma of online dating. You're not desperate if your mom signed you up. You just have an overbearing mother. And even though we're sure about 75 percent of people fake it and just use two e-mail addresses to sign themselves up, it still works out just fine. Those people can just keep on pretending all the way through, who's going to call them on it? The second is that we eliminate as much self-assessment bias as possible. We require five photos, and we don't ask a lot of subjective personal questions. It's more factual. How much do you make? What degrees do you hold and from where? How many times in the last month did you go to the gym? What magazines do you regularly read? Where did you go on your last vacation? All very yes/no and numerical. No questions like what's your favorite band. Favorite bands are not a good predictor of compatibility. And third, it's successful because most of what TheOne does is offline. You can't search our database of profiles, which means you're free of the hassle of trying to come up with a witty screen name and all that. What you get after someone signs you up and you or they provide all the necessary information about yourself is just an invitation to a party. That's it."

"So are the parties just geographical?" Lily interrupted.

"I believe this is the part where things get good," Robert goaded.

Rachel lashed back with what I'm sure she thought was flirtatious fervor. "You're exactly right, Robert. This is where things get good." Unfortunately, her flirtatious fervor sounded like real fury, leading me to infer that in addition to being insatiably hungry for male attention, she was among the poor, misguided souls who confused outright assault with coy banter. Akin to my problem of slight meanness in place of real flirting, but a much more virulent form of the disease.

"The way the parties are designed is the fourth pillar of our success," Rachel said. "We work very hard to get the right group of people at each party."

"So it's a program you wrote that matches certain characteristics?" Lily asked, trying to keep things on course.

"We're always refining the program, but the honest truth is that it's a lot easier to predict compatibility than people think. People who are similarly attractive are more likely to be compatible. People whose parents are still married are more likely to be good matches for other people whose parents are still married. People with similar incomes are more likely to be compatible, as are people whose parents had similar incomes when they were growing up. The list goes on and on. TheOne team did a lot of research, and we built it into our reviewing system, and that's how we decide who gets invited to what party. As I mentioned, we've been refining the system, so now every party has a few wild cards."

I winced inside as she went through her list. It sounded like I was supposed to move home and marry one of my second cousins. And even though I'd diagnosed the troubles between me and Robert on dozens of occasions, I hated hearing our compatibility so publicly condemned. And hearing his and Lily's so publicly affirmed. And seeing it so blatantly affirmed as well. They just seemed so natural together. Like I'd never even existed.

"Let's look at you two, for instance," Rachel said, gesturing toward Lily and Robert. My heart seized. Really? Was she going to say it all out loud?

Robert at least had the sense to intervene.

"Wait, I have a much better idea," Robert said. "Let's look at Dawn."

That wasn't exactly the intervention I had hoped for.

"Hold on, wait a second here, how did I get involved in all this?" I protested, panic clomping through me. "I'm an innocent bystander. My only role here is journalistic."

"We could look at you, Rachel, that could be fun," Lily said divertingly. Maybe Lily would be spared some discomfort of her own if we skipped analyzing me, but I was still grateful.

"Fine," Rachel said, ignoring both me and Lily. "Let's look at Dawn."

"Please don't make me go down the list and answer all of The One's questions. I can tell you that I've stayed in my apartment in Brooklyn for all my recent vacations."

"I'm going to guess a few other details," Rachel began. "Ivy League degree, creative professional, income—not high."

Ouch. And true.

"Parents . . . divorced? Not originally from New York."

I silently grimaced my assent. Was everything about me really that obvious? Did I reek of broken home and redneck America?

"So let me tell you who would most likely be at your party," Rachel continued. "It'd be men in the twenty-five-to-twenty-nine range. Well educated, either in somewhat creative fields or who score high in other 'humanist' areas like significant book ownership or playing instruments, things like that. They'd be decent looking. And to compensate for the fact that you're a redhead and that there's a significant minority of men who say no redheads, we'd tilt the ratio and throw in an extra man or two."

How generous. She said all this without even a hint of a pause, making it clear that categorization better than "decent looking" hadn't even flickered across her imagination, nor had much concern for the potential thwack to my feelings from her "no redheads" comment. You had to give it up to her for not mincing words, though. I felt myself slouching.

"And there'd be a lot of midwesterner-gone-east types," she continued. "Nice guys, middle-class families, that sort of thing. And then we'd throw in a few wild cards. A few well-educated folks from tougher backgrounds. A few doctors. A handful of engineers and banker types. One or two working-class characters. Maybe a surfer type. And you'd pretty much be guaranteed to find a good match at that party."

"Most of that sounds reasonable," Lily said. I was glad she said "most." "But I'm not sure you're describing Dawn's type."

What was happening? Based on the gravitational pull he'd

exerted on me for the last four years, my type was Robert. But were we really going to say that out loud? Or maybe, I thought again, Lily didn't even really know that.

"And she's still single, right?" Rachel replied, without a pause.

"Um, wait a second," I finally burst in, a little bit like a fireman axing open a door just as he realizes he left his hose downstairs. "I don't think we've established that I'm single," I fumbled. "I mean fine, I am. But Geez Louise."

"See that right there," Lily said. "I think that's why you have Dawn at the wrong party. Robert and I are the type of people who find 'Geez Louise' to be very cute. I don't think any of those bread-basket boys would appreciate it like we would. She should definitely be at our party."

This was getting worse and worse. First, she was announcing that she and Robert had collective tastes. And then she was making me sound like a collectible you could carry around in your pocket. Any minute now someone was going to comment on how well I cleaned up.

"I think you should send Dawn to the new immigrant party," Robert said. "Or maybe the hip-hop superstar party. Or wait, is there a party for people with aliases? That one would definitely do the trick. DJ McJammin, meet Kelly Burns." I peeked at the wine bottle across the table and noted both that it was sitting right next to Robert and that it was totally empty.

Rachel skated right past the Kelly Burns comment, which must have sounded like pure gibberish to her given the gibberishy ring it had even to those of us who knew about my pen name. "If she didn't find anybody she liked at the first party," Rachel said, "we'd start by sending her to another party along the same lines but with new people. And if that still didn't work, we'd put her in our wild-card group."

I didn't want to go to any parties. I just wanted to go home.

"So, let's sign her up and see," Robert said.

"Wait, don't I have to consent to be signed up?"

"Come on, it'll be an experiment," he said. "You can write an article on it."

I rolled my eyes. "About 482 people already wrote that article."

"Then you can write one of your little stories about it."

Lily interjected, "I can't believe you just called them 'little stories.' They're *not* little stories."

So Lily was sticking up for me now? Had I said anything to Robert directly, he would have said, "You're so sensitive. Why are you so sensitive? You need to be more confident. If you were more confident, you wouldn't care what anyone said. You know who's successful? Confident people." Like some *Glengarry Glen Ross* lecture he was warming up for the pretzel salesforce. And I would have gotten increasingly angry in the back-and-forth, and he would have retrenched even further into his position, and then I would have started crying, and then we would have broken up. I knew, because we'd performed almost that exact script more than once.

"Stories, short stories, great stories," he said, responding to Lily.

She gave him a slight approving head nod, and just like that we moved on. No escalation. No tears.

"But I agree with Robert," Lily continued. "I think you should do it, Dawn. It'll be interesting."

"Fine," I said. Partly because of the wine, and partly because all of this—the back-and-forth, the eagle-eyed watching for signs of Robert and Lily's blooming love, the attempts at conversation with Rachel—had dispirited me. I said fine to be done with it.

Lily clapped, and not like she was happy to be pawning Robert's old girlfriend (of whatever significance) off on some men from the Internet. Like she thought it was actually fun. "Done! We'll sign you up tonight!" she cheered.

Robert smiled at Lily, clearly admiring her enthusiasm.

Rachel, on the other hand, looked annoyed, or, rather, like a person who had been annoyed at some point in the past, a point that had corresponded perfectly with a swift hit to the back that froze her face that way. She'd then been covered in a fine glaze and put in a kiln overnight to set. She was the perfect annoyance-themed mannequin. It had, after all, been a full minute since Robert, or anyone for that matter, directly attended to her.

"So Rachel," I said halfheartedly, "Lily was telling me that you and her sister were roommates during college?" This turned out to be rather weak as far as annoyance interventions were concerned. Rachel barely registered that I'd said anything at all.

Lily hadn't missed the glassy Miss Texas look either, and being the gracious hostess that she was, she decided to rescue us both. "My sister was saying you just came back from a big trip to, was it Argentina?"

Cue Rachel's interest in showing off, obviously much greater than her interest in roommate stories of yesteryear.

"Oh, we went to the most amazing wineries," she cooed. And then she proceeded to extol the virtues of Argentina's terroir. The Andean watershed, the altitude, the Malbecs!

After dinner I could have escaped, but a sort of pious perversity bound me to the evening, like I was a saint, praying for more arrows to mortify my flesh. We all retired to the living room, where Robert steered us toward his all-time favorite topic: celebrity doppelgängers. He had long been convinced he was a dead ringer for Hugh Grant, and based on his belief, he brought up celebrity doppelgängers whenever possible, then just waited for the Hugh Grant comments to roll in. The slim percentage of the time they did gave him enough fire to carry on till the next go-round. There was a certain something about the lines around his eyes, his flouncy hair, his longish face, but dead ringer? If the ringing were so high only dogs could hear it, maybe.

Lily said I reminded her a little of Cate Blanchett, which I thought was very nice. Feeling a strange flare-up of reciprocal generosity, I gave her back a Kate Beckinsale even though it was only vaguely true. And then Rachel announced that she sometimes got Hilary Swank.

After Rachel wished us all good night, Robert said to me, "Stick around and help us do dishes." His voice was warm, like the night had been familial and fun and he hated for it to end. Lily added, in the exact same entreating tone, "We still have most of that last bottle we opened to finish . . ."

Was I the only one who hadn't been happy tonight? But I'd come in the first place. I'd stayed all evening, despite my misery. So why would I start listening to my feelings and leave now?

Robert sudsed up a large pan that, I knew from last winter when I'd adventurously roasted a pheasant for his birthday, fit only awkwardly in his dishwasher. Lily sat on the counter with a glass of wine in her hand. I leaned against the cupboard, closer to the door.

"More like Hilary Skank," Lily said, guffawing, apropos of nothing.

My eyes widened into round plates. The gracious hostess turning on her guest?

"Oh, come on," Robert said. "She wasn't at all skanky. Why is that the first thing women say when they want to criticize each other?"

"Robert, I appreciate your righteous feminist attitude," Lily replied earnestly. "You're right, she's not Hilary Skank."

So maybe Rachel wasn't skanky, but her laser focus on Robert and nothing but Robert hadn't engendered my affection either. I appreciated that Lily had noticed and commented on it. "More like Hairily Rank?" I offered.

Lily cackled again. Robert folded his arms, like a stern father preparing to chastise his overly rambunctious offspring.

"Fine, I was just trying to rhyme," I said. "But Robert, didn't you notice that the only person she was remotely interested in was you?"

"What can I say?" He unfolded his arms and kissed his biceps.

"Verily Stank?" I interjected, to no applause. "Okay, fine, that's a stretch. Anyway, I think she's one of those women who doesn't know how to interact with other women. They're the women who say things like 'I just get along better with men,' when what they really mean is that men pay attention to them because men pay attention to any woman who is remotely attractive, whereas women are discriminating. If you suck, we don't want to be friends with you."

"Exactly," Lily said.

"Exactly," I echoed, reaffirming Lily's affirmation of me.

"But Rachel is friends with your sister, right, Lil?" Robert said.

"Actually, more roommates, less friends."

"Why did they room together?"

"I think it was just a softball connection."

"Maybe she just likes men better because men are more fun," Robert said, flashing a showbiz grin.

I kissed my biceps and nodded. "That must be it."

When I finally gathered my things and moved toward the door a few minutes later, Lily asked with concern, "You're taking a cab home, right?"

I nodded, though of course I wasn't planning on taking a cab. A cab from the Upper West Side to my house might have been, what, forty dollars? I didn't know exactly, but I knew it was more than I had. Before Lily, on the nights when I'd stay late at Robert's but feel compelled to sleep in my own apartment, Robert had started out trying to force cab money on me. His face twisting with distress, he'd hold twenties out to me. "Just take the money," he'd say. And I'd flatly refuse. Robert taking me to dinner was one thing. Robert handing me cash felt like another. And besides, there was some pleasure in my showy refusal. *We aren't all pampered, we aren't all coddled,* I felt like I was saying, as if I were hardened and streetwise. Though whatever pleasure I took always faded over the course of the hour-plus I spent getting home on the subway late at night. After too many failed attempts, Robert had stopped holding out the cash. He'd taken on a resigned, withdrawn look, a take-your-chances, I've-done-all-I-can look, as if I were a recidivist junkie.

Tonight, he smiled pleasantly and waved me off, which turned my heart to sinking lead. His fussy, irrational worry for my safety had meant he cared. And just like that, the light blinked off, and his concern was all elsewhere, in his apartment, with Lily. The door closed and they retreated inside together while I waited for the elevator to come. I barely nodded at the doormen as they pushed the revolving door for me.

Ellen Poloma,

Northwestern University, 1970

THE PROBLEM SOLVER

Ellen loves the lab. A top-of-her-class biochemistry major at Northwestern, she plans to attend medical school after graduation. She's gained hands-on experience already, volunteering at a free clinic in Chicago. But even though she enjoys patients, the scientific aspects of medicine are her favorite. "I'm addicted to solving puzzles," she says.

Chapter Five

L abor Day approached, and at work in the basement again, with still no signs of anyone in the building but me and Ralph and no repeat visits from Secret Agent Romance, I took deep breaths of cardboard-scented air, stretched my dialing fingers, and began making phone calls in earnest. I spoke with Stephanie Linwood, a 1969 winner who became a lawyer and told me about staying in a boring job at a real estate law firm in New Jersey for almost a decade after law school before landing a position as counsel for a fair housing advocacy organization, then becoming a professor of housing law and urban housing policy at NYU.

"We get so used to thinking success means one thing," she said. "Like you can take a snapshot and see if you have it. It's not like that. It's your whole life, and you have years and years to work with. I always want to tell young people, don't be so hard on yourself. Life is long. Be patient."

Years and years to work with . . . The years and years part sounded daunting, but in general these were words that made me want to holler "Amen!" Being a pale girl from the Pacific Northwest, I did something more like nod and blink vigorously as I clutched the receiver, my eyelids acting as windshield wipers to whisk away the sudden mist.

"I'll tell you," I said when she finally paused, "as a young person I really appreciate hearing that."

"Well, it's true! Take it to heart," she answered.

In addition to being slightly crooked, my nose troubles me by turning red anytime my emotions rise. For what I was sure wouldn't be the last time, I thanked my lucky stars that this was a phone interview and that my nose could glow Rudolph-bright in this basement without a soul to see it.

After Stephanie Linwood, I talked with Kirsten Nantz, a 1982 winner and graphic designer who became one of the country's foremost creators of new fonts. She told me that she knew she'd made it when she started throwing away invitations to events that were printed in her fonts. "For the first couple of years, every time I got one I saved it. It was this rare thing, and it felt like I might never get another. But then, I remember, it was actually a birthday card from my insurance agent, I was thirty-eight, and somehow I was finally confident that this wouldn't be the last card I'd get with my font. Throwing that card away was a real personal milestone."

After that, I tracked down Ellen Poloma, who was now the Chief of Pathology at Cook County Hospital in Chicago. I told her she was one of the first winners I'd come across, working my way from the fifties forward, who'd gone into medicine. "I bet that's right," she said. "When I went to medical school it seemed like this outrageous thing to my family. And there were only a few women in my class. I felt like a trailblazer."

She told me a little about her job, the slides she examined, how fascinated she was by cell tissue, but when I asked about her life outside work, she grew much more animated. Turned out, she had two things she wanted to discuss. First, Randall; second, Japanese hair straightening. She and Randall had been married for just four years. "I thought I was *never* going to meet the man of my dreams."

She drew out each word with drama. "Little did I know I just had to wait for him!" Ellen and Randall had just returned from a trip to Antarctica, and while we continued talking, Ellen whipped off an e-mail to me, attaching a few photos of the two of them in pounds of coats, crouching near penguins. Then she moved us right along to her hair.

"You can't tell in the photo of me from *Charm*—they blow-dried and ironed my hair within an inch of its life—but I have the most ridiculously frizzy hair. It's been a lifelong battle. But then I discovered Japanese hair straightening. I've been doing it for about a year now, and it's revolutionized my life." Almost before she finished the words "Japanese hair straightening," she'd zinged another photo to my inbox, this one embedded in an article from Northwestern's alumni magazine, discussing the advances in pathology she had pioneered at Cook County.

She was right, her hair was marvelously straight and glossy, but I laughed to think it was her hair that she found remarkable in the article, not all the achievements chronicled. How telling, I thought, what seems like a given and what doesn't. I guess if you're a certain sort of strong-headed hard worker, of course you assume you'll have a great career. It's the more serendipitous things, like love and hair breakthroughs, that seem astonishing and noteworthy.

"We're planning another trip for the spring," Ellen said. "Uganda, to see the gorillas. I can't wait to have frizz-free hair in the jungle." We both chuckled, but I could tell how much she meant it.

It didn't take that many calls with the phone cricked between my shoulder and my ear, my fingers typing swiftly at the keyboard, before I realized I should have been stretching my neck before each call, not my fingers. I dialed extension 1 for Ralph. He couldn't have sounded happier to hear from me. When I asked if I could order a headset, he said, "You bet! We should be able to have one couriered over from the main office by tomorrow." Just like that, my first professional requisition!

When we were kids, at the start of each school year, my mom would order Sarah and me pencils with our names on them. I'd check the mail daily in the weeks leading up to school, hoping for the arrival of the pencil package. You wouldn't think ordering a headset, something that would allow me to perform the basic functions of my job without injury and with which Mandalay Carson rightfully ought to provide me, would have gotten me that excited. But for a moment, I was practically at pencil package levels. Just the fact that I had a job, and that that job entitled me to office supplies—it felt like a serious achievement.

Shortly after I placed my order with Ralph, I finally got an e-mail back from Helen:

> Dawn—unbelievable! I worried the Ten Girls contest would come back to haunt me . . . but I was absolutely wrong!!! I'm so glad my past caught up with me. What an absolute pleasure it was to get your e-mail. CONGRATULATIONS on the new job! I can't wait to hear all about it, and of course catch up with you.

She sounded like herself. Cheery and charming and wonderful. No explanation for the strange delay. And it had been strange. I don't think I'd ever waited for more than twenty-four hours for a reply from Helen, and this had been almost two weeks. I'd worried. Other than vacation (which would have resulted in an out-of-office message), what would keep Helen off e-mail for so long? But here she was. I e-mailed back instantaneously. Was she free later in the week? I'd love to do a "formal" interview, I said. I ended with "I hope all's well," just to leave the door a tiny bit open for her to speak up in case it wasn't.

It's a strange thing, being a "protégé"—Helen and I were like friends. We laughed like friends, we chatted like friends. But only sort of. The difference was when my college roommate, Abigail, or my sister, Sarah, gave me advice about where to live or what to wear to dinner, I turned around and gave it back to her on similar subjects. Helen didn't barricade her personal life off from me, nothing so stark as that, and, yes, she sometimes solicited my thoughts, but she wasn't really looking for advice. If she needed answers, she probably wasn't turning to me. Still, I could listen. Judging by my weeks at *Charm* so far, I was actually pretty good at it. When we talked, I'd do my best to open the conversational door and see if she stepped through.

You'd think this influx of good female cheer and wisdom and encouragement and office supplies would have made me feel fabulous, and it did, mostly, but there was something hanging around the edges. I decided it wasn't Robert and Lily and my disbelief in the face of mounting evidence that he had really moved on. I decided it was Rachel Link. More accurately, the disappointment or at least sense of unfinished business I felt because Rachel and I hadn't hit it off. Even if that wasn't really it, of the two choices, it was the one I could do something about.

What had Rachel really done, anyway? Had big hair? Been a little socially awkward and stuck on guys? Not cooed over our entire interaction? Maybe I was as much of an attention-craving baby as she was, and I was just upset that she'd paid more attention to Robert than she'd paid to me. Or that Robert had paid more attention to her or Lily or his green beans than he had to me. So maybe I verily stank too. All this I told myself as a means of building my resolve, prodding and haranguing that was intended to push me to actually call her. I had to do something to clear my funk. *New job, new job, new job*—I should have been feeling 100 percent fantastic. I'd finally gotten what I'd wanted. Maybe if I could just wipe away the Rachel smudges, I'd be able to see clearly.

I googled TheOne's corporate HQ number. I didn't have a plan, exactly, but I continued on with the self-encouragement. Three layers of receptionists later, when Rachel finally picked up the line, her hello sounded like the hello of a much smaller-haired person.

I told her I hadn't gotten a real chance to interview her at dinner, a much better intro than "I talked smack about you as soon as you left the party and am attempting, by way of this conversation, to redeem us both." After a little chitchat about her memories of her New York trip—the highlight for her was the backstage tour of *Rent* on Broadway, where she'd, of course, gotten the guy who played Mark to sign her arm—I finally got to a good question.

"So what made you found TheOne? You must have had other ideas for good websites along the way. Why a dating website?"

After a long pause, during which I swallowed and felt the sound of it cartoonishly echo in the silence, Rachel answered. "I could say lots of things about the size of the market and the cost structure, and on and on, but I'll tell you something, Dawn. My parents are very, very happy. Ups, downs, whatever, they're crazy about each other. They haven't been apart for more than three days in the last thirty-five years. My dad plants a rosebush every year for their anniversary, and their rose garden is unbelievable. Different colors and different scents. It's this wonderful maze of flowers."

And then she stopped. I was waiting for her to tell me that this all meant she believed in "the One," and that she'd created TheOne to help her find her One or to bring the sort of love her parents had to millions of people. In short, I was waiting for a rehearsed sound bite. But it didn't come.

What she finally said was, "I'll pick a good party for you, Dawn."

I felt like that sports commentator who, against his will, found himself rooting for Mike the-rapist-ear-biter Tyson after he found out dear Mike trained pigeons. Maybe she was a man-attention whore, and maybe she had created an entire dating empire in place of getting her own game in order, but whatever it was that had seemed so wrong at dinner, the flower talk shifted my feelings. Now I sort of wanted Rachel to win the Miss Texas pageant, or whatever cosmic contest she was in.

We said good-bye, and it took me a minute to realize I was staring blankly at my bulletin board, thinking about my favorite rose, a white hybrid tea rose called the Mrs. Herbert Stevens, which I'd discovered on a sniffing tour of the Brooklyn Botanic Garden (the eight-dollar cost of entry had felt like an indulgence, but as the graduation year mark came and went with me still unemployed, I'd had to start doing little things to keep myself from sliding into complete catatonia). Whoever she was, Mrs. Herbert Stevens must have been the best-smelling person around, because her rose's fragrance was unbeatable—like the standard rose scent, but simultaneously tangier and creamier. It was like the pied piper of smell. I hadn't thought of that amazingly fragrant white rose in months, and it was a nice thought, a comforting thought. Even if I never met anyone, even if I failed at this job, there was still a rose that smelled that good.

I flipped through my stack of TGTW copies and found the page with 1996 girls in their mom jeans and shapeless sweaters, Rachel smack dab in the center of the crew. I pulled a tack from my drawer and pinned the photo to my bulletin board.

Almost two weeks had elapsed since I'd seen XADI, and I wanted to remind her both that I was alive and that I needed to be paid, so I began crafting an e-mail. She'd only met me once, and this e-mail felt accordingly critical. First, it was too much of a blow-by-blow. Then it was a one-liner. Then it went back to being too long, but even worse, it was too long and too chatty. At last, a full thirty-seven minutes of foolishly wasted time later, it was reduced to an e-mail I deemed appropriately informative but not overly familiar, which seemed to be the balance most appropriate for communication with a woman like XADI.

> XADI,
> I wanted to update you on my progress. Attached is a spreadsheet with all the TGTW winners. It's sortable by name, year, school, phone, and current state/country, as well as field of work and date of contact. I have filled in the information for the few women I have located so far, and this will be the file I will be working from and filling in as I make contact with winners. Please let me know if you have any thoughts/suggestions.
> Thanks,
> Dawn

I was actually proud of the marathon of data entry I'd completed to compile said spreadsheet. Information had been helter-skelter, and now, here it was, nice and tidy. It was the same satisfaction I felt after neatly folding laundry or organizing my silverware drawer. Though perhaps my pace during this marathon had been less than astonishing, how could I be expected to do more than turkey trot when there, staring out at me from the page in her fancy pillbox hat and yellow gloves, was a darling 1962 winner who closer inspection revealed to be Barbara Darby, the bestselling thriller writer whose name and face I recognized from countless airport bookstore rotating racks? Or there in her flouncy floral dress and feathered hair, Dora Inouye, who one quick google confirmed was indeed, as I detected despite the hair, Dora married-name Wei, the mayor of Seattle, a politician whose every move featured in papers throughout Washington and seeped all the way down to my hometown in Oregon. And just a few pages over, TV-radio-book-magazine giant Gerri Vans, trademark dimples and not-so-trademark Rapunzelesque-length of curly hair—very Alicia Keys crazy curls. I wondered just when "Geraldine Van Steenkiste" cropped both her hair and her name.

After my extended labor over my e-mail to XADI, I felt like taking a summer afternoon nap on my laurels. But XADI wasn't really a summer afternoon type. Her reply instantaneously lit up my inbox.

"Looks good. Move ahead. XADI"

Her overly friendly, excessively lengthy e-mails were really getting out of hand.

I was about to "move ahead" as instructed when Ralph knocked gently on my door.

"Pay day!" he announced as cheerily as always, today with a yellow cardigan to match his mood. "It's direct deposit, but you still get the stub."

"Thanks," I said calmly, even though I felt like a vampire trying to keep my frenzy at the smell of human blood in check. He didn't linger, and I ripped open the envelope.

Here it was, the moment of truth. I'd gone this far without an inkling of whether this was an I'm-not-in-this-for-the-money situation where I had to lie to myself and everyone else and pretend I had the luxury of not caring about the paycheck, or whether this was actually a sweet gig chatting up old *Charm* ladies, plus, *finally*, freedom from the imperiled terror I tried to tamp down daily regarding my financial footing in the world.

I pulled the pay stub from the envelope, and ding, ding, ding, the winner was I'm-not-in-this-for-the-money. Oh, Regina. My paycheck left me a grand total of twelve dollars richer than I'd been as a seat-warmer temp. So nothing was better. I could say I had a job, and that felt good, but the check sucked away my dreams of relaxing and finally being able to count on paying my bills. Every month that went by I slowly but steadily built credit card debt. I'd been hoping to reverse that. More than hoping, I'd been *desperate* to reverse that, sick and churning about it every day for a year. I'd really thought getting a job would do the trick.

My motivation to "move ahead," unsurprisingly, faltered. I halfheartedly googled names from the spreadsheet for the next couple of hours, logging some phone numbers to try on Monday. But my real focus was on scattered, anxious, scheming thoughts of money and what I could do immediately to either spend less or make more.

This was familiar territory. Before I landed the lawn care writing gig and started bringing in a few extra dollars, I'd gone so far as to consider reusing mouse traps in my occasionally rodent-plagued apartment in order to save money. Stop and think about what that entails. I'd put off any such horrible measures thanks to the start of my Lawn Talk gig, but there'd been a backlog of questions then. I'd raked in the dough that month. Now it was slower and steadier. Still, it would help if I could go home and do some lawn care writing. Lawn care writing and trawling Craigslist for more evening and weekend jobs. *Lawn care, lawn care, Craigslist. Lawn care, lawn care, Craigslist.* I felt like my brain was a car with the tires lifted off the ground, the engine revving and revving and getting nowhere.

When I got home that night, despite my bout of panicky worry over my finances, I couldn't bring myself to log in to Lawn Talk. Though it was the one thing that might have made me feel better, I felt too keyed up. I went on a long walk through my favorite parts of Brownstone Brooklyn, my eyes alternating between examining the beautiful chandelier medallions on the parlor-floor ceilings of the town houses and glancing at the uneven sidewalks to avoid tripping. Somehow, despite the wonderful first hint of turning leaves and the scenes of Brooklyny domestic bliss—kids riding scooters with helmets and pads attached to their every joint, families sitting out on their stoops—my hands stayed balled up in the pockets of my jeans. Instead of melting into the happy picture, I felt like an outsider, gawking at a vision of stability and comfort that seemed impossibly out of reach.

Back in my own building, I flipped the switch for the dusty light fixture above the mailboxes. One bulb came on, and the other popped, the sound of a snapping filament. I climbed the four flights in dingy half light. Inside my apartment, things usually felt cheerier—I'd done my best to artfully arrange my secondhand Ikea and cardboard furniture and had framed a half dozen pages from a Matisse calendar and taped up a few big Rothko posters—but tonight, instead of noticing all those bright pops of color, I noticed the greige walls behind them. The walls and Sylvia's shot glass collection, which took up a full two shelves of our bookcase. I counted five from Cancún. Had she been there five times or just done a lot of shots on one visit? (Somehow, I suspected the latter.) I popped some popcorn for dinner and then ate it in bed while watching *Big* on my laptop. I hoped it would put me to sleep. It didn't.

In fact, sleeplessness was nothing new. I'd had nights of insomnia here and there through all of college, mostly when Robert and I were on the outs. But since graduation, it felt like a nightly plague. Even nights when my brain would go quiet, when I wasn't thinking about jobs, or applications, or money, or Robert, or my parents, or disappointment, or the future—even nights when I felt peaceful— my body didn't shut down properly. I spent hours in the dark holding very still, trying to trick myself into unconsciousness. I'd tried drinking, but I was too poor for that and it didn't work well anyway. I'd tried Tylenol PM and Benadryl and melatonin. I felt groggy and made from sludge the next day, but I still used them plenty of nights anyway. The few times I'd mentioned the sleep thing to, say, Robert or to my sister, they'd said Ambien. But it hadn't felt bad enough or regular enough to talk to a doctor about it in college. And now that I didn't have health insurance or unspoken-for funds, prescription drugs weren't that easy to come by.

Eventually, sometime after three in the morning, I fell asleep. But then I woke up again Saturday morning, much earlier than I would have hoped, at the first hint of sun through my windows. Despite the fried fatigue, I lifted my laptop from its storage spot right beneath my bed, where I wouldn't step on it in the night, and prepared for what I'd been procrastinating—Kelly Burns duty.

One quick Gmail check and I'd get on with the lawn business. Or at least that's what I thought until I saw the subject line "The One Invites You . . ."

I checked the clock to make sure it wasn't indecently early. It was, but I dialed Robert anyway. I guess I could have called some other friend, but I hadn't exactly been telling everyone I'd signed up (or passively "been signed up") for TheOne, and this was his doing, after all. Somehow, the arrival of this e-mail felt urgent enough to override the "Do Not Call" advisories my brain had been issuing for weeks now re: Robert.

It rang and rang and then, just when I was expecting voice mail, a surprise: Lily answered.

"Good morning, Dawn," she said with a sort of wry seduction in her voice, a fancy-meeting-you-here drawl. Not confrontational. Flirtatious, if anything. The voice you use on a friend.

"Lily," I replied, more woodenly.

"What has you up so early on a Saturday morning?" she asked.

"I'm so sorry to call so early," I said, though her tone hadn't been rebuking.

"No, no. Don't worry at all." A dog barked on her side of the phone, followed by some shouting. "We're in the park. Robert would have answered, but he's deeply engrossed in a Frisbee game right now. He signed up for an Ultimate Frisbee league, which sounds like it would be all chill and full of Frisbee types, but it's not. It's psycho."

I couldn't help but follow her bantering lead. "So it's psycho, like people getting up at six a.m. to play frisbee, or psycho like people taking dives into the grass and body checking each other?"

"Unfortunately, both. I don't know how I let him talk me into coming to watch. I'm sitting on some bleachers, trying to read the paper, but I either look like a soccer mom or a perv leering from the stands."

We both laughed, like friends.

"But I thought Robert believed sports were for people who couldn't win in the real world and needed an outlet for aggression," I said. Robert and I had, on numerous occasions, bonded over our shared antipathy for contact sports. After a full three years of braces in high school, I refused to risk my teeth. He refused to risk his dignity.

"Yes, that sounds exactly like something he'd say." Lily laughed. And rather than feeling unsettled by this exchange about Robert, somehow upset that Lily knew him enough to say anything about him at all, I felt comradely. I felt validated. *Yes, that was something he would say. Yes, wasn't it funny.*

"So what has you up so early?" Lily asked.

I felt sheepish saying it, but there was, in fact, a clear reason I had called. "I just got an e-mail from TheOne," I admitted.

"I love it!" she said with the exact same delight she'd exhibited at dinner when the subject of my TheOne enrollment had come up. "So what does it say?"

"Oh, well, it's just one of their party invitations."

"Read it! Read it!"

I balked, embarrassed. I didn't want to read it.

"Come on," she said, filling the silence.

I could have continued resisting, but instead I let myself be sucked in by her charm.

"Okay." I cleared my throat. "Dear Dawn, Please join us tonight for a get-together with a great group of people we think you'll really like. 8 o'clock. 4 Leonard Street, Apartment 18A."

"Wait, it's in an apartment?"

"Yeah, their parties are all in apartments. I skimmed an article on it. It's something about cost and exclusivity and this theory that it makes people more comfortable and blah-blah-blah."

"Do you know what you're wearing?" Lily asked, not letting me finish reading the e-mail.

"I don't think I'm going to go," I said, the repartee slipping from my voice. I didn't say it the way people say no when they want to be talked into something, the false bashfulness, the yearning for entreaty. I said it for real. I didn't want to go.

"Do I need to call Robert over here to give you a talking-to? Of course you're going."

Suddenly, her tone felt too familiar, too smothering. It had been there all along, this overfamiliarity, like an odor, and it was finally too strong for me not to pull away sputtering.

"No, I don't need to talk to Robert. I think I should let you get back to your game," I said.

I didn't care whether it would be awkward later. I was tired. I'd go so far as to say exhausted. I felt like I was going to cry. I just wanted to get off the phone. I didn't want to be one more of Lily's cheerful order-takers.

"Wait, Dawn," she said, "Robert's yelling something."

I could tell from the rustling that she'd lowered the phone. Then I heard Robert at a distance. "This is ridiculous," he grumbled loudly.

I should have hung up. But I also felt the curiosity and slyness that accompanies clandestine intrusiveness. How was this going to go? So yes, I wanted to hear, but I still felt the need to back away. The phone next to my ear felt like too much, like I was a heavy breather. I put the phone on the bed and hit speaker.

"What's the problem?" Lily said to him, her voice muffled and scratchy.

"I don't need cardio enough to put up with this," Robert answered, even more distantly.

"Really, you dragged me out of bed for this and now you're quitting!" She said it sharply, like she was truly furious. And then she continued, "Oh, you're outrageous. What, four, maybe five body checks and one bleeding knee and you're quitting? I'm in the middle of reading a great article on eyeliner!"

Robert, his tone not yet shifted, huffily said something about the stupidity of his teammates, something with the word "meathead."

"You're going to have to take me to some pretty great brunch to make up for this," Lily replied with faux hauteur.

"We're going," he said, but now with the same put-on anger. As if he, like Lily, were only playing at being upset.

I finally hit the end button and sat staring at the silent phone.

She handled him in an easy, second-nature way I couldn't imagine. Like it was fun. Had I been at the park, I would have undoubtedly tried to placate him, to talk through his feelings, encouraged him to get back out there, or encouraged him to quit if he felt like it, either way. But it would have been a touchy-feely mess. And he would have fumed and gotten worked up and snapped at me and we would have been stormy all day, Robert walking around feeling bad about being a jerk, me walking around feeling wounded. With Lily, neither of them felt anything bad. I could just see their brunch. They'd keep grousing until the mimosas arrived, and then they'd forget they were worked up about anything except fondness for each other. Robert had solved all his problems by finding the right person.

And I, the wrong person, was left with all of mine.

I reread the e-mail from TheOne. "A great group of people we think you'll really like." Why did that sentence turn my stomach? Was it the automated message masquerading as a personal communication? Or was it just the slashing truth that I was alone, not just on a break from Robert, but really really alone. And like TheOne was going to work anyway. Why not just skip the rocky ride of love and rejection by staying right here in my bedroom?

As you might imagine, this line of thinking really killed my shoulder-to-the-wheel Kelly Burns spirit, and I slipped into a morass of aimless Saturday morning puttering. I should have been writing. Not Kelly Burns writing. Dawn West writing. Real writing. That's what I needed. To work on a story. Something that mattered to me. That's what would turn everything around. But I puttered, called my sister, puttered, called my mom, cleaned my bathroom, puttered, and hated myself every second of it. Not too long after

I hung up on Lily, Robert texted: "Heard you're going to TheOne party tonight. Go get em." I didn't respond.

That night, instead of doing what I should have done after my failed day—locking myself in my bedroom and writing till I fell asleep—I put on a dress and took the subway to Tribeca. I felt miserable and frenetic. So why did I go? I guess because part of me really wanted to meet someone. I tried to tamp down that part. As if hope were the most humiliating thing imaginable. In fact, I was pretty sure it was.

Nothing is as bad as wanting and not having, whether it's love, money, fame, status, or work. Needing, wanting—they're universally despisable traits. They're for villains and weaklings and victims and pests and gold diggers. There's nothing more reviled than a woman who displays her naked want by throwing herself at men. And if you're poor, the only way to get applause is to proudly make do or quietly and sternly build yourself up, never letting on that you're desperate. Hope, want, need—you have to disguise them at all costs.

So I pretended I was going to the party to prove a point, so I could say "See, I tried everything, and it didn't work, you stupid, foolish romantics who believe love always works out." But in fact, I was going because I wanted them to be right. I wanted someone to fall in love with me. I wanted to fall in love back. Maybe I was like Robert—I just needed to find the right person to transform me.

Before I left home, I took five minutes and logged on to Lawn Talk. BlackthumbMary in Lincoln, Nebraska, had written in with a plea. Her kids were tearing up her lawn. She needed suggestions for grass that could handle four boys and their football league. "Perennial ryegrass," I told her. "It's what they use at Wimbledon— tough as nails. They can trample all over it, and it won't show a thing." And with that, I closed my computer and headed out for the evening, ready to be Dawn West, perennial ryegrass.

Jane Smith,

Baylor University, 1959

THE COLOR QUEEN

Jane pairs classic grace and beauty with youthful curiosity and unexpectedly bold wit. An only child, she grew up on a rabbit farm and fought timidity through acting and speech. Even appeared on local television. These days, always turns down roles in tragedies and snaps up leads in comedies, especially musicals: a special flair for Gilbert and Sullivan. An English major, adores Chaucer. Her fashion credo? "Never wear black." In full color, she maintains a crisp, sophisticated look with simple sheaths and elegant "no frills" jewelry. Prefers earrings and bracelets to necklaces. The result—every bit as vivacious and pulled together as Jane herself.

Chapter Six

*T*he doorman checked my name off his list and sent me up. I inspected myself in the elevator mirror. I'd suited up in a mod navy blue dress I'd lucked into back in the day at a "clothes by the pound" secondhand store near campus. It was demure on top, but short enough to be slightly racy on the bottom. And I'd really gone for it with the mascara. There was a time when I'd figured I had brown eyelashes, so I should use brown mascara. No more! Black black black, with plenty of eyelash curler action to give them an extra boost (thanks to my mom, I had both a pocket and regular-size Mary Kay eyelash curler). Plus, I'd done some blow dryer and curling-iron action on my wavy red hair, and it cascaded past my shoulders and down my back in a way that seemed distinctly sexy. I felt a bloom of confidence—I looked good. Just before the elevator doors opened, I winked cartoonishly at my reflection, then I sauntered down the hallway of the eighteenth floor.

Glass and polished cement walls soared twenty-five feet to a polished cement ceiling checkered with vast skylights, all of it softly lit by bulbs I couldn't seem to locate. Had I been the lighting designer who'd put this glow in place, I'd have immediately written a book called *Modern Ambience* featuring this apartment on the cover. A woman in a little black dress checked my name again and stepped aside to reveal a polished cement bridge spanning a shallow stream of water that cut across the corner of the room before disappearing behind frosted glass. Even with the music and the gabbing, the tripping of the water over the gleaming river rocks made the room sound like a spa. Pale-green-tinted lights beneath the water's surface uplit the entire affair—the perfect back cover shot for *Modern Ambience*. So, this was someone's house, and this was supposed to make me feel right at home? The only stream I'd ever had in my house was an unfortunate result of plumbing problems and a sloping floor.

As soon as I could tear my eyes away from the wonder of the water, I scanned the assembled Ones. Two possibilities immediately emerged: (1) All the parties were in kick-ass apartments and my poor-to-middle-class pals and I were simply basking in opulence, because why not meet your soul mate at a shindig worth talking about? (2) Rachel had wild-carded me into a slick, richy-rich assemblage to prove a point, that point being that this was going to be a disaster.

I looked around to assess my company. Just ahead of me a woman in a lilac satin camisole and a cream, summer-weight cashmere cardigan leaned against the back of a gray velvet armchair. Her skin was that flawless translucent sort of skin that has launched a thousand skin care product purchases by less blessed gals like me.

The man next to her glanced over. Lanky and sweet faced, he looked as if his inability to drag himself from the library had kept him from the barber for quite some time. Perhaps this was the right party after all. I caught the woman's eye and moved toward the group.

"I'm Liz," she said, scooting closer to our floppy-haired friend to create a space for me. I started to introduce myself at just the moment the hair guy opened his mouth to say his name.

"Oh, sorry," I sputtered. "It's the apartment's fault. It's sort of blowing my mind."

He smiled sympathetically.

"I know what you mean," Liz said, giving the room an impressed nod.

"Right? I feel like I should have worn my good jewels, only I don't have any." I laughed at my own little joke, per usual. Unfortunately, it was at that very moment that my eyes caught the glint of a giant yellow diamond cocktail ring on Liz's right hand.

"Doug," said the sweet-faced gentleman, putting out his hand. His wrist jutted out of his jacket, revealing gold cuff links. I didn't get enough of a look as we shook to say for sure, but I could swear they were Alexander the Great gold coin cuff links. Oh boy. Robert had a collection of "great men" paraphernalia, including Alexander and Caesar cuff links. You name your conqueror, he had him emblazoned on something. The whiff of wild card was in the air. Right before my very eyes Doug's hair seemed to flop its way on over from scholarly disarray to too-entitled-to-groom.

"So you're saying your apartment isn't a scene from *A River Runs Through It*?" Doug chuckled, leaning toward me. Hm. That was the sort of bad joke my dad would make. Maybe the cuff links were a gift. Having spent years developing the ability to smile at groan-worthy jokes, it seemed a shame to waste those skills. I gave Doug an amiable half grin.

"I hear this river thing is a new trend," I began, not really having thought through the rest of the sentence. "Only in the really trendy places . . . it's either chocolate or lava, not water."

He gave me a half-puzzled, half-amused look.

I wrote a whole paper in college about myths and fairy tales across cultures in which words turned to toads, gold coins, or other assorted tokens (turns out there were loads of these stories), and I could just see the warty toads tumbling out of my mouth as I tried to dig myself out of the lava/chocolate line totally unsuccessfully with further yammering about Willy Wonka and Indiana Jones, and oh, why couldn't I just stop? In normal conversation I could usually moderate my toad-speak, but the soaring cement walls and the room full of single-and-available strangers were putting me in peak form. Doug did his best to smile politely, but I clearly detected his darting glances to the left, to the right, to anywhere that would free him from the muck I was creating all around us. I finally bit my tongue and stopped the horror, and he politely excused himself.

I turned to Liz, figuring I'd try to croak out something at least halfway normal after the Doug Disaster.

"So, Liz, are you from New York?" As a nonnative New Yorker, I have found it is often flattering just to be asked the question, as if it were possible that little-town-me could be mistaken for a metropolitan type.

"I am, actually," she said. "West Village, born and raised."

"Wow, same apartment the whole time?"

"Well, sort of. My parents ended up buying the building next to ours, and we renovated, so I technically moved next door when I was eight. And then I went away for high school."

Ah, the crisp clarity of it all. Liz "went away for high school" the exact same way I "went to college in Boston," except I was going to be paying for "college in Boston" until I was fifty, and it was pretty clear that Liz's time at Exeter or St. Paul's or Groton or wherever wasn't keeping her up late tallying lawn care word counts. Was Liz here a wild card? Just a sweet New York prepstress all grown up and looking for crazy adventure in the form of a working boy from west of the Mississippi? As she shifted her drink I noticed the bag hanging from her arm—the nondiamond arm, that is. Small, sweet, and black, the bag was clearly the real version of a five-dollar bag I'd purchased in Chinatown solely for the amusement of its large "Prado" label. Liz's bag didn't say "Prado."

She took a sip of her drink, which gave me the chance to get another eyeful of the geological marvel on her finger.

"That looks like a good idea." I tipped my head toward her champagne glass. Sweet, sweet conversational escape.

She graciously nodded her good-bye, and I moved through the crowd, noting approximately three Indian women, no Indian men, a handful of Asian women, again, no Asian men, two black women, two black men, and an awful lot of white people in various states of highly cultivated dishevelment.

The bar was at the back, in front of one of the glass walls with a view of the Financial District. I gazed at these same buildings from Brooklyn, but from this new angle, I had to search the skyline until I recognized my favorites. There was one I especially loved, the American International Building, which had a sort of Gothic–meets–Art Deco spire that looked like the perfect spot for King Kong to hang out. I scanned and scanned, and ah, there it was. Architectural orientation complete, I got in line for crackers and cheese, piling a few baby carrots and olives onto the small plate while waiting. I smiled and said hi to the woman across the table and then did a double take at what I saw over her shoulder. At the door, the LBD with the clipboard waved her pen in front of a familiar face, the face of Secret Agent Romance, Elliot too-old-for-me Kaslowski.

I immediately spun around and pretended I hadn't seen him, sending carrots and olives flying in the process. I stared intently out the window as the long seconds ticked by—gosh, that one building, who doesn't love the lights of that one building, or . . . that other one. How long before I could slowly swivel back toward the party and hope that Elliot had moved on without seeing me? Just as I steeled my nerves to turn around, there was a tap on my shoulder. I startled and jumped, which finished off the flight of the crackers from my plate.

"Whoa, sorry," Elliot said, bending down to help me clean up the mess.

"Oh, hi." I smoothed my hair (my confidence talisman for the evening) and tried to smile like, hey, airborne crackers, no big deal. "Elliot, right?" I said, as if I hadn't been reading his columns and as if I didn't regularly walk through the aisles of the archives shelves with outstanding posture, just in case he should reappear.

Bent over in his jeans, light gray dress shirt, and almost black blazer, he looked like a professor who'd just dropped the notes to his lecture on "Modernists' Search for Meaning" and was shuffling through them on the floor. If he were lecturing, I'd sit in the front row every day.

When he stood back up and awkwardly handed me back my plate of floor crackers, we both laughed a little. "So, what brings you here?" I said, ever the charmer.

"I'm doing a column on setups. The theory that other people know you better than you know yourself . . . or do they? This is the commercial angle. Last night I went out with my mom's aerobics instructor's daughter. That was the personal angle. And you?" he said. "Won't John be surprised you're here?" He smiled slyly as he pronounced the final sentence.

There was only one thing Elliot could have been referring to.

"You Google-stalked me!" I said, clasping my hands together in front of my heart. "I'm so flattered."

Unless Elliot had stalked me for real, he must have come across a short story I'd published in the college lit mag. In the story a girl, who perhaps bore a more than slight resemblance to me, finds herself overwhelmed by the family of a boy, named John, who perhaps bore a more than slight resemblance to Robert, when she goes home with him for Thanksgiving. The story ends with her accidentally burning down his family's boathouse, watching in horror, yet with a vague sense of satisfaction. I was mildly ashamed he'd found it—anything from college now seemed touched with a juvenile taint—but I was also proud. I still thought the story was good, and I was glad, juvenile taint aside, that it came up as one of the top Dawn West Google hits, which wasn't a small feat given the far-reaching Internet presence of the Dawn West who lived in Ohio and headed cafeteria services for the Pawtucket school district. That story and various other bits of flattering Internet marginalia (awards, listings in various teams and organizations, a cute picture of me climbing over a snowbank from the campus newspaper) were the real reason I'd invented Kelly Burns. Not to preserve the image of a suburban man for the readers of Lawn Talk. No, to preserve my good Google.

"Stalked is such a strong word," Elliot said.

"Don't be offended. Google-stalking is an art," I said. "In fact, if I could be a superhero, I would be the Googler. 'No search is beyond her ability,'" I said in my best radio theater voice. "'She is . . . the *Googler.*'"

"So you're saying I shouldn't be messing with you in this department."

"Actually, that's very true. Case in point, this week I tracked down a Jane Smith who won Ten Girls to Watch in 1959. I had her name, Baylor University, and that's it. I couldn't resist trying to find her because her caption in the magazine said she grew up on a rabbit farm and they had her all decked out in a rabbit fur muff and something about it was just so ridiculous. Anyway, what do you know, I had her on the phone in fifty minutes flat. She lives in San Antonio. She has three kids. She owns a chain of scrapbook stores called Memory Magic. Her husband wants to buy a race car, but she thinks it's a bad idea."

"Well well," he said, giving me his most impressed look.

"Thank you, thank you," I said, blowing fake kisses.

"But you still didn't answer my question about John."

"Fiction!"

"I see." Elliot smiled, easily, adorably. Here was a man with teeth nice enough that, if he were my husband, I would have to insist that he too avoid contact sports.

"So then, Dawn, who's responsible for your presence here this evening?"

"Actually, an old boyfriend . . . and his new girlfriend."

Rachel was right, being able to say that someone else had signed me up was a huge relief. I felt myself basking in the I'm-not-overeager glow of it all. Maybe that's what made the people in TheOne ads glow—not impending romance but simple freedom from shame, or at least from the one little corner of shame associated with wanting but not having companionship.

"Does that mean that you're not just a Google stalker, you're a real stalker, and he needed to get you off his back?"

"Ha-ha. No." I glared. "Actually, turns out Rachel Link, the CEO of this fine operation, was one of *Charm*'s Ten Girls to Watch back in 1996." I explained the Robert–Lily–sister's roommate connection.

"I see," he said.

"So did you sign yourself up or did you make your mom do it?" I asked.

"Actually, is this bad? I made *Charm*'s intern do it."

"You didn't! That's like those TV shows where the horrible guy makes his secretary call up women and ask them on dates for him."

"Well . . ."

I rolled my eyes. "So did you give her any info about yourself and your preferences, or did you just tell her to make her best guess?"

"Are you going to report me to the *Charm* ethics board if I tell you 'best guess'?"

"She must not have checked the box that banned redheads," I said, then blushed. I quickly added, "I'm actually relieved to hear someone else answered the questions to get you here." I leaned in to whisper. "I don't know if you've talked to anyone at this party yet, but I had a chat or two on my way in, and I gave the crowd a little look-see, and I don't know quite how to say this, but I think we might be at the snotty rich-kid party."

"Dawn, I'm shocked to hear such harsh language from you."

"Appalling, I know."

"If this is the snotty rich-kid party, what are you doing here?"

"I think it's a Rachel Link social experiment gone awry."

"I see, I see. So if what you're telling me is correct, I think the answer may be to blow this joint."

"Are you suggesting we leave?" I fake gasped. "What about your article?"

"I'll tell the intern to try again." He tossed a look toward the bridge and the stream. "Come on, let's go. You and me, crossing the Rubicon."

What girl's heart doesn't just melt at a Roman historical reference? Answer, most girls'. But I swooned. The two of us, crossing over the proverbial point of no return? If we were in one of those subway ads for TheOne, it'd be the painting by Pierre-Auguste Cot, *The Storm,* in which the rococo lovers flee the coming storm, running down the Arcadian path, each holding a corner of the sail of cloth billowing above their heads to protect them from the rain.

"Done," I said, setting my plate on the table. And with that, Elliot turned and led me through the crowd.

Back on the street, he said, "Which way?"

"Isn't being some sort of nightlife guru part of your job description?" I asked.

"Oh, definitely not. I make the interns pick all my date spots."

"For real?"

"No, but nightlife guru would be a vast exaggeration of my expertise. Though I'm decent at picking spots in Brooklyn."

"You live in Brooklyn?" I said. "Me too!" Despite the fact that 4 million people lived in Brooklyn and that all on its own it would be the fourth-largest city in America, this little revelation seemed like undeniable evidence that Elliot and I were simpatico.

"Fort Greene," he said.

"Carroll Gardens, which means you've got me beat in the coolness department, but I have you beat in mafia hangout Italian places."

"So, let's head back to our fair borough."

"We could walk the bridge," I said. "We're not far." And it was true. Just a few short blocks and we'd walked our way to City Hall plaza and the entrance to the Brooklyn Bridge footpath. At which point I felt a serious twinge of dread. Why hadn't I realized you don't walk the Brooklyn Bridge with just anybody? It was romance incarnate. I'd practically asked him to go to the top of the Empire State Building with me. I might as well have just thrown in the suggestion that we bear children together. Everything had been going so well, and now I'd surely ruined it. But it was too late, we were already heading up the ramp, the beautiful lines of the bridge soaring above us, the silver lights of the buildings glimmering on the dark water. I glanced over, and he seemed unfazed, striding ahead as if the bridge were no big deal.

"So, Secret Agent Romance, what did you do before you were drafted into the service?" I asked, attempting to match his nonchalance.

"Well, there were the years of hard training, all the covert ops stuff . . . Actually, I started out after college doing management consulting. And then I decided I wanted to be a writer, which meant quitting the consulting job and doing a lot of odd projects. But then I realized the reality of abject poverty isn't nearly as charming as the idea of it, and I went back to consulting, but freelance. You're looking at the proud author of the Carbonated Beverages Report, the Vibrating Devices Report, and my favorite, the Cultured Milk Report. Did you know that the popularity of yogurt-based drinks is dramatically rising?"

"Wow. I had no idea. So, what other trends should I be looking out for?"

"Actually, I quit the consulting gig a while ago." He put his hands casually into his pockets, like a shy guy who was about to start kicking a rock. "I kept writing while I was doing that stuff, and I got lucky and published a book, which freed me from the shackles of consumer marketing research at least insofar as it helped me land better freelance gigs."

"You published a book?" I grabbed his arm. Genuinely impressed and excited, and also aware that it was an excuse to touch him. How had I failed to google this man?

We stopped and leaned against the bridge's railing, gazing out toward the bay and Governors Island.

"You're not familiar with my masterwork?" he said. "I assumed that with the literally *hundreds* of copies in circulation, surely you would have heard of me."

"So tell me about the book." I smiled. "I'll get a copy tomorrow, I swear."

"I don't know. They're selling for a steep $1.97 on Amazon these days."

"So are you going to tell me about it or not?"

He paused for a second and looked farther out at the bay. "It's all about divorce. More specifically, my divorce." And then he flashed a big smile. "It's a new genre I like to call the antiromantic comedy."

It was all queued up for my easy response. I was supposed to gracefully and almost imperceptibly acknowledge the revelation, then proceed immediately with the banter. But I couldn't do it. I'd never thought about dating someone divorced. At twenty-three, it just hadn't come up yet. And after my parents, it was the thing I scared myself with late at night. In the yellow glow of the furnace in Helen's glassblowing hut, during peak postgraduation Robert breakup season, I'd tossed around on my cot, thinking, *It could be worse. We could have gotten married. We could have had a whole bunch of kids, and then we could have ruined everyone's lives by getting divorced. Breaking up now is a blessing!* All the while smudging tears into my pillow. Now, in my crooked apartment, there were nights when I'd stare at the line of light under the door that meant Sylvia and Rodney were still up and think, *Who needs to date? You're better off alone. The highs aren't worth the lows. You know what dating leads to? Marriage. And you know what marriage leads to? Divorce!* Like divorce was an STD, and abstinence was the only surefire protection.

Hearing the D word scared me on a fundamental level, but more immediately, it put Elliot in a clear category. And that category was: old. He'd had time for marriage and divorce already. Obviously, I knew Elliot was older than me, but the gap suddenly felt like a chasm. Were this to progress any further, I'd be playing the part of the girl who needs someone older and wiser, telling her what to do.

When I didn't respond as expected, he seemed not to know how to proceed. He looked at me searchingly.

"Go on," I finally said.

He took a breath. "Well, I grew up in a really religious family, married young. Me deciding I wanted to be a writer coincided with a lot of things, including my wife and I realizing we disagreed about some fundamentals. And to be fair, she hadn't exactly signed up for life with an impoverished writer. So in the end, there I was, a twenty-six-year-old guy who went from working at a swanky firm and living in a beautiful apartment on the Upper West Side with his high school sweetheart–turned–wife to being a divorced guy living with strangers in a share in Bushwick and writing pharmaceutical copy and marketing reports. It was a lot, and a few years after the whole thing, I wrote a book about it."

"I'm looking forward to reading it," I said.

He leaned away from the railing, and I followed suit, the two of us continuing toward Brooklyn but now at no more than an amble.

"So, Dawn West, how did you become the Jane Smith googler for *Charm*?"

I laughed. "Go home and google Kelly Burns. You'll find some masterworks to rival the Cultured Milk Report, I guarantee it."

"And aside from these masterworks, you working on anything else?"

I wished I could say, *Yes, some great stories. Check them out in literary magazine X.* I wanted to impress Elliot. But the sad truth was I hadn't really written any fiction in months. I thought about telling him about the profiles I'd been writing about past Ten Girls to Watch winners, but that didn't feel like anything to talk about yet.

"Well, don't you just love asking the hard questions," I finally said. "Maybe I'm working on a few things here and there. Nothing too serious."

He gave me an inquiring half smile that clearly said *go on,* but I didn't. I felt suddenly, inexplicably, yet much too explicably, emotional. Like when you start crying for the smallest reason, like you open the fridge and see that you have no yogurt left, and your eyes suddenly puddle. Of course you know it's not the yogurt, it's hormones, or another breakup, or fatigue, or whatever. The rush of threatening teariness now felt similarly out of the blue, yet there was the obvious answer: Robert had been a great Dawn writing-career cheerleader—Robert had read and admired all my drafts. He'd cheered when I'd turned down law school and urged me to buckle down and write more. He'd known just what to say in a way my parents and other friends never had, how not to be pestering, and how to be positive without being pandering. And now Robert was gone.

Standing here on this bridge talking not with someone who knew and loved me, or who had once known and loved me, but with a stranger, more or less, and talking about writing, perhaps the area of my greatest need and want and aspiration, I couldn't varnish over my vulnerability as easily as I could with other things. Besides which, everything I'd tried working on for the last year had sounded whiny or maudlin. Unemployed college graduates suffering from *utterly tragic* heartbreak kept creeping into every story

I wrote—hardly golden material. The result was that I'd pretty much stopped writing. The tears pricking at my eyes made me want to cover myself back up. I wanted a shielding blanket. At the very least, I wanted to talk about something else.

Finally, I said, "I don't know if you ever felt this way before you published your book, but I feel like there's something terrible about being an aspiring writer. Like everyone smiles and says good for you but they're secretly cringing and hoping you never ask them to read anything you write, since they're assuming it'll be awful dreck."

"And are you worried they're right?"

I wrapped myself safely again in smiling, protective chattiness. "Of course not," I said. "My delusions of grandeur know no bounds. Every year when they announce the MacArthur 'genius awards' I read the press release very carefully to make sure that I don't miss my name, just in case. I imagine the lectures tenth-grade English teachers across America will give when they assign my books to their students."

"I see." He smiled. "What if I admitted that I clipped all the positive reviews of my book and anonymously sent them to my tenth-grade English teacher, just to show him he was wrong, advertising wasn't the best route for aspiring writers?"

It was official. I liked Elliot. Even if he was old and divorced. We both smiled and held each other's eyes, long enough to make it clear that something was happening on this bridge.

We'd made it just past the high point, the lights of downtown Brooklyn and the clock atop the Jehovah's Witnesses Watchtower twinkling before us (9:37 PM. 71°). And just then his phone rang, a ringtone that took me a second to place, but then, oh, place it I did.

"Is that 'Sexual Healing'?" I asked as he rifled through his pocket.

"Noooo . . ." he said in exaggerated denial. "I can't believe you'd even think that." At last he found the phone, pulled it out, and silenced the ringing without looking at the caller ID. Clearly, this was a special ringtone that required no caller verification.

"That was so totally 'When I get that feeling I need, uh, sexual healing.'"

He smiled, sheepishly but encouragingly.

"Was that a Boots booty call?" I said. "That had to be a Boots booty call."

"You've been stalking me through my columns!" He clutched his hands to his chest in an impersonation of my flattered pose earlier in the evening.

I flicked his arm. "Absolutely not!"

And right then he leaned in and kissed me.

"Where are you from?" I said, a moment after our lips parted and he drew back to see my face.

"Like what planet?" he asked warily.

"No, like what state."

"Nevada."

"I knew it. You have rectilinear western state written all over you." I leaned in and kissed him again.

Night lights have always made me feel dreamy. As a teenager I slept out on the trampoline and memorized the constellations using flash cards I got for Christmas. The first time I saw fireflies, which wasn't till college, I made Robert pull the car over and sat by the side of the road, staring into the field where they glowed for what must have been a full thirty minutes. Standing there with Elliot, the lights of the bridge, the lights of the city, the lights of the cars streaming along the Brooklyn-Queens Expressway—it was all so beautiful. I'd felt so exposed just a few minutes earlier, but now it was like the world was twinkling warmly at me. Elliot and I kissed and kissed and kissed until my chin was sore from his stubble, and then we finished the walk across the bridge—11:02, the Watchtower said. He walked me all the way to Carroll Gardens, slowly, stopping here and there, kissing me again and again, and when we finally got to my building he kissed me one more time on my doorstep.

I gave him my phone number. "Swear you won't assign it 'Sexual Healing.' You swear?"

"Cross my heart, hope to die. You have any preferences?"

"I want that Cake song, the one about the girl with the short skirt and the long jacket who has fingernails that shine like justice and who's touring the facility and picking up slack."

"The na-na-na-na-na-na one?" He sang the tune.

"That's the one."

We kissed again and I climbed my crooked stairs and walked into my crooked apartment and didn't notice the slant at all. I felt better than any TheOne ad. I was in a Chagall painting, and the yellow goat was playing the violin and I was floating, full of hope, with the village spread out behind me.

Patricia Collins,

Ohio State University, 1967

THE FARMER'S DAUGHTER

Patricia's good looks are as American as apple pie. The daughter of a dairy farmer, she won her town's Harvest Queen title in high school. In college, she can't shake her All-American smile but has added a new level of sophistication to her style with tailored coats and the latest above-the-knee looks. A history major, she's considering the Peace Corps after graduation. "I know I want to make a difference." We can't think of a better ambassador.

Chapter Seven

I almost forgot about Elliot's insidious Cankles Column until I got an e-mail from him Sunday afternoon.

> Dawn,
> My heartiest thanks to you for rescuing me from a night with the A-hole rich kids. I'm eternally in your debt. Let me at least try to repay you. Brunch when I'm back in town? (I'm heading to CA today to report on iPhone app competitions for *Grid.* Then a week in NV.) Say hello to fall with me in mid-ish Sept? S.A.R.

Not that I thought he was lying, but there was a part of me that worried he was delaying our next get-together not for work travel but because he was working on a column about me. He'd call me "City Slicker" and describe the way my face built up a less than alluring sheen as the night wore on. And what did "mid-ish" September mean anyway? Why was he already building in wiggle room?

But rather than being crazy (at least on the outside), I e-mailed back a short and sweet "Safe travels. We're on for the fall hello," and thereafter spent a while sprawled on my bed shamelessly fantasizing about crunchy leaves and belted cardigans and how cute I'd look in them on our future dates. It'd be Elliot's loss if he missed my autumnal glory.

My phone pinged with a message in the middle of my daydreaming. "So, did you meet 'the One' last night? ;)" Lily had written.

I wanted to ignore the message, but that felt like an unnecessarily passive-aggressive move toward a woman who had just gotten me a job and invited me over for dinner. "Nah," I wrote back. Then, sensing that was a little dismissive, I added a smiley face before sending it.

That evening I got one more notable message, from Helen.

Dawn, I would love to set up a time to talk. But even better, why don't we do it in person? My new book is coming out in a couple of weeks, and I'm doing a reading at the bookstore across the street from campus. Come that weekend.

Helen had been working for the last few years on a new book on the connection between women's suffrage and World War I. Like *Must We Find Meaning?* it also wove her personal history into the narrative. In her early twenties, Helen's grandmother had been a suffragist in Oregon, and prior to the 1912 referendum that finally gave women the vote in Oregon, she had traveled all over the state, putting on suffrage shows in movie theaters. Then, in 1916, at the age of twenty-five, Helen's grandmother had taken a train to Washington to stand in the sleet outside the White House with a banner that read "Mr. President, How Long Must Women Wait for Liberty." Helen and I had talked about the book-in-progress a little during my weekly thesis meetings senior year, and she'd finalized the copy during the months I'd been living in the glassblowing hut.

On one of the nights during my hut stay, when the September weather had turned unexpectedly chilly, I'd crossed the leaf-covered yard from the hut to the house, my jacket collar pulled up to my ears. I tapped on the back door, and when Helen answered I didn't say anything, just held up the little tin of gourmet hot chocolate I'd splurged on at the fancy import store down the road.

"Ooh, please do come in," Helen intoned dramatically, swinging the door open. She'd warmed the cocoa on the stove, and instead of talking about jobs or plans or Helen's work, we sat on the kitchen barstools, sipped from our mugs, and talked about a short story I'd given her to read. This one was about a woman who, after multiple miscarriages, makes herself feel better by putting on a one-woman version of *The Sound of Music*. I admitted to Helen that it was maybe 90 percent true and based on my grandmother, who'd done that very thing.

"I think it's a wonderful story," Helen said, "but I wonder what would happen if you made it one hundred percent true. Sometimes I think you're hiding behind the safety of fiction, Dawn."

It was advice straight out of her own playbook. That's what Helen did—tell the true story. It's what had made her career. It was flattering to hear she thought I could follow in her footsteps. But I wasn't sure the true stories in my life were quite as interesting as the ones in hers. Not just that, I wasn't sure I was ready to give up my dreams of writing fiction.

I gave a small, nervous laugh and took a big swig of cocoa. "I guess all I can do is try it and see," I finally answered.

But I hadn't done it. After I'd crunched back through the leaves to my cot that night, instead of working on the piece I'd e-mailed Robert. And so it had gone for a seemingly endless line of nights—not necessarily e-mailing Robert, but something, there was always something—and now the story had been lying in wait on my laptop for almost a whole year, untouched since that evening. Maybe reading Helen's new book would give me the shove

I needed to actually open the file again. Because clearly, I needed a shove.

E-mails flew, and before the night was over, it was all set. I made the vast commitment of booking a fifteen-dollar ticket to Boston on the Chinatown bus.

Back at work on Monday, when I arrived at my office door, I found a small box resting against the jamb—my headset! It couldn't have been later than eight o'clock. Apparently, Ralph, man of mystery that he was, got to work even earlier than that.

No one was bothering to check when I arrived or left work (unless Ralph was somehow security-cam-monitoring me), but I found my hours creeping outward in both directions anyway. I was excited to get started on Ten Girls to Watch every morning, and at the end of the day, I almost hated to go. Maybe this was because of the veggie patty dinners that awaited me at home, but I didn't think so. Ralph could have been arriving early for other reasons—I briefly imagined soap opera tragedies lurking in his life, his long hours at the office driven by the need to escape heartbreaking bedside vigils or scandals related to wanton stepchildren. But that seemed pretty unlikely. He was probably just a morning person.

Once I was all headsetted up, I picked a year in the middle of the pack—1982—and started working from there. By lunchtime I'd made a handful of contacts (and had experienced nary a neck kink). Jeneese Walker, an educator who'd just founded a new charter school in Atlanta; Kendra Fowler, who now ran the veterinary program at the University of Washington; Allison Bentson, a lawyer who had become the head of an environmental lobbying firm in D.C., and who had just had twins at the age of forty-five; and Elizabeth Irwin, who I adored the second she opened her mouth.

Elizabeth was from North Dakota and sounded just like Frances McDormand in *Fargo*. She'd become a pediatrician and gone back to her hometown, where she was immediately disturbed by the number of children she saw who were clearly being abused and the difficulty she had connecting them and their families with the social services they needed. Within a year she'd established a wholly integrated Family Center, complete with medical, social, and legal services, all housed in one facility. The number of child abuse cases reported in her county quadrupled within two years. Not because there was more abuse, but because people finally had a place to go to get real help.

She had two young children of her own, a husband who was a newspaper reporter, and a mother who had just begun to show the first stages of early-onset Alzheimer's. The closer I listened the more I could hear the edge of exhaustion under her High Plains clip.

"I know people hate this question," I said, "but I'm only asking because I'm wowed. How do you manage all of that?"

She laughed self-consciously. "It sounds like a lot when you summarize it, but I don't do all of it every day. If you want to know the truth, most days I feel like I'm miserably behind and only doing about half of what I should be doing. But when you look back you can see that you're building something. I think people who say 'Don't look back' are crazy. I wouldn't survive if I weren't looking back and patting myself on the back all the time for making it this far. I've been thinking about memory a lot more these days, with my mom and all. And I think dwelling in the past can be . . . I don't know, very good, I guess. I just know that if you look back at it, the days add up to something."

After we said good-bye, I stared at my screen for a minute. I felt like I'd just listened to an aria—the kind of quiet that comes after musical lines rise and fall, then resolve with a question still in the air. *If you look back, the days add up to something,* I typed. Then I pulled the photo of Elizabeth Irwin from my 1982 binder and pinned it to the bulletin board. Day by day, the past year hadn't felt like much, but looking back, I realized at least I'd gotten through it. I'd figured out how to rent an apartment in New York City, had installed my own air conditioner, and had managed to feed and clothe myself, perhaps not in high style, but nonetheless. And I was here now, working for *Charm*. Tracking down winners was slow going, but it was true, the interviews were adding up. The spreadsheet was spreading. This was all getting me somewhere.

I stood up to take a break (well earned, my affirmations assured me) when a strange thing happened—my phone rang. My first incoming call! I'd been leaving voice mails with women across the country, and a lot of my calls were scattershot. For women from the early years whose maiden names weren't coming up on the Internet, I'd been making White Pages guesses based on state, date of birth, and middle initial. Apparently, I'd guessed right with one Mrs. Carol N. Stauffer of Birmingham, Alabama.

I said approximately five words—"hello" and "I'd love to hear . . ."—before Carol cut me off and began drawling through the story of her post-*Charm* life. "Oh, dear, let me tell you!" she began.

Carol Newbold became Carol Stauffer nine days after college graduation, and she and her husband, Richard, moved to Birmingham, Alabama, where his uncle owned a pop music radio station. Richard worked for him, selling ads and balancing the books, and when the uncle was ready to retire, Richard and Carol bought the station from him.

"Our youngest was about ten at the time, and I talked Richard into letting me host the late-night show, after the kids were in bed." Carol paused here and there in full back-porch storytelling mode. "Just for two months, I said. Just to try it. And, oh, it was a riot. I loved it! And it turned out I was pretty good at it. My littlest one, when she was about fourteen, I remember her coming home and mimicking the kids at school: 'Your mom is so funny. We love your mom's show.' Goodness, how she hated that! What's so funny is that now she hosts the number one morning show in Tallahassee, after getting her start on our station."

Eventually, Carol told me, she and Richard bought two other stations, one a country music station, the other a news station. "He won't ever retire, despite my begging, but I don't exactly have room to talk, since I'm still producing a couple of segments myself, one on Alabama education, the other on local restaurants. I can tell you where to find the best fried anything in town!"

Throughout all of this, I barely prompted her. I laughed when she laughed and said "How great" a few times, but that was about it. Finally, Carol gave another bighearted chuckle and summed it all up: "I've always had fun," she declared. "If I had to tell you the secret to life, that's what I'd say. Just have fun. What more can you ask for?"

"Sounds like it's worked for you!" I said, unable to resist her enthusiasm.

"You try it! You'll see!"

I could have happily spent another half hour listening to her, but Carol announced she had an appointment at the salon to have her hair "set," so off she had to go.

There was nothing to do after hanging up but smile and feel a little bewildered. It was like a dust devil had touched down in my office, scattering midcentury southern belle charm everywhere, then spun off as fast as it had arrived.

I spent ten cheery minutes writing up Carol's profile, and then clicked into my e-mail. I'd received yet another loving missive from XADI:

Dawn, Let's talk at 3:15 today. I want to discuss coverage of TGTW.

I noted the absence of question marks in the e-mail.

My roommate, Sylvia, had e-mailed as well:

Hi Dawn, I hope things are going well at your new job. I wanted to let you know that I'll be moving back to Toledo on October 1. I'm happy to help look for a replacement.

Roommate abandonment? In two short sentences? Couldn't she have said something in person? Was she moving home for Rodney? We were hardly best friends, but we certainly brushed our teeth together some nights. I would have thought we'd have had at least one roommatey heart-to-heart about all this. And she was "happy to help" look for a replacement? It should have been promises that she'd take care of it entirely. If Sylvia didn't find a replacement ASAP, where exactly did that leave me? There was nothing plummy or plush or able-to-cover-anything about my bank account right now.

For the next solid chunk of the morning, I took advantage of the fact that I worked alone in a closet to put up a roommate-wanted posting on Craigslist for a "cute room in Brooklyn" (cute being the catchall word for things like sloping floors and plumbing with a personality) and to frantically scan the Craigslist jobs "ETC" section. In the past year, I'd participated in focus groups for razors, soda, and and air fresheners, each one raking in seventy-five dollars for a mere ninety minutes of my time. I would have done one every night if only I'd qualified. That was the thing, you had to pass all these screens, and marketers were only minimally interested in single, college-educated, white twenty-three-year-old girls too poor to actually buy anything for themselves or others.

I scanned postings: "Earn $70 for owning a Tablet PC." Alas, I owned a Mac. "Elite Egg Donation Agency Seeks GREEK Egg Donors." Alas, again. "Dealing with TOENAIL FUNGUS?" Thankfully, no. "Pretty Girls Needed For Thursday Foot Fetish Event." Maybe . . . uh, no. "Have trouble falling asleep? Adults 18–65 Needed For Paid Research $500+" What? Yes! I clicked through and immediately called the number listed for some place called Somnilab.

I explained that I'd seen the ad and was transferred straightaway to an "intake specialist" named Becky.

They were looking for people who had trouble falling asleep, but not trouble staying asleep, she explained. Was that me? Would I be willing to stay overnight in a sleep lab? Was I willing to take medication that had proved safe in trials but was not yet FDA approved? Would I be willing to undergo regular urine and blood tests? Yes, yes, yes, yes, I answered. Maybe I still had Carol Stauffer's chipper voice in my head, but somehow it all sounded kind of fun.

"Great!" Becky said, slipping out of her reading-a-form voice for the first time. She explained they had a six-week study she thought I'd be eligible for. Each week required one overnight stay in the sleep lab. I would be paid two hundred and fifty dollars per week, but there were progressive requirements each week, so I might be cut off at any point. If I made it through the full six weeks, that'd be fifteen hundred dollars. Either way, she wanted me to come in for the full battery of prestudy lab tests.

I felt like I'd discovered some vast hidden reservoir of talent, like I was a seven-foot-tall woman from the bush who'd been a local freak until basketball scouts discovered her and made her a star. An insomnia study was going to pay me almost as much as my actual job? Good golly!

I tried to maintain my cool until Becky and I said our good-byes, but my heart had scattered into a million pieces and was pounding ecstatically in every corner of my body. Fifteen hundred dollars?! I really hoped I'd pass those lab screens.

Though I also wondered what could happen from week to week to prevent my continued participation. Kidney failure? Sleep-drug-induced psychosis? But even those thoughts weren't enough to dampen my spirits. After what I considered the most fruitful Craigslisting I'd had in months, I gleefully settled in to track down some more ladies.

I got another one on the phone—Felicia Calandra, 1976, a teacher turned stay-at-home mom turned Poughkeepsie, New York, city councilwoman. She'd started attending council meetings when she and her husband were having trouble with permits for their home renovation, but even after their garage extension and their driveway worked out, she kept going. It was only a few months before the election and she said, what the hay, I can do this. And she did. She won partly, she thought, because she'd connected with so many people through teaching their children. And it didn't hurt that her father-in-law was Phil Calandra of Calandra's, the much-loved Italian food shop in downtown Poughkeepsie. "You're never going to go wrong being associated with good food," she said. "That's why everyone wants to slap their name on a recipe." She offered to help with the catering for the TGTW party if we needed it. I suspected chicken parm, though delicious, might not be what Regina had in mind for the gala menu, but I told Felicia I'd let her know.

And then it was three fifteen. I called the number in XADI's e-mail signature.

"Hi, Dawn," she said. "Let's just jump right in."

I'd hardly expected pleasantries, but that was still a faster entrée than I'd expected. "Sounds good," I fumbled, trying to recover.

"At our senior editors meeting this morning, Regina was very keen on discussing Ten Girls to Watch," XADI said.

I had a picture of XADI sitting in her interior office, door closed, talking to me through her speakerphone with only her steepled hands visible in the small circle of light from her lamp, like a James Bond villain.

She explained that Regina wanted to bump the coverage up to January so it could run alongside a big "Real-Life Makeover" feature. We'd be meeting with her week after next to discuss, but in the meantime, XADI wanted the full details on my progress. She said all of this without pausing, without so much as waiting for an "uh-huh." When at last she did pause, it felt like an appraising pause, as if she were leveling a look at me through the phone, trying to assess whether the rabble she had to work with could be made to perform at tolerable levels.

January was the first mention of any timeline. I felt that piece of information lodge in my brain, a painful wedge, splitting apart any sense of security I'd been amassing—so that was when I'd be back to scouring the world for employment. But I moved away from that thought and adopted my most efficient tone in order to give XADI the rundown. She'd seen the spreadsheet. I'd been working to populate it and had been making steady progress. I'd made contact, either by e-mail or phone, with thirty-eight women so far. Now that I was in the swing of things, I expected my pace to pick up.

"You're doing great work," she said in a clipped tone. Was that a compliment? It sounded so strange coming from her, like a yodel in an ice cave. I had half a second to revel in it before she'd moved on to telling me I should have a solid list of ideas for the anniversary event and coverage to present at the upcoming meeting—themes, possible keynote speakers, lots of ideas for titles and formats for the magazine—and that Regina wanted to have as much information as possible about as many women as possible before we met. XADI wanted to see it all by next Friday.

There was nothing to do but say yes, and with that XADI signed off. I gazed with unfocused eyes at the stacks of cardboard boxes beside my desk. The giddiness from Carol and the sleep-study phone call was a fuzzy memory. I had a lot of work to do.

For the next two weeks, while regularly pausing to jot down potential themes and TGTW story titles—"50 Years of Wisdom," though perhaps a little plain, was the one I kept returning to—I launched into all-day calling sessions and spreadsheet updates.

I spoke with Lucy Alexander, '58. She'd married the fellow in

the background of her photo in the magazine, a young man leaning against a truck with a cowboy hat tilted halfway over his face, a
little like the Marlboro Man's after a long day of lassoing.

Amy Brandt, '72, was a lawyer in Kansas. She'd set up her own
firm and now employed thirty-two other lawyers. She'd also taken
up dancing and was on the road almost every weekend now for
ballroom competitions.

Carly Schwartz, '67, had been a model, then a food stylist—an
easy transition, she explained, since the photographers she knew
as a model introduced her to the photographers who shot food for
advertisements and magazines. She and her husband had never
been able to have children, she confided, and the sorrow in her
voice when she explained this rang with feelings from another era.
She didn't cloak her emotion in humor and irony, and she lowered
her voice as she spoke in a way that assumed we all understood the
loss, the same hush you would use to break the news of a death.

I finally got Rachel Link's lost acquaintance, Donetta Allen, on
the phone. She was still a programmer in Silicon Valley. She'd also
been one of Rachel's first TheOne.com experiments. I told her
about my party experience, playing down the part where I'd fled
the scene, and she told me that Rachel had invited her to a party
where all the women had D names and all the men had B names.

"Deborah, Daisy, Danielle," she said, "and Bruce, Brian, Brad,
Bernie, Bob, Bill . . . Buster. All names like that. She was testing
out some article she'd read on people with names at the front of the
alphabet having similar traits. All I'll say is Buster was all busted. I
don't know how I ended up going out with him after the party. But
that was the end of me and TheOne." I poured forth pure sympathy.

Between calls, I labored over profiles. In the hurry XADI had
put me in, I didn't write them for every single woman, but some of
the women had stories I just had to take the time to record. Like
Patricia Collins, '67.

She ran a winery in Napa Valley, and when I asked her how

she'd wound up doing something so cool, she didn't answer right away.

"There's a short version, and a long version," she finally said.

"I'm up for both," I prompted.

"The short version is that I grew up on a farm and always wanted to get back to something like that. The long version is a little twistier."

After college, Patty's roommate had talked her into moving to Chicago, where Patty found a job in an advertising office. "That's where I met Henry," she said. "He was my boss's son, and he worked at a bank right around the corner." They started meeting for lunch, and then for dinner, and soon they were in love. And then Henry was drafted. He never came home from Vietnam.

"It wasn't as if I never got over him," Patty explained. "I did. But there was never anyone else like him." After that, Patty left Chicago and followed friends to upstate New York, where they lived on a farm collective. Eventually, she and a friend from the collective moved to Northern California and found jobs at a winery. When she turned fifty, she bought fifty acres and started her own winery: "H."

"My parents would never say this," Patty said, "but living on a farm, your life is very sensual. You're always tasting, touching, smelling, testing. And I think that's part of why I love this. Wine is such a pure experience. For a few moments the only question in the whole world is how does this taste? Forget about politics, disasters, your life, forget about your history, your future, all your feelings—focus for a few seconds on just the taste, the smell, the feel of the wine. Just for those few seconds. I think that's as close to heaven as we get."

Later that week, a bottle arrived for me in the mail. The label was beautiful, the *H* embellished in purple and gold, like one of those ornate cardinal letters in a medieval illuminated manuscript. "Try this," the note read. "I think you'll like it. I always describe it as 'crisp and full at the same time.' Can't wait to meet in person! Patty."

I thought about calling Ralph right then to see whether he had a bottle opener, but instead I set the bottle aside, in a safe spot beside my desk. There would be a perfect day for that wine. I'd wait till then.

LeAnne Marston,

Indiana University, 1991

THE ATHLETE

LeAnne powered IU's volleyball team to the National Title in this year's NCAA Division 1 Championships, demolishing records for individual "digs" and "kills" along the way (she's ranked number one nationally for both). A true scholar-athlete, the 6'2" biology major's near-perfect GPA puts her in the top 2% of her class. Off campus, she serves as a volunteer EMT and as a coach for the Special Olympics. "There's nothing like seeing my team score," she says. "You can just feel the joy."

Chapter Eight

Sarah had stayed close to home for college. The University of Oregon, just an hour up the road. She hadn't come home that much during her first or second year, but her junior year, my sophomore year of high school, things changed. That was the year of the divorce.

They'd waited till Sarah's birthday weekend, in February, to tell us. She'd come home for the day, and I suppose they figured it was a good time since we'd all be together. They'd even waited till after Sarah had blown out the candles and her cake had been cut and served. We were sitting around the dining room table, all of us dressed up for the occasion, Sarah especially so in a red shift dress and black patent heels I'd helped her pull out from the back of her closet that afternoon.

"Girls, we need to tell you something," Dad said timidly, both of his hands gripping the table, as if it might jerk away from him at any moment. "There are going to be some changes." He then looked to Mom, as if cueing her.

"Your dad is going to be moving to an apartment, in that complex by the freeway exit," she said. It was the first time she'd ever

said "your dad" instead of just "Dad." After that, she'd never refer
to him any other way.

Sarah blinked repeatedly. I could feel my own eyes doing the
opposite, turning buggy. For a second, I felt like I had 360-degree
vision. I could see the ice cream melting on the cake plates in front
of us. I could see the rain plinking on the sidewalk through the
window behind us. I could see the little lines around my mom's
mouth pulled taut. I could see my dad, shifting his heavy-lidded
eyes from me to Sarah and back, waiting for one of us to move this
forward since he couldn't seem to.

"Are you . . . getting divorced?" my voice creaked.

"We are," Mom said, trying to sound resolute but sounding
instead like her words were riding waves, the pitch wobbling
unsteadily.

It wasn't a surprise. But it was. I couldn't really remember our
parents ever being *happy* together. Mom treated Dad as if he were
some sort of petty villain, like he had a magic purse of gold coins
he kept hidden away and if he'd just fish it out, we could finally
live. Dad treated Mom as if she were a remedial student, her every
suggestion laced with a feeble-mindedness he disdained. Mom
would say, "I thought we could organize the garage on Saturday,"
and Dad would roll his eyes, but because they were both funda-
mentally passive, he wouldn't say no, he'd just be evasive, and she
wouldn't push it, she'd just go out and buy new shelves, and then
he'd be furious about whatever she'd spent on the shelves, and
she'd be furious that he wasn't helping her set them up. But it
wasn't like they yelled. They just set their jaws and looked at each
other with disgust and shot glances at Sarah and me that were
supposed to confirm our sympathy for their side. Then everyone
would tiptoe for hours until the contempt waned, though it never
waned for long.

Over the years, we got used to the buzz of tension. It just
seemed normal. That's how it had always been. Somehow, they

went about disliking each other quietly enough that I had assumed they would go on that way forever.

That evening when Sarah's ride arrived (a girl from her dorm who pulled up to the curb in her old Volvo station wagon and honked the horn), I walked to the end of the driveway and stood in the rain with her for a few seconds before she climbed inside. I didn't say anything, but I must have looked pathetic. Sarah put her arms around me. "I'm not going to leave you alone," she whispered in my ear.

Dad left that same night, just a couple of suitcases in his backseat. Mom put on a graying terry cloth bathrobe and stayed in it for what seemed like months. Alone in his new apartment, Dad didn't fare much better. He left an omelette on the stove and burned his kitchen wall. Later, he left the faucet on in the bathroom, and the mildew that sprang up in the soaked floor never seemed to subside. But through it all, that whole year and the next, Sarah came home almost every weekend. Most of the time she didn't spend the night—just day trips in cars she'd borrowed from friends—but she'd pick me up in the morning and we'd drive to the coast together. We'd get Styrofoam cups of hot apple cider and plastic sleeves full of powdered sugar donuts from a bakery we found in a strip mall near the beach, and then we'd park and walk to the edge of the sand, where we'd sit on rocks or logs overlooking the waves, our hoods up to keep the drizzling rain from our faces.

We talked about the whole Mom-and-Dad mess, but we also talked about school (Sarah had had all the same teachers I now had a few years earlier; "if you ask Mrs. Wilkinson for extra credit, she'll always come up with something," she offered) and we talked about boys (none for me at that point, something I attribute to my high school love of oversize sweaters and barrettes, but Sarah met her now-husband, Peter, in an elective called "Environmental Philosophy" that they'd both signed up for that spring semester) and about what we were going to do when we grew up. I said "lawyer," even though I secretly wanted to say "writer"; Sarah had gone from saying "singer-songwriter" to saying "music therapist." It never quite happened. After college, she took a job at a car rental company, which she stayed in up until the twins came. But even with full-time work, she kept singing with her band. It wasn't her Manhattan fantasy, but her life had changed, and her dreams had changed too.

Even when we didn't say much on those weekend drives, even when we just watched the yellow lines of the road and the green of the trees whizzing by, it still meant a lot that Sarah was there. She had kept her promise. I hadn't been alone. If her visits had petered out, I probably wouldn't have turned into a junkie-flunkie (much as they repelled boys, my barrettes also repelled kids cool enough to get into trouble; in inverse proportion, they attracted friends whose idea of a good time was really killing it on poster boards about photosynthesis). But without Sarah, I would have been sadder. I would have been lonelier. I would have missed out on a lot of stability—and hot cider—that I'd really needed.

I thought of all this because of an afternoon call with a 1991 Ten Girls to Watch winner named LeAnne Marston, a former volleyball star who'd gone on to become a coach.

"After college I wanted to go foreign and go pro," LeAnne told me, her voice sweeter and softer than I would have expected from such a hard-core athlete. "There was a team in Sweden interested and another team in France. Women's sports are bigger in Europe. But one afternoon I got a call from my old high school. They needed a biology teacher and a volleyball coach. It was a private school so they said they'd figure out all the certification stuff. I had really romantic notions about coaching. Mine were always bigger than life, and I kept thinking about all those movies where little high school or college teams fight the odds and rise to glory thanks to an amazing coach.

"But my little sister was just starting high school," LeAnne continued, "and that's what decided it for me. I think a lot of people right after school forget about their families. They're off to live their own lives somewhere else and that's it. But going home—I coached my sister in every game of her high school career. I helped her pick her prom dress and study for AP tests. All the things she watched me do, because she was younger, and that I would have missed out on if I'd gone somewhere else."

After her sister graduated LeAnne left the school and went pro on the beach volleyball circuit for a few years. "It was a total blast," she said, "but the WPVA went bankrupt in the late nineties, so that was that."

When I asked her about what she was doing now, she laughed. "I've got two daughters, six and four, and so far they're both giants like me, so I think there might be volleyball in their future. I'm only coaching part-time, but here's the funny thing, my sister is a coach too, and our schools play each other sometimes. There's a major family betting pool. Serious money changes hands over those games."

She paused again, returning to the thoughtful silence she'd slipped into earlier, then said, "I'm really lucky to have such a great sister."

I felt that way about Sarah. But there was also the flip side. What kind of sister was I? Sarah had been there for me, but when my turn at college came around, I'd booked it out of town on the first plane to Boston and barely looked back. Talking to LeAnne and thinking about Sarah, I felt . . . guilt. Not overwhelming guilt, but a dusting, like the powdered sugar from the donuts we'd shared, stuck to my fingertips.

After LeAnne and I said our good-byes, I took my hands off the keyboard and called Sarah. My cell phone reception was spotty in my basement abode, and though it made me feel a little out-of-bounds, I used my Mandalay Carson landline to dial. I was new at this job thing, but I assumed a personal call or two, even (scandal!) a long-distance one, had to be okay.

"Hello," Sarah answered quietly.

The girls must have been napping.

"Hi, Sar, it's Dawn," I said.

"Oh, good, I can whisper then." She dropped her voice even further. "What's up?"

"I was just missing you," I whispered back. "I thought I'd see if I could catch you and say hi."

"How are all the interviews going?" she asked.

I wanted to tell her about every single woman, but who knew how long this nap time would last. Instead, I picked just a few. I told her about Lucy Alexander, who'd married the guy in the Stetson from her TGTW photo shoot; I told her about Elizabeth Irwin and days adding up to something; I told her about Jean Danton and how you couldn't predict what you'd fall in love with; I told her about Ellen Poloma and Japanese hair straightening; and then I told her about Patty and her winery.

"I wish I could explain it just the way she did," I said, "but basically, it's that you have to take little moments, like when you're tasting a glass of wine, and savor them. They're pure experiences, and that's a rare thing in life."

"Do you know what we should do?" Sarah whispered. "Next time you're home, we should drive down to Napa, just the two of us. Just a couple of days. Wouldn't that be fun? We should go visit that woman's winery."

"That'd be great," I answered back, and I knew it would be. Sarah and I in the car together again. Just the two of us.

Finally, we both whispered "Talk soon" and "Love you."

I sent LeAnne a follow-up message to thank her for taking the time to chat and included a little P.S.: "After we got off the phone, I called my sister. Thanks so much for reminding me how amazing sisters can be."

She wrote back a few seconds later: "I love it! Just called mine too!"

I smiled and felt even rosier than I'd been feeling a few seconds before, if that was possible. I liked hearing that I wasn't the only one moved to thought or action by these phone calls, that these calls might be doing something for the winners as well.

———————

After a few more conversations with women from the nineties, I jumped ahead and sped my way through the girls of the 2000s. They were the easiest to track down, a few of them still in college, lots of others in grad school, their contact information usually turning up on some university club or organization's website. Some even had their own—MeghanMcNaught.com (songwriter), ReaganSimpsonInc.com (inspirational speaker). For others, I just called their parents, whose contact information we often still had on file—I'd discovered a treasure trove of boxes labeled "TGTW applications," which was ripe with such information (I had to keep myself from being distracted by the applications from the fifties and sixties, all of which rather unbelievably had blanks where the girls had been required to fill in their heights and weights and parents' occupations).

Two thousand four winner Kate Carlisle, whose nonprofit provided eye exams and glasses for people in the developing world, was roommates at Stanford med school with 2005 winner Simran Malik, who was continuing her research on enzymes and cancer. After *Charm*, 2001 winner Danni Chung won the Miss America pageant, which was a fun year out, she said, before she began her graduate vocal studies at Northwestern. She'd been performing ever since, and she'd just won a spot in the Metropolitan Opera's Lindemann Young Artist Development Program. Next, I went on a spree of Ten Girls winners who were current Oxford and Cambridge Marshall and Rhodes Scholars. I giggled hearing how many of them had developed faux-British diction. "You're putting together a party then?" one after another said in Madonna-style accents. By the end of my afternoon of calls with them, I was half-way to adopting the accent myself.

The overall highlight of the 2000s, though, was Tanisha Whitaker. She was working as an SAT tutor in New York while trying to make it as a stand-up comic. I hadn't spoken with her yet, just her mother, but Gayle Whitaker brought me up to speed on her daughter's post-*Charm* activities, including the ins and outs of her love life, which were manifold and of great interest to Gayle. Jason had been "fiiine." And Chaz was "a rat." Gayle had one of the richest, easiest laughs I'd ever heard, punctuated by little gasps and screams, and I could imagine why her daughter would have wanted to get her laughing whenever possible. As we chatted away she said, "Girl, you are a hoot. *Charm* sure found the right woman for this job." I wanted to keep her on the phone all afternoon.

It turned out I actually knew a few of the winners from the 2000s as well. I'd met Aditi Tyagi at a party in Boston. She and my friend Suresh had been dating at the time. He'd moved to New York after graduation. I didn't know about her, but I hoped they weren't dating anymore, since the last time I'd seen Suresh he'd had his arm around the waist of a brunette who was most definitely not Aditi. Another winner, Mei Li Chan, had been in a creative writing class with me in college. A quiet girl with thick glasses and a perpetual braid in her hair, she'd added little to discussions, but then she'd submitted devastating stories about maids and factory workers in nameless Chinese cities. She'd made me feel inadequate then, but now, Google quickly revealed that she'd turned those stories into a novel, which, despite the fact that she was a mere one year older than me, had just been published to significant fanfare. It made me want to quit trying, move home, and become a waitress at our local IHOP. Instead, I forced a big fake quavering smile and dialed her up. Thankfully, at least for the time being, all I got was her voice mail.

I hoped, a misery-likes-company hope, that one of the younger women would admit to mucking through the first years after college before hitting upon her supersuccessful stride. But no such luck. If they'd mucked through like me, they certainly weren't admitting it now.

During one of my daylong phoneathons, I got a special surprise.

"Boo," went my Gchat.

"Abigail!" I wrote back.

"Bus ride was totally worth it for your news!" she said.

"I'm at work right now! In my *office*."

"Fancy. I'm in an Internet café that also sells lottery tickets and fried dough. So, is the job as amazing as it sounds?"

I explained that I was, in fact, working on floor −2 in a corner of the Mandalay Carson world where fashionistas did not tread, but that my one coworker, Ralph, seemed nice enough. Then I rattled off a quickie list of some of the women I'd talked with: "Rachel Link, the founder of TheOne. This amazing woman who translates Russian poetry, a radio station owner, an epidemiologist, if I play my cards right maybe Gerri Vans . . ."

"Really?!"

Probably not, I explained. But she was a winner, and maybe at some point I'd see her from across the room.

"On to more interesting subjects," I wrote, "have you found love in the jungle?"

"Well . . . :)"

Apparently, she had. He was a graduate student, studying dopamine and its connection to birdsong in birds' brains, and he was in El Salvador for another three months, conducting field research.

"And when he's not in El Salvador?" I asked.

"He's in Michigan. Blech."

Abigail was from Wisconsin. Half the reason she'd wanted to go to El Salvador was to skip winter.

We chatted for another twenty minutes or so, enough for each of us to know the other was alive and well (or "well" in our own way—I was still poor and Abigail was still suffering from intestinal parasites, but neither of those facts was unexpected).

Once we signed off, I got back to real work. After each call, I highlighted the women who were particularly interesting to talk with in pink (e.g., Susan Frock, the woman whose information Kathy Knowlton had asked me to share; turned out Susan ran a 250-acre cherry orchard in the Ozarks and had a series of books about back-to-farm cooking). And I highlighted women who seemed particularly high profile in yellow (e.g., Jane Novey, president of the National Women's Health Coalition). For every woman I spoke to, I e-mailed one or two others whose e-mail addresses I'd sniffed out but whose phone numbers eluded me.

Patterns emerged. Lawyers and professors were the easiest to find. Their bios and contact information were published on the firm's or school's website. Doctors were cake as well. Bigwig businesswomen and leaders of nonprofits were easy too—their bios were online or at least their names and affiliations were featured in articles. Women from my college were a snap, just one easy check with the alumni directory. Women in later years were most likely to have kept their names or to have at least kept their last names as middle names. The women who were proving toughest were the women of the fifties and sixties. Betty Robinson, Pine Manor College '64, where were you? My whitepages.com searches were only proving so useful.

And then there were the surprises. Danica Day, '94, showed up in the *San Francisco Chronicle,* which wasn't remarkable, but the article itself was: it detailed Dani's murder conviction for killing her husband. They'd been separated, he'd come to her apartment, an argument had ensued, somehow a gun was fired. Both were medical researchers completing their PhDs at the University of California San Francisco. They'd both contributed to a paper published by a professor who was set to receive a Nobel Prize in Stockholm the week of the shooting, and they'd planned to attend the ceremony. Their tickets to Sweden went unused. The article didn't run a mug shot or any grisly photos. Instead, it included a smiling picture of Danica in her lab coat, the grin and the curls around her face unsettlingly similar to her TGTW photo. After finding Danica I moved right back to the safety of the unfindable women of the sixties.

There, I found Sally Crenshaw, '61, faster than I'd thought possible. Just a simple White Pages search, and there she was, still named Sally Crenshaw, still living in Illinois. I turned to her photo, the caption "Young watercolorist, swears she dreams Italian landscapes" in perfect line with the dark bob of her hair. How delighted she was that I'd found her, she said. How surprising it was to find a woman from *Charm* 1961 who'd kept her name, I replied.

"Oh, that," she said, her voice dropping. "I was actually Sally Henderson until last year. When my husband and I divorced I changed my name back."

I tried to lighten the conversation and told her I'd love to hear about her adventures over the years and what she was doing now.

"Well, Roger and I moved to Phoenix when he retired, but then last year, after everything, I moved back to Chicago to live with my daughter. She and her husband have a little apartment in their basement, which works for one."

"How terrific that you're able to be close to your daughter," I tried.

"Yes," she said warily, "it's something."

"Do your daughter and her husband have children? Have you gotten to do any fun grandmother duty since you've been back in Chicago?"

"No, they've decided to put that off for now. They're both filmmakers."

I was striking out here, but then Sally went on, sparing me from firing another cheery question into the void.

"Roger and I were married for forty-two years, and I never worked. I was home with the children, and then I took care of him, took care of the house. So it took me some time to find a job—I'm learning to use the computer, but I wouldn't be any good as a secretary. Since April or so, I've been at a Hallmark store in the mall near us. This is actually my first paid job. I'm supposed to wear jeans to work, which is a new thing for me. So I'm working on that." She followed this with a laugh, not one that savored the dark humor of working to build a professional wardrobe comprised of jeans after a lifetime of ladylike skirt-suits and slacks, but a hollow, sad laugh, the kind that is more like a hiccup before a jag of emotion.

"I have to tell you," I said, trying to be light, "new work wardrobes are tough. Before *Charm* I mostly worked from home. The fact that I can't wear slippers to the office is still killing me a little bit." Was this actually amusing given the circumstances that had pushed Sally into her new job? Probably not. She was gracious enough to chuckle a little anyway.

"I'd love to hear about some of your memories from the contest," I picked up. "You were in New York for a few weeks, is that right?"

"That's right. Every fashion and beauty company wanted to get our opinion. This was back before they did massive surveys, I suppose. So what they did instead was have girls like us all gathered in a room, and they'd show us all their latest products and see what we really oohed and aahed over." She paused, a break longer than the normal moment or two between thoughts, then she said, "I remember the Europe trip most of all. I couldn't wait for all those art museums. Which is funny now that I think of it. Roger is in Europe now, traveling with . . ." She stopped herself.

I asked a few more questions, said a few things about our plans for a party—we weren't sure exactly what or when, but I'd be in touch. Then we said our good-byes. I looked at Sally Crenshaw's smiling photo and tried to visualize her now. I imagined her still tall and lovely, her hair now shorter and gray, a smile pulled on her thin lips. But what I really saw was something more like a picture of the plains after a tornado, years of gentle building gnashed and dropped, broken timbers here and there among the scattered crops, ripped from the ground. There was a reason some wise prairie people built basement-only homes with tiny aboveground windows in a thin strip at the roofline offering a soil-level view from here to the horizon. I briefly conjured the other woman, dashing around Paris on the arm of her beau, this sudden whirlwind all giddiness and adventure for her. I didn't highlight Sally in yellow or pink, but I did tack her photo to the board above my desk.

The Friday of my check-in meeting with XADI rolled around. I sent her a document, we had a short phone call, and it was all dispatched in about five minutes, per usual. She liked my ideas. We were cleared for a meeting with Regina on Monday.

I should have been ecstatic—my return to the company of the lovely Regina and a chance to show off all the work I'd done!—and yes, I was excited. But my brain was much busier thinking about the fact that it was now officially mid-ish September, and Elliot Kaslowski had not yet e-mailed. Nor had he called or stopped by my office/closet.

Thanks to Abigail, who had decided back in college that if I wasn't going to heed her advice and break up with Robert (or stay broken up, that is), I should at least develop as much of a backbone within the relationship as I could, I had my very own copy of both *The Rules* and *Why Men Love Bitches*. Not a lot of good came of them on the Robert front, but at least they meant I knew better than to harass Mr. Kaslowski in hopes of rekindling whatever it was we'd had that night on the bridge. But that didn't mean I didn't look at my e-mail every few minutes and wonder what was wrong with me. It had to be either my looks or my personality, and neither was a good answer.

On the plus side, the results from my visit to the sleep lab earlier in the week had cleared me for takeoff, so though my weekend plans included nary a magazine columnist, they did include a date with an insomnia study. I considered that far from a bust.

I started gathering my things before realizing I'd forgotten to ask XADI a critical question. Calling again seemed excessively familiar, and so I e-mailed.

Hi XADI,
I'm looking forward to the meeting. In the meantime, I'm wondering if there's any sort of special process for VIPs. For example, would you prefer to call the mayor of Seattle or can I go ahead and give her office a ring? Other prominent winners I have yet to call, pending your input, include Robyn Jackson, Jessica Winston, Barbara Darby, and Gerri Vans.
Thanks in advance for your guidance,
Dawn

I reread the e-mail before I sent it and paused at the second sentence: "I'm wondering . . ." On one of the rotten days of the Dawn-Robert romance, Robert and I hit up the National Air and Space Museum together during a little D.C. trip. There was a fab-looking exhibit on Barbie in Flight, and after some time unsuccessfully trying to follow the arrows pointing to it, I approached a nice security guard and said, "I'm wondering if you could point me in the direction of the Barbie exhibit," which he obligingly did.

"Why do you always do that?" Robert asked as we were walking away.

"Do what?"

"Start every question with 'I'm wondering' instead of just asking the question."

We broke up later that night. Though we also got back together even later that night. I sent the e-mail to XADI exactly as it was, glad to wonder away freely.

XADI replied to my e-mail within three seconds: "Don't call. We'll discuss next week. X"

How had she even read my e-mail that quickly? Perhaps she'd hit send too soon and she'd actually meant to write yes, she thought I was the perfect person to chat up Gerri. Perhaps that message would be momentarily forthcoming.

Sadly, it wasn't. But it was now six o'clock, and my overnight bag and I exited the building and began a leisurely amble toward the subway downtown, where the sleep lab and an incredible fifteen hundred dollars awaited me.

"Broken hearts heal! But most of them aren't worth it anyway, so say no when the drummer asks you out."

—GENEVIEVE WOLCOTT, 1994

"People you've only met in passing will often come back into your life, so always be nice."

—SARAH SCOTT, 1958

"Stop tanning!"

—TIFFANY REYNOLDS, 1989

"You're not in a competition with every person you meet. Most of them are on your team. Lift up the people around you, and you all win."

—ARZA PATEL, 1996

"Don't make choices based on what you think *sounds* impressive."

—NICOLETTE RABADI, 2001

YEARS

Real-Life Role Models
the 50th Anniversary Issue

What advice do you wish someone had given you when you were 21?

> "You need to *find* your passion before you can *follow* your passion. Try a lot of things, and don't be embarrassed to call it quits if something isn't right for you."
>
> **—BETTY ROBINSON, 1964**

> "Don't wait till your jeans don't fit to stop eating the donuts.
> Jeans stretch!"
>
> **—SANDRA HORNE, 1975**

Chapter Nine

"You here for an overnight?" the Somnilab security guard said, giving me a once-over.

I nodded.

"Sign in and head on up," he said. "Somnilab's on ten."

The Somnilab building stood on a scrubby corner of far-west Soho, which, in fact, felt rather like the scrubby corner of far-west Hell's Kitchen where the Mandalay Carson archives resided. As I walked toward it, the building's lights cast a clinical glow out onto the dark street, all the more glaring because of the orange security lamps of the surrounding barbed-wire-protected parking lots. Given the generally ominous vibe, I was relieved to hear that Somnilab shared the building, meaning all ten floors weren't dedicated to the sleep-disordered (sleepwalkers on 2, night screamers on 3).

The elevator doors on the tenth floor opened to what looked like a normal doctor's office waiting room, with me as the lone patient in waiting. The receptionist placed a quick call back to the lab, and with that, the thin facade of normalcy fell away—a woman in green scrubs appeared and led me behind the doors to the "main facility," where we approached another reception desk, this one humming with activity. A man in an orange jumpsuit walked by followed by a woman in a blue flannel nightgown with lace around the collar. The flannel woman held a straight out of *The Matrix* switch box in her hand connected to a rope of electrode cords springing from the back of her head.

My bescrubbed guide checked a chart and led me to room eleven, my home for the night. When we arrived, the room appeared to be in the midst of an identity crisis. Was it a hospital room? Was it the Econolodge? The bed said medical, the lamp and desk said budget travel.

"Get yourself settled in and change into your pajamas," the woman instructed. "Your lab tech will be here in a few minutes to get you set for the night."

A camera mounted on the wall above the bed stared right at me, but I figured it probably wasn't on yet, and even if it was, oh well. I did a quick change into a raggedy sweatshirt and my favorite flannel pajama bottoms featuring monkeys holding bunches of bananas and the words "I love you a bunch" over and over, a Christmas present from my mother. I was pulling on some thick knit socks with crocheted butterflies attached at the ankles (again, courtesy of my dear mother) when after the quickest of knocks, in strolled a man in scrubs, pushing what in another context would have been a bar cart but which, here in the lab, was piled high with wires and tubes of glue.

So this was my lab tech. Young, with smooth coffee-colored skin, sharp cheekbones, black rectangular-framed glasses, and thick twists in his dark chin-length hair, he was, in short, superhot. He put out his hand and introduced himself—Raymond. I could call him Ray or Raymond, either way was cool. Had he just seen me change on camera? Although I regretted the butterfly socks, I was instantly grateful I'd kept my bra on.

"So it's your first night on this study, I see." He held some sort of chart. "Let me help you drag that chair over here and we'll get started." He explained that for the next hour and a half or so, he'd be hooking electrodes to my legs, chest, and head, so that he could then monitor my brain waves while I slept.

I nodded, feeling awkward in that junior high dance sort of way. He, obviously feeling no such thing, started right in on my unfortunately stubbly legs. I threaded the wires down through my shirt and waistband, then pushed them out the bottom of my pajamas.

"Just cuff those for me, will you?" he said, holding up some electrodes and glue. "I need access to your shins. We have to make sure you don't have restless leg syndrome," he said. Sure, sure, I nodded. No one had ever asked for access to my shins before.

While he glued we chatted. I tried to be cool, and as I settled in, the whole experience started to feel beauty treatment–ish, the sort of half-distracted conversation you have at the hair salon.

"So you don't sleep well?" he asked, as if he didn't know.

"No, not so well lately," I said. That topic covered, we moved right along. He'd started at Somnilab six months before. He was an architecture grad student, and this was the only job that didn't interfere with his academic schedule. Under a similar premise, I informed him, I had taken a 5:30 a.m. job at the campus paper my freshman year of college, stuffing the sports or culture section into the main body of the newspaper. It was true, I had no schedule conflicts . . . except sleep, which became sadly apparent when, the month after I started the job, I looked around my room one paper-writing afternoon and saw the wreckage of an empty two-liter bottle of Diet Coke, an empty six-pack, and two empty twenty-ounce Diet Dr Peppers. The rather critical sleep conflict became doubly apparent when I read the title I'd given said paper: "Longing and Loss in Bartelby the Scribbler." Raymond didn't really laugh. "The Scribbler? Not the Scrivener," I said. "Ha-ha." Nothing. We went back to him.

Architecture grad school was cool. He was working on designing a theater in the Red Hook neighborhood of Brooklyn. Cool again, and I had loads of questions, but before I could ask them I had to stretch the collar of my T-shirt way down so he could paste electrodes to my chest. The awkwardness of this derailed my ability to sensibly continue the conversation.

"What's with the guys in the orange jumpsuits?" I asked, leaping to the first thing that came to mind.

"Oh, that's a jet lag study. They fly folks in from Hawaii and keep them here for a week. But the deal is that they can't leave the sleep lab while they're here. Orange makes them easy to spot so we know if they're up to anything."

I nodded again, which, it turned out, was the last time I'd be able to nod for the next half hour, since Raymond was about to begin cementing electrodes to my head and taping others to my face. To complete the process, he twist-tied all the electrode wires together, a braid of wires coming from the back of my head, and plugged each of them into a master switch box.

"Let's give this a test run," he said, taking the switch box and leading me by the electrode cords to the bed (what girl doesn't have a romantic led-by-electrode-cords-to-the-bed fantasy?). I sat down on the edge, and he plugged the box into a docking station on the wall.

"What happens now? Is this when I start feeling electric shocks?"

He gave me a halfhearted laugh. "If everything's working, I'll get feedback from each electrode on my computer." Off he went to the control room and a minute later returned to redo the electrode on the back left of my head.

He checked his watch and returned with my little blue pill. "Gulp this, and then you can go to the bathroom down the hall and brush your teeth or whatever. You'll have a half hour till lights-out."

I gulped and joined the ranks of sci-fi characters walking the halls with their head cord tentacles in hand. Even though I tried, I couldn't quite keep an amused smile from creeping to my lips, which, if anyone was looking, probably made me and my elec-trodes look even scarier.

Back in my room, I read the latest Patricia Marx shopping col-umn in the *New Yorker,* and just as I finished and was about to turn to the movie reviews, Raymond returned to hook me up to the wall. As he left, he abruptly flipped off the lights and closed the door. A few seconds later I jumped as his voice crackled through the box on the wall—tinny, like a drive-through window. "Okay, now try to go to sleep. Just speak up if you need anything." Appar-ently, in addition to transmitting my brain waves, the box was a personal two-way radio system.

Although "now try to go to sleep" sounded like a taunt, I did my best, holding very still and counting backward from five hun-dred, and unlike every other night when this got me nowhere, it worked. I didn't remember falling asleep, but a few hours later, sometime in the middle of the night, Raymond opened the door and flipped on the lights, leading me to wake up, immediately sit bolt upright in bed, and in a weirdly delayed reaction, scream a full second later. Not a somebody-help-me scream, more of a holler, an instinctual little hoot, a halfway-to-singing "hooaah!" I stared at him with eyes that I'm sure looked like the huge nervous eyes of those lemurs they catch in photos at night.

"Whoa, sorry about that," he said. "I have to reattach your leg electrode. It fell off."

I was now awake enough to check my face for signs of drool or, equally bad, residue from dried drool. I was apparently drool-free for the moment. Raymond unscrewed the cap of the glue tube, and I pulled back the blanket and pushed up the leg of my pajamas. There it was again, my pasty calf—there's nothing quite as sexy as a glimpse of just-above-the-sock, just-below-the-knee stubbly, super-glo-white leg.

He reglued in silence, then went back to the computer room to check. "We're good," his voice came through the box behind the bed. A second later he leaned back into the room, flipped off the light, and closed the door. I put my head back down just as Raymond clicked into the box again. "Okay, now try to go back to sleep."

Thank you, Raymond. Thank you. Fortunately, it didn't take terribly long, maybe twenty minutes. And then it was morning.

"It's seven a.m.," Raymond announced, turning on the lights. "Time to get those electrodes out of your hair. Unfortunately, you're going to have to scrub for a few days. The glue is like cement."

After my shower in the bathroom's oh-so-cozy stall proved Raymond right, cement clinging despite my scrubbing and clawing and picking, I returned to my room for a quick once-over with the vital signs nurse. Check check, I appeared to be functional and safe to leave the facility. Another nurse popped into the room and gave me a bottle with a six-week supply of pills and printed instructions for calling my sleep times into the study's automated system every morning.

On my way out I passed the control room where Raymond had spent the night with a monitor full of my brain just as he happened to be putting on his jacket.

"You heading out too?" I said.

He nodded, and we caught the elevator, then walked to the F train together. Turned out he'd settled on an architectural project involving Red Hook because he lived in Red Hook, just over the border from my apartment in Carroll Gardens. On the train home, we talked about the neighborhood, the model he was building, the worst person he'd ever had to glue electrodes to (the story involved flatulence), and whether we'd sign up for the Hawaii–New York jet lag study given the opportunity. (Yes, we would. My "yes" became even more emphatic once Raymond informed me it paid four thousand dollars.)

After we got off the train at the Smith and Ninth Street stop, I was about to turn off onto my street when he said, "Would you like to see the model of the Red Hook theater? I'm almost done with it."

"Sure," I answered, and only then did it dawn on me that this would most likely mean stopping by his apartment rather than taking the train all the way back to the city to some model-holding room on campus. Was this sluggish cognition a side effect of the sleeping pill? I couldn't be certain, but I'd make note of it in my sleep journal just in case. More important for the moment, was going to Raymond's apartment a bad idea? The last twelvish hours seemed to indicate that he was not a psycho-killer rapist. So that was okay. And then there was the fact that he was hot . . . and that I clearly wasn't seeing anyone at the moment, despite hopes that I might have been seeing someone sometime around, say, mid-September.

I followed Raymond under the Brooklyn-Queens Expressway, past the twenty-four-hour Quick-E Lube, to a weedy building across the street from an old brick factory, now loft condos—a combination of derelict chic and actual derelict that typified Red Hook. Up two flights, his door swung wide to reveal a studio that was dorm-room-style squalor at its finest: a futon mattress lumped on the floor in the corner, the sheets rumpled, no bedspread in sight; an open pizza box full of crusts beside the bed; a grouping of camp chairs (he'd sprung for the fancy ones with cupholders in the arms) in front of the TV, which itself sat atop two plastic crates; clothes—T-shirts, boxers, jeans, more T-shirts—strewn about the room, some piled on the backs of the chairs, most deposited on the floor; and beneath the clothes, against the background of the flimsy black carpet, I wasn't surprised to see crumbs, but I was surprised to see coins.

"Should I be looking out for shards of a piggy bank?" I said. Ha-ha, ho-ho.

"Oh, yeah, that. I tipped over my change bowl one day and then didn't clean it up for a while. But then I decided it was kind of awesome to walk around on money, so now I just throw my change on the floor." To illustrate this point, he jammed his hand into his pocket and fished out some coins, then, grinning, opened his fingers and let the nickels and dimes run through onto the floor, like they were sand and this was the beach.

He swept some clothes off one of the camp chairs for me. I took a seat, and he pulled another one right up, so close to mine that the arms touched.

"Yep, so this is the place. Home sweet home."

"It must be great to live alone," I said, searching for a silver lining.

When he didn't say anything, I swiveled my head around in search of the model. A few boxes hulked on the kitchen counter, but they were jumbled in with dishes and crinkled paper towels, making it hard to discern their true nature.

"It is nice to live alone," he finally said, leaning over. And then, next thing I knew he was tracing his finger around the edge of the red mark one of the electrode patches had left on my chest. This would have been one part sexy, four parts hilarious had he done it with a sense of irony, but I double-checked his face—no irony, in spite of the slightly gummy edges of the mark. I adjusted a little, moving away and trying to laugh off the sexy electrode action. To no avail.

"There's just something special about a man and a woman," he said as he leaned in further to kiss me. It was instant make-out regret. Though it's hard to say something is regret while it's still happening. I was kissing a man who had just delivered a horribly embarrassing line, a line that also made no sense unless he meant that he usually made out with other men, thereby making this a special novelty. And yet, there I was, still kissing him. He leaned over even further so that his chest was pressing against mine at a strange angle.

I hate rejection, whether I am the rejected or the rejector. My strategy is *avoid, avoid, avoid.* If someone I'm not sure I want to go out with starts getting stammery and mentioning ideas for things to do, I start talking about the weather, check my watch, and then flee the scene. To my cowardly mind, this is somehow preferable to saying the word "no."

My weakling's flight mechanism usually kept me out of situations like the Raymond dilemma at hand. But now that we were already kissing, what was I supposed to say? "Excuse me, I believe I've changed my mind"? Probably, but that was hard for me. I started practicing saying something along those lines in my head while he continued his work with his tongue. After another minute, he took my hands, stood up, and started to pull me toward the futon mattress on the floor.

"No, no no no no no no." The word just spilled right out as I pulled my hands from his. "I mean, I think we should just be friends. You watch my brain waves. Doesn't that make this wrong?"

"How can this be wrong?" he said, his nonironic smile gleaming.

"Oh my goodness . . . I have to go." I grabbed my bag and jacket and waved from the door.

After I crossed back under the BQE, I ran the rest of the way home, my overnight bag banging awkwardly against my side. On my way up the stairs, I fixated on the thought of showering. I wanted another go at the electrode glue cemented in my hair, but I also felt rather biblically unclean. Maybe making out with a hot lab tech in a filthy apartment is part of what you're supposed to do in your early twenties. Maybe I was supposed to be stocking up on stories like that. But it didn't feel like awesome fun I'd be dying to recount later. It felt yucky. I felt yucky. I hoped some hot water could steam it all away. I also hoped there were more lab techs in the rotation so we wouldn't have to talk about—or worse, not talk about—my flight next week while he glued electrodes to my scalp.

But, as is often the case when you have roommates, the time you most want and need the bathroom is always the time it is unavailable to you. Sylvia had the shower and her shower radio going when I walked through the door. She sang along with Celine Dion, sputtering out here and there, but really holding the long notes with fervor. I might have found it sort of sweet had I not been a millimeter of patience away from pounding on the bathroom door.

Instead of pounding, I collapsed on the couch and checked my e-mail. And wouldn't you know it, there he was: Secret Agent Romance. The first time in a week I'd checked my e-mail without thinking of him, and ta-da, he appeared.

"It's Fall," read SAR's subject line. The entire body of the e-mail was the single word "Hello" visible next to the subject in the preview line. That was it. I didn't even have to open the message to read it in its entirety. American Express, up next in my inbox, much more dotingly wanted me to know that they valued me, so much so that they wanted to bring my whole family on board—why not earn more SkyMiles by linking additional cards to my account? It was a love fest compared to Elliot's three-word message.

That weak little "Hello" certainly didn't require an immediate response. I waited out Sylvia's shower and then shook off my clothes and turned the water up as hot as I could take.

When I got out of the shower, I had a text message from Robert. Really, wasn't today just the day? "U free tonight?" he'd written.

"Why?" I replied, feeling both savage and petulant. Not that he would pick up on my mood from that single word.

"Lily's in Chicago. I need dinner company."

Was this constant mentioning of Lily really necessary? The NYU freshman hadn't always been mentioned. She'd existed, but during that period Robert and I had had dinner, gone to movies, gone shopping, all sorts of things, and we'd both conspicuously avoided mentioning her. And though we didn't touch each other during the entirety of her stay in Robert's life, our silence felt like

TEN GIRLS TO WATCH ■ *171*

it signaled her future dismissal. Now, Robert's Lily dropping felt like a bullhorn announcing her permanent dominion.

"Fine," I typed, as if my lack of enthusiasm would crush him. Clearly, it had no impact, since he replied right back with a time and place.

I spent the rest of the day consciously not e-mailing Elliot.

When dinnertime finally approached, my feet weren't dragging; I actually felt feathery with anticipation. Maybe Robert irked me, but there had never been a time I didn't want to see him.

Sandra Seru,

Duke University, 1989

THE JOURNALIST

The Editor in Chief of the Duke *Chronicle*, Sandra recently accepted the Associated Collegiate Press's prestigious Newspaper Pacemaker Award honoring the *Chronicle*'s excellence. "I've practically lived in the *Chronicle*'s offices for the past three years, but it's been worth it!" Sandra says. Her dream job: reporting for the *Washington Post*. Other surprising talents: Sandra is fluent in Spanish and plays a mean jazz clarinet.

Chapter Ten

*A*s a tribute to the good old days, the Rollands kept Grandpa Rolland's shop in the Lower East Side up and running. It was right next door to a shop that sold only pickles. Pa Rolland liked to call it the saltiest street in town. The mirth with which his eyebrows leapt every time he told this joke was responsible for most of the laughs it garnered.

Robert and I had arranged to meet at a restaurant around the corner from the original Rolland's shop.

As soon as we sat down, even before the waiter brought the menus, Robert said, "I've been thinking."

Here he paused, his face sliding into a mask of restrained distress. My stomach lurched. Like the split seconds when people are falling from a building and seem to have all the time in the world to see scenes from their lives, my body seemed to expand the moment long enough to pound with the feeling of every single reunion Robert and I had ever had. In that fifth of a second, I imagined him saying he loved me in a dozen different ways. Not that my rational mind thought this was what he was going to say, but my every muscle braced in anticipation.

The pause ended. "I don't think we should see each other any-more," he said.

What?

"I'm sorry, what?" I said. "You invited me to dinner to tell me you don't want to have dinner with me? Also, we're not seeing each other. You're seeing Lily."

"I don't mean 'seeing' like 'seeing.' I mean seeing, at all."

How was it possible I'd been looking forward to this dinner? How was it possible that any part of me had imagined he was going to say something the complete opposite of this? If I had been a cool character in a movie, I'd have gotten up and walked away right then and never looked back, except maybe at the end of the movie when I was looking out over a crowd of my adoring fans, all holding up books or photos for my signature, and I'd see Robert among the crowd and look at him for one second before brushing right past him. But I wasn't a character, or if I was, I was more like a character in a horror movie, sitting inert in a room while the menace nears and the audience screams "Get out of there!" And so instead of making a glorious exit, I sat there and let Robert keep talking while I tore the paper napkin in my lap into tinier and tinier pieces. How did words like that actually come out of Robert's mouth? A friend breakup on top of all the actual breakups? He had superhuman abilities to offend.

"Seeing at all . . . uh-huh." I gulped down a lump in my throat.

"It's actually flattering to you that I'm saying this."

"Oh, really," I said limply.

"It's not forever. I don't want us to end our friendship forever. I care about you too much for that. It's just that I really like Lily. And when I spend time with you I get confused."

"I'm flattered," I answered sarcastically. But the problem was I actually was flattered. Or not exactly flattered. More like illic-itly enlivened. The part of me that wanted Robert to be in love with me forever, no matter how profoundly that defied reason and reality, the part of me that had just imagined he was about to declare his love for me again, after all the months apart, despite Lily, despite everything, that part throbbed with excitement when he said those stupid words. It was like my feelings had disconnected from the proper channels, like instead of working properly my heart sprayed a mess of blood with each thump-thump.

"So I want to take a friend break," he finished. "Just for a couple of months."

"That's fine," I said evenly. "Do you want to start the break now, or should we order dinner?" Darkness had fallen, and I was descending into full wallowing mode, the pleasure of misery and martyrdom bubbling their way up to full boil.

"No, of course I want to have dinner!" Robert's voice had turned flustered. "I just wanted to say everything now rather than at the end of dinner so you didn't look back and wonder why I'd waited to say it."

"Very considerate of you."

The waiter came by. I ordered a rare steak. Robert ordered the "fiesta salad."

"That's great that you like Lily so much. I mean, I like her too. I see why you like her."

"Dawn, don't make this hard," Robert said.

So what if there was an edge in my voice? He was the one who was making this hard.

"Well, I've been meaning to tell you," I continued. "I met someone."

"Really?" he said.

"You sound so surprised. Is it that shocking?"

"No, no, you're supposed to meet someone. I should have said 'great.'"

"Well then why didn't you?"

He ignored that particularly barbed question and proceeded

along with his most jovial tone. "So this new guy. What's his deal? Did you meet him via TheOne?" Robert's eyes lit up as he said "TheOne," like Pa Rolland's when he said "saltiest street."

"He writes for *Charm*," I said, leaving out TheOne bit of the story to avoid giving Robert that particular satisfaction.

"So now you're dating gay guys?"

"Oh, I hate you sometimes." Though I said it a little like I was kidding, it was true, true, true. "Why did I know you were going to say that? No, he's not gay. He's *Charm*'s dating columnist. His name is Elliot. He's very cute. I kissed him on my doorstep a few weeks ago and that was that."

"You kissed him or he kissed you? Remember, there's nothing worse than coming on too strong."

I wadded the whole stupid ripped-up napkin in my lap into a big ball.

"We kissed each other, okay. Oh, and la-di-da, did I mention that he's divorced?" I waved the words like a flag, as if Robert should be impressed, like I was now dark and dangerous, dating divorced men. I set my fork down and waited for his response. When it came, it was inadequate.

"Watch out. Married people get used to regular sex. That's probably why he's a dating columnist. So he can make his living while simultaneously satisfying his sexual needs."

"What is wrong with you?" I said.

"Did he try to sleep with you?"

"No, he did not try to sleep with me."

"Two things. One, that probably means he's at least a little bit gay. Two, as I have often said, novels don't make babies. So when he does get around to trying to sleep with you, put your laptop down and consider your options."

"I can't believe the things you say." I glared at him.

"I was being funny! Funny and true!"

The enlivened heart that had been spewing hot blood before

was now spewing something more like oily black muck. The sludge spread further each minute I stayed there with Robert.

"Can we not talk about dating, please? Can you please just talk about pretzels or something?"

"We signed a big deal with a distributor in China this week," Robert said, apparently not put off by the dismissive tone with which I'd said "pretzels or something."

"Seriously, huge," he went on. "Do you know how many pretzel-deprived people there are in China?"

He went into a lecture about China and how the real possibilities for growth were not importing from China but manufacturing and selling within China. I wished right then that he'd just go ahead and *move* to China to exploit that great opportunity.

When the check arrived, I let Robert take it. If I'd cared, I would have tried to split it, or pay the whole thing myself, laughable though that was. I thought of Elliot's column about Boots; checks were indeed fraught. I'd always tried to pick up my fair share of bills when Robert and I dated, despite the fact, or really because of the fact, that I didn't have a pretzel fortune of my own. I never wanted Robert to feel like that made anything different. Like I cared about that, or like I thought it should play into our dynamic in any way whatsoever. Now, whatever. I was poor, and he could pay. I didn't feel like pretending I was unaware of the difference between us.

That dispatched, Robert insisted that we stop by the pretzel shop. I glumly let him talk me into it, like a sad, kicked puppy still following the perp in the vain hope of receiving snacks and love. Inside, all the men working away in their white aprons and hats came out from behind the counter and out of the kitchen and peppered Robert with "my mans" and high fives that turned into arm grabs and then partial hugs/body checks. Robert was the king of the pretzel world.

"Two soft Bavarians, Georgie." Robert beamed. So at least there was a snack.

"And can we get some extra salt with them?" he said.

"What, for rubbing in my wounds?" I muttered.

"Ha-ha," he said.

"Ha-ha, indeed."

He handed me my pretzel, and we walked out into the warm September night. I said I was heading east, toward the subway, and he moved to hug me.

"Don't hug me," I said, backing away. "You don't get to hug me."

He looked like I'd uttered devastating words, like I was the one who'd hurt him this evening.

"I guess I'll see you after you and Lily are married, or something. Or not. Or never. Or whatever."

And with that, about ninety minutes too late, I turned and walked away.

My pretzel was warm, soft and a little tough, just as it should be. I licked up the salt crystals that had fallen into my hand and savored the tang as they dissolved on my tongue.

Not that I hadn't been mad at dinner, but on the subway I got angrier and angrier. And unfortunately for me, anger almost always translates to tears. What hadn't come out at dinner came out all over the place during the course of the next five subway stops in the form of embarrassing, grimacing, runny-nosed tears and sniffles that I couldn't wipe away fast enough to fool anyone on the train into thinking I was okay.

I hadn't exactly been polite to Robert, but the fact that I'd sat through that whole dinner, that I'd even been in a position to be having dinner with Robert in the first place . . . What was wrong with me? Why couldn't I shake my inordinate need to leave feathers unruffled?

I stopped crying after I got off the subway, and the walk from the subway to home calmed me even further. I felt like I'd cried myself clean. Like I'd had a revelation. I was going to be a new person starting right that minute. No more Robert. No more passivity. I was going to be a clear-eyed, confident woman who told the world what was what in clear-eyed, confident, nonhysterical terms on a regular basis. As I fell into a drug-induced sleep that night, I became more sure with every passing groggy minute that I was going to change everything.

Despite my big dreams, I didn't wake up the next morning feeling fresh and new and ready to take on the world. Instead, I stayed under the covers feeling like a shipwreck, barnacles of sadness clinging to my every surface. I needed some company, and unfortunately, this need revealed that I didn't have as many serious cry-on-your-shoulder friends as I maybe should have had.

In high school, I'd been part of a big group of girlfriends. We weren't the popular crowd or the jocks or the geeks. We were more like "the nice kids," the ones who babysat and got picked first for study groups, and to the extent we were competitive, it wasn't over boys or clothes, it was over things like who got to be president of the Spanish Club. But they'd all stayed in Oregon, and as soon as I got to Massachusetts I felt like they were on the other side of a wall. Every party I went to with tuxedoed waiters—and there were a lot of those parties in college—the higher the wall got. These days, I kept track of what they were all up to mainly through my mom's reporting. And while I had plenty of friends from college in New York, they were more the sort of pals who invited me to parties and plastered my Facebook wall with rabidly enthusiastic "HAPPY BIRTHDAY!!!!!!" messages, rather than close friends who'd heard me blubber enough times to make out my words over the phone despite whatever heaving tears might come. Plus, almost everyone I knew from college was just as close to Robert as they were to me.

Of course I had Abigail. The first day of freshman year, we'd pushed our furniture around into every possible arrangement, a task that required a fair bit of stamina given the weight of the old wooden desks and dressers, not to mention the fact that Abigail was a tiny Asian girl with arms the size of chopsticks, and I wasn't exactly a starter for the field hockey team myself. Halfway through, she was perfectly content with the setup and was ready to call it quits, but she kept shoving, just to make me happy. That had been the start of my adoration for her. In all four years of college, the number of breakfasts I ate either without Abigail or without Robert was probably in the single digits.

Despite the fact that she was from Wisconsin and I was from Oregon, one or the other of us had still managed to fly cross-country every winter break so we could spend New Year's together. My mother had given her multiple free makeovers, products included, and Abigail's parents sent me birthday cards in a timelier fashion than my own parents. All during college, Abigail had been an anchor of stability amid the stormy seas of Dawn and Robert, and I'd done my best to keep her safely moored as well, from going as her date to the freshman formal to trekking to Kinkos at two in the morning to help her print her thesis on biracial coalitions and the election of Asian-American legislators. Those years of connection and closeness meant a lot, but the whole rural El Salvador thing put a definite limit on her ability to offer real-time comfort. There was also the fact that she'd heard more than enough boo-hoo-Robert talk to last a lifetime. I sent her a woe-is-me e-mail anyway.

I guess I could have called Helen. If it had been a work or writing crisis, I wouldn't have hesitated, but even though we'd certainly crossed the talking-about-personal-things threshold (she once told me, "The real question isn't whether you like Robert, it's whether you like yourself when you're with Robert," which struck me both as wise and also as something I was entirely incapable of ascertaining, since I didn't know who I was without Robert for comparison purposes), I still tried to keep myself in some semblance of order when I talked to her.

There was my sister, but this would take more than five minutes, and finding longer than that in a twin household was tricky.

Who else could I call for romantic (or romantic-ish) advice? My mom? My dad? Ha. Raymond, the sleep lab guy? I didn't have his phone number, but if I ever dragged myself out of bed, he and his coin-covered carpet lived just down the street.

The fact that I basically had no one to talk with about the unpleasantness of this friend breakup made me feel all the more pathetic. I was left with my Craigslist roommate, Sylvia.

In my woeful state, I would have turned to Sylvia, the limits of our acquaintance aside, but unfortunately, Sylvia was nowhere to be found. Which was even more unfortunate because Sunday, the day after the downer dinner, was the day we were supposed to show the apartment to new prospective roommates who could take over when she left for Toledo.

The new me should have left Sylvia a message and told her to find her own gosh-darn roommate replacement, and then gone out and done something with my day. But the old me had already set up appointments with a bunch of people who'd responded to the apartment posting. Plus, I had to live with this person, whoever it was going to be. So, despite my new-me ideals, I went ahead and toured all the potential replacements through the place by myself. Each time I flipped on the light in Sylvia's room to display it to a possible tenant, I imagined Sylvia off flopping around town somewhere, her bralessness, which usually didn't bother me, suddenly seeming an emblem of flagrant disregard for others.

I was hours past making my pro and con lists for each roommate (the front-runner so far was a pastry chef who I hoped would bring home leftovers) when I finally heard Sylvia come through the door. Before I could get up and approach her with the tatters of the once billowing sails of my new in-charge attitude, she knocked on my bedroom door and asked whether I had a sec.

She cleared her throat. "I'm not moving back to Ohio anymore. I'm sorry to be so crazy and to change my plans last minute like this. But Rodney and I broke up, so I'm staying in New York."

"Oh, wow," I said. "I'm sorry. About Rodney, I mean. You're sure about this, though? I mean, you quit your job last week, right?" I asked partly for sympathy, but also to clarify, since an unemployed roommate who doesn't pay rent is far worse than a new roommate who, though maybe less neat or reliable with leftover pastry delivery than hoped for, would likely be on top of the bill situation.

Sylvia shrugged. "Yeah, but I couldn't stand to be in the same city with him now, so Toledo is out. I'm going to find another job here. I know you've been looking for other roommates. I'm sorry to have put you through all this. I can find another place if you want."

And then came the straight-up, rained-on, puppy-dog look. Her eyes whimpered.

"No, no, stay here. Definitely. I haven't told anyone yes yet, so stay. For sure. Stay." I smiled and nodded and was still smiling and nodding like a nice-roommate automaton when she turned on her heels and went back to her room.

In the wake of her businessy reporting of her breakup with Rodney and her immediate departure for her own space, I felt ridiculous for having imagined turning to her for a heart-to-heart. Clearly, she didn't need to talk, and she'd actually broken up with someone. I had only friend broken up. I felt more tattered by the second.

Con, I thought, *living with unreliable Toledan. Pro: will not be required to paint.*

First thing upon moving in, Sylvia had painted her room a ghastly Pepto-Bismol pink. I'd promised all the prospective roommates, who'd each gasped audibly when I'd opened the door, that it would be a nice taupe before they moved in. Funny how Sylvia hadn't offered to help paint it back to a normal color herself.

Earlier in the week I'd stopped by the hardware store and procured a couple of cans of paint and brushes. I could return the brushes, but unfortunately, once they've mixed you a can of paint, they won't take it back. Sylvia had disappeared to her room with such remarkable speed that I didn't dare knock. Clearly, she wanted to be alone. So instead of knocking I passive-aggressively made a lot of noise right outside her door, loudly loading myself up with the paint cans so that I could move them from our apartment to the basement. Unsurprisingly, my huffing and puffing didn't elicit an offer of help from her room. I should have knocked on her door. The fact that I couldn't bring myself to was pretty much the final death knell in the dream of a new me.

I'd only been down to the basement once before, after a blow dryer–blender–microwave usage trifecta had blown a fuse. On that occasion, I'd hunted around the apartment for a fuse box, unsuccessfully tried to reach my landlord when I couldn't find it, then, imagining the basement held the answer, descended the stairs. Approaching the basement door, a smell—two parts mold, one part decaying rat skeletons—had thickened the air. I'd opened the door anyway. And that was as far as I got. Peering into the reeking darkness, I'd decided I could handle a few hours without power. It turned out to be a full thirty-six hours, since my landlord is, how to put it delicately . . . somewhat unresponsive.

Today, though, I was glum and self-castigating enough to feel like the musty basement and I deserved each other.

I made it all the way down the stairs, breathing through my mouth on the final flight to the basement door. I pushed through and felt along the wall for a light switch. One dim bulb hanging in the center of the room lit up. Its reflection bounced back in the good half inch of water collected on the floor in the low part of the room, which seemed to include everywhere but the immediate vicinity near the door. So, I'd found the source of the mold smell. Rotted-out cardboard boxes lined one wall. An old bike with only one tire leaned against a refrigerator, which had no door but did have a bottle of ketchup on the shelf. Miscellaneous tools and jars of screws and hoses and cans overflowed a sodden particleboard workbench.

And then, as I calmly looked around, wallowing in the dankness, I heard a scuffle. Rat? Snake? Psycho killer? Who knew, but I guessed it had something to do with the carcassy smell. I semi-hurled the cans into the pile of miscellaneous buckets and canisters near the workbench, then double-teamed the stairs all the way up to my apartment.

Monday, the day of my meeting with Regina, I woke up ready to shake off the weekend. Just getting back to TGTW would help, I knew, but I also kicked it into high gear by completing every ritual I ordinarily skipped—curling my eyelashes, applying lotion after my shower, spritzing perfume. I hoped to impress Regina with my myriad exciting Ten Girls to Watch ideas, but I also hoped to convince her I was a paragon of style and grace. Maybe then she'd hire me for keeps. I felt a little like a woman who's trying to convince the guy who's told her he just wants to have fun that she's his forever girl, but frankly, I *was* desperate for Regina's employerly affections. I was somewhat desperate for any affections at all.

Before I'd have the chance to put on my show, though, I had to put in a morning of work at the warehouse archives. Down in my closet, I was chatting away on my headset with 1989 winner and journalist Sandra Seru, who had just returned from a two-month reporting project on miners in Argentina and was telling me all about her book on Latin American workers' collectives, when, to my great surprise, Elliot Kaslowski leaned his head into my office, all smiles. Panicky, thrilled hormones shot through my body, and I phased out for a second, missing part of the story Sandra was telling me about traveling with her teenage son—something about food allergies—and mouthed "Give me five minutes" to Elliot. He nodded, disappeared briefly, and was back in time to hear me give Sandra the excited spiel about our get-together. No firm plans for the TGTW event yet, but I'd be in touch again as soon as I knew anything. I couldn't help it—even though I'd now delivered my speech dozens of times, I still bubbled over. I really had been thrilled to talk with Sandra Seru. I really did hope she'd come to the event.

"They must love you," Elliot said as he perched himself presumptuously on the corner of my desk. I hadn't yet replied to his effusive e-mail message, and I noted that my inadvertent hard-to-get move was causing exactly the sort of reaction the stupid books promised.

"I'm very lovable," I said. I was grateful I'd curled my eyelashes that morning.

He smiled. "So what are you doing Friday?"

I paused. This was the weekend of the Helen Hensley reading. I had firm plans to go to Boston. I was very glad to have something to say other than "Uh . . . cutting my toenails and rearranging my socks," but I felt a momentary pang: he was going to ask me out, and I was going to have to say no.

I heard myself say, "I was thinking of going to Boston. Just visiting a friend." As if it were in some way tentative.

"Are you taking the train?" he asked.

"Wouldn't that be fancy!" The train was always at least a hundred dollars each way. "No," I said. "The Fung Wah Bus."

"Really? Why don't I drive you?" he said. "I broke up with the Fung Wah last year and got together with an old Honda Civic. Infinitely more luxurious."

"Are you kidding? You want to drive me to Boston?" I said, stunned.

"Why not? I've got some friends up there. I'll call and see what they're up to this weekend. That way I can catch up with them and also enjoy the pleasure of your company on the way up and back, if you'll have me."

I'd learned something about the East Coast, or at least New York. Rides were a rarity. In Oregon, offering a ride was common decency. A light, easy thing. Not in New York. Here, it was like offering bone marrow.

"That would be amazing," I said.

"Good, then it's settled," Elliot said. "We'll leave right after work?"

I nodded, unable to suppress my smile. He smiled just as much, the smile lines around his eyes stretching down to his cheeks.

There are moments, right in the middle of the normal passage of time, when you pause and think, *I'll remember this.* This was one of those. His eye crinkles were that beautiful.

As he rose from my desk, he briefly put his hand on top of mine, and then he was gone. I didn't make another call for a full ten minutes. I just sat under the glow of my lamp, gazing at the bulletin board. Gerri Vans and her fluffy curls smiled down at me. I noted, when I finally thought about Robert again, that I'd gone a full fifteen minutes without thinking about Robert.

Another few phone calls to past winners, half a peanut butter sandwich at my desk, and I began my final readying for my return to the Mandalay Carson building. I printed and neatly stapled copies of every document I could ever dream of sharing (including all my profiles, just in case), slipped on flats, and headed aboveground for the walk east, out of exile. Turning down the hallway on the ground floor, I ran into Ralph. Today, he'd transitioned to a royal purple cardigan. If I'd felt like the lord of my little basement dominion, Ralph's purple cardigan squelched that idea. He was king of this place.

"Gorgeous day out," he said, as if he saw me all the time and we'd exhausted every other topic of conversation.

"I know," I said. "I'm headed out into it!"

He nodded, and with that, I pushed through the doors and into the sunshine.

Upon arriving in the Mandalay Carson lobby, I forgot to pretend the silver tree sculpture didn't mesmerize me, which proved embarrassing when the woman behind me in line to go through the entrance gates slammed into me, not noticing that I had stopped to gawk at the delicate quaking metal leaves above. I did not particularly appreciate the icicle-through-the-heart glare she leveled as I offered my prolific apologies. I did my best not to take it personally. That said, I did take it personally. I always do. I read somewhere that redheads experience dental pain more intensely than other people. In my case, I think it extends to all physical pain, plus emotional slights.

The same tiny woman who'd been there on my first visit to the eighteenth floor once again sat behind the reception desk. I told her my name and said I was there for a meeting with XADI and Regina.

She slowly smoothed stray strands of her white hair up into the massive bun atop her head as she dialed XADI's office.

"Do you like mint?" she said when she hung up the phone. No segue, just straight to mint. She didn't wait for an answer. "I planted some mint in my garden this year, and it's going crazy, taking over everything. I step outside, and I feel like I'm in a tube of toothpaste."

"That happened to my parents' garden," I said. "Mint is nuts. But you know what's amazing? Mint in lemonade. You just put a few leaves in and it infuses the whole thing with that cool, crisp flavor. It's the most refreshing thing ever."

"Mm-hm, that sounds delightful." Her low voice quaked with pleasure, and then she closed her eyes and smiled, as if she were drinking mint-infused lemonade right then. But the thing is, she didn't open her eyes again. She hadn't had a stroke or anything; she was moving her head around a little, smiling. I guess she was just loving the moment.

My parents really had had an amazing garden. Maybe not quite on the order of Rachel Link's parents' roses, but they'd grown bushels of vegetables every summer. It had been the one thing they'd seemed to be able to work on happily together. After the divorce, my mom ripped it all out—the garden, the grass, everything—and replaced it with rock. Which might make sense in Tucson, but this was Oregon. Before that though, there was the terry cloth robe phase, during which the garden turned into a tangle of weeds, with mint covering huge swathes of the former flower beds. Only after she signed on to Mary Kay and got a sporty new haircut and several dozen new lipsticks did the plants come out. "No time for all that stuff anymore!" she'd said. I'd been both relieved and alarmed. Maybe I should have helped her pull out the overgrown garden, but I hadn't been able to stomach the idea and she hadn't asked for help. Instead, like a person peeking through her blinds at a suspicious neighbor, wondering whether a crime is unfolding but not wanting to get involved, I'd watched from the window of my bedroom as she yanked one bunch of flowers after the next.

XADI appeared behind the glass door, pulled it open, and waited for me, without saying so much as a word.

"Hi," I said awkwardly.

"Hi, you ready?" she answered abruptly. I nodded. Her black hair was shorter than the last time I'd seen her, but still every bit as severe, and she wore the same brusque magenta lipstick. And just like last time, she took the lead and I trotted behind. We went past her office, past the copy room, through the art department, past a conference room, and finally, lo and behold, we arrived in "The Pod." Which I knew was called "The Pod" (with capitals) because as we entered the area, XADI said, with great weight, "Regina's office is just off [pause] *The Pod*."

The room was the bright and airy room I'd imagined I was going to be working in, before I was summarily packed off to the archives. Or at least semirelated to the room I'd imagined. The desks were of the same mold as the receptionist's desk out front, but these white plastic desks and cubicle walls spanned the length of the floor. And while the lobby desk gleamed, while the receptionist there was a bit of a genie in her pristine bottle, here nothing was pristine. Stacks and stacks of black photo portfolios sat atop cabinets and desks, spread wide for review. Copious back issues of *Charm* were jumbled across shelves and desks. Half-closed cardboard boxes stuffed with sample products jutted out from beneath desks and chairs. Piles and piles of papers and folders perched on chairs and cubicle walls. And spread across each of the waist-high filing cabinets that ran the length of the walkway between cubicles was the most notable mess of all: food, food, and more food. I spotted a fruit tray with a few lonely pieces of cantaloupe, a box of donuts with only crumbles of a powdered jelly donut and a pink frosted donut remaining, bags of chips on a tray on the next cabinet down, and finally, cupcakes, cut in halves and quarters, crumbs trailing across the counter.

Women talked on the phone, typed, typed, and typed, and talked back and forth across desks. I recognized Rebecca Wagner, the platinum-blonde Charm.com beauty blogger, at a cubicle near the window. A few desks over was Allie Krezgy, dark curls, the health blogger who chronicled her every workout and meal. Her silence on the subject of cupcakes and donuts now seemed epic. For the first time, looking around at the mess, I thought perhaps I was lucky to be working in my quiet, comparatively orderly basement.

At the far end, which we were steadily approaching, a white silk bench flanked the door of an office. A rumpled assistant in very tall heels got up and closed the door, apparently under the impression that we would otherwise barge right in. "Regina will be ready in five minutes," she said to XADI, not even so much as glancing at me.

XADI took a seat on the bench, and with an ordinary person, I would have followed suit. But XADI seemed to demand more personal space than most. I stayed standing. Again, with an ordinary person, this might have been the time for chatting. XADI and I waited in silence.

Finally the door opened, three stylish women shuffled out, and XADI and I rose to shuffle in. Every bit as lovely in her office as she'd been at the garden party, Regina stood over her desk in a glowing white tuxedo, the jacket gorgeously tailored with a wide peak lapel and a plunging neckline. She wasn't the image of some languidly elegant movie star, though. She looked more like an athlete. Even before she moved, you could see her coiled energy.

"Dawn, it's so good to see you again!" she said. As if I weren't her lowest-level employee and were instead a friend she was just charmed to run into.

"Nice to see you too," I said, with demure surprise. I think I'd half expected her to not even remember who I was.

"XADI, how's everything?" Regina said, with the same warmth.

"No complaints," she replied, all business as usual.

We circled up around Regina's tortoiseshell office table, and XADI, in her shapeless black sweater and trousers, was like a black hole of fashion beside a radiant star. And even though she wasn't exactly nice to me, or someone I particularly wanted to grow up to be, I had a brief moment of amazement in regard to XADI. Here was a woman who was what she was, and no one, not Regina, not a whole office full of trends and niceties and people wearing much cuter outfits and augmenting their lives with smiley-face emoticons, was going to make her otherwise. She was the opposite of me. She did nothing to smooth her path in the world. And she was successful. I took note.

XADI kicked things off. "To start with, Dawn has a list of all the past winners we've found so far."

I passed them my copies of the color-coded spreadsheet and explained each designation. Regina nodded as she glanced over the first page.

"There are a few particularly high-profile women we haven't talked with yet," I continued, "but they're still highlighted, since we know where they are. Gerri Vans; Robyn Jackson, who is the CEO of Madison Capital; Jessica Winston, the opera singer; Barbara Darby, the writer . . ."

"Do we have a plan for contacting those women?" Regina asked.

XADI jumped in. "Figuring out how we want to use them and the best way to approach them is on my agenda for this meeting."

"Great, so does that lead us to the event?" Regina said.

XADI snapped her eyes to me, and I handed out the packets with event ideas.

Regina took hers, but without looking at it she said, "I've been thinking a lot about the event and the coverage . . ." Her voice trailed off for a moment before she launched into a full outline of her vision.

She wanted a gala dinner. She wanted Gerri Vans to keynote. She wanted a journalist-type celebrity to MC. She wanted to announce this year's winners at the event. She wanted a video featuring the most prominent past winners. She wanted Clairol, the longtime sponsor of the awards, to give a big award to Anitha Ming, the activist responsible for freeing countless girls from brothels in Thailand and Vietnam, and she wanted *Charm* itself to give a big award to the new female president of Harvard, Drew Faust. All the past winners should be invited, though *Charm* wouldn't cover any of their travel expenses. And she wanted a fancy press list, all the big names. The events team would get going immediately.

Regina could make you feel like you were chatting away over a pot of tea, but she could also clearly get down to business.

My list of ideas for a much less glamorous, conferencey type event were tidily tucked away.

Regina walked to her desk and pulled out her editorial calendar. "I want this in the January issue," she said. "I'm thinking 'Real-

Life Role Models' is the Hed. XADI, I think I mentioned I thought this would go well with the Real-Life Makeover special, right?"

XADI nodded.

Calendar in hand, Regina started announcing deadlines. "For the January issue we need final copy and layout no later than November 1. Which means at the very latest we need copy in the lineup starting October 15." My arithmetic skills revealed that October 15 was a mere nineteen days away. I sat in silence as XADI nodded smoothly.

"Let's make it easier and feature this year's winners in a follow-up story on the event in February's issue," XADI said.

Regina nodded. Plans continued to roll forth. A photo meeting was set for later that afternoon. Video production had to start rolling. I needed to get addresses firmly squared away so the events team could get invitations out the door.

By the time the meeting wrapped forty-five minutes later, my ears were buzzing. I was going to have to find a hundred-plus elusive women in less than two weeks and generate all sorts of copy while I was at it.

"Oh, last thing, Dawn," Regina said as we moved toward the door. "We need to start warming up all the big names. Call all of them except Gerri. I'll talk to her."

XADI didn't bat an eye, but I felt a ping of exultation. Who cared if XADI had worried I wasn't up for the big calls? Regina had declared me fit for duty.

"And as soon as possible," Regina added, "I want the names and bios of the ten women you think are most worth featuring."

The second we'd crossed back over the threshold, Regina's assistant swooped in and closed the door behind us.

XADI walked me back to the lobby and said she'd be in touch about follow-up. I was slightly rattled after the immense number of tasks Regina had just given us, but XADI seemed completely nonplussed. I took comfort in her authoritative calm. We could do this, no problem! As she parted ways with me at the door, she nodded a curt good-bye.

The second the door clicked closed, the receptionist, who seemed to have been waiting for XADI's departure as much as I had, smoothed another few hairs back into her bun and said, "How was your meeting?"

"Pretty good, I think."

"Good." She nodded, her voice with the same purring rumble from before. Then she suddenly sat forward and opened her eyes wide. "You know what I'm going to do for you? I'm going to bring you a mint cutting. You need some plants in your life! I can just tell. Next time you're here, I'll have it for you. Just you wait."

"I'd like that," I replied with reflexive politeness, but I could tell as soon as I said it just how true it was.

Tanya King,

Spelman College, 1985

THE FILMMAKER

"I've always loved movies, and we need more women behind the camera," Tanya says. She's off to a great start—her short film, *Regaling the Ritz*, about a jazz trumpeter, won top honors in Georgia's student film competition. A jazz trumpeter herself, Tanya plans to keep performing while attending film school in New York.

Chapter Eleven

*R*egina had given her orders, and so I began my calls to big, famous, amazing women I had no right talking to. I left messages with secretaries and assistants and plotted out possible questions in the event any of them actually called me back. *What do you know now that you wish you'd known at twenty-one? Did winning the contest affect your life in any unexpected ways?*

A few hours after I placed my first big calls, my phone rang, and I caught my breath, waited another ring, then answered as evenly as possible.

"Hello," said the voice. "This is Jessie Winston." Jessica Winston, soprano of Metropolitan Opera and perfume ad fame? Jessie Winston, on my phone?! Her voice sounded regal, crisp but luxurious at the same time, like a layered meringue dessert. I'd seen her just a few months earlier at the Met, descending into madness as Lucia di Lammermoor, trilling away with blood on her gown. The seats had been courtesy of Robert, pre-Lily. Since then I'd considered springing for my own twenty-dollar seat way up in the tippy-top of the theater, just to prove I could access the fine arts all on my own without Robert, thank you very much, but I hadn't quite gone in for the splurge yet. But here was Lucia di Lammermoor saying hi to me, no opera tickets necessary.

I told her about the anniversary, how excited we were and how we were hoping to bring together as many of the winners as possible. And then I said I obviously had a good idea of what she'd been up to for the past fifteen years, but I'd love to hear a little more about it. Just like that. Nothing more than a little shimmying open the window of invitation, and yet she started pouring her voice through the crack I'd created.

"I've been incredibly blessed," she said, her enunciation sparkling through the receiver. "Any singer who is able to spend her time performing has to acknowledge that. But I think I've also been blessed by the mind-body connection this profession fosters.

"Something most people don't think about is just how physical singing is, and I think that's what I'm most grateful for in my job. I rely so much on my body that I notice all the tiny differences. If I don't sleep enough, if I've eaten poorly or had a little too much to drink the night before, it comes out in my voice. You can hear my sins. The thing is, everyone relies on their bodies; it's just harder to hear the screeching when your job is writing or taking care of patients or crunching numbers. That doesn't mean it's not there. It just means that some people consider it part of their jobs to turn a deaf ear. I don't have that luxury. I have to take care of myself, and that's been a gift."

"Absolutely," I said, and she went right on.

"Taking care of yourself is one of the hardest jobs—don't ever let anyone tell you otherwise. It's much easier to take care of others. After almost twenty years in this business I still struggle with it, but at least I know I'm engaged in the right fight. So many people seem to think there's something honorable about hurting themselves—working through the night, drinking coffee and eating donuts and plowing through work, running themselves ragged. I've been lucky enough to have a job that has taught me to recognize that sort of toughness for the lie that it is. It's the easy way out. Diligently caring for yourself, now that's what's really honorable. All those bad habits, you can get by with them for a while, but in the long run, you hobble yourself."

Then, more quietly, her diction still lyrical and percussive at the same time, she said, "I had a cancer scare a few years ago. There was a growth on my liver. I felt the change in my body almost immediately. Fortunately, because we found it so early, the growth was very small. And even more fortunately, it turned out to be benign. But I think about that a lot. What a gift it is to know my body, to pay enough attention to it that I can feel every little shift."

At this point I concluded that even if she was a tiny touch self-righteous, I had just spent a weekend lying in bed and eating nothing other than bowls of cold cereal stolen from my roommate's Cap'n Crunch box when she wasn't looking. The part of me that considered this a reasonable way to deal with life needed to listen to Jessie Winston. I could sign up for all the weird sleep studies I wanted, but maybe if I left work a little earlier and went on a run every night, I wouldn't need those little blue pills. For so long, I had been thinking success was only attainable if I pushed myself to the breaking point. Taking care of yourself was so easy to dismiss as a self-absorbed silly modern notion, and I did, obviously, all the time. But it wasn't silly, and Jessie Winston was right, it actually wasn't all that easy.

We talked for another twenty minutes, about her early career, about how she knew opera was right for her and stuck with it, even when all the easy early breaks didn't come her way and she spent two years as a singing waitress and another year as an ESL tutor. Her early comments had chastened me, but I found this admission of youthful struggle supremely comforting. Not that I was going to blossom into an opera star, but that a year of fumbling didn't necessarily rule out stardom of some sort. Maybe I wasn't Mei Li Chan with a literary masterwork right out of the gates, but that didn't mean that there was no hope for my writing.

The call with Jessie made me feel buoyant. It was the same way I felt when talking with Helen—like the high flyer I'd just spoken with had shared some of the magical air that lifted and carried her.

I made more calls, both to regular and famous women, and the days passed with more amazing Ten Girls' life stories. Lacy Schwartz dropped out of medical school after her first year but then went on to be a playwright. It was fifteen rather painful years before her first play went up anywhere near Broadway. Her Pulitzer Prize for *Phaedon's Philosophical Smile* came, she told me, twenty-three years after she walked away from Duke medical school. Did she feel vindicated? Sort of, but not really. If she'd been a success the next year or in the next five years, she said, sure, that's what she would have felt. But twenty-three years later, it was just her life, not some point she was making. "It's not like I think medical school would have been a bad thing. It was just like I was wearing shoes that didn't fit. I had to get out of them," she said. Joyce Halverston was entering her sixth year as a federal judge in Ohio. She said one of the best things about her job was having to wear a robe every day so she never had to worry about fashion. Katherine Mack, the editor in chief of the *San Francisco Chronicle,* cracked that she was just grateful to have a job.

And on and on the conversations went. Most were wonderful, most filled me with huge excitement to meet the women in person. Every now and again, a call would make me feel like I didn't have much to show for myself (hello, winners with recording contracts at nineteen or jobs writing for TV shows at twenty-four). But mostly, they filled me with optimism. At this point, I knew that the *New Yorker* wasn't going to put me on any 25 under 25 lists, and I wasn't going to be one of those charmed souls who marries their college sweetheart. "Early Bloomer" wasn't going to be the title of my success story. But there were plenty of these women for whom that hadn't been the scenario either. There was Stephanie

Linwood, with her years at a boring real estate law firm; there was Ellen Poloma, who fell madly in love with Randall whatever-his-last-name-was in her forties. There were lots of ways to do this. I didn't want to say "hope" too loudly, but down in my basement storeroom, while no one was looking, I was starting to build a little stockpile of it.

Thursday morning, when I emerged from the subway in mid-town, my cell phone vibrated with a new voice mail. "This is Becky from Somnilab," the dreary voice said. Unfortunately, Becky continued, the sleep times I'd been phoning in every morning showed that I was sleeping too well. For this study they needed people with more severe insomnia. I would still be receiving a check for two hundred and fifty dollars to compensate me for my one over-night stay, but that was it. No fifteen hundred coming my way. I was out of the study.

I would have been grouchier about my dismissal except, it was true, I had been using the pills to sleep as much as humanly pos-sible. Also, the dismissal conveniently allowed me to avoid ever seeing Raymond again. Also, I got to keep the pills. Also, two hun-dred and fifty dollars was pretty good all on its own.

Back at the archives, an air of abandonment hovered in the hall-ways as usual. From the doorway of my closet, I spotted the blinking voice mail light. More voice mail? Great, what was this going to be? XADI telling me I'd been doing such a good job they decided they didn't need me anymore? Elliot telling me he'd decided he didn't want to be "friends" anymore either? (Maybe I was a little more disappointed by my sleep-study rejection than I'd let myself admit.) Fortunately, the voice mail was from Robyn Jackson's assistant. She'd called just a few minutes before I arrived. I dialed her back immediately, and she patched me right through to Robyn.

In 1968, Robyn Jackson became the first black woman ever to grace the cover of a major women's magazine. In the photo her skin was smooth, her cheeks peachy and glowing over the top of her burnt-orange turtleneck sweater. From her perfectly peaceful smile, you'd think it was nothing to crash through barriers. She was just another girl, heading to a football game. Except she wasn't. She never was. She started her own business as a teenager. By the time she was in college, the cleaning service she ran employed over a hundred maids, including her mother and all her aunts.

These days, she wasn't exactly famous, but she was if you talked to the right people. Anyone who knew money knew Robyn Jackson. Her company, Madison Capital, invested its gazillions in real estate, renewable energy, biotech, and retail. In my reading I even came across several reports of Madison's rumored bids for Mandalay Carson.

"So glad we're connecting!" Robyn girlishly chirped. I felt a little embarrassed for having imagined she'd have more of a husky Aretha Franklin voice.

After some initial chitchat, she told me the story of the magazine cover. The editor who took over *Charm* in 1967 apparently imagined a different approach than her forebearers; at her direction, in 1968 academics joined the criteria upon which the Ten Girls to Watch were judged, a factor that certainly helped Robyn.

That year each of the ten girls had been photographed individually during their weeklong trip to New York, and a few days later the editor called Robyn aside during one of their lunches and said, quick as can be, "Your photo is running on the cover. It was the most beautiful shot, hands down."

Robyn stopped her story at that point and said, "I always appreciated that—her emphasizing that the beauty of the photo was the deciding factor, not anything political. I think she was telling the truth, though it's now obvious to me that it was a little more complicated than that—she took a huge risk when she made that judgment. But she was devoted to beauty and empowering women, and I endlessly admire people who keep themselves to the standards they set."

I told her how exciting it was to see a woman at the top of what was so often thought of as a men's profession.

"Let me tell you, Dawn," she said, chuckling a bit, "money is power. Anyone who tells you it isn't—they're kidding themselves. Most women won't tell you they want power. There's something ugly in that word for women. And I understand that. Believe me, as a black woman I particularly understand that. But power is only a dirty word when you don't have any. Women are never going to rise up and take their rightful place as long as they're afraid of power."

I felt the weight of my fingers clacking as I typed her words. I wanted to say money didn't matter. I had really believed that as a college student, back when I didn't have money but had all the access to libraries and leather couches and boathouses and institutional legitimacy I could have ever wanted. But now, I was pretty sure she was right. I felt keenly aware that Robyn was only talking to me because I was calling on behalf of *Charm*, which was part of Mandalay Carson, which was rolling in dough. I tried not to think about how the conversation would, or rather wouldn't, have gone if I, Dawn West of Milldale, Oregon, had just called her up on my own.

But I was indeed calling from *Charm*, and so we continued pleasantly along and turned the conversation to Robyn's family. She told me about her daughter who'd just started college and wanted to become a journalist. Perhaps because this made me feel validated, even if my hold in the field of journalism was currently tenuous at best, I immediately offered up my contact information and the contact information of every friend from college who had gotten even close to having a journalism-related job. I hoped I offered not because Robyn owned half the office towers in Manhattan but because she crooned and giggled as she talked about her kid with such obvious adoration, but I couldn't be sure.

After Thursday's Robyn Jackson talk, Friday was all discouragement. E-mails sent to addresses that bounced back. Lost trails and fruitless phone calls. No bigwigs returning my messages. And the saddest story about a 1985 winner. On tanyakingscholarship.org, I found this:

> *My sister Tanya was my best friend. She taught me to love life and shoot for the stars. This website is dedicated to Tanya's art, to her memory, and to helping deserving young people who are following in her footsteps. It's also dedicated to raising awareness of depression and prescription drug dependence. Tanya didn't hold back in life, and I know she would want me to share her story in hopes of helping others through their struggles.*

The scholarship section of the website detailed the application process. Undergraduate women of color studying either music or film were encouraged to apply for one of three ten-thousand-dollar scholarships to be given out annually. "About Tanya" featured clips of films and shows she'd directed, including a number of episodes of the PBS show *American Experience.* In one short film, she strung together clips of dozens of women who remembered lynchings of their family members. "About Tanya" also included a section called "Tanya's Story" written by her sister.

In 1998, Tanya adopted a six-year-old boy, Anthony. In 2000, Tony disappeared from their Baltimore backyard. Two weeks later, his body was found mutilated and abandoned in the woods less than a half mile from their home. The murder case was still open when Tanya was killed in a car accident in 2002. Earlier that year Tanya had been caught seeing multiple doctors in order to receive multiple prescriptions for antianxiety medication, painkillers, and antidepressants. The morning she'd driven into the Patapsco River, the autopsy reported, she'd taken a massive overdose of Xanax. Tanya's sister encouraged everyone struggling through pain, battling depression, or feeling themselves in the clutches of darkness to reach out, to seek help, to pray. She then listed resources: narcotics anonymous web listings, grief counseling referral sites, suicide help lines, support groups for parents who've lost children. At the end of the page, she wrote, "My love, Tanya and Tony's love, and God's love to you all."

I slowly scrolled through the site with one of my hands half covering my face, as if not fully reading the words could somehow undo them. I'd been looking at Tanya's photo from the magazine, an artsy profile shot, expecting to have the beautiful woman from the picture on the phone any minute. Instead, I blinked the mist away from my eyes, then left my desk and walked aimlessly through the shelves of floor –2 for a while. When I returned, I made a simple note in my spreadsheet. "Tanya King: deceased." Then, thinking that wasn't enough, I added "music and film memorial scholarship: tanyaking scholarship.org." Maybe one of the TGTW winners for this year could apply, or perhaps we could invite Tanya's sister to the gala in her stead.

Finally, after a day of so much discouragement, five o'clock arrived, and Elliot once again knocked on my door, this time to take me to Boston. I'd been jumpy all day, imagining I was hearing his footsteps every time I detected the slightest rustle. I turned at what seemed like an imagined footfall, the hundredth time I'd turned thinking I'd heard him, but this time, I hadn't imagined him. I caught him a second before his hand touched my door. He knocked anyway, holding my eyes as his knuckles lightly rapped on the wood.

"Hey there," he said. "What do you say we blow this joint?"

"I was thinking I'd stick it out until six."

"*Charm*'s turning the screws?" He winked. "Oh, come on. We don't want to pull in at midnight."

"Okay, okay. Give me a minute to grab my stuff." I surrendered.

Elliot walked my way and perched on the edge of a stack of boxes.

I attempted to close out of my e-mail and stack my notes and printouts with some semblance of grace, but I couldn't shake the outside-myself awkward-actress feeling.

I had packed the night before with the greatest of care. I'd made white chocolate cranberry scones for Helen and tied them up in a box with a gold satin bow. I'd picked up the latest collection of Alice Munro short stories for her and nicely wrapped and tucked that in my weekend bag as well. I'd cleaned my shoes. I'd packed two possible outfits for the reading, one dress, one pants and sweater combination. I'd folded everything fastidiously, as if I were the butler from *The Remains of the Day.*

Finally, I dramatically pushed in my chair, picked up my bag, and said to Elliot, "All right, I'm all yours."

"Really?" he replied in a hopeful, flirty voice.

Eleven-year-old Dawn reared to life, and instead of flirting back, I ignored this comment.

"So are you parked near home?" I asked.

"You think I'm making you schlep all the way to Brooklyn?" he said. "How meager your expectations, my dear. I'm parked in the garage out back."

I gave him a wide-eyed look, and he nudged me with his shoulder. He took my bag and we rode the elevator up, silently smiling.

Then, just as we approached the lobby doors, Ralph rounded the corner. When he saw us, his friendly face took on an expression I'd never seen before—a smirk. A hot shot of humiliation flashed in my brain. Did *Charm* send all its marginal employees to work in the archives? Had Ralph seen Elliot do this precise walk with other girls before?

"My man!" Elliot said, putting his hand out to shake Ralph's.

Ralph returned the greeting. His eyes grazed right over me, as if walking with Elliot made me simply an accessory.

"Have a good weekend, Ralph," I said, trying to reclaim my place.

He mumbled something back. It might have been "You too," but I couldn't really tell.

In the elevator, Elliot leaned over and kissed my cheek. Despite Ralph, I felt the blurry buzz I'd felt on the Brooklyn Bridge creeping back into me.

When we arrived at his sensible blue Honda, he drop-kicked the front bumper and said, "Check this dent. I bargained seven hundred dollars off the price thanks to this baby."

Robert swore by BMWs. The contrast was enough to make me want to pull Elliot into the Honda, make out with him like crazy, then tell him all my bargain-hunting secrets: Honey Bunches of Oats are always cheapest at the drugstore; never buy anything online without searching for a coupon first; appetizers are large enough to serve as entrées at almost every single restaurant . . . When he opened the door, I acted on at least one part of my plan (sharing all my bargain-hunting secrets would have taken far too long). It was well after five o'clock when we pulled out of the garage.

We eked through traffic for a full hour before we escaped the city, but when we finally hit the Saw Mill Parkway, we started cruising. Until we hit the lights. How were there so many of them? Stopped alongside a construction site, Elliot said, "Have I ever told you about my lists? One of my best ones is my list of port-o-potty companies. Dr. John over there," he said, motioning to a green port-o-potty, "I've never seen him before."

"I keep lists too!" I said, thrilled to be able to come back with something I thought he'd find funny. "I've got a great misheard-expressions one: skimp milk, windshield factor. But I think my best one is my food spoof celebrity names: Tuna Turner, Catherine Feta Jones . . ."

"Oh, we're coming back to those, but first we've got to deal with Honey Bucket, Call-A-Head, Mr. John . . . Dr. John there is upping the game. He may be heralding a whole new age of honorific porta-johns."

We moved from one list to another as we finally broke free of the lights. Bond movie titles: Midnight Never Fades, Dawn Never Forgets (my personal favorite). Names I would consider should I ever become a romance novelist: Brooks Reverie, Constance Waters. Animal group names: pod of whales, pride of lions, murder of crows, clutch of doves. Bad company names: Krazy Kuts (Crazy and Cuts have the same first letter to begin with—why the switch? And does anyone actually *want* a krazy kut?), Bake My Day (confrontational muffins? No thank you).

This segued to bad ideas we'd executed on ourselves. We were passing through Waterbury, Connecticut, when I told him the story of the summer in college I decided to save money and eat nothing but Easy Mac. It was great, until July when I started looking pale and had three nosebleeds in a week. A lesson for the ages: Easy Mac is not a robust source of Vitamin C. It's a strange day when University Health Services doesn't even test to see whether you're pregnant; they just tell you you have scurvy, and it turns out they're right.

Elliot reported that he'd permed his own hair in high school.

"I give you scurvy and you come back with a perm? Weak," I said.

"I could get all serious and talk about bad marital decision making, but I don't think you want to go there."

I suddenly felt guilty that I hadn't read his book yet. Guilty and petty. I should have read it. I would have had I not been passive-aggressively reacting to him being "out of town."

I waited a second too long to reply, and he said, "Did I just do a Debbie Downer feline AIDS thing?"

"No, no, not at all," I said. "Or yes, sort of. I haven't read your book yet. I'm so sorry."

"Phew. Don't apologize. I'm totally relieved. That's the problem with memoir. You write it, and then it's all out there."

This was the flip side of Helen's "write the truth" advice. "I can only imagine," I said. "I'm scared enough when I write fiction. It's not like my mom *isn't* going to know the stories are about her. But at least we can all pretend."

"So true, Kelly Burns. So true."

"How did your ex-wife take it when the book came out?" I said, feeling a little daring at the direct mention of the ex-wife.

"I don't know, actually. Susan and I haven't talked since the day we signed the papers."

All I could think of to offer was another feeble "I'm sorry."

"Don't be," he said. "It's for the best."

"How long were the two of you together?" I asked.

"We started dating when we were sixteen, and we got married when we were twenty-one and then divorced when we were twenty-six. So ten years or five years, depending on how you count."

He said it all so easily, without ever looking away from the road. Like he was listing the classes he was taking or his favorite songs. And then he said, "There's part of me that still loves her. And part of me knows we could have made it work. But I guess the way I think about it is a little like binding your feet. You can wrap them all snug and maybe they feel fine for a while, but then your feet get bigger, and it's terrible. You can push through the pain and learn to do everything you need to do on your tiny feet. And maybe that's a prize-worthy choice. But Susan and I decided we couldn't do it."

Everyone seemed to have shoe metaphors lately, and they were all trying so hard to get out of their shoes, their relationships, their careers. I just wanted some of those shoes in the first place. I could struggle with outgrowing them later.

I said it must have been hard. He said it was. And though I didn't say it aloud, I wondered whether he and Susan had really decided together, or whether *he* had decided. Maybe in her mind she'd been lovingly holding him tight until one day he cut her off and threw her away. I mean, Robert and I always *both* knew we weren't working, but somehow it always felt as if he was the one saying it out loud and doing something about it.

"Are you in touch with all your exes?" Elliot asked, feigning nonchalance. Or at least it seemed like feigning to me, but maybe it wasn't. Maybe he had dated so many women that discussion of exes was nothing to him.

Once again, I was suddenly aware of our age gap. Clarifying that I only had one ex was like shoving my inordinate youth into a beaming spotlight. *Look at me, I'm practically an adolescent,* then jazz hands. In college, I'd never ached to be older, but now, my age was like a disability. When I said "twenty-three," people's voices turned creamy and condescending. "You're so young!" they clucked. Which essentially meant, "You're too young to do anything real, but it's cute that you think otherwise." One of the reasons I thought my Ten Girls calls often went so well was that my age wasn't immediately apparent over the phone.

"We're in touch off and on" was the response I finally settled on, hoping it had an easygoing and experienced ring.

Elliot waited for me to go on, and when I didn't he tried to take up the conversational slack. "*Charm* asked me to do a column where I called all my exes and asked them what they thought I should have learned from our relationship. I declined."

I laughed, and then attempted to change the subject. "So tell me about the friends you're visiting in Boston this weekend," I said. "Anybody special?"

"Say 'special' again," he said.

"What, do I say it weird?"

"Yes, say it again," he said.

"Special."

"God, you say it exactly like my mother. Where the 'sh' in the middle gets all the emphasis. I love it."

So I reminded him of his mother. I didn't mind since it sounded like he liked his mom. I also noted he'd conveniently avoided answering my question.

"Back off, fellow western-stater," I said.

He held up his hand. "Do you hear that?" he asked.

I listened. "No," I said. And then a moment later, "Yes." We both listened to the small rhythmic pinging, which quickly became both less rhythmic and less small. "That knocking?" I said, using what was now the only appropriate word.

"I'm going to pull off at the next exit," he said. But then, moments later, the knocking disappeared, just like that. The car sounded totally fine.

"Maybe it was just something kicked up by the tires that was banging around," I said. We exchanged doubtful glances but drove on anyway. For the next hour, half listening to each other, half listening to the car, everything was fine. I'd told Helen I'd be arriving by eleven at the very latest. I was still very much hoping this would be the case. And then, just as we cruised past the last Hartford exit, the pinging kicked in again with a fervor that made it clear the previous rat-a-tat-tat had been nothing but an overture. This was the real symphony.

The next exit was for Mashapaug, Connecticut.

"Do you ever feel like you're in a story?" he said. "Pulling off in a town called Mashapaug . . . You know nothing good is coming your way in Mashapaug."

"We've gotten ourselves into a real Mashapaug here," I said. "Ha-ha." Then I switched to my radio drama voice: "Dawn peered into the gloom. Was it possible? Could it be? A Mashapaug approaching through the mist?"

"I was thinking more like the high school football team is called the Mashapaug Marauders, and they haven't won a game in fifty years," he said. "But the Monster of Mashapaug is pretty good too."

The car pinged and knocked and pinged and knocked, like

an audience that starts clapping slowly and then breaks into wild applause. "Just keep your eyes peeled for a garage," Elliot said. I kept figuring that around the next turn the frontage road we were following would reveal a splash of lights, and then fast-food joints, a gas station, and a town would appear. But no. When the din of pings was just too much, Elliot pulled the car to the soft shoulder of the road and killed the engine.

He turned to me in the dark. "You don't happen to moonlight as an automotive expert when you're not on lawn duty, do you?"

"Sadly, no," I said.

"I'm just going to let the car cool down for a minute and then turn it back on and see what happens."

I tried to keep calm. This wasn't going to interfere with my plans to see Helen. Everything would be fine. We waited ten minutes, and the grand result was that when he turned the key the car didn't make a sound. At all. It was fully and completely dead. I checked my cell phone—9:03 p.m. I wondered whether I should call Helen. But I didn't want to yet. There was still time. Maybe this was going to be a quick fix.

One AAA call and thirty minutes later, Elliot and I were smooshed into the cab of a tow truck from the nearest real town, Sturbridge. Reggie, the driver, informed us that none of the garages in town would be open till Saturday morning, but Wilson's Automotive would take great care of us as soon as Mr. Wilson himself got in at eight the next morning.

I finally called Helen.

"Dawn! Hello! How's the drive?"

I told her the bad news.

"Oh, no! I can come get you," she said, and she sounded eager, like she meant it, but she also sounded tired, like I should say no.

I assured her she didn't need to do a three-hour round-trip drive to pick me up. The car would be fixed in the morning, and I'd be there bright and early.

"I can send a car," she said. The longer we talked, the more I could hear the weariness in her voice.

I felt terrible. Not like I was just inconveniencing her. Not like I was just going to miss out on some fun times for me. Like she really wanted to see me. That worry I'd had a few weeks earlier, when she'd taken so long to reply to my e-mail, crept back in.

"Helen, is everything okay?" I said.

"Of course! I'm just sad to miss you." I didn't quite believe her. She sounded too cheery all of a sudden.

"The car should be fixed in the morning. I'll call you first thing with an update. I should still be there in time for the reading."

"Don't worry," she said. "If it's not this weekend, we'll find another one."

"I'll call you in the morning. Sleep tight and see you soon," I said.

As we said our good-byes I turned back to Elliot. I felt terrible. I was supposed to be with Helen tonight. But I was surprised to find, once I was off the phone, that I also kind of didn't feel terrible. This little breakdown extended the time I got to spend in Elliot's company threefold, fourfold, who knew. Plus, me, Elliot, a hotel room in Sturbridge? Far worse things had happened. Though as we piled into the tow truck cab and the reality of the night descended on me, I turned clammy. I wasn't really sure we were at the sharing-a-hotel-room stage. Was this going to be a one-room, one-bed situation? A forthright and well-adjusted woman would simply have stated her preferences. That's what Robyn Jackson or Helen Hensley would have done. But I froze.

If I jumped in and said two rooms, I'd be a total prude. And if I said two beds, would he think I was full of myself, assuming he was planning to put the moves on me? And maybe one bed was just fine. One bed did not equal sex. Sure, the Mashapaug Marauders would probably go for a touchdown, but certainly I could intercept their passes. Or maybe this was going to be their big winning season? No, no, it wasn't. After all, it had taken Robert's team a year to get into the end zone. One little drive to Boston and I was supposed to bench my defensive team? No siree.

"The car repairs might be expensive," I said after the tow truck dropped us at the Black Swan Inn. "Let me cover the room."

"No way," Elliot said. "You wouldn't be stuck in Sturbridge if it weren't for me and my dumb car. This is on me."

He forged ahead to the counter. One room, he said, and when the clerk asked if we'd prefer a king or two doubles, he said doubles would be great. I liked that. A lot. When the bellman dropped us in our room, Elliot flopped onto one of the beds.

"I ruined your weekend. I'm so sorry," he said. "And I'm sure your friends are totally bummed too."

I flopped next to him on the bed. "It's okay, we'll get there tomorrow."

He leaned over and kissed me.

I kissed him back.

In most of my dreams, I am outside myself, watching the action, like a patron in a movie theater. In real life, the same distance sometimes creeps in, a protective removal—I see myself doing things. But with Elliot, I didn't feel any distance. There was just the warmth, the slight roughness of the edge of his fingers on my skin, the surprising span his palm and fingers covered. Just the bristle of his stubble on my neck. The smell of dryer sheets, deodorant, cologne, and beneath it all, as I ran my lips along the skin just above his collarbone, the smell of him, just him—faint, deep, masculine. I pressed my fingers into the muscles of his back. We only used one of the beds that night.

Alexandra Guerrero,

Harvard University, 1990

THE SHOWSTOPPER

She's played leading ladies from Lady Macbeth to Sweet Charity (she's even played the occasional leading man— we hear her Coriolanus is Tony-worthy). But that's just the start of Alex's theatrical feats. In the past year and a half she directed and produced five plays, and her debut as a playwright comes this fall, when her one-act play *Mango Ladies* hits the college mainstage.

Chapter Twelve

*C*ozily, as if we did it every day, Elliot and I brushed our teeth together in the bathroom of the Black Swan Inn.

"Have any interesting dreams?" he said through the foam in his mouth.

"You wan me thoo tell you dow?" I laughed, equally foamy.

I leaned my head on his shoulder, still working my toothbrush, and we both looked at ourselves in the mirror. I noticed a sprinkling of gray hairs amid the stubble on his chin. His reflection winked at mine, and I laughed and dropped my face to rinse away the toothpaste.

Once we were all dressed and ready he took my hand and held it as we walked the four blocks to Wilson Automotive. In the waiting room, despite the smell of tires and motor oil, Elliot drank cup after cup of coffee. Didn't the garage smell interfere with the flavor? I asked. He shrugged. His love of Styrofoam and prepackaged creamer seemed to know no bounds. By eleven his dented Honda was on the lift, and by eleven fifteen Mr. Wilson himself let us know he'd have to order in some transmission parts.

He could have a guy bring them down from Boston ASAP if we

wanted, but he had a bunch of cars in line ahead of ours, and he probably couldn't put any guys to work on the transmission until around two or three that afternoon. Elliot and I slumped back down in our chairs.

I'd been texting Helen with updates throughout the morning. Now I didn't quite know what to say.

Helen didn't give me much of a chance to say anything anyway.

"Don't worry, Dawn," she said. "We'll just have to figure out another weekend. I'd feel terrible if you left your friend all alone at a garage in the middle of nowhere."

I protested and spewed half-formed thoughts about car rentals and Amtrak stations. But she stayed firm.

I said okay, told her again how sorry I was, and wished her luck on the reading.

"I'm so, so sorry," Elliot said. I still could have called 411 and gotten the number for a rental car company in town. In fact, Mr. Wilson probably had the actual real-life Yellow Pages lying around somewhere. But I didn't. Neither did Elliot. He refilled his coffee, and when he sat back down and put his arm around me I snuggled in close.

When the car was back in working order at six thirty that evening, we drove back to Brooklyn. Elliot asked whether I needed to rush right home. No, I said. I just needed to do a little work—some lawn care posting and coming up with my list of the ten most interesting Ten Girls to Watch for Regina—but I could do that from anywhere. And so he took me to his apartment, which was spacious for a studio, and swankily decked out for a freelance writer, with massive bookshelves packed with fabulous books, and mod glass spheres with clear lightbulbs hanging at various heights over the dining room table. What I thought to myself was *This is much cooler than Robert's apartment.* What I said aloud was "You have excellent taste in lamps."

"The better to see you with, my dear."

I grimaced.

"Was that cheesy?"

"Yes," I said.

"Stop being so critical and come over here," he said.

I did.

After a Sunday morning spent in various states of lounging and making out with Elliot, I finally settled in at home, first to somewhat trudgingly answer lawn care questions, then to finish up my TGTW Top Ten bio compilation. During the weekend, in the lulls in the car-ride conversation and, later, the lulls in caressing, I'd been arguing with myself over certain women, making swaps, trying for diversity all around—age, geography, field of work, race. Now, after a few energetic rounds of cutting and pasting and comparing, I came up with the following:

Ten Girls to Watch 50th Anniversary— 10 Most Prominent/Interesting Winners

1. **Rachel Link,** '97, *Founder of TheOne.com, New York, NY*

2. **Cindy Tollan,** '90, *Two-Time Paralympic Games Gold Medalist for Women's 400m Freestyle Swimming, Internationally Ranked Wheelchair Marathoner, Phoenix, AZ*

3. **Rebecca Karimi,** '89, *Former Fighter Pilot, Current Caltech Physics Professor, Pasadena, CA*

4. **Jessica Winston,** '87, *Soprano, Metropolitan Opera, New York, NY*

5. **Dora Inouye,** '84, *Mayor of Seattle, Seattle, WA*

6. **Gerri Vans,** '83, *Talk Show Host, Media Mogul, New York, NY*

7. **Rita Tavenner,** '79, *Architect, President of Tavenner Associates (Merck Building, American Express Building), Chicago, IL*

8. **Robyn Jackson,** *'68, President of Madison Capital, New York, NY*

9. **Barbara Darby,** *'64, bestselling novelist* (Kiss Me, Kill Me, *etc.*), *Augusta, GA*

10. **Teresa Anderson,** *'57, retired after 40 years as a first-grade teacher, Madison, WI*

I'd left off another dozen women who could have just as easily been on the list. There was Alexandra (Andy) Benson, a 1978 winner, who'd been the saxophonist in Prince's band for over a decade. There was 1990 winner Anne Marie Chu, who headed the Los Alamos National Lab's Infectious Disease Control Computer Simulation Project. There was a 2004 winner, Kate Carlisle, whose Gift of Sight Foundation had made glasses available to thousands upon thousands of people in the developing world. There were big doctors and lawyers and even a winner from the sixties, Marcy Evans, who'd played opposite Sean Connery in a movie called *Hollywood Heartbreak*. And then, of course, there was Helen. I'd only left her off the list because although she was a famous writer, the novelist Barbara Darby had slightly better name recognition.

I wanted to call Helen, not to tell her I'd left her off the list, just to call. I did, and when she didn't answer, I left a message. "If there's any chance you're free tonight, what about finally having our formal Ten Girls to Watch interview?" I said, then offered one more round of apologies for the failed trip.

Even without Helen, I was pleased with the list. So pleased, in fact, that I sent Elliot an e-mail to tell him what a super job I'd done.

All he wrote back was "miss you already."

Robert was the first person I'd ever really dated. Up until the previous morning, he was my first and only toothbrush-time companion. He'd been the only one I'd ever shared a mirror with, my only mutual reflection gazing. It had been freezing the winter night he'd first leaned in to kiss me outside my dorm. We'd been on three polite dates, enjoyable absolutely, but restrained. But once he kissed me, instead of saying good-bye and going inside, I'd clung to him, and we'd stayed in the cold together, walking and talking and walking and talking, holding each other's gloved hands, the street feeling more private than either of our shared rooms. It was like our kissing had whisked aside the curtains we'd each been hiding behind.

"So when did you first like me?" he'd asked, beaming.

I looked at him slyly, as if I weren't going to answer, and then I broke into the same smile he had. "The morning we first went to brunch. You ate your fancy powdered-sugar waffles *so* daintily. After I got home, I told Abigail it was like eating brunch with Little Lord Fauntleroy. She still calls you that."

"I was nervous!" he protested, though his grin didn't fade at all. "You want to know when I first liked you?" he asked eagerly.

I shrugged, playing at being all cool again, but I could only keep up the act for about half a second. "Of course!" I said.

"First week of freshman year. I saw you across the dining hall. You were carrying this whole tray full of sodas—it looked like you were going to spill them all any minute, but you didn't and then you sat down and passed them around to everyone at your table. I signed up for that shift at the shelter just so we'd be volunteering together. I'd been trying to come up with ways to meet you for months." The words rushed out giddily, like he was an excited kid who'd been dying to share his secret.

I glowed, hardly noticing the cold anymore. The curtains were up, and there in the spotlights of center stage was this new thing. Us. Just like that, we were a couple.

The weekend with Elliot had been good. It had been great, really. But where that first kiss had illuminated everything between me and Robert, a whole weekend with Elliot hadn't shed any such light. Was Elliot my boyfriend? That seemed a reach. You can trip and fall pretty easily when you're fumbling around in the darkness. I was hoping to avoid bruising here, feeling bruised enough from Robert already. Even though I wanted to grip Elliot's "miss you already" like it was some sort of candle lighting the way to our golden future together, I decided to try to relax. We'd see. This was the way grown-ups did these things—cool, casual, easy come, easy go—wasn't it?

Afternoon turned to evening and Helen hadn't returned my message, and I began to feel a familiar desperate loneliness. The sort of loneliness that paws awkwardly for any sort of relief. Who could I call? What video clips could I watch? What could I do to make this ache go away? I couldn't call or e-mail Elliot. I'd just left him. And he wasn't my boyfriend. I couldn't call Helen. I'd already left my voice mail. I read the *New York Times* online. I watched some episodes of *The Daily Show* on Hulu. I called my mom, who didn't answer. I called my dad, who didn't answer either. I checked for more LawnTalk.com forum questions. I answered a few. The feeling didn't abate.

Finally, I started typing an e-mail to Robert.

In one of the lawn care books I'd checked out from the library, I'd learned something about soil. If you work it too much, you can kill it. Clumps are a sign of active fungi, helpful bacteria, and moisture that allow for chemical binding and nutrient transfer. If you break up all the clumps, if you rake it and turn it and rake it and turn it some more, eventually, instead of a tidy, tended-to plot, you end up with desolate earth. Thoughts of Robert were dirt I'd turned over and over. And now, even with whatever it was with Elliot flitting about in the air, Robert was still the territory my mind turned to in its loneliness. In fact, if anything, Elliot made me think of Robert even more. Robert and Lily. I wanted what I felt between Robert and me to be lifeless. I fantasized that if I turned it over one more time, if I raked my fingers through it, if I rubbed it between my hands into finer and finer grains, at last it would lose its power.

So I wrote an e-mail. I didn't plan to send it. I imagined how pathetic I'd feel if I sent it.

"I hope you and Lily had a great weekend."

That's all. It might as well have said "Please write to me."

I sent it.

After a weekend of Elliot, I shouldn't have needed it, but I waited another hour, then took a sleeping pill and fell asleep.

Monday morning, Robert still hadn't responded, and I was delighted to go to work, a place where I'd have plenty of other things to think about. On my way to the archives, I dropped a box in the mail for Helen—here was hoping the scones would still be fresh when they arrived.

Just like that, as if my package had cosmically summoned her, Helen appeared on my caller ID. I answered and asked whether she could give me five minutes, which I figured would be just enough time to hustle to my office, turn on my computer, and strap on my headset. She said five minutes was just fine, and I jogged the rest of the way to the warehouse. One more benefit of no coworkers (other than Ralph): no one to see me arrive at work sweaty and disheveled.

"Helen!" I said when she answered. "Before I ask you any questions, I just have to say one more time how sorry I am about the weekend."

She assured me once again that it would have been great to have me, but I should stop worrying about it. The reading had gone well, and she'd already put a copy of the book in the mail for me. After a few words about the car and its ultimate return to functionality, I steered us toward TGTW, beginning with my standard spiel about the upcoming party, then shifting to questions.

"So here's what I wonder," I began. "In 1972, what did you picture when you envisioned your future? Did it look like your life now? I mean, reading your profile, it sounds like you're going to end up running Greenpeace. Are you surprised that you became an academic?"

"This is going to sound a little grand," she said, "but I feel like winning the *Charm* contest changed what I imagined for myself. It really was a big deal. This national magazine, picking *me*. And meeting Betty Friedan was huge. When I was in college, if you wanted to change the world, marching and organizing was the first thing you thought of. But Betty Friedan changed the world with a book, and meeting her, seeing that she was a real person—I don't know. It realigned my thinking. I had always liked research and writing more than I liked marching, and thinking that I could make a difference through research and writing . . . that changed my direction. Actually, right after the contest, I got it in my head that I wanted to move to New York."

"Wait, I thought you stayed in Boston for grad school."

"I did. But I had this vision, and I'm not sure what I thought I'd do, but it wasn't becoming a university professor. I thought I'd be a *New York Times* columnist or something."

"Did you ever think about moving here and trying it?" I asked, surprised. This was the first I'd ever heard of anything even close to an unrealized dream in Helen's life.

"Well, I applied to history PhD programs in New York, but NYU and Columbia didn't take me. That's the real truth, I guess! And at Harvard, I kept up my bookish ways and got lost in history instead of current events, and there you go. So I think I actually had a much more glamorous vision of where I was going to be now when I thought about it back in 1972."

"That's so funny, since I think of you as pretty much the most glamorous person I know."

She laughed, then sighed.

I wondered whether maybe I shouldn't ask, but then I went ahead and did anyway. "Helen, I just wanted to make sure everything is okay with you. I've been worried. Not for any real reason. Just, I don't know . . ."

I heard her exhale.

"Dawn, that's really sweet of you. I'm fine. But you're right, I may have been a little . . . off." This next part she hurried through, like if she just said it fast enough, it would almost be as if she'd never spoken the words at all. "Paul and I have decided to separate. Just for the time being. But yes, I'm sorry if I've been preoccupied."

"Oh no, you haven't been preoccupied," I fumbled, trying to say the right thing. "Don't apologize. I was just worried."

Neither of us said anything for a second.

"I'm sorry," I finally said.

"Thank you," she said.

"Maybe I could come up for another weekend. And this time actually make it."

"Oh, don't worry. The Ten Girls to Watch party is happening soon enough and then I'll see you in New York." The vulnerability in her voice was gone. There had been just that streak of a shaking moment, but it had hurtled by and already Helen had steadied the table.

I could have asked her plenty more interview questions, and I could have asked her questions about Paul and how she was doing, I guess. But it felt like both those portions of our call were over.

"Well, I'll be thinking about you, just so you know." I cringed a bit as I said it. It was so little to offer.

Helen's voice vibrated with surprising emotion. "Thank you, Dawn. That actually means a lot to me."

After we said good-bye, I felt suddenly fidgety. It took a few minutes of straightening up my desk and tapping my pencil mindlessly on the arm of my chair before I snapped out of it and e-mailed my list of ten women to Regina and XADI.

While waiting for Regina's and XADI's replies, I began a

new line of investigation. During our loll about on Sunday morning, Elliot had seen fit to pass along some info from a piece he wrote for *Grid* about identity theft. Straight googling would get me nowhere. I needed Zabasearch.com. It was where all baby thieves started, he said, so I should see what it could do for me. I started typing the names of some of the women who had heretofore eluded me into the Zabasearch database. Within three minutes I had four numbers to try for Betty Robinson, Pine Manor College '64. And that was just the start of it. I searched away and came up with option after option for my mystery women.

I was vaguely aware that I was Zabasearching instead of thinking about Helen. I mean, I was thinking about her, in terms of sending her positive energy or whatever, but I hadn't really let her news sink in yet. I'd never known much about her and Paul. I knew he was an architect, that they'd been together for twenty-something years, that at dinner parties he told funny stories about clients and always had something to say about the new biography he was reading. I knew they liked to cook dinner together. They'd always seemed solid enough. But what did I know, really? I hoped she had someone else she was talking to. I was sure she did, I just wished I knew something more I could say or do. I said a little prayer for her. And then for him too. Though the prayer for her was bigger.

———————

By noon, Regina had replied with the list of winners she wanted highlighted in the magazine: everyone on my list. XADI came back with the basic format for the fiftieth anniversary article, a massive timeline of the past fifty years interweaving key dates in women's history with details about the contest and various winners. She gave a short sampling of the sort of women's landmarks she thought should be included:

TEN GIRLS TO WATCH ■ *229*

- 1960—the first FDA-approved birth control pills
- 1963—first woman in space
- 1972—Title IX bans discrimination against women in education programs and activities
- 1972—first female CEO of a Fortune 500 company
- 1975—Supreme Court rules that women can no longer be excluded from juries based on sex
- 1981—first female Supreme Court justice
- 1984—first year more women than men received bachelor degrees
- 1997—the debut of the WNBA
- 1997—census data shows women own one-quarter of all US businesses
- 2001—first year more women than men entered law school

She'd work with the photo department to pull images from the magazine archives. For now, she was leaving the actual writing and all the TGTW history to me. But getting the magazine copy in order was just the start.

I still needed to find as many of the remaining women as possible—and there were still plenty of them to find—both for "fun fact" purposes and to fill them in on the event. Plus, there was the small matter of selecting this year's new winners.

Shortly after XADI's first e-mail, outlining my assignments for the anniversary copy, she sent over this note:

> dawn, we need to select this year's ten girls to watch. i am messengering over the applications. please narrow the field down to fifty and messenger those back as soon as possible. XADI

Within the hour, Ralph hulloed from the hallway outside my door and began dollying box after box into my office, lining them up on both sides of my desk, creating a sort of cardboard pathway for me to navigate. I opened the first box. It must have had a hundred applications in it. By the time Ralph was done, I counted eleven boxes.

"Good luck," he said, with the sort of intonation that implied "You're gonna need it."

The very first application I pulled from the box was from a nursing student who'd lost 117 pounds, become a personal trainer, and launched an online fitness video company. She was the first in my "maybe" pile.

Over the coming weeks, sunset came earlier and I stayed at work later and later. First my departures crept to seven o'clock, then eight, then nine. Soon, the only real interaction I had with daylight was during my morning walk to the subway. Thanks to my new Zabasearch sleuthing method, I found and spoke with more winners every day. I also worked away at pulling snippets from old issues and tallying TGTW trivia: eight winners from military academies; eleven winners from Juilliard; twenty-seven winners from Harvard; 18 percent of the winners (that we'd found so far) had gone on to law school. XADI pored through it all and asked for more. When I wasn't doing all that, I read through applications.

I didn't have time to write postinterview profiles during my hours at work anymore, but I found myself wanting to write them in the evenings at home. For the first time in months, I fired up my laptop for something other than Facebook, YouTube, or Lawn Talk.

One of the women I couldn't stop thinking about was a lawyer specializing in divorce mediation, Alexandra Guerrero, though I'd expected my Google search to turn up something else entirely. Her profile in the magazine had been all about theater. I'd imagined playbills or an IMDb listing.

On the phone I'd started carefully, not wanting to hit the wrong notes in case Alexandra had been disappointed by acting and playwriting and turned to lawyering as a sort of sad last resort.

"So you're a lawyer! Sounds like you have a really interesting area of practice," I said enthusiastically, skirting the acting issue altogether.

"I'm sure you expected an actress, right?" She laughed. "Oh my God, was that ever ages ago!" She sure didn't sound disappointed. Though maybe that was still the actress at work?

"So, did you go to law school right after college?" I asked. If there was a story to the end of the theater dreams, that nudge seemed gentle enough for her to either indulge or ignore, her choice.

"Hardly!" she said. "After college I did what everyone expected me to do. I moved to New York and auditioned like mad. I did it for . . . well, it was about four years. Oh my God, I can't believe I did it that long. I remember my last audition. It was for a gum commercial. I had to pop bubbles and shimmy, and it was me in a line with a bunch of other girls who looked just like me, all popping away and shaking our chests. And that was it. I'd had it."

Turned out, the law wasn't a bummer of any sort for Alexandra. After the acting stint, she'd gone on to Stanford. "And now," she crowed, "I'm one of the happiest lawyers around!" Before I could start reconsidering the legal profession myself, Alex added, "But I'm glad I didn't go right out of college. If I hadn't had those years of trying to make it as an actress first, I would have always wondered."

"Do you miss acting?" I asked. "Was it hard to give up?"

She didn't have to think about it for even a second. "It's funny to say it, but even though giving up on acting was giving up on a dream, on a certain level it was also such a huge relief to let it go. I realized along the way that there was more to me than 'Alex the Actress,' and walking away from acting was like walking away from a chokehold. All these other parts of me could finally breathe."

She and her husband had three children. He was a furniture maker, but he'd put it on hold until their children were older. For now, he was a full-time dad while she practiced family law, with a focus on mediated divorce.

"Most people think being a divorce lawyer must be depressing, but I'll tell you two things about divorce," she said. "The first is that I feel like what I do makes a real difference, supporting people in what can be one of the worst times of their lives. The second is that families come in all shapes and cope in all sorts of ways, and sometimes there is nothing like a divorce to liberate everyone. Parents and kids, they lose this dream of the perfect family, but sometimes—not always, definitely not always—but sometimes it finally clears out the junk and lets people be who they ought to be."

In my apartment, my laptop open in front of me, I wrote about Alexandra and the surprise career she'd found in divorce mediation, but while I was typing I was thinking about Helen, wondering why the news of her separation had shaken me like it did. It was more than just sympathy and concern. Truth be told, I'd started counting on Helen in ways I'd stopped counting on my parents. I didn't look to them as role models anymore. Whenever I thought about them, I thought about how things had a way of falling apart—not exactly an inspiring conclusion—so I looked to Helen instead. Even though she was this glamorous intellectual now, I knew she'd started from a place awfully similar to mine, and she'd made her whole life happen. Usually, when I thought of her, it was like I was whispering to myself, *You can do it too.* But now? Now it seemed maybe things fell apart for everyone, no matter how smart you were or how hard you worked, no matter how far away you got from Milldale, Oregon.

With Helen's news, I felt like the kids in the families Alexandra described, losing this dream of perfection. But maybe the rest of what Alexandra said was true too. Maybe Helen's divorce was going to free her to be who she ought to be. I remembered the time she'd asked whether I liked who I was with Robert. Maybe Helen was going to like herself a lot better without Paul. I couldn't really imagine her being any more incredible, but maybe *she* could imagine it. Maybe in her inner world, she was clamoring to breathe free. I made a mental note: introduce Alexandra and Helen at the party. She probably already had a divorce lawyer, but knowing a good mediator never hurt.

A few days later I interviewed another woman I couldn't leave at the office, Candace Chan, a 1986 winner who'd debuted as a cello soloist with the Cincinnati Symphony at sixteen and gone on to be the star of Princeton's biology department. Now, she was an assistant professor of Molecular and Cellular Biology at Stanford, specializing in membrane-associated cell biological processes. None of that was why I couldn't stop thinking about her, though. The reason came after all the talk about the long haul she'd been on—six years for her PhD, four for her postdoc research, and though she was now in a tenure-track position, tenure itself was still a hurdle to leap—when she turned the conversation to her daughter, Ana, who'd just turned twelve.

"I can't believe I'm telling you this"—her voice shifted, emotion lifting her tone a touch—"but Ana is doing so well with her new stepdad. I'm so proud of her. Her father and I met during college, and we went all the way through our PhDs together. Life was just so intense for so many years, it wasn't until Ana was in school and we were both professors that we even came up for air and realized something was missing. More than something. Almost everything. I actually didn't realize it until I started playing the cello again. I'm a very analytical person, except when it comes to music—it's really always been this tool for me to access my emotions—and when I got back to playing, I started to feel how unhappy I really was. I thought maybe if I changed instruments it'd help. So I decided to learn the mandolin, and it helped, just not the way I figured it would. That's how I met Len. He's in a bluegrass band. He's also a lawyer for HP, but we met at a concert. Eric and I were still together, but with Len the world opened up. Everything sounded like music."

She paused for the first time. "Telling Eric was hard," she finally continued, "but telling Ana, knowing I was the one who made her cry like that, it was devastating. But it's been a few years now, and it still feels like I finally just opened the windows and let life in. And I think Ana can finally see that too. What kind of cheater says she's happy she set that kind of example for her daughter? But it's weirdly true. I want her to see that life is full of happiness if she's willing to risk it."

In some ways, her story reminded me of Stephanie Linwood, her reminder that life is long and you can't just look at one moment and judge your life based on that snapshot. If you'd looked at Candace with her first husband, things might have looked good. If you'd looked at her when she was having an affair, it might have all looked bad. But if you looked at the whole thing, a stretch of many years, you saw something else, a woman and a family emerging happier and more fulfilled. Sitting on my bed with my laptop on my knees, I realized that I'd pretty much been treating my parents as if their stories were encapsulated in a single snapshot, as if they were forever locked in place as the unhappy people they'd been when I was in high school. I needed to stop doing that. In the last seven years, I'd gone from being a kid who couldn't drive to being a college graduate who paid her own bills. It seemed quite possible that they'd changed a little too.

A thunderstorm had arrived in Brooklyn. I listened to the rain pummeling my window while rereading the profile I'd just written for Candace. Then I called my mom.

"Hey, sweetie!" she said. "It's late where you are!"

I told her I was still up working, and then I answered every single one of the million questions she asked. Usually, it wasn't all that long before I felt a little tired of describing, again, exactly what my office looked like or what I was wearing that day or recounting verbatim a conversation I'd had. But tonight, her rapt attention felt supportive and caring, not suffocating.

"So how many identical cardigans would you say he has?" My mom laughed, cherishing this detail about Ralph's wardrobe.

"I think I've seen it in five different colors so far, but who knows, there could be dozens more in his collection."

I asked her about all the latest at Mary Kay (they had a really exciting new lipstick/lip gloss hybrid that was supposed to be shiny but not sticky), and all the news in the extended family. (One of my cousins was having twins, just like Sarah. "You better watch out," she said. "You probably have the twin gene too." Impressive how she was always able to work in her hopes for my future child-bearing somehow . . .) Then, feigning a casual air, I asked if she'd been on any dates lately, a topic well outside our usual areas of discussion.

"Oh, there's no one around here!" she clipped.

"Did I tell you someone signed me up for TheOne?"

"You didn't!" she said, as if I'd just admitted to something truly outrageous, like streaking through Times Square or sneaking out of a restaurant with salt and pepper shakers in my purse.

I told her all about Elliot, though I left out his age and prior marital status and the part about us sharing a hotel room. Then I said, "You know what I think? I think I should sign you up!"

She clucked, a don't-be-silly sound. "I can't imagine there'd be enough people around here to even put together a single party."

"You might have to go up to Eugene for the party," I mused. "I don't know. But I'm sure TheOne has something. What do you say?"

"Let me think about it. I'm not saying no. Just, I'll get back to you," she wheedled.

As a family schooled in the passive arts, the Wests excelled in I'll-get-back-to-you avoidance tactics.

"Yeah, right!" I laughed. "I'm not letting this go that easy."

"Fine, fine!" she said, laughing too. "I'm serious. Just let me think about it for a little while."

"Okay. Take your time," I said.

She then asked me about Abigail and how she was doing. Last I'd heard, things were still humming along nicely with the birdsong guy, and the intestinal parasites seemed to have quieted themselves if not entirely moved on. My mom was glad to hear it.

After we said good-bye, I almost logged on to TheOne right then and there to create her profile. But I'd wait. I had a feeling after I gave her a little "time to think about it" she just might come around all on her own.

I fell asleep that night to the sound of the rain, pummeling away, and my mom's "I love you" still lingering in my ears.

The next week, I brought home yet another profile to work on. Allison Katz, a 1997 winner who at age twenty had already explored more previously unexplored miles of cave than any other US caver under thirty. She'd also become a professional photographer as a teenager, with photos she'd taken of rare cave rock formations in *National Geographic, Outdoors*, and a handful of other magazines.

She had just finished her PhD in geology at Cornell a few months earlier. I tracked her down in Mexico completing a postdoc fellowship at the University of Mexico City, researching the Yucatán's massive flooded caves. We talked for a while about Mexico, how great the food was, then somehow we got onto the subject of geology jokes—*Igneous is bliss; Sedimentary, my dear Watson, sedimentary.*

Finally, I asked her the obvious: "Isn't it scary? I'm sure you're used to it now, but was it ever terrifying to squeeze into all those dark, unknown spaces, or you're just . . ." I trailed off. "I dunno, fearless?"

She laughed. "I hate horror movies. Like if I watch one, I think there's something on the other side of the shower curtain for days, so, no, I'm not fearless. I just got started caving young. My grandpa died in a mine collapse, and I think my daddy didn't want me to grow up afraid of anything. So he took me hiking in caves starting forever ago."

I asked her what it had been like, caving with her father.

"I remember the first time I ever pushed through into new area," she said. "As in no map, and absolutely no one has ever been past this point before—and then there I was, my light shining into a whole new passage, my daddy yelling from the other side of the tiny space I squeezed through, telling me to describe what I saw. There's no bigger rush."

"It must be amazing to be able to call yourself an explorer," I said. "I mean, how many people can say that about themselves and mean it literally?"

Instead of laughing it off as a compliment, she answered back seriously. "I've actually thought a lot about this. Some people are creators. That's their thrill. I've got a quieter streak. I just want to uncover what's there, I just want to marvel at what's beneath my feet, this whole time it's been there, just waiting for me to find it. That's me. I think a lot of times people think explorers are the wild and crazy ones, but I don't think so. We're actually more reserved. We just want to find things and treasure them."

I'd never made a distinction between creating and exploring before, but now it made me think of my own writing. Which kind of person was I? I felt like these profiles and all the work I was doing on Ten Girls to Watch was something closer to exploring. There were these women out there with amazing stories. All I had to do was find them. In some ways, that's what Helen had been urging me to do with my own personal writing as well—find the truth and tell it. TGTW was a pleasure—really it was—I loved what I was doing. But it didn't feel quite the same as writing fiction.

When I wrote stories in college, sometimes I'd wake up in the middle of the night with a perfectly formed phrase in my head. I'd be walking down the street, not even really thinking about a story, and an idea for a scene would come to me. There was a magic feeling to it all. That didn't happen with the profiles I was writing now.

When Allison said she had a quieter streak, I'd instinctually nodded and thought, *me too*. After all, no one in the West family ever yelled, just silently seethed, and whereas Robert was the sort to noisily share his thoughts on things like the proper angle to hold one's head while conversing, I was more likely to keep such opinions to myself. But maybe these weren't the right comparisons. Maybe I had a loud streak, and I'd just never realized it. At night, when I couldn't fall asleep, behind my closed eyes I'd spin fantasies, and they usually circled back to a vision of myself with gray hair and a floppy hat, coming in after an afternoon of gardening in the yard to a bookshelf lined with books I'd written. I'd never thought about it until now, but that fantasy shelf wasn't full of journalistic nonfiction. Those books were novels. My novels. Maybe my loud streak translated to this: I didn't want to find other people's treasure. I wasn't going to follow in Helen's footsteps. I was happy to tell other people's stories sometimes, but in the end, I wanted a story that was mine. Even writing a true story about myself wouldn't cut it—I'd have to account for the people who'd shared the experience with me. If you make it up, though, it's all yours. Maybe I was an explorer for now. But what I really wanted, someday, was to be a creator.

After I finished with Allison's profile I took my copy of *Must We Find Meaning?* from my cardboard nightstand and pulled out Helen's card from inside the pages.

"D, I believe in you, and what makes me really happy is I think you're starting to believe in you too. Love, H."

I thought about Helen's advice to turn my short story into nonfiction. Maybe part of believing in myself was trusting my gut and *not* following her suggestion. That night, for the first time in more than a year, I opened the Sound of Music file on my laptop and started revising. I didn't conduct any interviews or call a soul to fact-check anything. I just wrote and wrote. Not that I made a lot of progress, a couple of paragraphs maybe, but they were mine—all mine—and finally, I was writing again.

———

During these weeks of hard work, neither Robert nor I ever acknowledged my pitiful e-mail, but throughout the days I occasionally sent Elliot funny tidbits about winners I'd talked to or links to events I thought sounded interesting and notes that said things like "Thought I might check this out. Care to join?" He almost always replied hours later via text message, reply being a loose description for his brief missives, which never directly addressed my attempts at making plans: "Hey there." "Hello you." "Guess who I'm thinking about . . ." "Paging Ms. West. Ms. West to the stage." When he did actually e-mail, it was things like a link to the song "Secret Agent Man." In the subject line. Body of the e-mail blank.

While Elliot's electronic communication skills were somewhat lacking, he continued to please in person. After my first crazy week, he made me Saturday brunch. Lovely, non-takeout huevos rancheros at his dining room table. The next week he took me out to a rooster-themed Peruvian place in Boerum Hill, pan flutes and salsa music alternating over the speakers as he introduced me to ceviche. He told me about accidentally dropping his keys down a subway grate outside his first New York apartment, then miraculously fishing them out with a wire clothes hanger. I told him about the odd jobs of my teenage years (bumper car attendant, ice cream scooper, janitor). He told me about his brother's years in and out of rehab. I told him about Sarah's twins. When we were together in public, we started holding hands. I didn't send any more e-mails to Robert (though I still spent far too much time agonizingly imagining him frolicking around the city with Lily).

One night, Elliot invited me over to his place and cooked dinner for me. He poured the olive oil with dramatic flair and stirred the sautéing onions and garlic not with a spatula but with a flick of the pan that tossed them through the air, an ironic show-offy smile on his lips the whole time. When he was done, he plated the mushroom fettucini, adding pretty sprigs of parsley. At the dining room table, we both tucked into the delicious pasta, and he started telling me about an article he was working on, an investigative piece on bat flu versus bird flu. In the middle of talking, he stopped and put his fork down, his face suddenly stricken.

"What's wrong?" I asked anxiously. Had I said something? Had I *not* said something?

Sighing, he answered, "Do you ever worry that things just aren't going to work out? I mean, I had these big dreams. Famous writer: Elliot Kaslowski. The more time passes the more I'm sure that's not happening, and if that's not happening, what else isn't happening?"

"Are you kidding me?" I said. "I worry about that all the time. I have this perfect vision of me alone at age fifty-five, selling Mary Kay, which is so mean to say, because that's what my mom does and that's like saying she's a failure, but she actually really likes it! And she's really good at it. And she has kids! But when I picture it, it's just me, all alone with boxes and boxes of antiaging serum, and then I start hyperventilating."

"I see this big billboard flashing FAILURE," he said. "And I'm from Nevada, so when I say flashing, I'm talking megawatts."

The few times I'd ever tried to describe what a looming fear of failure felt like to Robert, he'd had no idea what I was talking about. "But that's crazy," he'd say. Or even more helpfully, "Just don't think that." Elliot, on the other hand, seemed to understand this deep part of me.

We finished our pasta and the bottle of wine we'd been working on and then we retired to the couch, and my chin got rawer and rawer with more stubbly kissing, and when we pulled back and looked at each other, I wanted to tell him I loved him. I didn't love him, not yet, and even if I did (which I didn't), it would have been too soon to say anyway. I still wasn't even sure we were really a couple. With Robert, I'd known it right away: curtain up, lights on, actors on the stage. With Elliot, I could tell we were in a theater and the overture was playing faintly—but those stage curtains were still tightly drawn. There was a chance I would never see behind them. Maybe there was nothing behind them at all. Still, the pesky words clomped loudly in my brain, like little rebels trying to defy my gag order by making so much noise that Elliot would hear them through my skull. I missed saying those words. More than that, I missed saying them and meaning them.

We never got around to doing the dishes that night. But who cared if they sat overnight? Before bed, Elliot took out his iPhone and replied to a bunch of e-mails. But who cared if he never answered mine? Answer to both questions: Dawn West, but then Elliot pulled my hair aside and gently, gently kissed my ear . . . and I certainly didn't care right then.

Candace Chan,

Princeton University, 1986

THE MUSICIAN

Candace debuted with the Cincinnati Symphony Orchestra at 16 and has been a working cello soloist ever since. Now a double major in biology and chemistry, she represents the undergraduate community on the university science council. While she spends more hours in the lab than the practice room these days, she still finds time to perform with the Princeton University orchestra. "I come alive when I'm playing," she says. "Music is what keeps me in balance and gives me perspective. Without it, nothing else in my life seems to make sense."

Chapter Thirteen

With the arrival of November, I reached a predictable challenge in the Kelly Burns calendar, which I had nonetheless failed to foresee: the end of lawn care season. Sure, I still got a few questions from eager souls curious about when to stop mowing for the winter or from procrastinators who wondered whether it was too late for a fall fertilizer application. But their traffic was but a sorry little trickle. Why did I only seem to attract readers in cold-weather climates? Where were the Floridians when you needed them?

Unfortunately, the November chill also coincided with a fascinating vanishing act on the part of my roommate. I would have worried about her, except there were signs of Sylvia all over the apartment—dirty dishes in the sink, celebrity photo-stalking magazines on the floor by the couch, the double-fast diminishment of my shampoo—yet she never seemed to be in the apartment when I came home from work. In the mornings her door stayed closed and a steady silence poured from under the crack. Weekends were even weirder—no sign of her at all. Maybe Rodney was back from Toledo and she was shacking up at his place? Who knew. But what I did know was that she needed to pay her part of the rent.

I started with a nice note on the fridge, tacked in place with a pineapple magnet (a goodwill gesture, the pineapple being the universal symbol of hospitality and all):

I don't know how we keep missing each other! I hope every-thing's going well with the job search! Just a quick reminder that I have to send in our rent check tomorrow, so if you could just leave a check for your part on the table, I'll be sure to get it. Thanks!

No check appeared. Though several of my grapefruits disappeared. I went ahead and sent in the entirety of our rent on time, scrupu-lous tenant that I am, which slimmed my bank account to double digits until my next paycheck. I considered another note, but my sister, in a rare spare moment, had recently e-mailed me a link to a favorite new blog of hers, passiveaggressivenotes.com. Her fav pick:

Hay ladies,
(particularly Jaime . . . you know who you are) Last night, as Ames knows, I was *extremely* drunk. Yet I still washed my shot glasses and put them away. I happen 2 know some of u are mormons so you aren't drunk when cooking. So the mess you so often leave in the kitchen is just inexcuseable. Please, rep the amazing strong young women that you are and clean up. Lots of love, Pamela.

With this reminder that roommate notes are a dangerous game, I decided further missives of this sort should be avoided. And so, the morning of November 6—six days, I waited six days!—I held off until nine o'clock, then knocked gingerly on Sylvia's door. No response. I knocked louder. And then a little louder.

She cracked her door open and leaned out, her hair in a matted mess and her eyes only half open.

"Hey," she said.

"I'm so sorry to wake you up," I said in my hangover-friendliest quiet voice. "I just wanted to see if there's any chance I could get you to write me a rent check."

"Oh yeah, sorry, sorry," she said, opening her door a bit more and shuffling over to her desk. She pulled out a checkbook, and a minute later I was on my way with her $950 check in my pocket.

I continued on my merry way to work, feeling quite proud of my direct approach and its great success. This sense of accomplishment expired exactly three days later, when Sylvia's check bounced.

November heralded another change too: Elliot landed a few big article assignments. In addition to his *Charm* column, he was writing a piece for *Grid* on the future of brain chip implants and a piece for the *Atavist* on a scientist and an industrial designer who had teamed up to try to build an underwater air-filled terrarium that could sustain human life.

I imagined the editors at *Charm* and *Grid* receiving doting five-word e-mails and texts from Elliot. Someone had to be, and it wasn't me. At least before when he'd ignored e-mails, we'd seen each other in person, which more than made up for it. Now we turned into something that looked less like a romantic relationship and more like voice mail pals.

"Dawn West, I miss you," his message would say. I'd listen on my way out of work at eight or nine o'clock. He worked late and turned his phone off so he could concentrate, so he claimed, so when I called back his voice mail answered, and I'd say things like "Elliot Kaslowski, are you eating fettucini without me?" I wondered why he didn't come by after he finished writing for the day. Or why he didn't ask me to come over and read in a corner while he worked. In college, Robert and I were never apart for long, even during finals we had studied across the table from each other in the library. "Let me know if you want me to come over and keep you company" was as far as my voice mails ever went in asking for such an arrangement. Days went by and he never "let me know."

Meanwhile, I was as busy as ever in my basement. XADI and I finally filed the magazine copy. Next step, the TGTW video. Regina looked at a draft treatment XADI had put together, jotted a few notes, and passed it back to XADI. The major theme of her notes: Scrap the treatment. If the film was to be a show-stopper at the gala and a hit on the website thereafter, we'd need in-depth, in-person interviews with each of the ten women we'd chosen to highlight. Since it wasn't feasible to send XADI on the road for any duration without large sections of the magazine falling apart, she'd stay put and cover the New York crowd—Robyn Jackson, Gerri Vans, Rachel Link, Jessica Winston—while I'd travel with the film crew and their cameras to interview the rest: Dora Inouye, Rebecca Karimi, Rita Tavenner, Cindy Tollan, Teresa Anderson, Barbara Darby. A business trip! The very idea of it made me giddy.

While I worked out a trip itinerary and set up filming dates with each of the women, the events team began to pull together the plans for the gala. Gerri Vans signed on for keynoting. They booked the Morgan Library, a museum in the East Thirties that housed J. P. Morgan's art and book collections and which had just been updated with a soaring glass gallery between the old and new wings. The space was stunning, but it also fused historic and contemporary architecture in a way that felt just perfect for our gathering.

I forged ahead with my reviews of this year's TGTW applications too. I was still several boxes away from the finish line, and the files looked like confetti thrown around my office, with various degrees of "maybes" sprinkled all over the floor. I couldn't believe the women I was putting in the "no" pile. Volunteering at a school for girls in Mali? Meh. Did you also found the school? Oh, you were a basketball star at your university? Was the WNBA talking about drafting you? A gene therapy discovery? How big a gene therapy discovery? What was obvious from my brutal culling was that I never would have stood a chance in this competition. Though I suppose that thought could have made me feel bad, it didn't. Strangely, I felt something closer to relief. I wasn't in college anymore. I wasn't even in my first year out of college anymore. I was in a different category from these girls. Reading about all their undergraduate accomplishments, I felt . . . older. I liked the feeling.

I started staying at the archives later and later every night, partly because I was busy and excited for the work, but also partly because I didn't want to go home. With Elliot's deadlines and ensuing silence, the nights just seemed so long. Late one Thursday evening, I finally finished reviewing the last box of TGTW applications, having winnowed the field from 1,211 hopefuls to the fifty XADI had asked for. As my final yes, I tossed in the application of an MIT student who had invented a portable and affordable disaster relief shelter, complete with a self-contained water supply, electricity, and an air filter, which was now being manufactured by a company in Denmark. She was also president of the MIT undergraduate association and the director of a science-focused after-school program for low-income children. I was switching out of my heels and into my sneakers (who I thought would be impressed by my heels down in the basement was unclear) when my phone rang. "S.A.R.," said the caller ID.

"Hi, Elliot." My voice sounded leery—it had been a full week since we'd actually talked—but he didn't seem to notice.

"Hey there."

"Are you home?" he said.

I told him I was heading that way, and he said, "Don't go home. Come over to my house instead."

"It's so late," I said. Had I been imagining the slow fade of Dawn and Elliot? Had it really only been a matter of collective busyness?

"But I have a surprise," he said.

Walking up the stairs to his apartment, I smelled popcorn. When he opened the door, the whole room was dark except for the lamp beside the bed.

"Is the popcorn the surprise?" I said.

"Nooooo." He pulled me toward the bed until he fell back onto it, pulling me down with him. He rolled me over and took off my coat and scarf, kissed me quickly, then said, "I got a book deal today."

"What? I had no idea you were even working on a book," I stammered, then said, "Congratulations!"

He smiled, stood up, and brought over the popcorn. "It's a collection of short stories."

"You write fiction? Is not telling me this stuff part of some weird Secret Agent complex?" I socked him in the arm.

"It's a new thing for me. I didn't really want to tell anyone unless it was real. And now it's real." His eyes were almost manically wide and bright.

"Are you going to let me read them?" I said.

"Not right now. You're busy right now," he said, kissing me.

"What a clever distraction," I said, kissing him back. I unbuttoned his shirt and kissed his neck, then his shoulders, then moved down to his chest. I kept my face pressed against his curly chest hair, surprised that for a flash of a moment I thought I might cry. I hadn't written anything in months and months, other than TGTW profiles and my one night with the Sound of Music story. This despite the fact that Helen's new book had arrived, and that I'd read it, and that I'd meant to work on my own stories the second I finished it. This despite the fact that she'd written "Can't wait for your book! Love, Helen" on the inside cover. This despite the fact that being a writer was supposed to be my reason for living. Didn't Elliot know, this was *my* dream? *I* wanted to call someone and tell him *my* stories were being published. If I'd dared say so aloud, I was sure he'd tell me to just wait, I was still so young. But I didn't want to hear about how young I was.

I pulled Elliot down so he was lying next to me on the bed. "Remember how uncomfortable that bed at the Black Swan Inn was?" I said. We laughed, we tumbled along, soon it was just his body pressed against mine, my whole body pretending I wasn't jealous.

I woke up the next morning in Elliot's bed, the first time I'd spent the night there in weeks. The clock said 6:16, and when I couldn't fall back asleep I sat up. It was only a minute or two before Elliot roused and nuzzled me with his head.

"Morning," he said, barely opening his eyes. Then he yawned and said, "Did I tell you I'm going home this week?"

"You didn't," I said, nuzzling him back, in part to cover my surprise.

"I decided to bump up my Thanksgiving ticket," he said.

I asked when he was leaving, and he said, "Actually, I think I leave tomorrow."

I gave him a wide-eyed look, and he said, "I've got to write. And I think better out there." In what was supposed to be a feather-deruffling offering, he added, "I'll be back the first week of December."

December?! I screamed in my head, amazed that he was heading to Nevada for two weeks and hadn't thought to mention it. I wasn't going home for the holiday. Tickets were stupidly expensive, and since I didn't get paid vacation days, every day off was money forfeited. I was hitting the road to interview TGTW winners of yesteryear right after Thanksgiving, so add that to Elliot's surprise time away, and I'd probably never see him again. But that was all inside. Out loud I said, "That'll be great for you to have a solid chunk of time out there."

I tried to imagine that we'd call and e-mail, and everything would be fine. Reality on the telecommunications front was that Elliot's phone was now sometimes off for days at a time. Voice mail pals didn't work one-way. Then it wasn't voice mail pals, it was just me, marooned on a desert island, throwing message bottles into the waves and watching the stupid bottles wash right back up onshore. The answer was to stop tiring out my arm with all the pointless throwing. I was going to wait for him to contact me. He needed to be the one hurling messages for once.

That night, after a day spent nonstop calling and e-mailing TGTW winners, all so I wouldn't dwell on Elliot, I took two steps through the door of my apartment and smelled something off. Swiveling my nostrils toward the living room, I immediately identified the source: Sylvia, draped all over the sofa. I hadn't seen her since the morning she wrote her check. In fact, I now realized I hadn't seen any of the usual roommate debris around the house, which meant she may well have not left her room for days.

But Sylvia was clearly out now, complete with body odor and the sickly sweet smell of dried sweat and unwashed sheets. Her hair was past greasy to the ratty, matted stage that takes a lot of work for white girls. And then there were the clothes. Rodney's NASCAR boxer shorts (I'd seen him wearing them on a morning I still try to forget, since they didn't quite contain all of him) and a yellowing Old Navy T-shirt all stretched out at the collar. The television, tuned to a juicer infomercial, murmured indistinctly in the background. I watched while she picked up a pint of ice cream from the coffee table, dipped her fingers in, and completely sans utensils scooped out a mouthful.

I put my bag down and asked if she was okay.

"Fine," she said, wiping away tears. She was past the point where they were a fresh spring. They were an old river that had been running steady for what had obviously been some time. And thus began the roommate intervention.

Rodney was an A-hole. There was some girl in Toledo. She hadn't slept in days or showered or changed clothes, or, I detected as I pulled up a chair next to her, undertaken any sort of dental hygiene. She was broke (sadly, I already knew this—after the first check bounced she'd written me another one, which hadn't gone through either). She'd quit her job, and she was too depressed to even get out of bed. How was she going to find another one? What was she going to do?

I said a shower was always a good place to start, went and turned on the water, then returned, took her arm, and led her to the bathroom. "Use one of my towels hanging on the back of the door," I said. "The one on the right is clean."

Maybe I should have let Sylvia deal with her own problems. Maybe this was a slippery slope and I should have stopped sliding the second she failed to present her check on time. But clearly, Sylvia was in need. While she showered I turned off the TV, put away the ice cream, and opened the windows to air things out a bit. Next stop, Google. "Free psychotherapy Brooklyn" turned up some surprisingly decent options, as did "temp agencies Manhattan."

"Next on the agenda is real food," I said when she returned to the couch wrapped in my towel, her hair dripping every which way. She wiped away more tears but nodded yes when I suggested Thai.

After another hour or so of talking we finally got around to therapists, temping, and calling her parents. Just for a little help to tide her over . . . and pay her rent so we wouldn't get evicted. After she finally got dressed I helped her change her sheets (a task that taxed my mouth-breathing abilities). I sat outside her door while she called her parents. Then I told her everything was going to be okay, brought her a glass of water, and turned out her lights for the night. After a half hour or so of quiet cleaning, listening to make sure she was all right, I left the apartment with my phone in hand. Maybe I should have called Elliot, or my mom, or Helen, or tried to track down a phone somewhere within a day's walk of Abigail's village. Instead, I called Robert. He was the person I'd called in emergencies for years. It didn't make sense to call him now, it really didn't, but somehow I just couldn't help myself.

Lily answered.

"Dawn! Hi, it's Lily. Why haven't we seen you lately!"

"Oh, hi," I said automatically. "How are you?"

"Great! How are you?"

"Okay," I said, more feebly than intended.

"You want to talk to Robert?" she asked.

"That'd be great," I mumbled.

"Hold on, let me get him."

A few seconds later, Lily was back on the phone.

"Sorry, Dawn. He's in the middle of something. Can he give you a call back in a bit?"

I could picture the exact scene, Robert silently mouthing "Tell her I'm busy."

"No, tell him no worries. I was just calling to say hi."

"Well, don't be a stranger!" Lily said.

"Take care!" I said with as much cheer as I could.

Lily answered Robert's phone now? It was okay, I didn't need to talk to Robert. I knew exactly what he'd say anyway. He'd say call the police if she's suicidal. Otherwise, don't get involved. The last thing you want to do is get involved.

Why would I want to hear that when "involved" was exactly what I already was?

I spent the weekend frantically cruising the Craigslist ETC section looking for gigs where I could, say, dress up on Saturdays as a penguin and hand out frozen yogurt samples or taste four varieties of orange soda and tell the committee which I preferred, all the while feeling incredibly grateful for overdraft protection and aware that I was awfully close to the point where even that couldn't help me.

Monday morning, Sylvia showered, put on pants and a bra (at my timid suggestion), and accompanied me to midtown, where I dropped her at the office of Hunter, Inc., Professional Staffing Services. And then, at last, I went back to the safety of the archives, a nice, insulated basement where no one was crying. At least not at that very moment.

That week at work I scrubbed the address list for invitations and started the process of pulling in archival footage of winners for the video. Every time one of the gals had appeared on the *Today* show, which gave the contest a regular slot for years, we wanted the clip. Every time one of them made the local news, we wanted the clip. We wanted clips from the debut episode of Gerri's talk show, clips from Jane Novey's testimony before the senate on Plan B and women's reproductive rights, clips from Marcy Evans's movie, photos of Robyn Jackson's *Charm* cover, the pencil drawing of her they used whenever she appeared in the *Wall Street Journal*. We wanted it all, and finding it fell to me. To start, I reached out to ABC, CBS, and NBC, then I followed the trail to affiliates around the country.

My work phone was busy, but my cell phone was free as can be—Elliot didn't call. Nor did Robert, who must have still been "in the middle of something."

On the Wednesday before Thanksgiving, Regina came back with her picks for the ten new winners. I'd sent my fifty along to XADI, and she'd sent twenty to Regina, and Regina had made the final selection. XADI sent the briefest of missives: "pls interview each and write profiles for the mag and event program." I'd get to it after the holiday. Elliot still hadn't called. I deleted his number, thinking that would show him.

When one thirty hit—the official close of the half day—I put on my coat and trudged toward the elevators. On the main floor, just as I was about to exit to the lobby, Ralph (in a navy blue cardigan) came from the other direction, as if he'd been monitoring my position on a security camera, just waiting for my arrival. It would have been creepy, except he was holding a pie.

"Happy Thanksgiving," he said, handing the cellophane-wrapped tin to me.

The sudden appearance of this gift made my eyes well up.

"It's pecan," he added, in case all the pecans on top weren't a giveaway.

"Thank you," I said. I thought of hugging him, but I didn't. I just said thank you again and wished him a Happy Thanksgiving too. But even though I'd restrained myself, inside I was overflowing with delight. Ralph had baked me a pie?

Although I'd deleted it, of course I still remembered Elliot's number, and out on the street I opened my phone and texted: "Ralph just gave me a pie."

"What kind?" came his immediate reply. Ah, here was the responsiveness I was looking for.

"Pecan. Rich, gooey pecan," I wrote back. "Any pie for you yet?"

And then I waited, waited, and waited for a reply. The waiting didn't entirely wipe away my feelings of shock and gratitude at Ralph's pie presentation, but it did dull the shine. The next day I got the generic "Happy Thanksgiving" message Elliot sent out to who knew how many people. Disappointing. But what didn't disappoint was the pie. The filling, not too sweet. The pecans, lightly browned so their flavor pushed forward in my mouth. The texture of the nuts, not soggy at all, the perfect resistance, then give, as they splintered with each bite. And then there was the goo. Soft, smooth, brown sugary perfection. Ralph could bake!

Sylvia's parents had graciously paid for her flight home—though they had yet to graciously pay for November's rent. The Wests, minus Dawn, were all in Oregon. Without Ralph's pie, I might have felt pitiful being alone, but with it, I tried to convince myself I felt urban and independent.

When I did call home, my mom rattled off the names of all the cousins who'd driven down to Milldale for the day, and my sister quietly griped about the way Aunt Belinda jumped into the kitchen and started bossing everyone around, as if it were *her* kitchen. For my part, I was grateful that I'd missed Aunt Belinda's Thanksgiving special and that come Monday, I'd be on a flight to California to kick off the interviews for the TGTW video with Rebecca Karimi.

I knew my dad was spending the holiday with his brother, my uncle Larry, and his family in Portland. I was planning to call in the evening, when he'd be back home, but he called me midday.

"Just here with everyone, and we were all talking about the big New Yorker," he said, landing on "big New Yorker" with a don't-get-too-big-for-your-britches sort of inflection.

Apparently, cooking was still under way, but he slipped away to Uncle Larry's study to talk. He'd just finished the latest Theodore Roosevelt biography. "Did you know Theodore Roosevelt was shot point-blank in the chest at a campaign event and he survived because the bullet was blocked by the folded-up text of his speech? Powerful words!" he chortled.

He asked what I'd been reading and I told him about Helen's book and about the interesting history of women's suffrage in Oregon. "Did you know voting rights for women were on the ballot in Oregon six times before they were finally voted in?" I asked. "The first time was 1884, and it didn't pass until 1912. That's forever."

Dad said maybe he'd put Helen's new book on the extra-credit reading list for his Advanced Placement US history students. I could hear his voice switching into wrap-up mode, but before he could end the call I jumped in. "Hey, Dad, have you ever thought about writing a book?"

It was actually something I'd been thinking about for a while, and Helen's book seemed like as good a segue as any. If my parents' stories weren't over yet, maybe the next chapter of my dad's involved an exciting new project. No one loved American history more than he did.

He laughed. "No. I like reading them, not writing them."

"So you say, but I don't know. Coolidge and Hoover both need better biographies!"

"You're right, there." He laughed again. "And what about you?"

I blinked with surprise. He never asked about my writing. "Well, I'm not much further along than you are. But remember that story you told me about Grandma, how when you were a kid she had that one-woman show of *The Sound of Music* and she made you travel around town with her, working the lights and handing her different hats when she needed them?"

"I remember it too well!" he said.

"Not that it's a book, but I'm thinking about trying to write a short story sort of based on that." I'd never actually shown anyone in my family my stories. They knew I'd written some, but they hadn't clamored to get their hands on copies, though, in fairness, it wasn't like I was advertising their availability. Nor had I ever said the words "I want to be a writer" to any of them, including Sarah. But maybe I'd show my dad this one when I was done with it.

"That sounds interesting, honey," he said. Not the most encouraging thing he could have said, but not exactly discouraging either.

"Well, I better let you get back to your kitchen duties," I said.

"That's right," he said.

I spent the rest of the day writing a little and then watching TV shows online, and even though this was a classic lonely-person activity, after my phone calls with my family, I didn't feel as much of a sad solo ache as I'd expected. In fact, after the Sylvia intervention and all my weeks of working, a day off and the apartment to myself felt downright luxurious.

On Friday I put a package in the mail for Helen. Just a goofy Thanksgiving card and a small pumpkin pie I'd baked, but Ralph's pie had made me so happy, it seemed only appropriate to pass along the pie-related good cheer. Overnighting the package turned out to be a little pricey (twenty-seven dollars!), but you had to do what you had to do.

On Saturday a book arrived for me in the mail. *Bachelor Stew and Other Recipes for the Lonely Life,* by Elliot Kaslowski. Even though Elliot had told me not to read it, after he'd left for Nevada I'd finally ordered a copy. I read the first line. "I was twenty-six before I made my first proper meal for myself." Ridiculous. The secret ingredient in bachelor stew was capricious unreliability, and I didn't want to read any more about it.

Helen sent me a text Saturday afternoon: "THANK YOU!!!" I wrote back with a smiley face.

Somehow, I made it through the rest of the weekend, and Monday, before I left for work, I left Sylvia, who was set to return that day, a note on the fridge:

> *Hi, Hope you had a good trip! It'd be great if you could send in the rent check this month. I left an envelope with the address and a stamp on it on the table. Thanks and talk to you soon!*

I knew it was a long shot, but here was hoping.

Teresa Anderson,

University of Wisconsin, Madison, 1957

THE BREEZY CHARMER

A true midwestern beauty, Teresa loves sporty casual looks, but has learned to counterbalance her sprightly breeziness with the occasional gravitas of tailored jackets and elegant A-line skirts. Shiny black pumps are an "absolute must." Other musts: plenty of time with her fiancé—they'll be married next month—and just enough time for her university office job and her studies (a Dean's List honors student, she makes do with "just enough time" quite nicely). In the few hours left each week, you'll inevitably find her reading. "There's no escape like a good book!" says Teresa. We couldn't agree with her sentiment more.

Chapter Fourteen

*T*he woman at the front desk of the Super 8 in Burbank, California, handed me my room key. I'd never stayed in a hotel room by myself before, but I pretended I was always on the road for work. Business travel—old hat! I'm a pro! Then she looked to Joel and Danny, the cameraman/producer team from the film company *Charm* had hired. They stood surrounded by piles of equipment they'd just lugged in from our rental van. "I'm only showing one room for the two of you," she said. "Is that right?"

Charm had seen fit to book us on a 6:00 a.m. flight from JFK with two layovers, first Cincinnati and then Denver. I didn't mind, but Joel and Danny had grumbled. But, apparently, Joel and Danny were too beat to grumble about this latest injustice. Joel just shrugged and took their key. The fact that we'd left behind the November gloom of New York for mid-seventies sunshine may have helped cushion the blow.

Late that afternoon we loaded up the equipment again and drove over to Caltech in Pasadena. Our interviewee, Rebecca Karimi, '89, was a tenured astrophysics professor who'd also been one of the air force's very first female fighter pilots. The book she published in the late nineties about discrimination in the air force and why she ultimately chose to leave the military didn't break the bestseller lists, but it had landed her on a slew of talk shows. I'd seen all the footage. She had straight-ironed the bejeezus out of her hair on every single appearance except a single MSNBC interview where her natural curls leapt fiercely out at the camera. Never having achieved aggressive hair myself, I loved that footage.

I hadn't actually spoken with Rebecca. I'd left messages, but she'd always e-mailed back instead of calling. In the recent photo she'd sent, her brown hair was now streaked with gray, and hair product technology had at last advanced enough to grant her lovely waves. She'd mentioned her father was Persian, and I thought I could see it in the architecture of her face, even in the fact that her face could be said to have architecture. Despite the softened hair, her photo looked formal and imperious.

Which was why I hadn't believed her when she'd warned that her office was not exactly film-friendly. Imperious people weren't slobs. Except, apparently in her case, they were. The office assistant showed us to a small, dark, cluttered cubbyhole of an office, every surface piled high with books and papers, the sort of disarray that prompted office Secret Santas to gift things like "Genius Is Messy" cross-stitch samplers or mugs featuring cartoons of offices in disarray and captions like "Out of Order" or "It's Shovel Ready!"

Further evidence that I'd misjudged her formality arrived the second she opened her mouth. "So sorry I'm late. I had to pee. I'm pregnant"—she framed her belly with her hands—"and this little guy loves hanging out right on top of my bladder."

She had a deep, almost masculine laugh and blunt gestures thanks to her large wrists and stubby fingers, something I hadn't noticed in any of the film footage of her. "God, this office is a mess," she half shouted, a sliver of Gilbert Gottfried in her voice. "Also, it makes me look fat. Just kidding. I'm pregnant. Every-thing makes me look fat." She wouldn't have stood a chance in the contest's dainty, poise-and-polish days, but here she was, one of TGTW's brightest stars.

"Outside is better, right?" she said. Joel, the lead producer, agreed, and luckily he'd believed her warnings about her office and had wisely gone to the trouble to get a film permit from the Caltech Public Affairs Office. Off we went to the lawn outside the physics building. Joel and Danny did their setup, a process involving endless cords and connections, while Rebecca and I chatted. Her partner, Keisha, was a few years younger, but Rebecca had wanted to be the one to carry their first child. "She can have all this fun next time around." Rebecca smirked. Even though she was already six months along, the January event in New York was just before her no-fly cutoff. "I'll be rolling in, but I'll be there!" she promised.

We were all ready to film when a police chopper parked itself in the air a few blocks away. We chatted some more while waiting for the helicopter to carry out its business. I asked her about the timing of her book—she'd waited until she'd been out of the military for six years before she put any of her experience to paper.

"It took me that long to get my head on straight." She laughed, her voice raised a little to be heard over the helicopter. Then she leveled an appraising look at me. I passed whatever inspection she gave me, apparently, because she went on in a more serious tone. "I had a revelation after I became a professor here, and it's basically this: sometimes there are excuses, and sometimes there are reasons. Even though I successfully flew missions for two years, I felt like such a failure when I quit. It wasn't until I succeeded at something else and saw that I was exactly the same, it was the circumstances that were different, that I could even start to think of my experience in the air force as anything other than a personal failure. That I wasn't just making excuses and that there were real reasons I left. I don't know why most women blame themselves first, but we do, and it was a total revelation for me to look outside myself and see some other folks who deserved some blame."

Rebecca then laughed her great big laugh again. "You remember the Lawrence Summers Harvard controversy? When he said that maybe it was women's fault—their limited abilities—that was the reason for so few female scientists? I couldn't believe it when I heard that. I was like 'For real? You've all been running things for how long, and you're actually going to get up there and say it's our fault?' No wonder we women get stuck blaming ourselves for everything—everyone else is blaming us. What else are we supposed to do?"

On e-mail she mentioned that she'd lost her copy of the '89 TGTW issue, and so I'd color-copied the entire issue for her. When I pulled it out of my bag she gasped, then lunged for it. "No frickin' way," she said, thumbing through the pages. "This is amazing." She wrapped her arms around me and pressed me into her stomach.

"Oh, this was hilarious," she said, opening to the page with her photo. "The magazine asked us all these questions about balancing a career with motherhood. We were all these dumb twenty-year-olds pontificating about something we knew absolutely nothing about. I think I said something like 'Women can have it all!'" She did Rosie the Riveter with her arm as she said it.

"Actually that's exactly what you said." I laughed, pointing to the quote next to her photo.

"Yeah, right. All I can say is that now I'm forty and I can barely balance being pregnant. Thank goodness I have an amazing partner, but even with both of us pitching in, things are going to get real interesting when this little rascal comes out of the easy bake."

The helicopter finally moved on, and the boys hooked Rebecca into her microphone while I stepped outside the shot. We wanted the video to open with a run of all the women saying what they did, so that was the first thing I asked her to say.

"I'm a professor of physics at Caltech. My area of expertise is observational high-energy astrophysics, which means, basically, that I scan the universe for things like gamma-ray bursts and neutron stars, and then try to draw inferences based on those observations. And before I was a physicist, I was one of the very first female fighter pilots in the US Air Force." She looked away from the camera toward me. "How was that?"

"Awesome," I said.

The guys nodded.

She looked back to the camera, then turned sideways to highlight her belly. "And I'm also pregnant." She beamed and raised her fists in the air like Rocky.

Back at the hotel I changed into my pajamas and pulled out my laptop. Even though lawn care questions were only trickling in at this point, I was still responsible for the trickle. I answered a question about how to fight moss (answer: aerate the soil and cut back on the overwatering), and then I opened the Sound of Music story file. I reread the opening paragraphs as they stood so far:

> *On one of Elsie's turnaround days (her name for the days when she finally kissed Ron again and forced herself to put on a dress, set her hair, and pat on lipstick), right between her fourth and fifth miscarriages, she went downtown to Brennan's Music to pick up new piano books for Laura and Michael's lessons.*

> *She hadn't meant to buy anything other than Laura and Michael's books, really she hadn't, but behind the register, a cover had caught her eye. A woman, arms out, twirling on a green hilltop. "I'll take that too," she said to Mr. Brennan, impulsively, gesturing to the title above his shoulder.*

> *That night, after dinner and dishes, she pulled her purchase from its brown paper bag.* The Sound of Music Songbook!

*declared the cheerful green lettering atop the cover. Acting
happy was the first step toward being happy, Elsie always said,
and so she opened the book and played and sang through one
song, and then the next . . .*

I thought about what Rebecca had said that afternoon about
excuses versus reasons. For the past year, I'd been coming up with
excuse after excuse not to write, which segued right into berating
myself for being so lazy or undisciplined. But maybe they weren't
all excuses. It had been a hard year. Maybe there'd been some
reasons hiding in there too.

That night, I worked and worked, long into the hours when I
should have turned out my lights and gone to bed. I'd still been
following the thread of what I knew to be the true story, but now I
added scenes that were pure invention. Elsie writing a newspaper
ad to publicize her first show, Michael helping his mother cut the
fabric for her nun's habit. Now that I wasn't writing about my actual
grandmother, something that had been stuck came unstuck. Elsie
could be as difficult or beguiling as the scenes demanded. I realized
that another reason I might have put off working on the story for
so long was fear of real-life hurt feelings if the "nonfiction" version
were ever published. We Wests were sensitive. What most people
would think of as an innocuous description of, say, a warbling singing voice could strike my family members as purest insult. But now
that I was straying farther and farther from reality, I ran free.

The next morning Danny, Joel, and I hit the airport predawn
and arrived in Phoenix at seven thirty. We'd made a trade—a night
of rest after our cross-country flight in exchange for doubling up
and interviewing Cindy Tollan, Paralympic gold medalist and
world-class wheelchair marathoner, in Phoenix that morning and
Dora Inouye, mayor of Seattle, in Seattle that afternoon. Danny
and Joel felt put upon by the fast and furious flying. I, in contrast,
felt like a glamorous globetrotter.

When I'd called Cindy Tollan to set up an interview time, I'd timidly suggested something around eight o'clock. Rather than balk, she'd said eight was absolutely perfect. She would have just gotten back from her morning run, which is what she called it, she said, even though it was actually a morning wheel, because who called it a morning wheel?

So that was that. Danny and Joel's only recourse for expressing their displeasure at our second early morning in a row was hitting up a drive-through Starbucks and ordering gigantic coffees and excess amounts of pastries, all on *Charm*'s tab. I couldn't believe we were allowed to order coffee on *Charm*'s tab in the first place. Business travel was really doing it for me.

Cindy Tollan had been nothing but lovely over the phone, albeit perhaps a little on the perky side, but I'd been secretly dreading the meeting anyway. I worried that I'd come off as an exploitative twenty-something interviewer asking the paraplegic athlete to testify for *Charm*.

"You must be Mr. Tollan," I said to the tan man in the golf shirt who opened the front door of the ridiculously vast stucco home.

"'Deed I am," he said, shaking my hand. "You must be the folks from *Charm*," he said, then hollered, "Ciii-ndy."

"Co-ming," she hollered back. Hollering was good. Usually people who hollered didn't fault naive twenty-somethings for phrasing their questions imperfectly.

From the entryway, we could see out the living room windows, or, more properly, the living room wall, which was all windows and which overlooked a gorgeous lawn and terraced garden. Here were the warm-weather readers Kelly Burns needed! In the middle of the yard an inordinately long and thin pool, almost like a canal, sliced through the grass. Plantings of succulents, light green and dusky purple, thrived along its edges, height added here and there by lime-green ceramic pots.

"Good morning," Cindy said as she wheeled into the living

room. "Come in, sit down." Her voice sounded a little lower than I remembered. Earthier. Almost before I could take in her face, I noticed the ropes of muscles in her forearms. Her husband slid open part of the window wall and said, "Why don't ya'll come out here on the patio. It's such a nice morning." We did, and moments later, Joel and Danny found their shot: Cindy facing south with a backdrop of yucca plants and silvery green Russian olive trees.

As luck would have it, I didn't say anything dumb, and Cindy didn't come off as even one bit ickily inspiring. She was just a carefree jock. If she were in ads for sunglasses or watches, the people of America, me included, would go wild for her shades and time-pieces. She talked about racing (hard-core), her husband and their going-on-twenty-year relationship from college straight on through (soft-core), and competition in general.

"I'd been an athlete for a long time before Ten Girls to Watch," she said. "I started swimming right after my accident, when I was eleven, and I was used to winning competitions, but not that kind of competition. I was going to have my picture in *Charm*? *Me*?" She laughed. "I felt stupid even sending in an application, and then, what do you know? I won. It started this whole chain reaction where I started doing things I'd never thought I could do. I married Mark. I took up marathoning. We left the Midwest and moved out here. We designed and built this house. I decided to try my hand at coaching. On and on, all these things that seemed scary or crazy or impossible, and I really feel like Ten Girls to Watch was the start of all that for me."

When it was finally time to go, Mark and Cindy sent us on our way with cheek kisses all around, plus little Ziploc bags of nuts from their cashew tree.

———

Shockingly, the sun was shining when we arrived in Seattle four hours later. Nice light glinted through the windows of Dora

Inouye's office as her staff gave us the rundown. Gesturing to a big American flag in front of a slim chair with yellow silk cushions, her chief of staff said, "That's setup number one." He then pointed to the window. "The other option is this view behind the desk. If you set up the camera at an angle, you get a shot of the Space Needle."

I was a little cheesed-out by the flag (nothing but love for America, but it felt a touch over-the-top), but Danny said "Lighting's better by the flag" and put down the tripod.

Dora herself was running a little late, the chief of staff informed us. She was walking back from the Seattle Climate Change Conference.

Even though Seattle is mostly a car city, everything I'd read about Dora highlighted the fact that she never drove; she took public transportation or walked to and from every meeting, even in the rain. At the previous year's Climate Change Conference—Dora had held one every year since she took office—college students from the University of Washington picketed the conference, up in arms about Seattle's new "Bridges to the Future" campaign, which planned to widen several of the major bridges around Seattle in order to improve traffic flow. Each bridge would include a dedicated bus lane, but the students felt that was an inadequate gesture. Among the signs bobbing up and down in the protesters' hands were "Bridges to our DOOM," "The A-BRIDGED Plan: Destroy Seattle," and less bridge-based but perhaps more to the point, "Light-Rail NOW!"

When she walked out of the session and found herself confronted by the crowd, cameras trained on her, Dora looked beatifically upon the protesters, broke from her entourage, approached the student with the "Light-Rail NOW!" sign, and asked whether she could borrow it. With the sign and the students right behind her, Dora told the TV stations nothing was better than seeing civically engaged young people, that she had been urging the city council to adopt Light-Rail all along, and that if it hadn't been clear already, the good people of Seattle overwhelmingly supported this measure.

The last was not technically true. Most of the good people of Seattle still wanted to drive and weren't eager to fund rails they didn't think they'd actually use. Later, when one of the city council members confronted Dora on that, her reply was that she'd said the good people of Seattle, not the bad ones. She didn't say it in a press conference, just a boring old meeting, but one of the Seattle papers ran the line anyway. In most cities that would have caused a holy ruckus. In Seattle, apparently, most people felt guilty enough about driving already that there was barely a peep—one or two letters to the editor, nothing more.

The chief of staff's BlackBerry buzzed. "Dora's coming up the stairs," he said, an edge of frenzy in his voice. And indeed, not ten seconds later Dora strode into the room. She had never looked like a typical political woman. No pearls or skirt suits. Short and athletic, she wore her long, black hair loose and usually outfitted herself in easy linen. Today's shade: lavender. The political woman emerged in force, however, when it came to circling the room and pumping our hands. When she got to me, her grip came with fierce eye contact.

"Dawn," Dora said, "it's so wonderful to meet you in person." And even if she was a politician, she said it with such earnestness that I felt warm and rosy.

After Joel hooked her into the mic and her team settled her into the yellow chair, I started with what I thought would be a warm-up question.

"So how did you first hear about the contest?"

Dora, apparently, needed no warming up. "I remember the exact issue of *Charm*. I still have it, in fact. I was in eighth grade, and we were on family vacation at my grandmother's place. I was lying in the hammock on her back porch reading *Charm*'s College Issue, and there in the Ten Girls to Watch section was an Asian-

American woman, Grace Chang. She was a scientist, and she was wearing a lab coat in her photo. And I remember thinking, I'm going to be one of those girls. I'm going to be like Grace Chang. And I started right then to do the things I needed to do to be ready to win. I was a journalist, not a scientist, but she was most definitely my inspiration. And you know, eight years later when I won, *Charm* arranged for me to meet Grace Chang. It was wonderful to get to tell her how much she'd meant to me."

I'd been on the phone with Grace Chang a few weeks before after tracking her down at UT Austin, and Dora and I briefly compared enthusiastic notes. In addition to building vehicles for surface exploration in space ("cars for Mars," she said), Grace was also a recreational drag racer and had adopted three children. She and Dora apparently called each other on their birthdays every year.

Before running for office, Dora spent seventeen years as a reporter for various Seattle newspapers, the last ten years covering the Seattle political beat. We talked about her time as a journalist, and then I asked what made her decide to run for mayor.

"I'd been following the political scene for so many years that I knew it inside and out," she said. "You can only write so many editorials trying to convince people from the outside. I finally decided it was time to go inside." And then after a short pause, she said, "It turns out it's exactly the same energy, the same drive, that gets you a spot in the Ten Girls to Watch that can one day get you a job as the mayor of Seattle." Dora beamed as she said this. She knew it was gold. Thirty minutes from start to finish, and Dora was out of her mic and off to her next appointment. I couldn't wait to get back to New York and watch the footage.

Our next stop, Chicago. We planned to take the red eye, check into our hotel, interview star architect Rita Tavenner, drive the two-something hours up to Madison, Wisconsin, interview Teresa Anderson from the 1957 class of winners, then back to Chicago for the night. Bright and early the next morning we'd fly to Georgia for our final interview with Barbara Darby and be back home in time to sleep in our own beds in New York that night. And all started off according to plan.

Rita Tavenner's office was a gorgeous corner spread on the thirtieth floor of a downtown building, and better yet, it overlooked the Merck Building, which she'd designed. Perfect shot for our cameras. Rita herself was a tall, lean woman with short, no-nonsense salt-and-pepper hair and simple clothing but for a blue silk scarf tied elegantly around her neck, and she settled into her chair in front of the cameras comfortably, one more woman at ease in the hot seat. I asked her the standard questions, and she was smart and charismatic, everything you'd expect. She'd been the 1979 pick for the TGTW *Today* show interview, and I threw in a question about her TV interview just for fun.

"Do you know that's how I met my husband?" She grinned. "*Charm* used to have a big party for all of us winners, and we spent all week getting ready for it—new hairdos and dresses, the whole works. And for the party, *Charm* arranged for each of us to have a nice college boy as an escort, someone cute we could dance with all evening. I was on the *Today* show a few days before the party, and what do you know, Ed was watching. He decided he had to meet me. And somehow in those two days he made enough phone calls and pulled enough strings that he wound up as my escort to the *Charm* party. I had a boyfriend at the time, but that didn't matter to Ed. A year and a half later we were married. It'll be our twenty-seventh anniversary next year."

"That story is crazy," Joel said to Rita after the interview.

"So crazy," she said, showing him a picture of her family. "Here we are," she said, turning and handing the photo to me. And there, courtesy of *Charm,* was Rita with a handsome husband and two children.

As she handed me the photo, she looked different than she'd

looked on camera. She was clearly delighted, but there was something a little more delicate too. Maybe even something nervous, like she was handing me a photo of the one thing she wasn't quite sure she deserved. Everything else she'd worked for. Everything else was hers. But this? Pure serendipity. And maybe that made it the most precious thing of all because it could so easily not have happened. Maybe, once chance plays so big a part in your life, you realize more is out of your control than you'd like to think.

Serendipity made me think of Robert. That had seemed fated. And then Elliot. I felt silly even saying it now that it had been thirteen full days since we'd spoken, but the circumstances had felt special. There he'd been, just waiting for me in the basement, and then there he'd been again, waltzing into TheOne party. But just because it felt like fate didn't mean it actually *was* fate.

As we drove up I-39 toward Madison in our white Chevy minivan, Joel at the wheel, me in the shotgun seat, Danny in back with all the equipment, I said, "So guys, I need your help. I'm working on a new list. It's a list of superheroes that don't exist but should. My best one so far is the Emasculator. She's a superhot chick who goes around to bars cutting cocky men down to size. I also have Wingman. He does what your average wingman does, just a lot better. And maybe he wears a chicken costume or something, which makes his ability to warm up prospects all the more impressive. Any other ideas?"

"What?" Danny asked, sounding genuinely confused.

"Ideas," I urged. "Any ideas for new superheroes?"

Joel jumped to the rescue. "How about the Cabbie. His superpower is intuitively knowing which streets will have the least traffic so he always gets you where you need to go just like that." He snapped his fingers.

"I like it, I like it," I said. "Okay, I've got another one," I continued. "The Pope Tart. He looks like an ordinary breakfast pastry, but when there's danger, he kicks into action and starts hurling blessings right and left. Eh? Eh?"

"I don't know about that one," Danny said.

"Okay, maybe we should go back to the job theme. Like the Cabbie. That was a good one."

We all sat in silence for a minute until I jumped in again. "Ooh, ooh. How about the Cow Hand? He actually has a cow for a hand. Which totally scares criminals when he takes off his gloves, and which means dairy whenever anyone needs it."

"You are a unique individual, Dawn." Danny chuckled.

Joel flipped on the radio, and thus ended the superheroes list. I'd been hoping to prove Elliot was nothing special when it came to car conversation, and by extension, nothing special in general. I'd failed, but I was still pretty pleased with myself for coming up with the Cow Hand.

———

When we arrived at Teresa Anderson's home, she showed us into the kitchen. The whole house smelled just like my grandparents'— a mix of lemon cleaning products, leather, and baked goods—and the kitchen gleamed in red and white, the table itself a vision in light green Formica. The Andersons, it appeared, had succeeded in waiting out the trends of the seventies, eighties, and nineties. Now, their sixties kitchen was retro chic. Every frugal instinct in me rejoiced.

In 1957, Teresa had been the pretty girl in the blue velvet tea-length dress, peeking out from under an umbrella held by the fellow in a tuxedo. She was seventy now, but her white hair was cut to the chin in almost the exact same style she'd sported in the magazine, and she still had that same look of investigation about her. When she trained her eyes on you, you felt her attention keenly. She was really looking, and you couldn't help but notice the energy of it.

I got her to deliver her opening lines, prompting her just the way I'd prompted everyone else.

"I'm Teresa Anderson, I was one of *Charm's* very first Ten Girls to Watch back in 1957," she said, "and I retired eight years ago after teaching first grade for forty years."

For a few minutes she told tales of that first year of the contest. *Charm* had organized a party for the girls at the penthouse of some famous designer. Teresa had never seen a home so opulent. It had curved staircases like the ones in the von Trapps' house in *The Sound of Music,* and wildest of all, in the center of the party was a splashing fountain of perfumed water. "The entire place smelled of White Shoulders," she said, giggling.

They'd spent a month in the city and another two weeks touring Europe. They'd been the toast of the town—concerts organized for their benefit, outings put together for their amusement—and they'd gone home famous. For years, she'd carried her *Charm* reputation with her. When she'd started teaching, all her students' parents had clamored to meet her, the famous and elegant *Charm* girl.

I asked her about teaching all those decades, what kept her going. Forty years of anything amazed me.

"I suppose I just never got over the pleasure of watching a child learn to read. You're watching the world open. It's a miracle every single time."

"Was that what drew you to teaching in the first place?" I said.

"This might sound funny to a modern ear," she said. "But I feel like teaching was a calling for me. I've always been good with children. Maybe I'm just too patient." She laughed. "That was the start, and then to be honest, I prayed and asked God to tell me what I should do with my life."

There was no way a thread about prayer was making it into the final video, and I could practically feel Danny and Joel giving me the evil eye when I kept her going. But she was quieter, calmer, surer in a way than any of the other women. I wasn't going to cut this short.

"And then you just knew?"

"I remember when I was in college and I just couldn't stop thinking about teaching. It was just always there, in the back of my head. I have always been a voracious reader. I always loved school. So that was the start of my answer. And then we had a nice life here. Three kids, and my husband owned a car dealership just down the road. The rhythm of the school year was just the rhythm of life. And I guess that was the rest of the answer. And it still is in a way, now it's just all about our grandchildren. I take care of my daughter's children most afternoons. You're sitting at the home-work table right now."

She smiled, and then she went on. "It's just in me. I'm always going to be a teacher. Actually, once I thought of trying to be a writer like you, Dawn."

My heart tightened when she said my name and "writer."

"But it didn't last. I didn't want it enough. And when I got over that, the idea of teaching was still there. And so that's who I became."

So many of the other winners had had these larger-than-life ambitions and careers, and truth be told, Teresa Anderson wouldn't have made the cut in 2007's contest. But the scale of her achievement seemed as great as anyone's. How many children had she taught to read over all the years of her career, after all? There was such radiant purpose in Teresa Anderson's modesty. Here she was, fifty years later, clearly fulfilled and at peace with her choices. Next time I started fixating on splashy success, I wanted to remember the sense of steadiness and contentment I felt sitting at Teresa's table.

I could have stayed with Teresa all day, but we had a flight to catch. We finished the interview, and after Joel and Danny packed up their gear she walked us to the door. I'd hugged all the rest of the women—I was an instinctual hugger—but Teresa put her hand out, and we took turns shaking her hand farewell. The formality of it felt right. I even bowed my head just a little bit as we walked out through her front door.

———————

After yet another flight and yet another drive, we set up the shot for Barbara Darby, spy novelist (and former CIA agent), in her Augusta, Georgia, garden, surrounded by Spanish moss.

"Of course you know when I won the contest, it was a best-dressed contest," Barbara said with pride, as if to say, *Who cares about all my bestselling books. What really matters is that I look fabulous!* And it was true, she did.

She won the contest in 1962, which meant she had to be in her sixties. But she didn't look it. She looked more like a mysterious forty-something, draped in a beautiful red silk shell that showed off her triceps.

"I spent months sewing my outfits," she said. "One school outfit, one weekend outfit, and one party dress. I had to wear them all in a fashion show in the dining hall while a bunch of department heads, deans, and club presidents scored me."

I barely had to ask any questions. She just rolled along.

"I think I won the school contest because I wore a white wool skirt suit with kick pleats, red piping, and red spangle buttons. I was this close to wearing a brown herringbone skirt and jacket. I really couldn't decide. But at the last minute I went with the bold choice. Ever since then, when I have a hard decision, I ask myself, 'What's the red spangle button choice?' And whatever it is, that's what I do."

She laughed a little, which made her sleek brown bob and square-cut bangs swing a bit. Her cheekbones sat so high and full that I couldn't look away. Whatever her age, Barbara still had the loveliest facial structure I'd ever seen. Until meeting her, I'd disbelieved the cheekbones theory of beauty, but she stood as such a compelling case that I was now entirely convinced.

I didn't know how, but I hoped upon hope we'd be able to get that spangled-button line in the final video.

Before I could say anything, Barbara went right on. "You know I was on the cover in 1962? Well, the day I hit the stands, I got eleven calls for modeling jobs. And that's what started it all.

"I meant to turn the jobs down," she said. "I talked it over with my fiancé, Tom, and we decided that's what I would do—say no and get right back to Augusta. But that's not what I did. I told him *Charm* had invited me to stay on for another couple of weeks, and I scheduled every last one of the jobs, one after another. But of course they just turned into more jobs, and at the end of the two weeks, I had to fess up. Later on, when they first approached me about spying, I thought, no way, I could never carry on that kind of double life. I couldn't lie like that. But I thought back to what happened with Tom, the way he would call and how I would tell him all about what the *Charm* editors and I had been up to that day even though I had spent all day on a modeling job, and I knew, actually, that I could lie quite well."

Danny, who was holding the boom mic, was starting to tremble, the boom, an extension of his arm, shaking with exaggerated fatigue. I wanted to give him a rest, but I didn't want Barbara to stop.

"I imagine you get this question all the time," I asked, "but how close are your books to your experiences in real life?"

She smiled, her ample cheeks moving up toward her deep gray eyes. "I'm sure you can imagine that's a very hard question to answer," she said. And after lingering with that smile, she winked, brushed her hands across her lap, and said, "I'm getting awfully hungry, aren't you?"

Tanisha Whitaker,

Vanderbilt University, 2003

THE COMEDIENNE

Her goal: to be the head writer for a hit comedy. Her track record: Winning the National College Improv Tournament as part of Vanderbilt's team inspired Tanisha to found "Schooled," an improv after-school program for underserved teens. In two years, over eight hundred Nashville-area high school students have participated. This summer, Tanisha interned at the *Late Show with David Letterman* and performed at the famed comedy club Carolines on Broadway. "Comedy can change your life," she says. "It stretches your mind in surprising ways."

Chapter Fifteen

"Weather Delays, See Agent," read the Departures board at the Atlanta airport. Everything had been so smooth till then. Although the drive from Augusta to the airport in Atlanta featured a long stretch where only talk radio stations came in, that constituted comparatively minor trouble. I was still getting quite a kick out of the whole business-travel thing, and even when the agent told us there were no flights in or out of New York for the foreseeable future due to high winds and rainstorms there, my mood remained relatively buoyant. This just meant *Charm* would foot the bill for some TCBY and magazines while we waited. Four hours and three TCBYs later, I was scraping bottom and reading the recipes in *Silver,* that magazine for hip retirees. When it finally became clear we weren't making it out that night, the airline gave us vouchers for forty-five dollars off a hotel room, and I finally began to see that business travel might have its occasional downsides.

Before we retired to our rooms, we sat down in the bland bar of the Airport Quality Inn. Danny asked Joel how his wife had taken the news of the delay.

"She said she didn't care, as long as I was home tomorrow in time to make flan for our dinner party with the McCallisters," Joel said. "Come to think of it, she didn't seem that concerned about me actually attending the dinner party either. Just so long as there was flan."

"And how about you, Dawn? Anyone anxiously awaiting your return?" Danny asked.

"Anyone?" I said. "Why, absolutely everyone!"

That got the smirk it deserved. Finally, I said, "No one, really. Maybe the guy outside my subway stop who hands me the *amNewYork* every morning?" And it felt very sad and true. Maybe Ralph, I thought to myself.

Friday arrived, and the morning flights were canceled just as the previous night's had been. But finally, after five more hours of semimiserable airport waiting, we brushed the Dunkin' Donuts crumbs from our laps and boarded our plane home.

Now that it was December, the dreary sun disappeared in New York at four thirty, and the cab I caught at five o'clock carried me home over dark, wet streets. Outside my building, a branch, apparently cracked by the wind, perched precariously atop a garbage can.

I lugged my bags up the stairs, expecting to be greeted by Sylvia sprawled on the couch, with or without sad-girl ice cream, I wasn't sure. But upon opening the door, I found no such greeting. The lights were off, and the apartment was almost silent. Except it wasn't. It sounded like the faucet was on. Except it wasn't. I flipped the light switch by the door, but nothing happened—no light. Then I stepped from the front entryway toward the kitchen.

As my eyes adjusted to the dim light shining in from the streetlamp outside the front windows, I found the source of the sound—a thin stream of water cascaded from the light fixture over the kitchen table, forming a river that careened down the sloped floor toward the couch. At that end of the room, the water was at least half an inch deep, high enough that the reflection of the couch and coffee table shimmered in the pool. I opened my bedroom door and threw my bags on my bed—the apartment's high ground. Standing at the edge of the water, watching as it visibly crept higher, I dialed my landlord.

"You've reached Carroll Gardens Realty Corp.," his wife Mary's voice mail answered. The number was Mary's cell phone, and Carroll Gardens Realty Corp. didn't actually exist. It was just Bob and Mary. But Mary liked to sound official. Whenever she picked up the phone, regardless of the music in the background, the sounds of the television, the chatter of the people in line around her in the grocery store, she always said, "Hello, this is Carroll Gardens Realty Corp." It usually made me laugh—what charming pretense!—but as I stepped up the slope to keep my feet dry, I wasn't laughing.

"Hi, Mary and Bob, it's Dawn in apartment 4," I said. "Call me as soon as you get this. The roof is leaking and my apartment is flooded."

I hung up, grabbed a big soup pot from the cupboard, and started bailing water into the kitchen sink. But the water poured down from the ceiling as fast as I bailed it, quickly making the fruitlessness of my endeavor clear. I hung up and dialed 311, the city's nonemergency number.

"My roof is leaking. Not really leaking, pouring," I told the dispatcher after I made it through the automated navigation system. "Yes, I have notified my landlord. No, he hasn't yet responded." The dispatcher informed me he could aid me in filing a complaint and put my building on the list for an inspection. When I said the situation might be more urgent than that, he suggested hanging up and dialing 911.

Nine-one-one? It wasn't like I was being *murdered* by the pouring water, but I did as instructed. And so it was that the fire department knocked on my door at 10:32 p.m. By then the rain outside had stopped, and the cascade was more of a dribble. The good men of the NYFD mostly waved their flashlights, tromped around, walkie-talkied in some codes to whomever they talked to on the other end of their contraptions, and asked whether I had another place to stay while my landlord attended to this situation.

I said yes, but the actual answer was no. I could have called Elliot—he was back in town by now, wasn't he? But I wasn't going to. I could have called Robert, but I wasn't going to do that either. It wasn't too hard to fake, though. I told them I'd head to a friend's, and they gathered up their things and left. But not before Trevor, a particularly pleasant—and muscular—firefighter from the great borough of Staten Island, took my phone number. He would doubtless never use it, but I felt a tiny bit grateful to have received some personal attention.

Monday afternoon, Mary, the landlord's wife, left me a message.

"Hello, this is Mary from Carroll Gardens Realty Corp. calling. I wanted to let you know that we fixed the problem with the roof and that a cleaning service will be taking care of the water in your apartment later today. I also wanted to let you know that, unfortunately, we have yet to receive your check for December's rent. Please send the check as soon as possible. As you know, we assess late charges of twenty-five dollars a day for any rent paid past the fifth of the month."

I'd been too busy bailing water to notice if the please-pay-rent note was still on the fridge. Wherever Sylvia was, she had apparently not paid our rent.

Before I left work that night, after approximately thirty-one calls from me to Sylvia with no answer and no response to my messages, her Ohio number finally lit up on my screen.

"Sylvia, are you okay?" I asked.

She apologized, but after Thanksgiving, she said, she just hadn't been able to bring herself to leave home again. She was staying in Toledo. Permanently. Would I mind shipping her a few things?

"I know this has been a really difficult time for you, but . . ." I'd intended this to serve as a segue, just an opener for further, firmer statements along the lines of "It might be hard for me to deal with all your stuff" and "I need your rent check *now.*" Sylvia, however, jumped in before I could proceed.

"I knew you'd understand," she said, barging into the middle of my sentence. "I'll e-mail you with the list of things I need. Everything else you can just throw away or give away or whatever. Maybe the new roommate will want it." And with that, she abruptly hung up the phone. When I called back, she didn't answer.

I returned from work to Brooklyn that night to find a musty yet frigid apartment. Open windows hadn't quite dried the place out, but they seemed to have allowed several pigeons to peck around and leave "gifts" on the floor. In good news, I could see the "gifts" clearly now that the electricity worked again. In bad news, the Carroll Gardens Realty Corp. cleaning crew obviously left something to be desired.

I scrubbed the floor, then retired to my room, where the odor of mold held the least sway. I posted a new roommate ad to Craigslist. Inspired by the deeply unfresh scent of my apartment, I wrote my lawn care column for the week: "Say Good-bye to Snow Mold." I e-mailed Abigail. "If a guy hasn't e-mailed or called in two weeks, would you say he's passively broken up with you?" I asked. She'd weigh in eventually.

Finally, I opened the Sound of Music file. I wanted to work, and I read over the document and tried tweaking a few words here and there, but my eyes kept losing focus. Really, what I wanted to do was cry. I wished there were a storm of tears I could release, and whoosh, once they were gone, I'd feel all better. But I didn't have a pent-up flood inside. If anything, I just felt foggy, like I'd fallen into some sort of ravine and I knew my prospects were bad, but it was too misty to see just *how* bad yet. Eventually, the air would clear, and I'd get a perfectly crisp picture and panic. For now, I simply gave up on the story and curled into a ball in front of the laptop's glowing screen, unable to really fall asleep, but unable to pretend to work anymore either.

"I don't think I'll be able to make it home for Christmas this year," I said apologetically into the phone the next day. In many families, this would have been a moment for parental intervention—tickets purchased, holiday happiness ensured—but that's not how the Wests worked. I was a grown-up. I was supposed to buy my own tickets. Even in college, I'd paid for every flight with work-study earnings. Certainly, graduating was supposed to have made me more able to do that, not less. "We'll sure miss you," my dad said. And then he told me all about the tree he'd just finished putting up and how much he was enjoying his new recording of the *Messiah* and the fine details of Teddy Roosevelt's near death from blood poisoning while exploring the Amazon. La-di-frickin'-da.

I next called my mother to break the news and she said, "Oh, honey, are you sure?" Though no offer of help was extended as part of the "are you sure" package with her either. When I said I was sure, she said she understood. Yeah, yeah, great. That's what I wanted to hear. Except it wasn't. I wanted weeping. I wanted offers of bake sales to raise funds to bring me home. I wanted moaning that it wouldn't be Christmas without me. Except that, apparently, it would be. For them.

In fact, I wanted a great deal more than moaning about Christmas. I wanted someone to rescue me from this mildewy apartment. I wanted someone to find me another roommate. I wanted someone to send a lump of cash to my bank account. I didn't want to take care of all this on my own. After some unsatisfying wallowing, I picked myself up and took a page out of Elsie's *Sound of*

Music playbook by slapping on some lipstick and heading to the store. When I got home I attempted to manufacture cheer by baking a bunch of cookies and hanging the cheapest strand of lights they sold at CVS along the wall above the couch.

My sister sent me a text later that night: "U sure ur not coming home? :(" Had she offered me a ticket, I would have taken it. But she only offered me a frowny face.

"Sad but true. Miss you tons," I wrote back. And I did miss her. In fact, I felt like I was pretty much missing everyone in the world right then.

The next day I returned from work to find a large square box with my name on it next to the mailboxes. No return address, and my name and address appeared on a printed postage sticker, so no handwriting either. Whomever this mystery package was from, it was heavy. It took a couple of tries before I had it successfully hoisted onto my hip. Four flights of stairs later, I set the box on the table and cut through the packing tape.

Up came the cardboard flaps and out came a few air pillows, and there, under cellophane, was something unexpected: a big basket of fruit. I pulled the basket out of the box and ripped off the rest of the wrapping. Inside the brown wicker were pears, apples, oranges, even a pineapple, and tucked in between a pear and the pineapple was a card. Who would have sent me a fruit basket? XADI? Ralph? The gracious Teresa Anderson?

I opened the envelope and removed a small white card with a drawing of a bottle of champagne on the front. Inside it read: "Happy Holidays, Love Elliot."

What? I stood there staring at the card. A fruit basket? Had Elliot filed me away in his BlackBerry as a *Charm* staffer? Was I part of his "Work Contacts—send holiday gift" list? But who signs a holiday gift card to work contacts with the word "love"? Did that make this a romantic gift, even after such a prolonged radio silence? And if it was, *a fruit basket*? And again—*love*?!

I'd been trying to pretend that every day that went by without Elliot calling or e-mailing didn't freeze-dry a new portion of my heart. But a pretense it had surely been. Was this basket of fruit supposed to thaw my feelings? Did he think I'd be all defrosted and ready to go when he returned? *Love?* He signed it *love?* Did he *mean* to do that?

I had no idea what to do. I ate a pear. I started to write a text message. "Thank you?" I typed. I looked at the basket and looked at the message and then hit send. I waited the rest of the night for a reply, but one never came.

Fortunately, during all this, XADI kept me nice and busy. The film production team came back with thirty minutes of what they thought was the best footage. I transcribed it all, and then XADI and I patched together pieces and sent our suggestions back to them for actual editing. Day after day we sent text revisions and were greeted the next morning with a new video to further trim. We started playing with music and fade-ins. I liked the Beach Boys and Van Morrison. XADI favored a Christina Aguilera instrumental remix. Regina's remarks for the event needed attention, and I contributed by supplying snappy yet inspiring lines on each of the new winners. I somehow became the designated keeper of the RSVP list. With excitement, I added name after name as the invitation reply e-mails and phone calls rolled in. Helen officially RSVPed, and I typed her name into the yes list with a real smile. It'd be good to finally see each other.

On the home front, I spent the second weekend in December once again interviewing possible roommates, and once again, everyone balked at the pink walls. "You can paint them when you move in," I said limply to one potential future crazy roommate after another. "I have paint, in the basement." At last an NYU anthropology grad student and I shook hands. Chelsea would be moving in January 10. Until then, she'd be in Belize, studying something I was embarrassed to realize I already couldn't remember. Till her January arrival, it was just me, the must, and Sylvia's piles of junk.

Finally, that Sunday, my phone buzzed with a message from Elliot. "In NV thru X-mas. xx" No mention of my "Thank you?" text. No mention of his "love" card. No "How are you?" or anything that invited a response. Did he think we'd just resume when he got back? What *was* this? Just as I had with the card, I cocked my head and stared at the screen. Maybe this was what dating was like when you were out of college, just busy people, fitting romance in where they could. I threw my phone at the bed, as if that would push all Elliot-related thoughts from my head. It didn't work.

On the *Charm* front, we reached our RSVP drop-dead date. XADI signed off on the printed programs for the event, featuring a complete listing of all the winners from the past fifty years, photo highlights, fun facts, profiles of this year's winners, and, of course, the order of events for the actual celebration. Regina signed off on the photo selection for giant blowup images to be placed around the hall. And then, at last, the video. The film production company went off to make hundreds and hundreds of copies. The president of Clairol, Gerri Vans, Drew Faust, Anitha Ming, and Jessica Winston all reconfirmed their attendance. And then everyone else went home for Christmas.

While they were away, I went to work every day. Ralph and I passed in the hallway. He was roasting a goose for his mother for Christmas. He'd found a delicious-sounding sour cherry stuffing recipe on SuperRecipeCollection.com. One day he wore a red cardigan. Another day it was mulberry, close to red, but definitely a different sweater. I told him I was spending the holiday with friends. A big fat lie, but better than eliciting a pity invitation to Trenton, New Jersey. I made fudge, using my mother's fluff and chocolate chip recipe, and brought in a plate for him. He looked stricken with pleasure, and I realized that though our interactions were few, I was really getting to like Ralph.

Abigail finally made it to San Salvador and an Internet café. She found me on G-chat and the forty minutes we spent felt like a Christmas miracle. Mr. Birdsong had gone home—his three months of grant-supported research had ended—but then he'd flown back, just to see Abigail. I told her a little bit more about Elliot and his disappearing act. "I'm sorry, hon," she said. To the fruit basket news, she replied, "WTF!!!!!!????" I was tired of thinking about him, so I moved along to regaling her with TGTW stories. After all, there were some good ones. She couldn't believe I was going to be in the same room with Gerri Vans in real life. "Can you please touch her dimples? I've always wanted to put my fingers in them," she said. "What is wrong with you?!" I wrote back.

I called my family Christmas Day. I got about ten solid minutes with my sister, in which I briefly mentioned Elliot, but unlike in my chat with Abigail, this time I framed it as if we were still together. After all, maybe we were?

"Did you say he's thirty?" she said incredulously.

"What? It's not that old," I said. "You're almost thirty."

"That's exactly how come I know how old thirty is," she said.

After that I watched *It's a Wonderful Life*. I ate a Swanson's turkey dinner. I felt lonely and pathetic. I flung myself around on the furniture as if I were a nineteenth-century maiden dying of consumption. I thought again about trying to track down Raymond. Gross, for sure, but maybe bad kissing was a small price to pay for human companionship . . . Surely, though, he'd gathered up all that change from his floor and used it to buy a plane ticket somewhere for the holidays.

In the quiet days after Christmas I should have been writing. Was I not an aspiring *creator* after all? Or I should have been running—why not take some inspiration from Cindy Tollan and make this the year I trained for a marathon? Or at the very least I should

have been reading some trashy yet engrossing thrillers by Barbara
Darby or volunteering at a soup kitchen or . . . something! But
no. The closest I got to interacting with other humans was when
I smiled overenthusiastically at the clerk while swiping my credit
card at the grocery store.

Instead of doing anything really worthwhile, I hauled a bunch
of crap, including Sylvia's sagging particleboard bookcase and
some broken shelves, down to the basement. It was a huff-and-
puff effort, and the exertion felt good. Once I got to the basement, I still wasn't bold enough to really brave the murky depths,
so rather than stacking everything neatly, I sort of hurled it into the
dark. After that, I went back upstairs and dusted. Truly, a person
is desperate when she turns to dusting as a source of solace and
entertainment.

As New Year's approached, there were multiple parties at
friends' places in the offing. The trouble was, given our intertwined
worlds, Robert and Lily stood a pretty good chance of sashaying
into whichever party I chose. I resolved to tough it out at home,
which had the added benefit of frugality, and I would have done
exactly that had I not gotten a Facebook friend request from Ms.
Tanisha Whitaker.

She was the stand-up comic–cum–SAT tutor, and although I'd
chatted with her mother and received Tanisha's e-mail RSVPing
yes to the gala, we'd never actually spoken.

I accepted the friend request and minutes later a message
arrived in my Facebook inbox:

Looking forward to the Ten Girls to Watch Gala! This is last minute, but if
you're in town, I'm having a New Year's Eve show. I can put you and a friend
on the comp list if you have any interest!

Maybe Tanisha thought I was a bigger deal at *Charm* than I actually was and that inviting me was a good PR move, but whatever

delusion had led to this, I decided to take her up on it. The show was free to me, Robert certainly wasn't going to be there, and I really needed to get out of the apartment. Wasn't this what Jessie Winston was talking about? You had to take care of yourself. If you were a famous opera singer, that probably meant lots of sleep and warm tea and cashmere scarves to protect your throat. If you were me, it meant *get off the couch and reenter civilization.* I wrote back to tell her yes, though I failed to mention I'd be going solo. Until I knew Tanisha a little better, there was only so much loserdom I was willing to cop to.

I put on the same short navy dress I'd worn to TheOne party, this time with thick black tights and tall black boots. I curled my hair. I blackened my lashes. My mother had sent me some of that new shiny-but-not-sticky lipstick/lip gloss for Christmas, and I lacquered my lips with it. Then off I went to catch the subway to the East Village.

The show was in a small auditorium behind a bar, and even though I was thirty minutes earlier than the time Tanisha had told me, the lights were already out and a comic was already onstage (apparently, it was a marathon show, and Tanisha was buried deep in the middle of the lineup). Folding metal chairs were set up in rows, and I had to slink by half a dozen people to get to a free seat near the back, "slink" being a poor description for anything done in a puffy winter coat.

Onstage, a wiry man in a tweed fedora said, "How many people with ADHD does it take to screw in a lightbulb? Oh my God, is that a spider? You want to go get a drink?"

Next up, a guy with a thick handlebar mustache pretended to be a cabdriver from Canarsie who took people places he thought they should go rather than where they asked him to drive. Agonizing silence greeted most of his lines.

Finally, it was Tanisha's turn. Even though it had been a few years, she looked just like her photo from the magazine, big smile with blazing white teeth, huge brown eyes, and a mass of curly black hair down to her shoulders.

"So, I'm an SAT tutor," she began. "Everyone out there take the SATs?" She waited for a reply. "Did you hear that? I think the only one who whooped was the bartender. See where college can get you, kids? You need to study those SAT words! So anyway, yes, rich people hire me to help their kids do better on the test. And the problem I have is that after I spend all evening drilling these kids on their vocabulary words, I can't really cut it off. I'll try to go on a date after. It'll be some guy I met on the Internet, and we've got beers, and he says, 'What do you do?' and I say, 'I hasten the retention of ephemeral vocabulary in my obdurate wards.' 'Come again?' 'Cajole callow kids into amassing verbal adroitness. I only do it because I'm impecunious.' Oh my God, are you guys groaning? I hear groaning. I am sorry for this tedium. I'm just tenacious!"

The crowd warmed up a little more when she moved on to jokes about the woes of finding roommates on Craigslist. "People should have to have those little disclaimers, like pharmaceutical ads. Like mine would be 'Tanisha Whitaker is nice, funny, and neat.'" Then she switched into a fast, low voice: "Tanisha Whitaker has also been shown to clog drains with her hair and to eat all your food when drunk. Other side effects of living with Tanisha Whitaker may include a television perpetually tuned to the Food Network, strange men sneaking out of your apartment at the crack of dawn, and unexpected visits from Tanisha's mother."

She then turned all perky. "Is anyone out there looking for a roommate? No really, I need a place."

After her set, another three comics went onstage before there was a break. Finally, intermission arrived, and I pushed my way through the crowd toward the front, thinking maybe the comics would return from wherever they disappeared to backstage. I waited until just before the lights dimmed again, but no Tanisha (though I did get a number of up-and-down, checking-me-out looks and smiles in my direction while standing there, which was a helpful little boost to my self-esteem just then). The show ended at about eleven thirty, and I pushed up to the stage area once again, but either Tanisha had been whisked away somewhere or she and the other performers were planning to ring in the New Year backstage.

I might have felt depressed, disconsolate, dispirited (clearly I was still channeling Tanisha) leaving a bar alone at 11:45 p.m. on New Year's Eve, but I didn't. The crackling cold air felt clean and bracing, the opposite of my stuffy apartment and the crowded club, and I knew I'd get a chance to talk with Tanisha eventually. Walking past packs of people spilling out of bars and restaurants, I thought about her act. I'd laughed plenty, but I was an easy audience and it wasn't as if *everyone* was falling out of their chairs. Still, she was working on it. And to have to "work on it" so publicly . . . wow. Despite my initial disappointment at being exiled to the archives, I took such comfort in my quiet basement office, where no one was around to overhear (and presumably judge) my phone conversational abilities. I was going to work on a short story in the privacy of my bedroom for weeks on end before even thinking of showing it to anyone, and then I certainly wasn't going to stick around and watch their faces while they read it. But Tanisha got up there in front of a room full of people and sometimes got laughs and sometimes got . . . nothing. Brutal, instant criticism. I thought it was one of the bravest things I'd ever seen.

I reached the subway at 11:59 on my cell phone clock and decided to give it a minute before I headed down the stairs. Seconds later, a roar from a bar across the street went up, and I looked at the numbers again: 12:00. *Happy New Year,* I said to myself. Before I even really thought about it, a resolution popped into my head. *This year, you'll do brave things.* I didn't quite know how, or what that would entail, but I said it again, a little vow: *Dawn West, you will be brave.*

———

At last, January 2 arrived. Back at work, the TGTW anniversary party was only a few days away. I double-checked the spelling of every place card. I picked up the programs and delivered them to *Charm*. I fielded calls and e-mails from TGTW winners confirming time and place and dietary restrictions. I sent Tanisha a note to thank her for the show, and she wrote back apologizing profusely that she'd gotten stuck backstage and hadn't had a chance to see me. I switched her seating assignment so she'd be at my table for the event. I had the feeling that when we actually got around to talking in person, she and I were going to be friends. Finally, the night before the event, the giant photo prints delivered to the Morgan Library, the gift bags (which included the hot-off-the-presses January issue) all assembled, I got off the subway a stop early to enjoy the unseasonably warm evening.

The clouds hung low over the city—the weather predictions all said a storm was brewing. I loved the pink blanket of sky, all the lights of the buildings and bridges held close and reflected back down on the streets. It was cotton-candy noir, and I wanted more. I didn't walk straight home and turned instead down toward the Union Street bridge, toward the gritty urban splendor of the Gowanus Canal. I leaned against the iron railing, watching the lights of the low-slung warehouses along the canal's banks waver in the purply murk, the scraggly weed trees standing stiff in the windless air. The air was chilly but damp, and my coat felt far too heavy. I loosened my scarf and finally turned back toward home.

I showered, put on my love-you-a-bunch pajama bottoms and my gray sweatshirt, drank some warm milk, and tucked myself into bed with the *New Yorker*. Sleep hygiene at its finest. Except that after I finished the issue and turned off the lamp, no brain wave transformation took place. My thoughts scuttled around in their regular conscious fashion for first a half hour, then an hour. I'd exhausted my Somnilab drug supply, and Benadryl had groggy consequences. Round and round my visions of the TGTW gathering swirled. I imagined introducing Helen Hensley to Barbara Darby and Tanisha Whitaker to Rebecca Karimi. I imagined Regina pulling me up to the podium after the event to introduce me to Gerri. I had to be at the Mandalay Carson building at nine the next morning. I kept imagining sleeping through my alarm. I was still awake when the storm's first lightning flashed. Somewhere around two in the morning, my fantasies veered—Jessica Winston sang, as planned, but then she pulled me up for a duet . . . and then, at last, I slipped into sleep.

I was traveling through a dream about moving back into Helen's hut when a sharp smell that didn't fit in with the dream urged me awake. When I opened my eyes my room was completely dark save for the little green glow of my cell phone charger and the pulsating white light of my MacBook, and completely silent save for the sound of rain battering the window. But it was undeniable, there was something in the air.

I sat up and turned on my lamp, then started sniffing around my room. The smell was stronger when I opened the door and walked into the living room. Smoke. Maybe. It was four o'clock in the morning, but I dialed Bob and Mary anyway. "Carroll Gardens Realty Corp.," the message said.

I went back to my bedroom and sat on my bed. I wanted to think I was just being crazy, that everything was fine. I didn't want to be the paranoid neighbor who overreacted and called the fire department in the middle of the night. I'd already been the crazy neighbor who called the fire department because her roof was leaking. I sat there for a good five minutes, sniffing and deliberating.

Finally, I slipped my bare feet into sneakers and walked to the front door, where the smell was strongest of all. I sniffed again. Then I opened the door. Instead of the usual hallway, the door opened to a solid curtain of smoke. I should have slammed it shut, but I didn't. I gently pushed it closed, as if I were trying not to disturb the smoke. It took a second for sensible thoughts to form, but when they did, I grabbed a coat and scarf, wrapped the scarf over my nose and mouth, opened the door, and bolted down the stairs. I knocked on the doors of the third- and second-floor apartments as I went, yelling "Fire!" loudly at each. I was on the ground floor before I had the inane thought that I should have grabbed my laptop. I'd backed up my writing, but the backup was in my apartment too.

Had I been rational, I might have thought of grabbing my wallet, or my phone, or, gosh, even something like my passport or my glasses. Or being a humanitarian and really banging on those neighbors' doors. No such thoughts crossed my mind. *My writing, my writing, my writing,* blared my lone panicked, pumping thought. I ran back up the stairs. Even while running I realized how stupid I was being, but I couldn't bring myself to stop. I pushed past one flight and the next. Finally, back in my apartment, I got down on my knees and pulled my laptop from under my bed, where I always tucked it away so I wouldn't accidentally step on it if I sleepwalked in the night.

But that wasn't enough for me. I spent more precious time grabbing the wastebasket beside my bedroom door, pulling out the plastic grocery bag liner, and shaking out the scraps of paper, receipts, and wads of hair. All so I could shove my laptop inside in hopes of it keeping dry in the rain.

Now that that was done, I could go ahead and escape my burning building. For a second, I even felt elated, like I'd rescued the only thing that mattered, so who the heck cared if the rest of it burned. I coughed, choking on the smoke, and took as deep a breath as I dared through my scarf before opening my door once again and charging into the stairwell.

Could the stairs really take so long to descend? They felt like Escher stairs. I banged on the other apartment doors again, just to be sure. And then, at last, I reached the front door and tumbled out into the pouring rain. Across the street, I joined the huddled collection of neighbors, people I recognized from mailbox interactions, but none of whom I actually knew beyond pleasantries. Still, a quick survey of faces was enough to know we were all out. Another quick survey—this one of the building—was enough to know we weren't going back inside. Actual flames lit the windows on the first and now the second floor.

We talked to one another with surprising calm, as if this were a fire drill, not an actual fire. The guys from the ground floor had 911 on the phone. We watched the fire climb for another minute. It was like watching one of those fireplace DVDs, logs charring on your TV screen—that's how removed it felt from any actual peril or trauma. I looked down at the way the light from the fire lit my hands. The glow on my skin looked warm and cozy, except for the plinking raindrops that ever so slightly ruined the effect. We heard sirens in the distance.

Two neighbors had been smart enough to grab umbrellas, and I joined the mass pressed together for protection from the storm. Here I was, the twisted version of Teresa Anderson peeking out from beneath her umbrella in the inaugural TGTW photo spread. Velvet dress replaced with monkey pajamas, tuxedoed date replaced with burly, bathrobed neighbor. No need to reach from under the umbrella to check for rain. How strange it was to watch a building burn in the midst of a deluge.

By the time the trucks showed up in force, Mohamed, the owner of the twenty-four-hour bodega on the corner, had taken our shivering, sloshing mass of humanity into his store. As it grew apparent that our building and all our worldly possessions were quickly becoming nothing but soggy ash, he even started taking orders for egg sandwiches. Whatever style we wanted, on the house. When his griddle momentarily burst into a ceiling-high grease fire, I didn't move a muscle, except for the contraction of my stomach, gasping with a shocked half gasp, half laugh. Luckily, Mohamed wasn't laughing. Moments later, fire extinguisher clouds and fumes filled the bodega. Our huddled mass returned to the sidewalk.

Eventually firefighters and neighbors from up and down the block mingled among us. By that point, rain still gushing down, most of us had given up on umbrellas. I was leaning against the iron fence across the street from what had been my apartment, waiting for emotion but still feeling blank. It was like I'd blistered over, a haze insulating me from the injury for the time being. The haze was helpful. I was staring out into the rain when Trevor the firefighter ambled by.

"You again," I said.

"I'm so sorry," he said.

"Don't be," I deadpanned. "It's fate bringing us together."

He froze.

"I'm kidding," I said.

He nodded seriously. "This happens way too often in old buildings. Water damage and electrical fires."

"I thought electrical fires were made up," I answered, my voice flat, the energy required to make it otherwise beyond me.

"Well, they don't usually burn buildings to the ground. But this one started in the basement, and it looks like there were lots of flammable materials down there. Paint stuff, scrap wood."

Paint stuff and scrap wood? The paint stuff and scrap wood I'd hauled down there in Sylvia's wake? I hadn't cried yet, but now the tears started. Luckily, the rain rendered them invisible. Trevor ambled along.

By five thirty or so, the Red Cross arrived to dole out coats, shoes, whatever we needed. Except umbrellas, no umbrellas. Also no fancy dresses for gala events. I took a pair of socks instead. As the fire crew and Red Cross volunteers mingled among us, news spread—flooding rain was overwhelming the subway pumps.

Water on the tracks meant F train service was suspended. The A train was still running, but who knew for how long. Really? It was almost funny at that point, except it wasn't at all.

During the hours in the rain, I realized that without my cell phone I knew exactly two numbers: Robert's cell, and my childhood home phone. Perfect since Robert wasn't answering my calls and was probably off on a holiday vacation with Lily somewhere. Doubly perfect since my mom had disconnected that line and only used her cell phone now, a number I'd never bothered to memorize. I also realized I had nothing in this world but the "outfit" I was wearing, the laptop in the plastic grocery bag under my arm, and the stuffed animal collection I'd wisely kept back in Oregon. This included having no money. Not even any access to the thirty-one dollars I had in the bank—paying my January rent had proved to be a poor decision.

I might have tried to talk the subway booth operator into letting me through the turnstiles, even without a card. But apparently, thanks to the flooding, that option was out. If I'd had a few bucks in my pocket I might have tried to hail a cab or flag a livery car. But that option was out too. So finally, I just started walking. At first I wasn't sure where, and then a few blocks in, I realized. I was heading to midtown, to the Mandalay Carson building. It was, for now, the only place I had left to go.

Danni Chung,

Yale University, 2001

THE DIVA

Fluent in French, Spanish, and Mandarin, this multi-talented East Asian Studies major is also a gifted soprano. After founding the Yale/China Summer Academy, which provides teaching opportunities for Yale undergraduates and offers courses that encourage critical thinking among gifted high school students in China, she spent the past two summers as the program's student director. This summer, Danni will be joining the Apprentice Singer Program at the Santa Fe Opera. "I want to be one of opera's great performers," says Chung.

Chapter Sixteen

*T*he cloud cover kept the morning unseasonably warm, but even at fifty-five degrees, I'd been shivering standing around outside my building. Now, walking, I was sweating beneath my sopping coat. The heat of my body against the cold of the rain made me feel like I had the flu, that feeling of blazing away under a heavy blanket, knowing chills are coming any second.

Trudging along Court Street toward the Brooklyn Bridge, I also started to feel like the star of my very own postapocalyptic movie, everyone else vanished, just me and whatever other marauders I would undoubtedly come upon, traveling the open road. It actually *was* my own postapocalypse. Everything really was in ashes.

By the time I hit the bridge, the red brake lights of cars and trucks trying to get into Manhattan despite the flooded roads were backed all the way to Cadman Plaza, and I started randomly cataloging my losses. My favorite family photo, starring me and my sister as perfect little versions of our adult selves, my hands in fists at my side, she standing behind me with her hands on my shoulders. My diploma. They replaced those, but still. My retainer. I still wore it sometimes when I felt out of sorts. No more. The pillowcase my grandma embroidered for me. My books. Sure, I could buy them again, but the new copy of *Must We Find Meaning?* wouldn't have any of my underlining or Helen's "I believe in you" note tucked away inside. And there was no re-creating my journal from seventh grade with its details of the triumphs and traumas of my gym class badminton. Then of course there were all the important files I'd scrupulously kept—my taxes, my immunization records, my student loan documents—gone. I'd recently upgraded to some nicer mascara. That was certainly twenty-two dollars wasted.

I hugged the plastic bag that held my laptop tight against my chest. Here I was, everything else gone, clinging to the files on my computer. It was just me, a bunch of profiles of *Charm* girls, and the Sound of Music story. For the second time that morning I thought of Teresa Anderson. She became a teacher because she just couldn't stop thinking about teaching. It was the idea that stayed in her head after all the other ideas were gone. Maybe the fact that it was just me and this laptop meant something? The idea that there was some cosmic message here made me want to shake my fist and yell, "Hello, Universe! You didn't have to burn my building down! There are less aggressive ways of communicating!"

The geometric splendor of the bridge never failed to capture my attention, but on my walk across now, I didn't look up even once. I barely glanced at the Manhattan skyline approaching, the lights of buildings still glowing in the predawn gray. I passed the high point of the bridge, the exact spot where Elliot and I had first kissed, and I didn't stop to wallow. I walked right by. But I did think, with some satisfaction, that this was the first time he'd so much as entered my brain that morning. I hadn't fantasized about him rescuing me. Good for me. Except the second I thought about him not rescuing me, I thought just how happy I would be if he and his dented Honda were warm and waiting for me on the other side of this bridge crossing. But they weren't. I kept my pace, and soon enough I was in Manhattan.

I could have kept walking, but I decided surely all the city's subways couldn't be out. As many people were walking out of the City Hall 6 train stop as were walking into it, but I went down the stairs anyway. I didn't have a MetroCard, but I figured eventually someone would walk out the emergency gate and I could slip in. In fact, this happened almost immediately, a whole stream of passengers leaving the packed platform, finally giving up on waiting for the delayed train. I pulled the ropes of my drenched hair into a ponytail and wrung out what felt like gallons of water. I wiped my face. I waited for the train.

It took thirty minutes for a train to come, but I had the time. Finally, after another short walk from the subway, I arrived at the pristine clean of the Mandalay Carson building. The lobby glowed out through the windows, the tree glistening, the floors radiantly white. You could have told me the marble was actually unicorn horn in that moment, and I would have believed. Outside the windows, I ran my hands down the arms of my coat to squeeze out as much water as I could.

It was just after seven thirty when I pushed through the revolving door. Water squished out of my sneakers with each step. The guard eyed me. If he'd had a gun in a holster, his hand would have been on it.

Despite my hair wringing, water still dripped on the counter as I leaned forward and cordially said, "Hi, I work for *Charm*. But it turns out my apartment building burned down this morning, and I don't have my ID with me since it was in the building, with the fire. My name is Dawn West. I'm not in the directory because I'm a freelancer."

The words all came out surprisingly easy, as if I were explaining a minor mishap. Like oops, forgot my keys at home. It felt for a second like I could minimize the trauma this way. Say it breezily enough, and it hardly hurt.

"Is there someone upstairs I can call?" he asked warily.

I told him to try XADI. If anyone would be in early, it was XADI.

"I have a woman down here," he said when she answered. "Dawn West. Says she works with you?"

He hung up and begrudgingly nodded. "Up to 18."

I could have been upset that he hadn't been more sympathetic, given my situation, but I was just happy to be inside. I took some deep breaths in the elevator and moved away from tears.

XADI was waiting at the doors. Instead of her usual magenta lipstick, today she was wearing bright red.

"My building burned down," I said. This time it didn't feel so easy to say. It felt like I was coming in from the snow, the way your hands melt and hurt as the numbness leaves your fingers. I was, in fact, coming in from the cold, and my body shivered all over as it took in the warmth. "My building burned down," I repeated, feeling even more pain.

"Come here," she said, and that was all, she didn't ask anything or say anything more. I walked toward her and she put her hand on my shoulder, the first time she'd ever touched me. A hand to the shoulder was XADI's version of a hug. After she lowered her hand, I followed her through the deserted hallways to her office. "Sit down," she gestured to a chair when we arrived.

"Are you sure?" I asked, holding out the arm that wasn't holding my laptop so she could see the water dripping.

"Sit," she ordered. "I'll be back."

In the dark of her interior office, the circle of light from the single lamp on her desk felt cozy. I felt warmer. And grateful that XADI was XADI. Had she reacted with cooing or real hugging or shock, I would have cried. But with her steady, calm distance, I could maintain.

She returned with two towels, a pair of jeans, a sweater, a dress, and shoes. To my inquiring look, she replied, "The closet." Which I knew had to be strictly off-limits for borrowing, but apparently XADI didn't care.

That dry towel against my wet, goose-pimpled skin felt like an angel pat-down.

She sat at her desk and dialed a number, pressed a few more numbers, then hung up.

"There'll be a car for you downstairs in five minutes. Our block of rooms at the Hilton—we booked an extra for staff. Give them my name at the desk. See you back here at nine."

She stood up, which was my signal to stand up too.

"Thank you," I said.

She nodded.

Swiping the key card and entering the hotel room, I felt swaddled by neutral comfort. Perfectly balanced, blank, no smell, no personality, a room that asked for no emotional response. It was exactly what I needed. I stayed in the shower for twenty minutes, long enough to return even the most deeply frozen parts of myself to warmth. I used the blow dryer on my underwear, then turned it on my soggy coat. I looked at myself in the mirror, and I felt almost normal, as if the only thing wrong with the world was my lack of bra and mascara. I turned on my laptop and held my breath. It powered up no problem, like it had been sitting unmolested in this hotel room all along. I shut it down again and stowed it in a drawer in the desk.

I hadn't made much headway drying the coat, but the inside felt warm enough, so I put it on anyway, borrowed an umbrella from the hotel concierge, and walked the few blocks back down to the Mandalay Carson building. Ninety minutes since I'd last been there, the office now buzzed. When I arrived, the receptionist at the front desk stopped me and said, "Child, how did you get here today? Everyone has a horror story!"

"A little walking, a little subway," I said, and left it at that.

"Woo-wee!" she said. "I never would have made it if I hadn't stayed over at my sister's last night! My cats are at her place too! I caught a car down from Harlem. Never ever would have made it in from Brooklyn. We stopped and picked people up all along the way. We had six of us in there by the time we got to midtown!"

When I arrived in the pod, XADI nodded at me but didn't say anything, and I slipped in among the hands XADI and the events manager were rallying to head down to the Morgan Library to help with setup.

At the library, in the soaring atrium with its four stories of windows and its crisp modern lines, everything was behind schedule. The tables hadn't arrived yet. The flowers were late. The rain, the rain, everyone said the rain. Finally, at noon, the rain lightened up. And then it stopped. The flowers came. The AV and light crews arrived and began their elaborate ministrations.

We arranged, we hustled, we ran here and there, and I felt calmed by it all, like I was swept up in a wave and as long as I didn't fight it, my head would bob just above the water. At four thirty, everything was in place. The tables perfectly arranged. The lights just right. And huge images from the magazine hung around the room. Helen in her Muppet coat. Gerri with her crazy curls. The 1958 girls who were "The Best in You from Sea to Shining Sea." Robyn Jackson and her history-making cover. The girls of 1996 in their mom jeans. It would be an hour or two before any of the women arrived, but I could already feel the energy in the room.

After we all returned to *Charm* HQ, XADI motioned me over with her hand, and I followed her back to her office. I wondered if she was going to tell me to go home. I melodramatically imagined saying "But XADI, I have no home."

What she finally said when she closed the door behind us was, "Do you have your wallet?"

I shook my head no.

"Pay me back as soon as you do," she said, reaching into her purse, opening her wallet, and sliding two hundred-dollar bills across the desk. My first thought was that of course XADI was a person who carried hundred-dollar bills.

With anyone else I would have effused thanks. But this was XADI, and so I just nodded. On the way back to the hotel, I bought a bra at Victoria's Secret and some mascara, lip gloss, and green eyeliner, a la Helen Hensley, at Duane Reade. I finally tried on the black dress XADI had handed me that morning. It hung a little roomily around my body, but it worked. The shoes were perfect. There was an Express around the corner and I bought the least trashy yet still sparkly earrings I could find and the first black belt I picked up. With it cinched around my waist, I actually felt pretty, in a semitragic-heroine sort of way.

Cocktail hour didn't officially begin until seven o'clock, but when I returned to the Morgan Library at six thirty, a dozen or so past TGTW winners were already milling about in the lobby. Before I could check in at the name tag desk, I locked eyes with a woman in an emerald-green silk skirt suit. Approximately one second later, I pegged her: Candace Clarke, '82 winner, UW Madison grad, advertising executive, ultramarathoner, and mother of two. In her TGTW photo, her hair had been feathered perfection. It was cut short now, but she looked just like herself anyway.

"Candace," I said, reaching for her hand, "it's Dawn West."

She gripped my hand in hers. And I barely moved from that spot for the next hour. Woman after woman filed by, and I knew them all. Maybe the photos had been thirty years old, but there they were: Dorothy Wendt, Wanda Linden, Jane Novey, Monica Medina, Donetta Allen, Simran Malik. Every last one of them lit up when I said my name, and I lit up in return. I'd helped bring all these women together. I sank into the warmth of the party. Hugging and chatting with all the winners I'd found was like slipping on blinders—everything before and after this room was blinkered safely away. I spotted Rachel Link across the room, and I wanted to give her an oh-Rachel punch in the arm when I saw that she'd affixed herself to *Charm*'s advertising director, one of approximately three men at the party. But I was also a touch relieved to see her so fully occupied; it meant I wouldn't have to tell her how truly unsuccessful TheOne party had been for me.

And then, I watched as Helen Hensley pushed through the revolving door wearing a smart black velvet tuxedo with an elegant pale blue bustier beneath. She smoothed her hands over her white hair, which she'd cut since I'd last seen her, not short, but to a perfectly swingy shoulder length. I watched her look around, get her bearings, and head toward the check-in table. She didn't immediately see me. I excused myself and made my way across the room. When her eyes caught mine, she hurried over and pulled me into a Chanel-scented hug.

I felt like I'd just taken a warm drink, when you can feel it coating you with warmth all the way down.

"How are you?" she asked enthusiastically.

I'd tell her after. If I told her now, I'd turn to worthless jelly. "I'll tell you what," I said. "I'm sure happy to see you!"

XADI came by and suggested we start moving to our seats. "I'll see you after dinner?" I asked Helen.

"Of course!" she answered.

My seating chart in hand, I launched back into the crowd to direct women up, down, and over, continuing to accept the hugs and kisses as I went. I watched Regina and Gerri take their seats next to each other at the head table. Gerri looked precisely like her television self. Rather than making me feel like she had entered the real world, it made me feel like this was all TV. I watched Helen take her seat one table over.

At my table, things seemed less televised. I was seated next to Tanisha Whitaker and Rebecca Karimi. The weeks had treated Rebecca well—in her empire waist navy blue dress she looked like the princess of the pregnant people.

"You're stunning!" I said.

"This is the only time I've ever had a nice rack," she answered, sticking her chest out further. "I'm taking full advantage of it."

Tanisha jumped in. "I still haven't thanked you properly for coming to my show the other night. It was so sweet of you! I'm so sorry I didn't get to see you after, but I definitely spotted you in the crowd."

Before we could say much more, Erin Burnett, the journalisty celebrity MC we'd rounded up for the occasion, crossed the dais to the podium, and the room started to quiet.

"Ladies," Erin began. "And the one or two lucky gentlemen I see out there . . . It is a tremendous honor to welcome you here tonight. We're here to celebrate an absolutely amazing group of women. Five hundred *Charm* girls who've grown up into doctors, lawyers, mothers, preachers, teachers, writers, singers, dancers, executives, engineers, scientists . . . girls who have grown up into *women*. If all the winners of *Charm's* Ten Girls to Watch contest who are here with us could please stand, we need to start this night off with a round of applause for you."

More than half the room slowly pushed back their chairs, put down their programs, and rose to receive their ovation. I felt like I was in the middle of the Oscars.

When the applause died down, Erin picked up again. "This is going to be a night of inspiration, and to start off our program I want to invite up a woman who continually inspires me with her talent and grace, Regina Greene, the editor in chief of *Charm* magazine."

Regina's gorgeously draped black dress swished as she walked toward the podium. It would have been suitable all on its own, but she'd topped it off with a heavy swath of a turquoise necklace and matching chandelier earrings. Bulbs flashed.

"Thank you, Erin," Regina said, taking the microphone. "Fifty years ago the editors of *Charm* had an idea. They wanted to pick ten young women who could serve as role models, young women they could feature in the pages of the magazine who would inspire readers. When the contest started, the editors weren't thinking of where these women would end up someday. They were thinking of image—who carried off the *Charm* look best. Little did they know there was more than meets the eye to the women they chose. *Charm*'s best-dressed girls, the first decade of winners of the Ten Girls to Watch contest, went on to become superachievers. Turns out there's just something about women who enter a contest. Once they enter one, they're going to be entering them again and again, formal and informal, for the rest of their lives. Women who are willing to compete are the women you want on your side! Anyone here ever heard of Barbara Darby?"

Applause broke out. "I thought so."

"How about Marcy Evans?" More applause.

"There are dozens of others you may not have heard of, but they're quiet heroes. Take Teresa Anderson, one of the first class of winners. Here is a woman who taught first grade for forty years. She changed the lives of close to a thousand children. Day after day, year after year. Teresa, are you here?"

At a table just to the right of the head table, Teresa rose. In a tailored dove-gray pantsuit and red scarf, she was a vision of elegance. Applause thundered. Teresa gracefully nodded and took her seat again.

"The competition changed into the scholarship contest it is today in 1968, and the winners who came after 1968 made great use of the foundation the earlier winners had laid for them. They went further and they rose faster than any of us could have expected. Among the girls who grew into outstanding women, we have opera singers, media moguls, air force pilots, space transportation engineers, elected political leaders, heads of nonprofits, composers . . . you name it, they've achieved it.

"Here at *Charm* we've been lucky enough to spend the last few months getting reacquainted with all of you. And we've even been lucky enough to sit down with a few of you in person. Before we announce this year's winners and welcome them to the fold, we want them and all of you to understand just what an amazing sisterhood they're entering."

She nodded to the back of the room, and on cue the lights dimmed, the video screen came down behind her, and then, there they were, our girls on the big screen:

"*'I'm the president and CEO of Madison Capital.' 'I'm the mayor of Seattle.' 'I'm a soprano with the Metropolitan Opera Company.' 'I'm a novelist.' 'I'm a physics professor.' 'I'm the founder and CEO of TheOne.' 'I'm the president of Vans Media.' 'I retired eight years ago after teaching first grade for forty years.' 'I'm an internationally ranked wheelchair marathoner.' 'I'm an architect; I design skyscrapers.'*"

From there it was seven minutes of glory. The images, the interviews, all filled in with clips of Regina talking about the history of the contest and what it meant to *Charm*. I was even proud of the music we'd settled on. Spirited and decade-appropriate songs in the background, like "Little Deuce Coupe" by the Beach Boys and "Reelin' in the Years" by Steely Dan. At the end of the video, the magazine profile pictures of every single one of the five hundred winners flashed one after another across the screen. The applause quickly broke into whistling and happy hollering.

When it was over, Erin Burnett returned to the mic and had to make several attempts to speak before the tables were finally quiet. "That was amazing, Regina," she said, and the room broke out in another round of applause. "We'll be taking a short break while dinner is served, but before we do, I want to introduce two very special women. Jessica Winston of the Metropolitan Opera and Danni Chung, one of the Met's young artists-in-training."

We applauded as the two women stood and a member of the AV crew handed Jessie Winston a roaming microphone. Danni wore a simple purple sheath dress, but Jessie's dress was more ornate—a full-length brown satin skirt with a matching jacket, a look that was two parts mother of the bride, one part divalicious.

3 1 6 ▪ C h a r i t y   S h u m w a y

Paired, they were a lovely picture of mentor and protégé. Jessie smiled beatifically and put her hand on Danni's arm.

"Danni and I knew each other six months before we made the *Charm* connection, but once we did, we couldn't stop talking about it. There is something about this contest, about being singled out by the magazine you grew up reading, that everyone grew up reading. It gives you confidence you can lean on for years. Eventually, you gain your own confidence, but until then, while your faith in yourself is still shaky, you can always look back and say, all those people at *Charm* couldn't have been wrong. I must be *something*. Danni and I have both felt that along the way, and I know I speak for all of the Ten Girls to Watch winners when I say thank you to *Charm* for the wonderful gift you gave us."

She then handed the microphone to Danni. "Jessie and I thought a lot about what to sing for you today, and we ultimately decided on the flower duet from *Lakmé*. Not because of what the song is about. But because we both just love the music. If you speak French, pretend you don't. Just listen to our voices."

The pianist began, and then they sang. Their voices rose and intertwined, fell and danced around each other. They caressed the notes. In some moments I couldn't tell whose voice was whose, and in others it couldn't have been clearer. They wound together and then unwound. They rippled. They were sweet, smooth, ecstatic, floating, twirling. The resonance shook my heart.

I could feel all of us hold our breaths as Danni and Jessie held the final note. We collectively jumped to our feet the moment their harmony shimmered away.

My hands hurt from the clapping, and still we clapped on and on, for the performance, yes, but also for the joy of seeing and hearing two generations of Ten Girls to Watch winners, so beautifully lifting each other up.

At last Erin thanked them and thanked *Charm* for spotting two such stars. When she left the podium the waiters began to circle the tables.

Rebecca sighed. "Now that was something," she said.

Tanisha lifted her head. "Mm-hm," she hummed, as if speaking would pull her too roughly from the dream that still held her.

I didn't say anything, just took a deep breath.

The waiters were still tables away when at last I plunged us back to reality. "Now may not be the time, Tanisha," I said. "But at some point I'm going to need you to tell me all about the SAT tutoring racket."

"Oh, absolutely," she said, laughing. "It's a great racket. But you know what I think we should do now? Peek in the gift bags."

"There's some good stuff in there," I said. "Herbal Essences shampoo and conditioner, earrings, the TGTW anniversary issue of the magazine, some fabulous white tea lotion, gym passes—"

"Shh," Tanisha interrupted. "You're ruining the surprise." She rustled through the bag, then pulled out the magazine. Rebecca followed suit, giggling with excitement.

"I've been dying to see this," she said.

In the end, the entire TGTW anniversary had only been awarded eight pages, but I knew every one of them by heart, having spent weeks slaving over every caption and photo. Still, I pulled my copy of the magazine from the bag so I could look through the pages with my table mates. I pointed out my favorite photos: the 1964 girls all in a cheerleading-style pyramid, the 1970s turban mania. As they settled in to actually read the article, I flipped through the rest of the magazine. The issue had only arrived yesterday, and the bag stuffing had been a timed drill, which meant I hadn't had a chance to look through anything else, including Elliot's column.

The magazine fell open to "Winter's Bold New Lip Glosses," then to "A-List Alert: Military Jackets," and then to . . . "Relationship Report, Secret Agent Romance's Dispatch from the Front Lines."

I shouldn't have wanted to read it. I should have skipped it. Or ripped the "Dispatch from the Front Lines" out of the magazine and crumpled it up, then shredded it, and then torched the shreds. But I didn't. I read the first line, and then the second, and then I sickeningly plunged headlong into the fire.

My uncle, a wise man, once told me marriage should be a refuge, not a battle. What I think he meant was that the right relationship is comfortable, easy even. If the person who sparks your passion also sparks your fury and frustration, enjoy it while it lasts but don't try to build a life on such an unsturdy foundation. Practical though this advice may be, it struck me then and it strikes me now as a downer. Forget about fiery romance, forget about being challenged. Isn't that why it's called "settling down" after all?

Boots called me two weeks ago. Boots, who is unequivocally a category 2 sparkler—oh, who am I kidding, she's a stick of dynamite. She hadn't spoken to me in months. Meantime, I'd been seeing someone easy. No, not that kind of easy. The kind of easy where I wasn't constantly watching myself, on edge waiting for her reactions. I could guess her reactions, at least enough to know they would be warm, funny, and sweet. It was comfortable. It made me think of my uncle's refuge. But the second Boots called I was on that edge again, and I remembered the heart-pumping thrill of it.

Boots asked whether I wanted to have dinner. After dinner she asked whether I wanted to have another drink at her place. In the morning, she was out of bed before I was even awake. She left a Post-it note on the bathroom mirror—"I'm at yoga. The keys are on the hall table. Lock up and leave them with the doorman. XO." What was it about the rough edges of that note that did me in? I should have bristled. She was so sure she could boss me around. And bristle I did. But I could scratch an itch with those bristles. I'd show her. The battle was on.

I lounged around in bed. I showered. I ate breakfast. And when she got home from yoga I was on her couch, reading the paper. "Still here?" she said when she came in the door, an almost perfect impersonation of nonchalance.

"You bet I am," I said, "and I'm not going anywhere."

She smiled and sauntered my way.

Here's to fire and fury. Here's to dynamite. To passion. To Boots. Maybe we're not settling down together. And maybe not settling is the best part.

I didn't actually cry until the last sentence.

I wiped my eyes quickly, hoping my face hadn't gone too red but knowing it had. I said I'd be right back without making eye contact with anyone at the table. The bathrooms were in the basement, and I didn't even make it halfway down the stairs before the tears were truly spilling. I pawed them away as fast as they came at first, then just let them flow.

I pushed through the bathroom door, and within seconds I had locked myself in a stall. I wasn't sobbing. Once in college, I'd cried so hard over Robert I'd thrown up. This was nothing like that. I was like Sylvia on the couch that day, silently pouring everything out of herself, the cascade of tears noiseless but beyond control.

I tried not to, but I couldn't help but do the calculations. The latest the article could have gone in was November 1. Elliot hadn't even gotten his book deal at that point. Were we still cuddling up and talking about our failure complexes when he wrote that column? He'd typed all that and sent it to his editor, probably done some revisions too, and then ordered me up a frickin' fruit basket? Did he send consolation fruit baskets to all the girls he wrote about? Had Roller Girl and her thick ankles cried themselves to sleep with a pineapple? Even after I should have been sure it was over (whatever "it" had been), I'd eaten that stupid pear and hoped it wasn't. And whatever our status had been, did he really think a column in a national magazine was the best way to officially end things? Not a phone call? Or even a text? "We're over 4ever" would have been infinitely better than the "Dispatch from the Front Lines." Where once I'd felt like a woman serenaded by Chagall, now I felt like the desperate illuminated figure in Goya's gruesome *Third of May*, the rifles of the firing squad leveled at my heart. What kind of idiot was I that I'd ever believed any of it? That the word "love" had even come into my head, not to mention that part of me had wanted to read the fruit basket card as a sincere declaration—how humiliating.

Slowly, I began to feel worst of all about the fact that Elliot was what broke me down. Not my apartment building burning. Not the evisceration of my every worldly possession. A man, one I'd barely known at the end of the day. I was down here crying over him. I was down here feeling hopelessly flawed because this stranger didn't love me. I was down here missing the event I'd worked so hard on for months. If I was going to be hiding in a bathroom, crying, it should be over something good. I thought of the letters my mother sent me while I was at college, only four of them, but each one had said in one way or another how happy she was for me, off in Boston, having my life's adventure. I'd stowed them all carefully in a black and green shoebox, and now every word was gone. Thinking about that, I cried harder, but still, I wasn't really crying for the letters.

I'd already soaked through the first wad of toilet paper I'd stuffed against my eyes and nose. I grabbed another wad and leaned my forehead against the cold metal wall of the stall. When I lifted my head I saw that I'd left an oily mark. The sight redoubled my tears. I let out my first audible sob and quickly pulled it back in.

I'd graduated, found a job, started seeing someone who wasn't Robert, managed a roommate fiasco, kept things together financially . . . all these things that had been so hard. And now it was all falling apart. The job was ending, clearly that whole "relationship" thing hadn't worked out, and I could hardly call my building burning to the ground a successful resolution of my roommate problems. I tried to do a "Pick yourself up, soldier!" thing inside my head. It didn't work.

Finally, after a solid fifteen minutes I left the stall and looked at my face in the mirror. My eyes and nose were red, but I wiped the smudges from under my eyes, pinched my cheeks, and fluffed my hair, trying to pretend all I needed was a little sprucing to look chipper and cheery. I went for the door, thinking I'd slip back into dinner and no one would notice a thing. But before I even reached for the knob I was crying again.

My hotel room key was in my coat pocket, hanging in the coat check at the top of the stairs. I'd have to traipse through the corner of the gala unnoticed and hope no one watched as I collected the coat and slipped out. And that's just what I did. The party buzzed with conversation and music (we'd found several of 1978-winner-and-Prince's-saxophonist Andy Benson's solo CDs and discovered they made classy background soundtracks), and I don't know what I'd expected—someone to chase me down and tackle me as I quietly opened the door and walked into the night? But no one did. Helen was going to be worried, but I couldn't help it. I had to go. Outside on the street, I cried my way north, cold wind drying the tears on my cheeks almost before they fell.

Geraldine Van Steenkiste,

Columbia University, 1984

THE BROADCASTER

Founding WQRK ("Quirk" to those in the know), Columbia's first student-run TV station, wasn't enough for her. This English major also wrote, directed, and starred in Quirk's first soap opera, *Low Life* (named for Columbia's Low Memorial Library), which went on to win the College Communications Association's first prize for television drama. After graduation, Geraldine hopes for a future in national broadcasting: "Television is a medium that's only going to get more interesting in the coming years!"

Chapter Seventeen

I'd been curled on the bed, still in my dress, for a good two hours, staring at the phone. At this point, even the last of the stragglers had to be home from the party. I sat there a minute longer, my face stiff with tear residue, then picked up the phone. I should have looked up Helen's phone number and written it down that morning. I just figured I'd see her at the party, and we'd go from there. But that obviously hadn't worked so well. I hoped Helen was among the hundred-odd women who'd taken advantage of our block of rooms. I called reception. Helen Hensley? Yes. They patched me through. Helen answered.

I said about fifteen words, including "fire" and "breakup," and she told me she'd be right there.

I swiped a washcloth across my face so I'd look half decent before she arrived. After I answered the door, she hugged me and then quietly walked over and sat on the foot of my bed. I took up my position against the headboard again, but now instead of looking out at an empty room, there was Helen.

"You missed Gerri and all the awards, and I don't think you got any dinner either," she said, as if those were the greatest of my worries. I appreciated her starting small.

"I don't know what's wrong with me," I said.

Still in her tuxedo, Helen pulled her legs up and sat Indian style, like a fifteen-year-old settling in for a long talk at a sleepover. She looked at me with soft eyes that said "go on." And so I did.

"Did you see the magazine? Not the Ten Girls to Watch part. That part was great."

"It was," she said.

"Secret Agent Romance. He's the guy I was with when the car broke down and I couldn't visit you for the weekend. Did you see his column?"

She reached for the gift bag sitting on the floor beside the bed— because I was crazy I'd brought it home with me. She found the article, and then we both sat silently for a minute as she read it.

When she finished she looked up at me with a pained and sympathetic expression.

"I'm a sucker." I wiped my nose on the back of my hand, and she reached for the tissue box and handed it to me. "Thank you," I said quickly before continuing my rant. "I am a pushover who puts up with rotten guys who don't love me. Actually, it's not just guys. I put up with everyone. I let my deadbeat roommate skip out on rent, and that's actually part of why my building burned down. A bunch of her dumb furniture caught fire in the basement. It's my fault. If I'd had some backbone, maybe I wouldn't be homeless right now. I've got nothing except for this stupid computer and the stupid stories on it, which I ran back upstairs into my stupid burning apartment building to get. It's all so stupid." And with that I threw my face into my pillow and let loose a muffled yet nonetheless resounding sob.

"May I say something?" Helen said, her voice sympathetic but also a touch arch, clearly responding to the melodrama being enacted before her.

"Yes," I said, lifting my head and wiping my nose and eyes.

"You're wrong about everything," she said. "The fire wasn't your fault. This guy doesn't know what he's saying. And you've got more backbone than almost anyone I know."

I tried to smile gratefully.

After a few seconds Helen spoke again, her voice quieter now. "Dawn, he got one thing right. You are sweet. Through and through. Every time I get one of your e-mails, it makes my day. You don't know it, but it does . . ." She trailed off for a minute.

"Sweetness is not a liability. In fact, I would argue it's the exact opposite. I wish you could have seen the room tonight through my eyes. I saw you, beautiful and strong *and* sweet, and I saw hundreds of women who opened their hearts to you exactly because you are those things. They wouldn't have talked to just anyone the way they talked to you. That video? The things they said? They said them because of you, because you made them feel comfortable enough to say them. Everyone I talked to, Dawn, every last one of them was touched by your sweetness. I think it's a gift. You can hide it and try to kill it off if you want. But I wouldn't if I were you. I'd risk it and see where it takes you."

I didn't know what to say. I didn't say anything. I put my head in my hands and looked down at the bed.

"I'll tell you something else. What you need right now is a good night's sleep, probably not a lecture, but try to listen anyway. You were very stupid to run back upstairs and get your computer. You're going to think I sound like an old woman when I say this, but your safety is the most important thing, so don't run into any more burning buildings ever again." She paused, leveling a stern look at me. "That said, the fact that you rescued your stories says a lot to me. Don't forget how much you care about writing, Dawn."

I couldn't look her in the eye. "I think the problem is I care too much," I said quietly.

Helen obviously knew I wanted to be a writer. Why else had I shown her my short stories during college? But I'd never said it aloud in exactly that way. We had a sort of code. Even her "I believe in you" note had addressed my ambition only obliquely. It was that shame-of-naked-hope thing.

"I remember how much I wanted things when I was young," Helen said gently. "And I remember how scared I was that nothing would work out the way I wanted it to. But things will start to work out. It gets easier, Dawn."

I finally met her eye.

"It also gets harder in different ways."

Yes, things got harder. I knew that. I didn't know anything about what it felt like to lose a decades-long marriage or the step-by-step frustrations of building a career, not just flailingly attempting to start one. Surely, my twenty-three-year-old woes were hardly worth these tears. Now, if I could just get myself to stop crying . . . But before Helen's words settled into chastisement, she went on.

"Experience is like evidence. When you're young and you don't have much experience yet, you don't have much basis for confidence. All you really have is hope, and that can get shaken pretty easily. But as years go by, you start to gather this evidence. You made it through this or that and you did okay, maybe not perfectly, but okay, so when you stumble, which you will, you can look back and say 'Well, I survived that, so I can probably survive this.' Or there will be things you're really proud of, evidence of your abilities, and you can look back on those things and say 'I did it then, I can do it again.' Right now, you're just building up those experiences."

It felt like Helen was walking around the room, picking up my scattered, desperate feelings and handing them back to me in shapely order. But I also felt a little like Humpty Dumpty, not quite sure the assemblage would hold.

"And then, later on, when your life and your career get more complicated, which they will, you'll have more to look back on for guidance. At least that's the best I can figure it. I mean, I certainly don't have all the answers. Clearly, I don't."

We sat for a few moments. Everything wasn't better. But, like

Helen had said, I could see how it could be. How it might be. How it would be.

"Thank you, Helen." I reached and put my hand on hers for a second.

"Well, like I said, you probably need sleep more than you need anything I can say, but when you get to a certain age lecturing is like breathing."

I smiled.

A few seconds later the hotel room phone rang.

I sat up and gave Helen a questioning look, then reached to answer it.

XADI said hello on the other end of the line. "A few people are downstairs in the hotel bar having a drink, and I'm hoping you'll join us," she said, as straightforward as always.

I cleared my throat. "Of course," I answered. Because that was what I always said to XADI. "I'm with Helen Hensley. Would you mind if she joined us as well?"

"Please bring her," XADI said.

Helen gave me the same questioning look I'd given the phone a moment earlier.

"My boss, XADI. She wants us to join her for drinks in the bar downstairs."

Helen looked at me with assessing eyes. "You're not too tired?"

"I *am* too tired," I sighed. "But I think we should go anyway. Really. I think you'll like her." What I didn't say was that even if having a drink wasn't number one on my list of fun ideas right now, I owed XADI.

I brushed my hands quickly through my hair, and Helen said, her voice serious again, "You're going to be just fine, Dawn. I know you can't see it yet, but I can."

I scooted down to the end of the bed and just sat there, my shoulder touching hers, for a moment. Then I got up, put on some fresh green eyeliner, and we went downstairs.

When we arrived at the bar, XADI stood and waved us over. There were two other women at her table: Regina Greene and Gerri Vans.

On another day I might have been short of breath. After everything that had happened in the past twenty-four hours, though, I just opened my eyes a little wider for a second and followed Helen's lead. Even at the evening's event, Gerri had looked to me like she was on TV. But I was about to sit down with her. That was not TV.

"Helen, so great to see you again," Regina said, affectionately leaning in to kiss Helen's cheek.

Regina then turned to Gerri and motioned to Helen. "And you two met earlier this evening, right?"

"Absolutely," Helen said, shaking Gerri's hand. "I'm such a fan, and it's such a delight to get to enjoy your company twice in one day."

"Right back at you!" Gerri said, her dimples dazzling as always. On-screen, her skin looked airbrushed. In life, her skin also looked airbrushed. I tried not to stare. I couldn't really believe it was her.

Then Regina introduced me. "And this is Dawn," she said to Gerri. "She and XADI made everything for today's celebration come together."

For just a second I imagined watching this scene in a movie. The warm light, the cozy bar, this table of women, and me, somehow with a seat at the table. It was my *G-Talk* dream, from my first phone call with Regina, come true. Except XADI and Helen were here instead of Bill Murray, which to my mind was more than a fair trade, though Bill would certainly have been welcome to pull up a chair too. I felt thrown out of time, like I was looking at a picture I wanted to be in, not one I actually *was* in—it was the odd sensation of feeling envious . . . of myself.

"So nice to meet you," Gerri said, shaking my hand. Her hand seemed like it should have been big-screen-size, but it was a normal, human-size hand. Now, whatever else happened, I could always say I'd had a drink with Gerri Vans. Forget calling my parents to tell them my apartment building had burned down. I needed to call them to tell them I'd met Gerri.

"Dawn, can you believe you did it?" Regina crooned. "All those women. And oh, they loved it. Women lined up halfway back the ballroom to meet you! Every single one I spoke with said something about how great it was to get your call and how much they enjoyed talking with you."

"That's really kind." I waved my hand. "But XADI was the one who kept everything on track."

"Seriously," Gerri said, "hearing all those women go on about you, I was jealous I didn't get to meet you earlier."

Gerri Vans had wanted to meet me? Maybe she was a liar, but if she was, she was my favorite liar ever.

I felt myself blushing. These were women who didn't have to be generous. They could demand anything they wanted. At best, they could choose to mostly ignore me. Yet here they were, being wonderful anyway. I realized, feeling the warmth they created around us, that if I ever became someone, if I ever had it in my power to demand anything at all, I'd still want to be like them, like Helen. Helen was right. Sweet wasn't so bad.

"How did you find your way to *Charm* in the first place, Dawn?" Gerri asked.

Before I could answer, Regina jumped in. "You should ask her to tell you about lawn care."

Gerri arched her eyebrow with interest.

Regina went on before I could explain. "I met Dawn at a party last summer, and without any experience she'd been running the advice forum on this lawn care website, totally on her own, just researching the answers for everything. I could tell how bright and resourceful she was, and I thought she'd be perfect for the TGTW anniversary project. I just had to snap her up."

I felt like warm butter, so flattered and pleased that I could barely keep myself from melting into the table. Regina had been impressed by me? Obviously, she'd given me her card and then given me a job, but I'd figured so much of it was circumstantial. Certainly, there had been luck involved, but the words were like an affirmation: I hadn't just been in the "right" place with the "right" people. *I* had stood out to her.

"I love stories like that!" Gerri said. "So what are you planning to do next?"

This time Regina didn't answer for me. I didn't know what to say. What *was* I planning to do next? Cry because it'd never occurred to me to get renter's insurance? I decided to focus on the question Gerri thought she was asking, not the more immediate where-will-I-sleep-tomorrow question I was asking myself.

"I'm not sure." I shrugged, and then what I said next surprised me. "The stories all the Ten Girls to Watch winners have been telling me are amazing. I keep feeling like there is so much more than just the eight or nine pages we could fit in the magazine. I mean, you can't talk to that many incredible women without turning up some amazing material, so I guess part of me would love to see if there's more I could do there. I've actually been writing some longer profiles of winners along the way . . ."

"I would love to see you work on that kind of project, Dawn," Helen said. Her eyeliner gleamed in the candlelight. How glad I was she'd entered that contest in 1972.

"I would too." Gerri nodded. I turned to her, still shocked that Gerri Vans was saying anything to me at all, let alone something like this.

"Really?" I asked. Helen was supportive, I was sure, but certainly Gerri was just a charming conversationalist.

"Yes," Gerri said. "And I think there's a market. Regina, think about it. The fun of those old photos and the old magazine copy, and the stories of where those women have gone and what they have to teach young women. It's *Charm* at its best. Total inspiration. Maybe it's a coffee table book. You could run the archival profiles from the magazine followed by a profile of every woman, where she is now. You could do all these great sidebars with quotes from the magazine over the years and stats about women in the fifties, sixties, and today. The photos alone are almost enough to seal the deal."

I glanced, and her wineglass was still mostly full. Was she really pitching Regina on this idea? And were they really going to hire me to work on it?

"Really?" I asked again.

"Yes, really," Gerri said. "I think this might be just the sort of publication I'm pushing Vans Media toward. Glossy but meaningful. Regina, are photo rights a problem?"

"Not at all. We own everything." She nodded with excitement.

Gerri took out her BlackBerry. "Hold on," she said. After a quick moment of thumb-typing she looked back up. "There, I just sent Allen, the head of the book division, an e-mail. We'll get this rolling!"

I looked at XADI. She gave the slightest nod. It made me feel like she was the director, overseeing this whole play. In fact, I was pretty sure she was.

"This is great." I barely got the words out before a huge lump rose in my throat. Gerri wasn't telling me I should write short stories about the TGTW women. She wasn't telling me I got to be the author of some dream book. At the most she was telling me I might get to weigh in on some sidebars in a coffee table book. But still. I felt my eyes well up.

Helen must have been watching me, because she reached under the table and gave my elbow two squeezes, then graciously turned the conversation to the music at the gala. For the next few minutes, they rhapsodized about the duet and then the rest of the program.

After I recovered, I added a comment to the evolving discussion here and there, but mostly I just listened and tried to take it all in. I felt drunk, like everything was hitting me a half second after it really happened. When we finally stood and said our good-byes, XADI leaned over and quietly said to me, "Take tomorrow off, but meet me in my office at nine o'clock on Friday."

I nodded as efficiently as she had.

"You did a good job," she added.

I wasn't sure whether she meant tonight, or today, or with everything. Whatever she meant, I knew, coming from XADI, that she'd just given me what was probably her best compliment.

I nodded again and bowed my head a little.

After that, I followed Helen back to her room. She'd graciously offered to let me use her cell phone for the rest of the evening, rather than racking up crazy hotel phone charges. While I used her bathroom, she changed out of her tuxedo and into pajamas and the plush hotel robe. Even though I'd lived in her backyard for two months, this was the first time I'd ever seen her in night clothes. It felt a little like the time she'd said "Call me Helen." I mean, you don't just wear your pajamas around anyone.

"Helen, I haven't even asked how you're doing," I said as she sat down on the bed.

Her face went through a range of expressions, starting with a smile like she was going to laugh, but the laugh never came, and she finally settled into a crooked half grimace that didn't reach beyond that one corner of her mouth.

"The book is doing well. I'm working on some exciting glass projects. The seminar I'm teaching on the women's suffrage movements in the US and UK is coming together. Everything is great. But I think you mean how am I really doing."

"Yes, that's what I mean." I turned the desk chair all the way around so I was fully facing her.

"We're not just separated. We're divorcing."

I waited for her to go on.

"We were married for twenty-three years."

She didn't say it, but no math required—they'd been married as long as I'd been alive.

"Like I said, Dawn. Life gets more complicated."

I nodded as if I understood.

"Sometime I'll really tell you about it," she said.

We sat there quietly for a second. "The house feels too empty," she finally added, "but I'm adjusting."

"Not that this will help all that much," I offered, "but I'd love to invite myself up for another weekend, this time with a more reliable transportation plan."

"I'd love that." She smiled.

We sat for a long, good moment, and then she put her hands on the bed to push herself up. "You must be exhausted. And you still have some calls to make."

I stood up with her cell phone in hand. "It's true, I do."

She walked me to the door and gave me a hug. "I'll see you tomorrow."

"Thank you." I squeezed her hand.

"Sleep tight," she said, squeezing back.

It wasn't as if I'd suddenly become Helen's confidante, and there was a good chance she'd talked about what was going on with her, albeit briefly, as much for my sake as hers. But still, I took the elevator to my room feeling glad to have had at least a moment where it was about her, not about me.

Back in my room, I wrapped myself up in a warm hotel bathrobe and turned on my laptop to search my e-mail for phone numbers. I jotted them on the hotel notepad, then started by dialing my sister at home.

"It's Dawn," I said when Sarah answered.

"Hey. Where are you calling from?" she asked.

I'd called in the middle of Pacific time zone toddler bedtime, and as I told her what had happened, I listened to the machinery of her evening seize up, with all the grating and yowling of gears thrown off the tracks.

"Hold on," she said. I heard her mumble something to her husband and then heard the girls shriek and bawl as she walked out of the room.

And then she was someplace quiet, and she asked me everything: Exactly what happened? Where was I? Was I okay? Had I gotten anything out of the apartment? What was I going to do? What did I need from her? After just a few of my answers, she decided what I needed from her was a rescue visit.

I hadn't felt like I could ask her to fly out, but now that she had offered, I cried and said yes, please.

Sarah put the phone down for a few minutes to go back to the girls' room and talk with her husband, and when she came back, she kept me on the phone while she booked her ticket. She'd be arriving at JFK the next afternoon. Peter was going to take a few days off work to stay home with the kids. All the grandparents were around too. She was sure it'd be fine.

"Have you called Mom or Dad yet?" she asked.

"I was going to call them next," I said.

"Do you want me to call them instead?" she offered.

Just when I'd thought I couldn't be any more grateful to her than I already was . . . The answer was yes, I wanted her to call them. I didn't think I could describe the whole thing again, let alone twice again, and there was a good chance their reactions would be either over-the-top or underwhelming, neither of which was exactly what I needed. But I stopped before I said yes to Sarah's offer. Part of treating my parents as if their stories were over was seeing them as fixed characters, as if they would always react in perfectly predictable ways. I should call them. I should give them the chance to surprise me.

"It's okay, Sarah. I'll do it. But thank you, seriously, thank you."

"Okay, see you tomorrow," Sarah said.

"See you tomorrow," I answered, with warm, leaky tears.

First, I called my mom. When I said "fire," her voice went red with panic. She asked if I'd been to the hospital to get checked out. She asked if I'd saved my immunization records, which I took to be her panicky stand-in for important papers of all sorts. She asked where I was staying that night. The more questions I answered, the calmer she became, and it was only a few minutes until she was comforting me instead of the other way around. I told her about losing her letters, and how it wasn't even the biggest deal, but how I felt so sad about it.

"Sweetie," she answered, "I just want to hug you and sing you to sleep. I'm hugging you right now. Can you feel it?"

I really *could* feel it.

"I can be on the first flight in the morning," she said. I knew this wasn't really true. Some Mary Kay ladies drive pink Cadillacs, but some, like my mom, were lucky if they could pay their health insurance every month. She wasn't in the position to buy last-minute plane tickets.

"Sarah is coming tomorrow," I told her, realizing I should have let her know that very first thing.

"I'm driving over there tonight with some things for you, then," she said.

"That'd be great," I said. I wasn't sure what she meant. Old clothes or banana bread or a Mary Kay face mask. But whatever it was, I'd be happy for it.

When I called my dad, as soon as I told him what had happened I told him Sarah had already booked a flight.

"I'll come too," he said.

Maybe this is exactly what I should have expected. What kind of parents don't offer to fly across the country when their daughter is in real need? But I hadn't actually thought they'd be so ready to get on a plane. Not that they didn't love me, just that I knew traveling wasn't a matter of whipping out the frequent flyer miles or the platinum card for them. But deeper than that was a feeling that had started with their divorce and then intensified when I'd gone so far away for college and stayed so far away after: I'd stopped thinking that I could count on them. Yet here they were, proving just how much they were still there for me. They weren't going to buy me an apartment or serve as my healthy-marriage role models, but they loved me and Sarah, and they were good people worth emulating in plenty of ways.

I talked my dad out of coming. I told him maybe next week, after Sarah had to go home.

Finally, he said, "Do *you* want to come home?" He'd had to work hard, waiting so long to say it.

I paused and considered. What *was* keeping me here? Not friends or love or the pain of packing. I was free to go. But as I thought about leaving, my brain jumped to an image of the night on the Brooklyn Bridge with Elliot. Scratch him from the picture, and the edges of the city still stood bright against the water, doubled in their beauty. The taxis still trailed over the bridge and zipped up and down the avenues like golden fireflies. The glittering lights still felt like countless pinpoints of potential. So much could happen for me here.

"I want to stay," I finally answered quietly.

"Okay," he said in a sweet, soft voice. Like he was finally accepting it, not just for this moment, but for good.

I hung up feeling like an overwatered flower, all droopy with love and fatigue.

I should have gone to bed then, but I decided to make one more phone call. Up-in-flames apartment buildings overrode friend breakups, or so I figured.

I didn't have to look at my notepad to dial. I knew Robert's number.

I counted the rings. Three, four . . . voice mail.

What sort of message was I supposed to leave? My apartment building (sob) burned (sob) down (double sob)? I considered it, then I just said, "Call me, will you?"

I'd imagined he might not answer, and for that reason, I'd also jotted down Lily's number. It was late, but I dialed anyway.

Three rings, four rings . . .

"Dawn, what a surprise," Lily answered. The way she said it, it didn't sound like a happy surprise.

"Oh, hi. Sorry, I'm not calling too late, am I?"

"No, it's fine," she said, but again it didn't really sound like it.

Usually Lily was more of a firecracker of friendliness.

"Well, I'm actually trying to track down Robert. He wouldn't happen to be with you, would he?" I tried to sound casual.

"Funny you should ask. I guess that means he didn't tell you he dumped me."

"Uh, wow, no, I'm so sorry. I had no idea." And then I added, as if I needed to explain further, "We haven't really been talking lately."

"Yeah, well, we actually broke up earlier tonight," she said. "I thought he might have called you."

"No, he didn't."

On the other side of the phone, she sniffled, and I was pretty sure she was crying.

"Lily, are you okay?"

"What a stupid thing to ask," she scoffed.

She sure was good at speaking her mind.

"You're right. I'm sorry. It's just . . . are you all by yourself tonight?"

"I'm fine," she said, but her voice broke as she said it.

That morning at five o'clock when I'd been huddled in the bodega on my corner watching my second fire of the day, if you'd asked me how many bars I was planning on hitting up that night, I would have said zero. Apparently, the answer was two.

An evening of magnanimity from Regina Greene, Gerri Vans, XADI Crockett, Helen Hensley, and my sister and parents had primed me for generosity. After a few more minutes, Lily conceded that yes, she could—sniff, sob—really use some company. I changed out of my bathrobe and back into my black dress and hailed a cab, grateful once again for the cash XADI had given me that morning. I'd never expected to be in the position of comforting Lily, but here I was, headed her way.

A lot has changed
in the past fifty years —

1950s

Winners are chosen for "glossy, gleaming" hair and "posture and poise"

1957—*Charm* kicks off "Ten Girls to Watch," originally a contest honoring "the best dressed college girls in America"

1959— Lorraine Hansberry's *Raisin in the Sun* debuts, the first play by a black woman ever performed on Broadway

1960s

Ten Girls to Watch goes academic, focusing on achievement rather than fashion

1960—The FDA approves the first birth control pill

1963—A Russian rocket launches the first woman—Valentina Tereshkova—into space

1968—*Charm* puts winner Robyn Jackson on the cover, making her the first black woman ever on the cover of a major women's magazine

1970s

Winners march, with the environment, Vietnam, and women's issues topping their concerns

1972—Title IX passes, opening the world of college athletics to women

1972—Katharine Graham is named the first female CEO of a Fortune 500 company

1975—The Supreme Court rules that women can no longer be excluded from juries based on sex

1981— Sandra Day O'Connor is sworn in as the first female Supreme Court justice

1980s

Winners take aim at the glass ceiling, zeroing in on careers in business

1984— Gerri Vans makes her national press debut as a TGTW winner

1990—For the first time, a woman, Darlene M. Iskra, takes command of a US Navy ship

1990s

Winners volunteer more than ever before, founding nonprofits around the world

1996—We get our first female Secretary of State, Madeleine Albright

1997—The WNBA kicks off its first season

2001—The balance tips, with more women than men now entering law school

2000s

As everything from artists and entrepreneurs to researchers and athletes, Charm's Ten Girls to Watch continue to wow.

2007—The House of Representatives gets its first female leader, Nancy Pelosi

2007—TGTW turns 50! Let's hear it for all 500 winners!

Chapter Eighteen

*P*redictably, Lily lived on the Upper East Side, and although the plan was for me to meet her at her place and then take her out for a drink, as soon as she opened the door it was clear from the mascara dripping off her chin that we wouldn't be going anywhere.

It was also clear that I'd underestimated the size of her trust fund. The apartment sprawled in all directions, including a sizable terrace off the living room.

"It's three bedrooms," she said, following my eyes. "I know, it's ridiculous, but my parents thought I should have 'room to grow.' Do you know what Robert said when he broke up with me? He said he thought I was too dependent on my parents."

"Oh, that's rich, coming from him," I said.

"That's what I said!"

We sat down on the couch together.

"So what's the plan? Rogue Taxidermy?"

"I haven't gotten that far yet." She laughed. "Though we should definitely look up their latest offerings. Pickled sheep brains might be just the thing." Then she looked toward the kitchen. "Do you want something to drink?"

"Well, maybe something like hot chocolate," I said.

"Me too," she said. "Or hot chocolate with bourbon."

We went to the kitchen and heated up some milk over the stove. Lily took a box of Kleenex with her, and as we leaned against the cupboards, she proceeded to wipe her tears with tissue after tissue, dramatically wadding each one and throwing it to the ground when she was done. By the time the bourbon cocoa was ready, the floor was covered.

We finally got around to what was going on with me, and I started with Elliot.

"You're fucking kidding me," she said. Then her outrage seemed to crystallize. "You're going to write an article back. Even just a letter to the magazine. You have to. He does not get the last word in print."

"I might get around to that eventually," I said, "but I probably have some other things to take care of first. Uh, well, uh, my apartment building also burned down this morning?"

I said it like a question. Like I wasn't sure it was actually true.

She slammed her bourbon cocoa on the counter and gave me an openmouthed look of incredulity, with a cocked eyebrow that said "You're crazy." Not so much that she didn't believe me, more that she couldn't believe I'd told her about Elliot first.

I giggled a little. And then she laughed, and soon, weirdly, we both started howling uncontrollably. Eventually, there was some crying mixed in, but even then, it was minutes before we could keep the laughter down.

We slid to the kitchen floor, pushing aside wadded Kleenex, and then, with our backs leaning against the cupboards, we talked for another hour. Lily firmly believed that Trevor the fireman and I were meant to be together. Right after she ghost-wrote my retaliatory article about Elliot, she was going to engineer a way to bring us back together, even if it required arson.

Finally, I sighed and said I really had to go.

"That's insane. Would you look at this place?" she said. "I have two guest bedrooms. Would you please do me a favor and take one of them?"

I spent the night.

The next morning I had breakfast with Helen, who offered to stay another few days to help me, but I reassured her that Sarah and I would be okay. I promised I'd call her with updates. Just before she got in the cab to go to the train station, she hugged me and said, "Someday you'll write about this."

I thought she was probably right.

I met Sarah at JFK that evening, and instead of a hotel, we stayed with Lily, who'd insisted it was the least a decent person with a three-bedroom apartment all to herself could do.

Sarah opened her suitcase in the living room. "Mom sent this for you," she said, handing me a stuffed horse with yarn hair. Part of the stuffed animal collection I'd wisely left in Oregon. Instead of giving the horse an actual name, at age nine I'd just called him "the white stallion."

"Look who's here to save the day?" I said, laughing and tearing up.

Friday, at nine o'clock I left my sister at Lily's place and went to XADI's office, as requested.

She was wearing a bright green top, the first time I'd ever seen her in anything but black. I liked it on her.

Thanks to my sister, I was able to give her an envelope with the two hundred dollars cash I owed her.

XADI tucked it into her desk drawer without a word and said, "There's an editorial assistant position opening up. I'd like you to apply for it."

"Here? In this office?"

"Your desk would be in *the pod*," she said, ironically inflecting the words.

"Wow," I answered, half seriously, half with the same tone XADI had just used.

"It's not glamorous. You'd be answering my phone and keeping my calendar and expenses. But you'd also have some chances to write for the magazine, and you'd get some experience editing features. The pay is not much more than you've been getting as a freelancer, but it's full-time, so you'd have benefits, and you'd be on the masthead."

The masthead—that page at the front of the magazine that listed the editorial staff. A page everyone but people who worked in publishing skipped right over. A page I was dying to be on.

"I'd love to apply," I said.

"Good, send me your résumé. And whatever happens with the Gerri project, we'll make sure you have time to work on that." And that was the end of our conversation. She stood up, her usual signal that that was all, I was dismissed.

Back at the elevators, the receptionist tucked a pencil into her big white bun and crooned, "I've got something for you, honey. Remember that mint I promised you?"

She lifted a tiny pot with two sprigs of mint poking out of the dirt. "I knew I'd see you again soon," she said, handing the plant to me.

"Thank you!" I said, putting the mint to my nose, the bright and cool scent making me instantly tingle with memories of home. "Wow, just, *thank you!*"

She hummed her deep "mm-hmm" and leaned back in her chair.

The next day, Sarah and I went to the DMV and got me a new driver's license, we went to the library and got me a new library card, we replaced all my bank cards and credit cards, we got me a new cell phone, and we went on an Old Navy, cheap-but-acceptable-clothing shopping spree.

After everything she'd done for me, that night I channeled Sarah's take-charge attitude and tried to do something for her. Following a quick dinner at a falafel place on Bedford Street, I pulled her a few blocks over to Cornelia Street Café, a little West Village spot known for its open mic nights. We listened to five or six numbers, and then I nudged Sarah toward the stage. She resisted for about half a second before she borrowed a guitar from the guy who'd gone just before her and settled into place in front of the microphone. I didn't know what she'd play or sing. For a moment, she looked out into the crowd of tables, her dark hair hanging loose around her shoulders, her eyes wide, and it seemed like she might not play or sing anything at all. Then, without strumming a single note, she sang the first aching, soulful phrase of James Taylor's "That Lonesome Road."

Walk down that lonesome road, all by yourself. The room fell silent except for her breathy, beautiful voice. She lifted up another a cappella phrase, arching her voice up and down the steps between notes—*Don't turn your head back over your shoulder.* Only then did she join in with guitar chords. It seemed to me that even the waitresses raised their eyes from their trays to watch her. In the same way certain frequencies can make glass quiver and even break, I felt my whole self vibrating with the sound of Sarah's singing. When she sat down beside me again, I squeezed her hand. She squeezed mine back.

Later, in the cold air on our way to the subway, we shivered as our misty breath mingled in front of us, and Sarah said, "Thanks for that, Dawn."

"You were the best act all night," I answered honestly.

She shrugged and gave a little I-don't-know-about-that laugh, but then, after another minute she said, "Next time you come home, I'm going to make you drive to Portland with me, and I'm going to do that again."

Back at Lily's apartment, Sarah and I changed into our new matching pajama bottoms (no monkeys, but very cute end-of-season-sale penguins) and started trawling Craigslist for apartments. When Lily saw what we were doing, she piped up with her usual tenacity.

"Would you please just stay with me? I'll charge you like five hundred bucks a month and we'll call it a day."

And that was how I came to be Lily Harris's roommate.

I sent Sarah back to Oregon a day earlier than she'd planned, but only if she promised to get on Skype with the girls and say hello when she got home. She did, and we sang half a verse of "The Wheels on the Bus" together before the twins bolted, but it was still great, and we promised to do it more often. I told my dad not to come quite yet, and instead we planned a trip, his first ever to New York, for the February school break.

The next week, XADI called to tell me the job was officially mine if I wanted it. I did. I e-mailed Lily to tell her the news, and when she walked in the door that night, she was brandishing a bottle of champagne.

"This is to celebrate all the cool parties you're going to get us into in the future." She winked.

"I'll do my best." I laughed.

I'd brought home Patricia Collins's bottle of wine, and while we waited for the champagne to cool, I decided this was the perfect occasion to sample it.

"It's supposed to be crisp and full at the same time," I said, pouring.

I told Lily all about Patty, and then we did our best impressions of wine connoisseurs, taking in the bouquet with our noses and rolling the wine around in our mouths. By the time we poured our next glasses, I'd regaled her with a handful of other TGTW winners' life stories, including Tanisha Whitaker's.

"We should go see her show," I said. "You'd like her."

"One better"—Lily raised her glass—"let's just invite her to dinner."

And so we invited Tanisha and a couple of Lily's girlfriends over for dinner that weekend, and just like that, I was on my way to having three new friends. Not college friends. *New York* friends.

The assistant to Allen, the head of Gerri's book division, called. I went in for a meeting. I was almost as nervous and excited as I'd been that first day at Mandalay Carson, but XADI had been good prep—no one would ever be as intimidating as she had been. As I waited in the reception area I thought about how Helen was right, once you have an experience under your belt, you're more confident ever after. When Allen walked toward me, I stood nice and tall and shook his hand with a good, firm (but not weirdly firm) grip. It might have also helped that Lily loaned me her pearl earrings. We didn't settle on anything that afternoon, but Allen promised he'd be back in touch after another internal meeting or two. For my part, I'd never imagined feeling so excited about sidebars.

My last day at the warehouse archives, Ralph must have been monitoring the security cameras again. I hadn't seen him since I'd gotten the new job (or during any of the days I'd been in the office since the gala, for that matter), but XADI had cc'd me on the e-mail where she explained the timeline of my transfer from the archives to the main office, so he knew I was packing up. I gently took everything down from the bulletin board and placed it in a file folder, then tucked it in a bag with the rest of the files I planned to take with me to the pod, and not ten seconds after I'd finished this and stepped into the hallway outside my basement office, Ralph appeared.

I didn't know whether Ralph bothered to read any of the magazines he added to the archives every month. He probably hadn't seen Elliot's latest *Charm* dispatch, but maybe he had. At the very least he must have noticed Elliot had been scarce around the building. I'd thought back to the smirk on his face the night I'd left the office with Elliot, and I'd constructed all these scenarios for what he'd say to me now. It went something like "He didn't deserve you" or "I could have told you he was no good months ago" or "In your honor, I'm going to rip that page out of the archival copy."

Of course he didn't say any of those things.

"Dawn," he said, putting out his hand for a shake, "it's been a pleasure working with you."

He wasn't smirking now. He was smiling warmly, though there was still something not entirely straightforward about it. Suddenly I realized I'd miss Ralph. Chances were the little lingering something in his smile was the fact that he'd miss me too.

"I have the key for you," I said.

"Terrific," he answered.

"I also have something else for you," I said. I juggled my bags and pulled a plastic-wrapped pie from the canvas tote on my arm.

"It's pumpkin, probably not as good as your pecan, but I did my best."

He took it graciously, his head slightly bowed, as if I were handing him something noble like an heirloom family sword.

"Anytime you need anything from the archives, you just call me," he said. And then, just like he'd walked me in a few months earlier, Ralph now walked me out. He gave me a little hug at the door, and I noticed that he'd shaved his neck hair.

———

When I finally e-mailed Abigail to tell her about the fire, I made it sound like a big, funny story. Which it wasn't quite yet, but was on its way to becoming.

A couple of weeks after I moved in with Lily, Robert got around to calling me back. When he appeared on my caller ID, Lily was in the kitchen and I was in my bedroom. I could have easily flipped open the phone and closed my door. But I didn't. Once, I might have screened out that first call and then eventually called him back, and we would have begun our whole stupid cycle again. Now I didn't call for a week, and then another week, and then a month. I still haven't called.

Lily wants to sign us both up for TheOne together. I haven't said yes yet, but I'm considering it. I told my mom, and she promised she would if I would. It's winter now, but it won't be forever, and Lily and I are also making plans for a garden on the terrace. Or more properly, I am making plans for the garden, Lily is making plans for garden parties. "I know it's crazy," I've told her, "but I want to have at least one planter full of grass, even if I have to trim it with scissors." She has assented.

I got my first real paycheck for my new job, and I groaned when I saw the after-tax amount. I was a grand total of forty dollars a week richer than I was when I worked in the basement. And XADI hadn't been lying—the job *was* largely an exercise in secretarial drudgery. But at least I was on a path. Not a straight shot to literary fame, but it was like so many of the Ten Girls to Watch women had told me—each door you pass through opens the next, and sometimes you don't know what's on the other side till you get there. Saying no to law school had led me to Lawn Talk, which had miraculously led me to Regina. Now I was officially part of *Charm*. Someday an assistant editor position would open up, and although working at a magazine wasn't the same as writing novels, for now, it was a way to write and get paid.

In the meantime, I was doing my best to inch myself along from explorer to creator. I finished my new and improved and radically fictionalized version of the Sound of Music story and sent out two copies: one in an e-mail to Helen, the other in a crisp manila envelope to a little lit mag called *17th Letter*. With Helen's I included a note. "Remember this story? I decided *not* to follow your advice. It's more fictional than ever. Huge mistake? I'd love your thoughts."

She wrote back that very night. "Ignoring me was a genius move! This has turned into a gorgeous piece!" I beamed with pride.

A few weeks later, I got a rejection in the mail from *17th Letter*, but at the bottom, after the standard thanks-but-no-thanks text, there was a note, scrawled in blue ink:

This isn't quite right for us, but please send more. I like your voice. You're a writer I'll watch for.

The editor's name was signed below. Not an acceptance, not even exactly the promise of a future acceptance, but an editor out there thought I was someone to watch.

———

Maybe the real progress started when I met Regina, or Lily, or when I spoke to my first Ten Girl, or on some other small occasion I hardly noticed at the time. In fact, I'm sure it did. But I felt so up and down during all those months that I couldn't see what was happening. In fact, I don't think I saw how far I'd actually come until I peeked out of the bombshell crater of Elliot and my apartment fire.

The night of the fire and Elliot and the gala, at the bar with Regina, Gerri, XADI, and Helen, there'd been a moment when someone or another's laughter had blown out the small candle on our table. The waitress struck a new match, the flame returned, and all our faces glowed again. It was just this tiny moment. I'm sure no one else noticed it. I probably only did because I was half drunk with fatigue and famous-person sensory overload. But I remember thinking that it was the exact opposite of my naked and glowing TheOne nightmares. I wasn't exposed or alone. There were all these wonderful women, and we were glowing together. I remember leaning back in my chair and feeling an actual ache of relaxation move through me. The voices at the tables around us blurred into an easy din, fading into the music.

In spite of the moment and the glow of the table and the warmth of the women around it, I knew I would wake up the next day and the day after that, for who knew how long, unsure of almost everything. And it's true. That's exactly how I wake up, still unsure. Still young and scared. I wake up in a nicer apartment now, and I go to a nicer office, and I have forty more dollars and a future in sidebars. Also health insurance. And when I get home, I have a roommate who not only wears a bra and eats all her ice cream with a spoon, but who is also an actual friend, I hope for life. But still, I'm muddling my way through at best.

That night at the candlelit table, though, I looked over at Helen, Helen who was so sure everything was going to be okay. When she finally looked back at me, I gave her a small smile and held her gaze, long enough, I hoped, for her to know that maybe, just a little bit, I was starting to believe her.

Acknowledgments

T he greatest debt of gratitude goes to my dear friend and agent, Kristyn Keene, for her patience, intelligence, sensitivity, and will-power. She believed in this book more than anyone, and it exists because of her.

I am grateful to everyone at Atria Books for taking a chance on me, but especially to Judith Curr, for her incredible support of the book, and to my brilliant and wonderful editor, Sarah Cantin, for bringing her transformative insights, grace, and energy to bear on the manuscript. My special thanks also go to Jaime Putorti for all her work on the design, and to Hillary Tisman, Julia Scribner, Diana Franco, Cristina Suarez, Stuart Smith, and Lisa Keim for their love of this book and the great efforts they've put into sharing it.

I am grateful to *Glamour,* in particular to Cindi Leive, Susan Gooddall, Lauren Smith Brody, Katherine Tasheff, Lynda Laux-Bachand, and Daryl Chen, who gave me the nonfictional opportunity to connect with fifty years of amazing women. And to all those amazing women themselves, for their generosity in sharing their stories and their wisdom.

My thanks to the college professors who made me hyperventilate over the course catalog in real life, Elaine Scarry and Laurel Ulrich; and to my actual thesis advisors, Suzanne Berne and Marjorie Sandor, both of whom have been better teachers and mentors than any character I could ever dream up.

Another huge thank-you goes to my wonderful friends, especially Kelly Irwin, who has talked me through every high and low; Erika Decaster, who knows the Kelly Burns side of me better than anyone; Desiree Lyle, my amazing coworker; Wendy Oleson, my ideal reader; Matt Swanson, who asked to read my stories way back when and believed in me enough to drive me all the way to Oregon; Aimee Schick Hardy and Eliot Schrefer, each of whom provided great insights on drafts along the way; Nicolette Rabadi Jaze, who shared her harrowing apartment story with me; and Helen Thomas, who was sure this was going to happen long before I was.

To my family, thank you not only for reading early drafts, but also for laughing at all the bad jokes in them (and in real life).

Finally, thank you to my husband, Greg Starner, for his love, his humor, his support, and his unfailing encouragement. The night we first met, I made him listen to a full synopsis of the plot of this novel. He asked me out anyway. I am outrageously lucky.

Photo Credits

TEN
GIRLS
to
WATCH

Charity Shumway

A Readers Club Guide

INTRODUCTION

Dawn West knew life would be hard when she moved to New York. She just didn't know it'd be this hard. On top of being broke, jobless, and living in a shabby Brooklyn apartment—complete with a slob of a roommate who won't pay rent—Dawn is struggling to get over her ex-boyfriend Robert, who is blissfully dating a girl Dawn wants to hate. Making a pittance from her gig writing for a lawn care website under a pseudonym, Dawn is thrilled when a chance to freelance for *Charm* magazine comes her way. Her assignment? To track down the past winners of *Charm's* annual Ten Girls to Watch contest and plan an event to honor their achievements.

As Dawn tracks down each of these extraordinary women, while experiencing the highs and lows of being twentysomething in the big city, she begins to question much of what she thought she knew about success, friendship, love—and ultimately—about herself.

QUESTIONS AND TOPICS FOR DISCUSSION

1. Read each of the Ten Girls to Watch profiles interspersed throughout the novel. What do you think Dawn learns from each of these women when she speaks to them, years after those profiles were printed? In your opinion, does she successfully take their advice to heart? What story or piece of advice stayed with you?

2. Of all the prior Ten Girls to Watch winners that Dawn interviews, who was your favorite? Why?

3. Rebecca, one of the contest winners, tells Dawn: "'I had a revelation after I became a professor here, and it's basically this: sometimes there are excuses, and sometimes there are reasons. . . . I don't know why most women blame themselves first, but we do, and it was a total revelation for me to look outside myself and see some other folks who deserved some blame.'" (p. 265) Do you agree with Rebecca's conclusion? Why or why not? Do you think Dawn is too quick to blame herself?

4. Reflecting on her sister, Dawn says, "Sometimes I felt I was living in New York for both of us. And sometimes I thought I was in New York out of some sort of perverse sibling rivalry." (p. 33) What do you think of Dawn's view of Sarah, their relationship, and her own reasons for being in New York? Does their relationship remind you of any in your own life?

5. How do the themes of sisterhood, friendship, and female empowerment that emerge through the stories of the Ten Girls to Watch winners relate to the relationships in Dawn's life? Consider Abigail, Lily, XADI, Sarah, Helen, and Dawn's mother.

6. At the Ten Girls to Watch gala, Regina says: "'Turns out there's just something about women who enter a contest. Once they enter one, they're going to be entering them again and again, formal and informal, for the rest of their lives. Women who are willing to compete are the women you want on your side!'" (p. 314) Do you agree or disagree with this statement? Do you consider yourself to be a competitive individual?

7. How did you react to the way Dawn handled her relationship with Sylvia? How did their interactions speak to Dawn's character? What would you have done if you were Dawn? Were you reminded of any similar roommate horror stories?

8. At one point in the book, Dawn reflects: "Robert had solved all his problems by finding the right person. And I, the wrong person, was left with all of mine." (p. 105) How does Dawn amend this statement by the end of the novel?

9. Dawn has two romantic relationships through the course of the novel—Robert and Elliot. Compare and contrast the two men. How does Dawn change as a person when she is with Robert? With Elliot? What do you think Dawn learns from the two relationships? What does she learn about being single? Do you think she should do as Lily advised and fire back at Elliot for the awful way he ended their relationship? Would you?

10. The philosophy behind Rachel's dating site is to assign people to different parties based on the data and personal information they

provide. Do you think this is an effective way to match people? Why or why not? Would you ever go to a party hosted by TheOne?

11. What potential do Lily, Regina, and Helen see in Dawn that she has a hard time seeing in herself? How does Dawn's own perception of herself change as the novel progresses?

12. Pages 158 and 159 of *Ten Girls to Watch* offer snippets of advice that the contest winners wish someone would've given them when they were twenty-one. What advice would you give to someone ten years younger than yourself?

ENHANCE YOUR BOOK CLUB

1. Write your own winning Ten Girls to Watch profile, as it would've read back when you were eighteen. Then, create your profile as it would read today. Compare the two. Are you surprised by how similar or different they are?

2. If *Ten Girls to Watch* was being made into a movie, whom would you cast for each role?

3. Dawn's grandmother was inspired by *The Sound of Music,* which in turn inspired Dawn's writing. Get together for a *Sound of Music* movie night, complete with some of Dawn's snack foods like popcorn and Cap'n Crunch. End it by listening to the "Flower Duet" from *Lakmé,* the song performed by Danni and Jessie at the gala.

4. Author Charity Shumway writes a blog about "growing and cooking in the city" called Spade & Spatula (www.SpadeSpatula.com). Browse through the posts and choose either a planting project to do with your book club members or a recipe to cook for your next meeting.